About th

Award-winning author **Jennifer Hayward** emerged on the publishing scene as the winner of Mills & Boon's So You Think You Can Write global writing competition. The recipient of *Romantic Times Magazine*'s Reviewer's Choice Award for Best Modern of 2014 Jennifer's careers in journalism and PR, including years of working alongside powerful, charismatic CEOs and travelling the world, have provided perfect fodder for the fast-paced, sexy stories she likes to write.

Tara Pammi can't remember a moment when she wasn't lost in a book, especially a romance which, as a teenager, was much more exciting than a mathematics textbook. Years later Tara's wild imagination and love for the written word revealed what she really wanted to do: write! She lives in Colorado with the most co-operative man on the planet and two daughters. Tara loves to hear from readers and can be reached at tara.pammi@gmail.com or her website tarapammi.com

Susan Stephens is passionate about writing books set in fabulous locations where an outstanding man comes to grips with a cool, feisty woman. Susan's hobbies include travel, reading, theatre, long walks, playing the piano, and she loves hearing from readers at her website susanstephens.com

Princess Brides

December 2024
Enemies to Lovers

January 2025
A Second Chance

February 2025
A Marriage of Convenience

March 2025
Friends to Lovers

April 2025
A Cinderella Story

May 2025
A Royal Baby

Princess Brides: Enemies to Lovers

JENNIFER HAYWARD

TARA PAMMI

SUSAN STEPHENS

MILLS & BOON

All rights reserved including the right of reproduction in whole or in part in any form. This edition is published by arrangement with Harlequin Enterprises ULC.

This is a work of fiction. Names, characters, places, locations and incidents are purely fictional and bear no relationship to any real life individuals, living or dead, or to any actual places, business establishments, locations, events or incidents. Any resemblance is entirely coincidental.

This book is sold subject to the condition that it shall not, by way of trade or otherwise, be lent, resold, hired out or otherwise circulated without the prior consent of the publisher in any form of binding or cover other than that in which it is published and without a similar condition including this condition being imposed on the subsequent purchaser.

® and ™ are trademarks owned and used by the trademark owner and/or its licensee. Trademarks marked with ® are registered with the United Kingdom Patent Office and/or the Office for Harmonisation in the Internal Market and in other countries.

First Published in Great Britain 2024
by Mills & Boon, an imprint of HarperCollins*Publishers* Ltd,
1 London Bridge Street, London, SE1 9GF

www.harpercollins.co.uk

HarperCollins*Publishers*
Macken House, 39/40 Mayor Street Upper,
Dublin 1, D01 C9W8, Ireland

Princess Brides: Enemies to Lovers © 2024 Harlequin Enterprises ULC.

Marrying Her Royal Enemy © 2016 Jennifer Hayward
His Drakon Runaway Bride © 2017 Tara Pammi
In the Sheikh's Service © 2016 Susan Stephens

ISBN: 978-0-263-39771-0

This book contains FSC™ certified paper and other controlled sources to ensure responsible forest management.

For more information visit: www.harpercollins.co.uk/green

Printed and Bound in the UK using 100% Renewable Electricity at CPI Group (UK) Ltd, Croydon, CR0 4YY

MARRYING HER ROYAL ENEMY

JENNIFER HAYWARD

A special thanks to Captain Steve Krotow, USN (ret), for his insight into naval aviation. You were so helpful and fascinating! Now I really want to land on a carrier someday.

And to my brother Andrew for being the most awesome brainstorm partner.

CHAPTER ONE

So THIS WAS what freedom tasted like.

Princess Styliani Constantinides, or Stella, as she had been known since birth, lifted an exotic rum-based cocktail to her lips and took a sip, the contrasting bitter and sweet flavors of the spirits lingering on her tongue before blazing a fiery path down to her stomach, where they imbued an intense feeling of well-being.

The perfect combination for this particular moment as she sat in her friend Jessie's tiny, local bar on the west coast of Barbados, halfway around the world from her home in Akathinia, contemplating her future.

Sweet, given the burnout she'd been suffering from after the hundred-plus public appearances she'd done last year, in addition to her work chairing the boards of two international youth agencies. *Bitter* because her brother Nik had accused her of running away from the issue at hand.

As if it had been just yesterday she'd ditched her Swiss finishing school to spend a month in Paris when she'd thought the stifling formality of her studies might suck the very life out of her. As if every sacrifice she'd made since then had meant nothing…

"How's that?"

The testosterone-laden, dreadlocked bartender rested

his forearms on the gray-veined marble bar and cocked a thick, dark brow at her.

"On the nose." The smile she gave him was the first real one she'd managed in months. He offered a thumbs-up in return, then moved on to serve another customer.

Relaxing back in her stool, she cradled the tulip-shaped glass in her hands and studied the fiery jewel tones of the cocktail glowing in the fairy lights of the beachside bar. She deigned to disagree with her brother, the king. She was not, in fact, running, so much as drawing a line in the sand. She may have given up her childhood dream for her country and sacrificed the freedom that was like oxygen to her, but her brother's latest request was over the line. Untenable. Out of the question.

She wouldn't do it.

Her breath left her in a long, cathartic exhale. Pulling in another lungful of the salty ocean air, she felt her limbs loosen, the band of tension encircling her skull ease, the tightness in her chest unwind. The release of pressure unshackled something inside of her that had been knotted and twisted for weeks.

When was the last time she'd felt she could breathe? As if the forces conspiring to turn her life upside down were not in control, but *she* was. As if the insanity that had driven her to this Caribbean paradise had simply been a vexing nightmare that an airplane ticket purchased under an assumed name and a lifetime of skill in eluding her bodyguards could fix.

A smile curved her lips. It had been a compelling game. Almost as fun as the ones she and Nik had used to play on the palace staff. Convincing Darius, her ex-special ops bodyguard, to let her leave the palace alone and dropping an arch hint she was headed for a secret tryst, when, in fact, a man was the last thing she wanted in her life, had summoned a blush to the hardened serviceman's cheeks and an agreement to "overlook" her departure from the palace. Boarding a commercial flight in a Harvard T-shirt and sunglasses and making the getaway from the pink-sanded Mediterranean island paradise she called home had been even easier.

The only rain on her very slick parade had been the text from Nik. She'd sent him one to say she was fine, that she needed time to think. His blunt, admonishing reply had made her turn off her phone.

Her brother could, of course, find her if he wanted to. But she knew he wouldn't. Once her twin royal rebel, Nik knew the price it had cost her to clip her wings. He himself had made the ultimate sacrifice in taking their brother Athamos's place as king, giving up the life he'd loved in New York when Athamos had been killed in a tragic car accident that had rocked Akathinia. He would allow her this time to find her head, *herself. If* she even knew who she was anymore.

"Need a menu?" The bartender waved one at her.

"Please." There were no paparazzi lying in wait to chase her from the bar, no Darius watching her with eagle-eyed precision from ten feet away, nor did anyone have a clue who she was in jeans, a T-shirt and sunglasses. Since Jessie wouldn't be free until the dinner rush was over, she might as well eat and enjoy the superb sunset from one of the patio tables.

"I hear the calamari is spectacular."

The low, textured voice came from her right, delivered by the male who slid onto the stool beside her. She froze, breath jamming in her throat. The hairs on the back of her neck rose to attention, a sense of unreality washing over her. *It couldn't be.* Except that voice carrying a Carnelian accent, infused with a Western inflection, that richly flavored, deeply masculine tone, could belong to only one man.

Noooo. Every muscle in her body tensed in rejection, her heart shutting down in coordination with her breathing as the earthy, sensual scent of him slammed into her senses. Her toes curled in her shoes, ordering—*begging*—her to run. But she had never been, nor would she ever be, a coward, so she looked up at the king of Carnelia instead.

Tall and muscular, he dwarfed the stool he sat on, as if he went on forever, the sheer brawn of him riveting; *intimidating.* But what was perhaps more hazardous to a woman's health was how all that sheer masculine power was cloaked with a civilized veneer that had always set him apart from his savage of a father. That had once made her believe he was different.

Kostas Laskos lifted a hand to capture the bartender's attention, an unnecessary action when everyone in the bar was staring at him. The women because his hawkish, striking face, set off by his short-cropped black hair, was just that arresting. The men because anyone that dangerous was to be inspected and sized up immediately.

"The oldest Mount Gay you have," the king requested.

Diavole. Her stomach retracted in a visceral reaction only this man had ever been able to elicit. Stunning, as he had been the last time she'd seen him, in ceremonial uniform at the Independence Day ball in Akathinia, tonight in jeans and a shirt rolled up at the elbows, he was compelling in a way the sunset staining the sky outside was—an utterly unavoidable, spectacularly beautiful product of nature.

His long, powerful fingers claimed her attention as he lowered them to his side. He had lethal hands—ones that could snap a man's neck as easily as they had crushed her eighteen-year-old heart. Hands that purportedly seduced so skillfully that women lined up for him to do it, but she wouldn't know because he had saved his cruelest rejection for her.

Her teeth sank into her lower lip, the effects of him reverberating through her. He had kissed her with that beautiful, sensual mouth of his, the only soft part of Kostas that existed, to comfort her after her dreams had come crashing down around her. He had stripped her of her innocent defenses, shown her what true fire could look like, then walked away, making a mockery of her teenage idolization.

She *hated* him.

He was watching her, analyzing her every reaction to him in that deadly way of his. She forced herself to speak past the blood pounding in her ears. "Shouldn't you be home ruling over that band of ruffians you inherited, or did your jet run out of fuel?"

A corner of his mouth lifted. "You know why I'm here."

She set down her glass with a jerky movement, liquid sloshing precariously close to the sides. "Well, you can refuel and be on your way. I gave Nik my answer. I wouldn't marry you if you came with a dowry of a hundred billion euros."

"I think you have that the wrong way around."

"I think I don't. I'm the prize in this scenario, am I not? Or you wouldn't have flown halfway around the world to harass me."

"I wouldn't have had to if you'd given me the time I'd requested."

"I refused what was on offer."

His whiskey-soaked gaze glittered. "How can you

know what you don't want when you don't even know what's on offer?"

She pressed her fingers against her mouth. "Let's see… *Hmm.* A barbarian for a husband, living in the enemy's lair, a union with a man who didn't even have the guts to try to stop his father when he tried to take Akathinia? No, *thank* you."

His jaw tightened. "Watch yourself, Stella. You don't have all the facts."

"It's a year and a half too late. I no longer care." She pushed away from the bar and slid off the stool. "Go home, Kostas."

"Sit down." The words left his mouth with the fine edge of a scythe. "Do me the courtesy of hearing me out. The time for tantrums is long past."

Customers turned to stare. Jessie, who was seating a table, looked over, eyes widening as she took in the man beside her. Stella waved her off and sat down because she didn't want to cause a scene and blow her cover. *Not* because of the inherent command in the king's voice.

Kostas pinned his gaze on her. "Have dinner with me. Listen to what I have to say. I promise if you do, I will leave and accept whatever decision you make."

Accept whatever decision she made? Had he always been this arrogant? How could she once have thought herself so blindingly in love with him she'd willingly made a complete fool of herself over him?

Heat smoked through her, singeing her skin. *"Kala,"* she drawled in her most agreeable voice. "You're right. This conversation is long overdue. Why don't you order us a good bottle of Bordeaux, find a table, and we'll discuss it over dinner like two civilized adults?"

She slid off the stool and sashayed toward the washrooms.

* * *

Kostas knew the moment Stella turned on her heel that she wasn't coming back. He knew *her*. Had known her since childhood, when the royal families of Akathinia and Carnelia had crossed paths at official celebrations, at the dozens of royal occasions that marked the season in the Mediterranean. His family had had a measure of respectability then, as his father's tendency toward a dictatorial rule had been less pronounced.

He had watched Stella grow from an undeniably attractive teenager into a spirited, often recalcitrant young woman who spent so much of her time flaunting the rules he wasn't sure she could see past her insurgency. Except of late. The past few years had seen the Akathinian princess turn herself into a respected global philanthropist, her rebellious edge muted if not entirely eliminated.

And for that, he was glad. It was her will he had always respected, found himself irresistibly drawn to. Her strength of character. It was a quality he required in a wife, a woman who could accomplish extraordinary things with him—change the very fabric of a nation that had suffered greatly. Few would have the courage to take on the challenge he was about to offer her. Stella had been born with it.

He caught the proprietor's attention, secured a private table outside on the edge of the patio, then returned inside to lean against the wall opposite the washrooms, arms crossed over his chest. When Stella emerged and headed directly for the exit, he cleared his throat.

"I thought you might need help finding the table," he offered in as benign a tone as she had drawn him in with. "Château Margaux okay?"

Her eyes widened, then narrowed, a series of emotions flashing across her arresting face as she formulated an alternate game plan. “Lovely,” she announced, swishing past him into the restaurant.

He followed, a surge of amusement filling him as he contemplated her better-than-average backside, set off to perfection in formfitting blue jeans. He couldn’t remember the last time he’d felt alive, awake to the zest of a life he’d lost his taste for. It figured Stella would be the one to snap him out of it.

Guiding her to the table on the patio with his fingertips at her elbow, he held her chair out for her. She sat down, allowing him to push in the chair. He deliberately let his fingers brush her shoulders as he lifted his hands away, eliciting a visible flinch from the princess. *A test.* He recorded it with satisfaction. She wished it to be hate, but he knew it was anything but.

He fixed his attention on the woman sitting across from him while he waited for their server to uncork the impressive bottle of Bordeaux. Devoid of makeup, with her hair pulled back into a tight ponytail, the bold, strong lines of her face were a challenge in themselves. Not classically beautiful, but unforgettable when paired with her ice-blue eyes and blond hair.

Where every other woman had eventually faded to a blurry replication of the last, Stella had remained unique. The one he couldn’t group with all the rest. The one his twenty-three-year-old self had somehow resisted with an impressive display of self-control. *Just.*

The waiter left the wine to breathe. Kostas laced his fingers together on the table and addressed the land mine that lay between them. “I’m sorry about Athamos. I know how much you loved him. I understand the grief you and your family must be going through.”

“Do you?” She lifted her chin, fixing those spectacular blue eyes on him. “I don’t think you could possibly

understand the grief we feel because you are alive, Kostas, and Athamos is dead."

He drew in a breath at the direct hit. He had expected it. Deserved it. Had spent every waking moment since the night Athamos had died wishing he could turn back time. Wishing he could bring Stella's brother, the former crown prince of Akathinia, back to his family. But he couldn't. The events of that night would always be a waking nightmare for him. A reminder of his flaws. All he could do was forgive himself for his mistakes and attempt to move on before he destroyed himself, too. With a country resting its hopes on him, that wasn't an option.

He held her cold, bitter gaze. "He was a friend as much as a rival, you know that. Our relationship was complex. I need to take responsibility for what happened that night, but both Athamos and I agreed to that race. We both made bad decisions."

Fire disintegrated the ice in her eyes. "Yes, but *you* were the ringleader. I've heard the stories about you two in flight school—they're legendary. You egged him on until neither of you could see straight past your obsession to win. But you weren't collecting points to be top dog that night, you were gambling with your lives. How can I forgive you for that knowing Athamos was following in your trail? In your suicidal *jet wash*?"

"Because you need to," he growled. "Because bitterness won't solve anything. I can't bring him back, Stella. I would if I could. You need to forgive me so we can move on."

"It's too late for forgiveness."

He closed his hand over hers on the table. She yanked it away, glaring at him.

"What was so important you couldn't have come to us and explained what happened? What was so *impera-*

tive you needed to walk away without putting us out of our misery?"

"I should have." He closed his eyes, searching for the right words. "What happened that night rocked me...shattered me. I needed time to process what had happened. To pick up the pieces..."

"And that was more important than the precious peace and democracy you preach?" She fired the words at him, her hand slicing through the air. "While you were *finding* yourself, we were living in fear, *terrified* your father would annex Akathinia back into the Catharian Islands. How could you *not* have intervened?"

His fingers curled around the edge of the table. "My father was the king. Short of overthrowing him, spearheading a mutiny against my own flesh and blood, the only thing I could do was try to reason with him. It wasn't working near the end. He was losing his mental faculties, suffering from dementia. I had to bide my time until I took control."

"So you put yourself into a self-imposed exile?"

"I went to Tibet."

"Tibet?" Her eyes widened. "You went to live with the monks?"

"Something like that."

She stared at him as if searching for some sign he was joking. When he said nothing, she sat back in her chair, eyes bleak. "Did your *sojourn* afford you the forgiveness you craved? The absolution? Or perhaps it was *peace* you were looking for. Lord knows we've all been searching for that. We didn't even have a body to bury."

He brought his back teeth together. "*Enough*, Stella."

"Or *what*?" She tossed her hair over her shoulder. "I am not your *subject*, Kostas. You can't fly in here, interrupt the first vacation I've had in years and order me around like your dictator of a father loved to do. You're the one walking on very thin ground right about now."

He was. He knew it. "Tell me how I can make this right," he growled. "You know we need to."

The waiter arrived to pour their wine. Dispensing the dark red Bordeaux into their glasses, he took one look at their faces and melted away. Stella took a sip, then cradled the glass between her palms, eyes on his. "What happened that night? Why did you race?"

His heart began a slow thud in his chest. Every detail, every minute fragment of that night was imprinted on his brain. He had promised himself he wasn't ever going there again, and yet if he didn't, Stella would walk out on him, he knew that with certainty.

"Athamos and I met a Carnelian woman named Cassandra Liatos. We both had feelings for her. She was torn, liked us both. We decided to settle it with a car race through the mountains—the winner got the girl."

Her jaw dropped. "You had a *pink-slip race*, except the prize was a woman?"

His mouth flattened. "I'm not sure that's a fair comparison. One of us had to back off. Cassandra couldn't make the call, so we did."

"So she was merely a pawn in the game between two future kings?" A dazed look settled over her face. She rubbed her fingertips against her temples and shook her head. "That wasn't my brother. He didn't treat women as objects. What was *wrong* with him?"

His gaze fell away from hers. "It was not a rational night."

"No, it was a deadly one." The rasp in her voice brought his eyes back up to hers. "Where is Cassandra now? Were you with her after Athamos died?"

"No. It was…impossible to move on from there."

Stella looked out at the sunset darkening the horizon to a deep burnt orange. The convulsing of her throat, the slow deliberate breaths she took, told him how hard she was fighting for control. When she eventually returned her gaze to his, she was all hard-as-ice composed.

"Are you *done*? Have you said all you need to say? Because if you think I'm going to marry you after hearing that, Kostas—sign on to be another one of your pawns—you are out of your mind."

He leaned forward, resting his forearms on the table. "It was a *mistake*. I made a mistake, one I will pay for the rest of my life. What I am proposing between us is a partnership, not a chance for me to lord it over you. An opportunity to restore peace and democracy in the Ionian Sea. To heal the wounds we have all suffered."

Her mouth curled. "So I should *save* you after everything you've done? Allow myself to be used as a symbol you can flaunt to the world in some PR exercise you are undertaking to restore Carnelia's credibility?"

The animosity emanating from her shocked him. "When did you become so cynical? So unforgiving? Where is the woman who would have done anything to fight for a better world?"

"I *am* fighting for a better world. Every day I do that with my work. It's *you* who seems to have lost your compass. *You* are not the man I once knew. That man would have stayed and fought your father tooth and nail. *He* would not have jumped ship."

"You're right," he said harshly, bitter regret staining his heart. "I'm not the man I was. I am a realist, not an idealist. It's the only thing that's going to save my country from the mess it's in."

She regarded him over the rim of her glass. "And how do you intend to do that? Save Carnelia?"

"My father has driven the approval ratings for the monarchy to historic lows. I plan to hold elections to turn Carnelia into a constitutional monarchy in the fall, which will include a confirmation by the people they wish the monarchy to stay in place. There is a very real possibility, however, before I can do that, the military junta who backed my father will seize control. You marrying me, joining Akathinia and Carnelia together in a symbolic alliance, would be a powerful demonstration of the future I can give to my people if they afford me the opportunity. A vision of peace and freedom."

An air of incredulity surrounded her. "You're asking me to marry you, to walk into the enemy's lair, where a powerful military faction might take control at any moment, and transform a country, a government, with you?"

"Yes. You have the courage, the strength and the compassion to help me take Carnelia forward into the future it deserves."

Her eyes flashed. "And what about me? Am I supposed to lay my happiness down on the altar as I've done everything else? Marry a man I can't stand for the sake of duty?"

He shook his head. "You don't hate me, Stella. You know that's a lie. And it wouldn't be like that. You told me once your dream was to become a human rights lawyer, to effect widespread change. Becoming my queen would allow you to do that. You would be altering the course of history, bringing happiness to a people who have suffered enough. Can you really tell me that's not worth it?"

Her lips pursed. "Pulling out your trump card, Kostas? Now I know you're desperate."

"We both know that isn't my trump card. We've proved we could be very good together. *More* than good."

A deep red flush stained her chest, rising up to claim

her cheeks. "That was ten years ago and it was just a kiss."

"One *hell* of a kiss. Enough you jumped into my bed in flimsy lingerie and waited for me until one o'clock in the morning, while the entire party thought you were ill."

A choked sound left her throat. "You are such a gentleman for bringing that up."

"No," he countered softly, "I was that when I tossed you out. You were Athamos's little sister, Stella. *Eighteen.* I was the son of the dictator. Kissing you was the height of stupidity when I knew the pedestal you put me on. I tried to end it there, but you wouldn't take no for an answer. Sometimes cruelty is kindness in its most rudimentary form."

Her sapphire eyes blazed a brilliant blue beam at him. "You should have spared me the pity kiss, then."

"It was far more complicated than that between us and you know it." She had been wrecked by her parents' refusal to allow her to accept the Harvard Law School admission she'd been granted, where Nik had studied. Devastated, as her dream had evaporated. *He* had not been prepared for the chemistry that had exploded between them.

"Would you have preferred I'd taken you?" He held her stormy gaze. "Walked away with a precious piece of you and broken your heart?"

"No," she huffed, fingernails digging into the armrests of her chair. "You did me a favor. And now that we've confirmed you're a heartless piece of work I'd never consider marrying, I think we've said all there is to say."

He studied the emotion cascading through her beautiful eyes, regret sinking through him. He had hurt her. Perhaps more than he'd thought.

She stood up in a whirlwind of motion, snatching up

her purse, pushing back her chair, as if a hurricane was sweeping down the Atlantic headed straight for them.

"Breaking our deal?" he drawled.

"The deal was to hear you out. Suddenly, I find myself without an appetite."

He stood, then reached into his pocket, pulled out his wallet and extracted a card from the marina where he was staying. She flinched as he tucked it into the front pocket of her jeans. "Don't make this decision because you hate me, Stella. Make it for what you believe in. Make it for Akathinia. If the military isn't handcuffed, they will seek to finish the job they started when they took that Akathinian ship last year. Lives will be lost."

Her chin dropped, her lithe body tense, caught in the middle of a storm. "I know you," he murmured. "You'll do the right thing."

"No, you don't." She shook her head slowly, a wealth of emotion throbbing in those blue eyes. "You don't know anything about me."

CHAPTER TWO

KOSTAS COULDN'T KNOW her because she clearly didn't know herself at this moment in time. The fact that she was even *entertaining* his proposition was ludicrous.

Stella paced the terrace of Jessie's oceanfront villa, smoke coming out of her ears. How *dare* he come here? How *dare* he throw that guilt trip at her? She had come to Barbados to get her head together, to figure out what she wanted to be. Instead, he had dumped the weight of two countries on her shoulders; issued that parting salvo that had her head spinning…

If the military isn't handcuffed, they will seek to finish the job they started when they took that Akathinian ship last year.

Her stomach plummeted, icy tendrils of fear clutching her insides. Five crew members had died when a renegade Carnelian commander had taken an Akathinian ship during routine military exercises in the waters between Akathinia and Carnelia last year. If Kostas lost control of Carnelia and the military seized power, Akathinia was in danger.

But to marry him to protect her country? Commit herself to a union of duty, something she'd vowed never to do?

She halted her incessant pacing. Leaned her forearms

on the railing of the terrace and looked out at the dark mass of the sea, a painful knot forming in the pit of her stomach. At least she knew the truth about Athamos now. It didn't explain why Cassandra Liatos had been so special that he'd engaged in a death race with Kostas over her—why he'd been so foolish as to throw his life away over someone who didn't know her own mind.

Unless he'd loved her...

Frustration curled her fingers tight. *Had he?* Was that the answer to the mystery that plagued her? She wanted to pound her fists against the big barrel of her brother's chest and demand an answer, but Athamos wasn't here. Wouldn't ever be here again.

Bitter regret swept through her, hot tears burning her eyes, threatening to spill over into the sorrow she'd refused to allow herself to feel lest it disintegrate what was left of her. Somehow she had to let him go. She just didn't know how.

She was pacing the deck again when Jessie came home, high heels clicking on the wood, a bottle of wine and two glasses in her hands.

"What is *Kostas* doing here? He nearly blew your cover. I had to convince a regular you were a friend from church."

She could use a little higher guidance right about now. "He wants me to marry him."

Jessie's eyes bulged out of her head. *"Marry him?"*

"Open the wine."

Her friend uncorked the bottle, poured two glasses and handed her one.

She took a sip. Rested her glass on the railing. "It would be a political match."

"Why?"

"I am the symbolic key to peace and democracy in the

Ionian Sea. A way for Akathinia and Carnelia to heal. A vision of the way forward."

"Are you expected to walk on water, too?"

A smile curved her lips. "It would be a powerful statement if Kostas and I were to marry."

Jessie fixed her with an incredulous look. "You can't commit yourself to a marriage of duty. Look what it did to your mother. It almost destroyed her."

All of them. Her parents' marriage may have been a political union, but her mother had loved her father. Unfortunately, her father had not been capable of loving anyone, not his wife nor his children. The king's chronic affairs had created a firestorm in the press and destroyed her family in the process.

"Kostas worries about the military junta that backed his father. He plans to hold elections to create a constitutional monarchy in the fall, but he's afraid the military will seize control before then if he doesn't send a powerful message of change."

"And you being the poster child of global democracy will give him that."

"Yes."

Jessie eyed her. "You aren't actually considering this?"

Silence.

Jessie took a sip of her wine. Leaned back against the railing as she contemplated her. "Can we talk about the elephant in the room? You were in love with him, Stella. Mad about him. If this isn't you repeating history, I don't know what is."

"It was a childish crush. It meant nothing."

Jessie's mouth twisted. "You two spent an entire summer with eyes only for each other. It was predestined between you two… Then you finally act on it and he slams the door in your face."

She shook her head. "It was never going to happen. It was too complicated."

"Does that discount you measuring every other man by him? This is *me*, hon. I knew you back then. I know you now. You looked shell-shocked when he walked into that bar. You still do."

"I can control it."

"Can you? You once thought the sun rose and set over him. He was the newest superhero to join the party, sent to rescue all of us from the bad guys."

What an apt description of her teenage infatuation with Kostas... Of the heroic status she'd afforded him for his determination to bring a better democratic way to his people. Her belief he was the only one who could recognize the bitter, alienating loneliness that had consumed her, because, she'd been sure, he'd carried it with him, too.

But that had simply been a manifestation of her youthful infatuation, she conceded, her chest searing. Her desperate need to be understood, *loved*, rather than seeing the real flesh-and-blood man he had been.

"I know his flaws now," she said, lifting her gaze to Jessie's. "His major fault lines..." She no longer harbored the airbrushed image of him that had once steered her so wrong.

"The thing is," she mused, her subconscious ramblings bubbling over into conscious thought, "I haven't been happy in a long time, Jess. I've been restless, caged in a box I can't seem to get out of. Everything about my life is charmed, *perfect*, and yet I'm miserable."

Jessie gave her a rueful look. "I was working my way around to that. But why? You do amazing work. *Meaningful* work. Doesn't it give you satisfaction?"

"Yes, but it's not truly mine. Other than my support for

the disarmament issue, it's the sanitized, gilded, photo-op version of philanthropy the palace directs." She shook her head. "You know I've always felt I have a higher calling. The ability to effect widespread change because of who I am, the power I have. And yet every time I've tried to spread my wings, I've been reined in. Athamos and Nik have taken precedence. *I* was the one left to toe the line."

Jessie was silent. "I hear what you're saying," she said finally. "But this is *big*, Stella. Irreversible. If you marry him, you're going to be queen. You will be taking on a nation. You're going to be walking into a very delicate situation with no real control."

But weren't those the kind of challenges that made her feel alive, despite the inherent risk involved? Wasn't this what she'd been craving all her life, a chance to make her mark?

She and Jessie talked late into the night. When her friend finally pleaded exhaustion and drifted off to bed, Stella stayed on the terrace, tucked in a chair, the fat half crescent of a moon, tossed in a sea of stars, her silent companion.

She didn't question her ability to do what Kostas was asking of her. She'd walked through war zones to promote peace in countries where young people were the innocent victims of conflict. She'd met and challenged tribal leaders to find a better way than destroying each other. What she was afraid of was *Kostas*. What he could do to her in a political marriage with her as his pawn.

Tonight had proved, a decade later, she was far from immune to him. In fact, it had illustrated the opposite; revealed the origins of her stunningly bad mistake with Aristos Nicolades last year.

She had worked her way through a series of men whom she'd discarded one after another without allowing any of them to get close. When that had proved unsatisfactory, she'd fixed her sights on Aristos to prove she could win a man every bit as unattainable as Kostas; as elusive and undeniably fascinating. She'd sought to exorcise the ghost of her most painful rejection, to prove she was *worth* more than that. Instead, Aristos had broken her heart and, worse, fallen head over heels in love with her sister and married her.

She wrapped her arms around her knees and hugged them to her chest, the pang that went through her only a faint echo of what it once had been, because she'd anesthetized it, marked it as mindless self-pity.

She was destined to be alone. Had accepted that love was unattainable to her. That she'd been too badly scarred too many times to view the concept as anything but a destructive force. Which would almost make the suggestion of a political match bearable. Practical. If it was with anyone but Kostas.

Tying her fate to a man who could destroy her, if the forces threatening to splinter Carnelia apart didn't do it first, seemed like another bad decision in a long list of many. *Unless* she neutralized his effect on her.

If she was to do this—marry Kostas—and survive, she would need to bury her feelings for him in a deep, untouchable place where he couldn't use them against her.

The question was…could she?

"The princess is here to see you, Your Highness."

Kostas looked up from the intelligence briefing he was reviewing, his heart climbing into his throat. It had been two days since he'd thrown all his cards at Stella, hoping she'd see the light. Two days with no response. Due to return to Carnelia tomorrow for a regional summit of leaders, he'd started to think his penchant for risk taking had been his downfall. That he had overrated his negotiating skills when it came to a princess who harbored a very personal anger toward him.

He betrayed not one ounce of the relief flooding through him as he nodded to his aide, Takis. "I'll go up."

Taking the steps to the upper deck of his old friend Panos Michelakos's yacht, anchored in Carlisle Bay while its owner took care of business in the West Indies, he found Stella standing at the railing of the impressive seventy-foot boat, looking out at the ocean.

She was silhouetted against the dying rays of the sun, her hair, the color of rich honey, hanging loose down her back. Her slim body was encased in a white skirt and caramel-colored tank top. She looked every inch the cool, sophisticated golden girl she was reputed to be, except he knew from experience Stella was anything but cold. She brought passion to everything she did.

He was fairly sure the image of her in bloodred lingerie, curled up in his bed at the Akathinian palace, would forever be imprinted on his brain. Stored there to torture him with the memory of the one woman he had never allowed himself to have; the one who had never left his head.

A slow curl of heat unraveled inside of him as the erotic image painted itself across his brain. It had been late, the early morning, when he'd climbed the stairs to his room after a palace party, head hazy from too many shots of *tsipouro*. He'd let himself into his suite unaware anyone else was there, stripped off his clothes, left them in a pile on the floor and collapsed onto the king-size bed.

It was only when his splayed arm had touched silky soft female skin that he'd become aware he wasn't alone. He'd thought maybe he had drunk too much and dreamed up the lingerie-covered Stella until she'd started talking, telling him he was the most exciting man she'd ever met, that their kiss earlier in the library had been incredible and she wanted him to be her first.

His twenty-three-year-old brain had nearly exploded. She was every red-blooded male's fantasy come true with her high, perfect breasts and mile-long legs. His body had definitely not been in tune with his head. She'd been too innocent, too pure, too full of her ambitions to change the world for a man caught in a struggle to define himself as different from his autocrat of a father to ever pursue. A man unsure he could ever live up to the lofty ideals she'd built around him.

Somewhere in his liquor-soaked brain, he'd summoned up the sanity to scoop her up, carry her to the door and deposit her on the other side, telling her to go kick sand in her own playground. He'd been sure someday the shattered look on her face would be worth it when she realized he'd spared her a broken heart. That women, for him, were fleeting pleasures meant to be enjoyed, then discarded in the must-win, must-conquer existence that had characterized his life.

But after that night, he sensed his callousness had dug far deeper than he'd believed in a tough, resilient Stella. That his need to underscore he was not the man for her, not the man for any woman in their right mind, had hurt her deeply.

She sensed his presence before he revealed himself. Turning, hands curling around the rail, a charge rocketed through her. Her soon-to-be fiancé was studying her with an intense curiosity in his hawk-like gaze that seemed to strip the layers from her skin, deconstructing every one of the protective barriers she'd come armed with.

Her chin dipped as he moved toward her. "Planning your next move, Kostas?"

"Admiring you. You still have the power to stop me in my tracks."

Her stomach folded in on itself, a renegade wave of heat spreading through her in places that needed to remain ice-cold. "No need for flattery," she said, injecting some of that much-needed, cool composure into her tone. "You know why I'm here."

"Honesty," he countered as he came to a halt in front of her, "is something you will always get from me, Stella. Whether you like what I have to say or not."

Another veiled reference to his humiliating rejection of her? A current of awareness zigzagged through her as she took him in. In a short-sleeved shirt and trousers today, the fading light of the sun illuminating the deep lines etching his eyes and mouth, there was a life experience imprinted on the hard contours of his face that lent him a somberness she didn't recall. A *knowledge.*

If those deeply embedded marks that had taken purchase on him made her wonder what the forces had been that had changed him so, had driven him to Tibet on a soul-searching expedition, she pushed that curiosity aside. She was here to negotiate her future.

"I'm good with honesty," she drawled, holding his dark gaze. "It's always been my forte. Along with sticking to my principles and reaping the messes I sow."

He ignored the gibe. "What changed your mind?"

"You were right. Notorious dissident that I am, I cannot turn my back on our two countries. Nor on my big dreams, because yes, I do still have them. But there are conditions attached to my becoming your queen."

He leaned against the rail and folded his arms over his chest. "Let's hear them."

"I will not be a figurehead…smothered by the patriarchal establishment. You will give me real power and status."

"Do you have any advance thoughts?"

"A seat on your executive council."

His gaze flickered. "That would be most…*unusual*."

"Say yes, Kostas, or this isn't happening."

He gave her a long look. "*Kala.* You can have a seat on the council. But I warn you it will not be an easy ride. Akathinia may be enlightened, but Carnelia is still stuck in the Dark Ages."

"I like a challenge. Clearly. Second, I will continue my work with the current organizations I support unless my schedule proves to be excessive."

"I have no problem with that. You do great work. What you *cannot* do is waltz around active war zones. It's too risky."

Heat lanced through her. "I do not *waltz*, Kostas. The photograph of me with those children raised millions of dollars toward the support of a regional disarmament treaty."

He tilted his head. "An unfortunate choice of words. But the fact remains, I need my queen alive."

Not because he cared, because she was of *value* to him.

"Third," she continued, "you will not take a mistress. Should you do so, I will have the power to divorce you immediately. It will not require a decree signed by government."

"I'm not your father, Stella. I have no intention of indulging in affairs. Why would I when I have a woman like you in my bed?"

Her gaze rested on his. "Speaking of which, this will be a political marriage. As such, I will not be under duress to sleep with you."

His gaze narrowed. "That might be a problem given the fact I need to produce an heir *quickly* in order to secure the Laskos line. Also, your fourth point seems to be in direct contradiction to your third. I can't have a mistress, but we aren't going to have sex?"

She waved a hand at him. "The heir—we can make that happen."

"How does that work?" He took a step closer, dwarfing her with his height and breadth. "We have *conjugal* visits? I seek you out when the *temperature* is right?"

She tilted her head back to look up at him, every cell in her body going on high alert at the proximity of such blatant masculinity. "Something like that."

A dark glitter filled his gaze. "Setting yourself up as a martyr, Stella? The sacrificial lamb sent to slaughter for the king's pleasure?"

Her chin lifted. "I would not be the first princess to sacrifice myself to the call of duty. History is littered with them. We are valued for our beauty and poise, our *compassion* and *empathy*, but in the end are viewed as nothing more than glorified broodmares."

He gave her a long look. "I am offering you far more than that. This would be a true partnership."

"Along with the heir you so *urgently* require."

He flicked a hand at her. "What happens when you are not acting as my *broodmare*? When I have normal male urges?"

Her cheeks flamed at the erotic image that spurred in her head. She *knew* what he looked like from that night she'd waited for him in his bed…knew how heart-stoppingly virile he was in every respect. It made the blood coursing through her veins fizzle with heat. Singe her skin.

Diavole, but this was not how this was supposed to

go. She lifted her chin higher, a belligerent expression on her face. "That's not for me to figure out, Kostas. That's *your* job."

"Is it?" His gaze touched her fiery cheeks. "I think when you let go of the past, when you finally forgive me, when you acknowledge how good we are together, we will be as potent a match in the bedroom as we will be ruling my country."

"No," she said, even as a pulse of electricity ran between them, magnifying the sizzle in her blood. "That isn't going to happen. Women are objects to you. I am a means to an end. I would be stupid to forget that and cede power to you."

"You will be my *wife*, the woman by my side, not an object." His dark lashes arced over his cheeks. "And who said you would be ceding power? Just because I walked away from you that night didn't mean I didn't want you, Stella. That I haven't replayed that scenario in my head with a far different outcome. You would have equally as much power over me if we went to bed together, maybe more."

Her stomach muscles coiled. It was a seductive, beguiling thought to imagine he might want her. That her desire for him hadn't been as one-sided as she'd imagined it to be. That by exploring that revelation, she might wipe away the rejection that stung even now in a place that had never healed. But her head, the part of her she was operating with now, realized his tactics for what they were. *Negotiation. Manipulation.*

She lifted her chin. "It will be an act, conceiving your heir. Nothing more. I've lost my taste for megalomaniacs housed in beautiful packages."

"Megalomaniacs?"

"Yes—*you*."

He studied her for a moment. "Are you including Aristos Nicolades in this esteemed group?"

She lifted a brow. "Following my love life, Kostas? Aristos was simply the last kick at the can." Her voice took on a nonchalance that hid the steel underpinning her insides. "I've decided to make myself as impenetrable as you when it comes to relationships, as *unaffected*, because I've found, in the end, it's just not worth it."

He frowned. "That's not you, Stella. You live by your passion."

"Not anymore I don't. You should be happy about my new outlook, by the way. It's the only reason I'm marrying you."

"That and your desire to do the immense amount of good I know you will."

"Don't patronize." She took a step back because oxygen was necessary for breathing and she couldn't do that near him. "I'm already on board if you agree to the conditions I've laid out."

He nodded. "Agreed. Shall we go over next steps, then?"

Her head spun. *This was actually happening.* "Go ahead."

"I fly back to Carnelia tomorrow for a summit of regional leaders. It would be ideal if you accompanied me so we can make the engagement announcement and begin preparations for the wedding."

Tomorrow? She had been craving this time to herself so badly.

He read her dismay. "General Houlis, the chief architect behind the military junta, has put his campaign into motion, marshaling strength behind the scenes. His support is by no means solid—he still has a long way to go. We need to neutralize him while we can."

"I'm assuming the coming elections will be a major weapon at your disposal?"

"Yes. I will announce them at the summit this week. There will be a large media contingent in attendance. Nik will also be there. We will provide a united front."

"And our engagement? Do we announce that before or after?"

"I will double-check with the palace PR team, but I was thinking this coming Friday. Start the week with a bang at the conference, end the week with an equally strong commitment toward the future."

"And the wedding? When would that happen?"

"Within two months. Six weeks, I'm thinking. Those who can make it, make it."

"Six weeks?"

"The events team will make it happen. You just need to show up."

Like her role in all of this. A chess piece to be moved around at will.

His expression turned conciliatory. "I know it's traditional for the engagement party to happen in Akathinia, but in this instance, I think it needs to be in Carnelia with all the key figures in attendance.

Her mother was going to have a fit. A deviant streak reveled in the thought. She enjoyed every opportunity she had to push her aloof mother out of her comfort zone. A latent lashing out against her childhood perhaps, at the attention she'd never received.

"That's fine." She watched her dream sabbatical fly out the metaphorical window. She could hardly relax on a beach now knowing what was ahead of her.

"Good." He reached into his pocket and pulled out a ring. Caught off guard, she was blinded by its brilliance. A square-cut diamond set in an exquisite platinum filigree, it dazzled in the sunlight. Upon closer inspection, she saw it had the Carnelian coat of arms interwoven on both sides.

"You were that sure of me?"

"Hopeful. This was my mother's ring. One of the few remaining mementos I have of her."

Her chest tightened, a sandpapery feeling invading her throat. "She died when you were very young, I remember."

"When I was four. I have no real memories of her."

She studied his impassive expression. What must it have been like to grow up without any warmth in his life? With only his universally despised tyrant of a father to guide him? Had he had someone else to confide in, to love him—a grandmother, a godmother? She couldn't remember him talking of one. Or had he always been alone?

Athamos had once remarked Kostas was the only man he knew who could look alone in the middle of a crowd. It was something she'd never forgotten. How could she?

"Your hand," Kostas prompted, pulling her back into the moment.

She held her hand out, her fingers trembling ever so slightly. He slid the ring on, his big hand engulfing hers. The enormity of what she was about to do lodged in her throat as she stared at the stone blazing on her finger. It was a ring that not only symbolized the commitment she was making to Kostas, but also the weight of a nation that now lay squarely on her shoulders.

Kostas held her gaze in his dark, unfathomable one. "*Efharisto*, Stella. *Thank you.* I promise you won't regret this. We will make a powerful team. We will give Carnelians the future they deserve."

His energy pulsed through her. Sank into the very heart of her. Her future was now inexorably intertwined with a man she had vowed to hate, a man for whom she now realized her feelings were far more complex than she'd ever anticipated. But there was no looking back now. It was done.

CHAPTER THREE

THE DAYS FOLLOWING Stella's return to Akathinia passed in a blur, likely a good thing given the magnitude of what she'd committed herself to. She knew her decision to marry Kostas had been the right one, knew this was the challenge she had been looking for. It was the *noise* that was getting to her.

Everyone seemed to have an opinion on her upcoming nuptials to the king of Carnelia, from her hairdresser, who pronounced him "a real man among the current flock of pseudo-men," to her sister, Aleksandra, who agreed with her hairdresser, referring to Kostas as "one sexy hunk of a man," to the celebrity press, who'd dubbed their pairing "the most exciting thing to happen to royalty in decades. Camelot has come to Carnelia."

The traditional media, on the other hand, Kostas's harshest critics, were taking a wait-and-see approach. Not all of them were convinced King Idas's son, the thirty-two-year-old Oxford-educated proponent of democracy, could turn his legacy around. Rumblings of military discontent were rippling across the country, approval ratings for the monarchy were down and all bets were off as to whether Kostas could win the hearts and minds of Carnelians.

But there was also hope. The Carnelian people seemed

guardedly optimistic, as spontaneous parties broke out in the streets as the first elections in the country's history were announced for the fall. Those celebrations continued with the news of the king's forthcoming match to the elder princess of Akathinia. For the great majority, she appeared the bright, promising light Kostas had painted, but for others she was an unknown quantity in a culture historically closed to outsiders. *Not* a Carnelian.

That would have to be overcome, she thought grimly as she flew to London for an official appearance the week before her engagement party. The future of a country, the self-determination of its people, depended on it, though they were so wounded at the moment, they weren't sure what they wanted.

The oppressive media coverage dogged her as she attended a charity luncheon in support of one of the major hospital's cancer units. What started out as a peaceful affair was hijacked by the news of her upcoming nuptials. Irritation chasing a beat up her spine, she apologized to her hostess. It was only a taste of the wedding madness, she knew, and it left her in an exceedingly cranky mood as she returned to Akathinia for a dress fitting with her sister-in-law, Sofía, and sister, Alex. A designer who was making her name on the world stage, Sofía was creating both her engagement party and wedding dresses.

"What do you think about this?" Sofía held up a sensational sapphire-hued backless satin gown in the bright light of her palace workshop at the front of the white Maltese stone Akathinian palace.

"Too obvious."

Sofía returned the dress to the rack and pulled out a white chiffon gown for her inspection.

"Too virginal."

Her sister-in-law flicked through the row of dresses and held up an elegant, midnight blue lace number.

She shook her head. "Just…not right."

Alex eyed her. "What are you, Goldilocks?"

At least there was a happy ending to that story. She ran a hand through her hair. "Sorry, I know I'm being a pain. It's been a bad week."

Sofía folded the dress over her arm. "You don't have to do this, you know. Nothing has been done that can't be undone."

Her sister-in-law should know. She'd been an ambitious, career-driven dress-shop owner in Manhattan before she'd fallen in love with Stella's brother, been swept up in romance and taken the unlikely path of becoming queen. But the road to happiness hadn't been an easy one for her and Nik.

"I'm doing the right thing." She said the words more vehemently than she felt them at the moment.

"For you or for your country?"

"For both."

Alex stayed quiet and she knew why. Her sister was blissfully happy with Aristos, who'd mellowed out from his jungle-cat personality to something approaching civility of late. Stella was happy for her, she really was, but it was like being slapped in the face with her own romantic futility every time she saw them together.

A knock on the door brought their heads up. Her brother strolled in, jacket over his arm, tie loose. He gave his wife a kiss, then glanced at the dress rack. "How's it going?"

Alex made a face. "How's it *not* going, you mean."

Nik took in Stella's dark look. "Can you give us a second?"

His wife and Alex left, clearly happy for a breather.

Her brother turned his ever-perceptive gaze on her. "Everything okay?"

"Never better."

"This was your decision, Stella."

"It's not that." She waved a hand at him. "I needed a challenge like this. I was dying inside going through the motions. It's this media circus that's getting to me. You'd think I'd solved world hunger instead of getting engaged."

"Think of it as good for Carnelia. People are excited."

"I know." She raked a hand through her hair. Strode to the window to look out at the glittering, sun-dappled Ionian Sea, across which her fiancé was attempting to manage the media firestorm he'd created. She wondered how he was doing. She'd talked to him on the phone a few times, but she'd mostly been working with Takis, his personal aide, on logistics, while Kostas attempted to hold a faltering country together.

"Kostas is a good man. Survivor's guilt is a hell of a thing to deal with. Give him some leeway."

She turned around. "You absolve him of any responsibility?"

"I have chosen to let go. You should, too."

She wasn't sure she was as enlightened as he was.

"I wanted to mention something else. Darius is going to accompany you to Carnelia. Permanently."

"I can't ask him to do that—he lives here."

"He wants to go. His loyalty to you has always been unquestionable."

She adored Darius. He'd kept her sane at times when it felt as if her life was just too *much*. "Does Kostas know about this?"

"He's in full agreement. I trust Kostas implicitly—he *will* take care of you. It's when he's not there I want an Akathinian, a known quantity, with you."

"Why? You think I'm in danger?"

"I think it's a smart precaution. You're walking into a very tricky political situation."

She didn't like how he hadn't answered the question. But then she'd known taking on this challenge was full of risk.

"Kala." Fine.

Nik's gaze softened. "I think you're very courageous to do this, Stella. I'm proud of you. Remember you are not alone. You are never alone. We're with you every step of the way."

Her heart softened. Her rock, Nik was. Passionate, idealistic like her, the yin to Athamos's rock-steady yang, she'd had to get to know him in pieces. He'd been sent off to join Athamos at boarding school when Stella was four, leaving her with only her nannies and tutor to keep her company while her mother immersed herself in her charity work as her marriage imploded.

She'd seen her brothers on holidays, had eagerly eaten up any time she'd had with them, missing them desperately when they left. When she'd gotten old enough to travel by herself, she'd visited Nik frequently in New York, hoping someday to join him there with her studies. But her parents had axed that dream.

She held his gaze now, as Constantinides electric blue as her own. *"S'agapao." I love you.* "You know that."

"Ki ego s'agapao." I love you, too. He enfolded her in a warm hug. "Now pick a dress. The party is days away."

Sofía and Alex returned with coffee and biscuits. Stella eyed the tray. "You think it's my blood sugar."

"We're working all angles," said Alex.

She smiled. Eyed the dresses. Felt her old fighting spirit rear its defiant head.

"I'm thinking the sapphire blue."

She was going to dazzle. She was going to shake things up. She was going to seize every ounce of her destiny and accomplish what she'd set out to do. The king had no idea of the storm headed his way.

Her storm surge was downgraded from a hurricane to a tropical storm by the time she made landfall at the Carnelian palace. Perched on a chain of mountains overlooking a vast green valley in one direction, with the Ionian Sea in the other, the cold and forbidding Marcariokastro was every inch the imposing medieval castle.

It conjured up the dark, suspenseful tales of her childhood, with its square ramparts, circular, capped turrets, moat and drawbridge, although the moat and drawbridge, it was to be noted, were no longer in use. Instead, a beautiful, pastoral lake surrounded the castle.

Stella had visited the massive, gray stone castle with her family years ago when relations between Akathinia and Carnelia had been peaceful; friendly, even. It had seemed a place of immense excitement and mystery to her then, its dungeon and weaponry rooms and long, stone labyrinth of hallways the perfect place for hide-and-seek.

She had always been the bravest of the kids, lasting the longest in her hiding spot, her goose bumps and chattering teeth nothing compared to the thrill of victory. Not even the brave Athamos had liked the dark. But settling into the spacious suite down the hall from the king's wing, where she would stay until she and Kostas were married, it suddenly felt more unnerving than exciting. Perhaps because the thought that this was now her home filled her with trepidation. Perhaps because she would miss Nik, Sofía and Alex terribly.

Immersed in meetings until late on the night of her

arrival, Kostas had left word he would see her the next morning. By the time he deigned to make an appearance as Page was doing Stella's hair for the party, the day had come and gone, the apprehension she hated herself for having once again kicking up a storm in her veins.

Nodding her head to Page to admit the king, she felt her stomach fill with a thousand butterflies. Clad in a bespoke, light gray suit and white shirt that emphasized his good looks, with his dark hair scraped back from his face, the sleek, powerful impact of him knocked her sideways.

She'd told herself she'd have her response to him firmly under control by now, but the spacious suite suddenly felt as if it had shrunk to the size of a shoe box when he strolled over to stand by her side at the dressing table, his gaze meeting hers in the mirror.

Moistening her lips, she searched for a smart remark but, for the life of her, couldn't think of one. His gaze slid to her mouth, as he appeared to absorb the evidence of her nerves, then dropped to the plunging neckline of her silk robe that had seemed respectable until he'd walked in, but now made her desperately want to pull the edges together.

She resisted the urge to do so. *Somehow.* The color riding his high cheekbones, the dark heat that claimed his whiskey-hued eyes as they lifted to hers, ignited a slow burn beneath her skin. Sparked a chemical reaction that climbed up into her throat and held her in its thrall.

He bent his head and brushed a kiss against her cheek. Unprepared, or perhaps *overprepared* for the press of his firm mouth against her sensitized skin, she flinched.

Kostas straightened, a dark glitter filling his eyes. Her gaze moved to Page, who was watching them with unabashed curiosity.

"Leave us," the king bit out quietly. Page scurried

from the room as if he'd been Zeus himself raising one of his thunderbolts.

Stella lifted her chin defiantly as the door closed and the room went silent. "You will need," he instructed tersely, "to learn to hide your very…*distinct* response to me when we're around others, when the cameras start flashing tonight, or this isn't going to be a very productive exercise."

Her chin lifted higher. "I don't *plan* it, Kostas. It just happens."

The glint in his eyes deepened. "Maybe we should do it again, then, maybe a *real* kiss this time, *practice*, so it doesn't happen tonight."

"I don't think that's necessary."

"Why not? Are you afraid of how you might respond?"

"Hardly." The pressure on her brain pushed her temper to its very edge. "But why stop there?" she challenged. "Why don't we *do* it right now? Up against the wall while Page is waiting… Would that *satisfy* you? Would that be enough of a *reaction* for you? To have the whole palace abuzz with how you keep me in line?"

He leaned his impressive bulk against the dresser, folding his arms across his chest. Dark amusement melted the ire in his eyes. "Is that the plan, Stella? To make me pay for entrapping you? To bait me until I fall over the edge? You forget how well I know you, how you deflect when you are stressed, when you feel *cornered*, how you use sarcasm as a weapon because that sharp mouth of yours is so very good at it."

She lifted a shoulder. "You have to work with the tools you're given."

His mouth curved. "Why don't you just tell me what's eating you?"

"Oh, what would be the fun of that? I'm enjoying

your amateur psychology course *so* much, I think *you* should tell *me*."

He pursed his lips. Eyed her. "It's been a trying two weeks. We've both been analyzed beyond endurance. Most of the Carnelians seem ready to welcome you, but some are reluctant to embrace a foreigner. Tonight is the night you must prove to them you belong. You wouldn't be human if you weren't feeling the pressure."

Remarkably spot-on. "I've been brought up in the media glare. I can handle it."

He inclined his head. "Regardless, I appreciate how you've risen to the occasion."

She had no smart comeback for that, so she left it alone. He flicked his gaze around the elaborately furnished, if exceedingly dark, suite. "How are you settling in?"

"Fine. Except honestly, Kostas, you were right. It's like you're caught in the Dark Ages here. Everything is cold, unforgiving stone. There's no warmth to the rooms, no *life*. How in the world do you live like this?"

"It's remained untouched since my mother died. My father refused to make changes. I agree, though, it needs massive renovations. It's hardly the kind of place I want to bring our children up."

There it was again. *Children. An heir.* She wished they could just forget about it for a while.

"What was it like?" she asked to distract herself. "Growing up here?"

"Lonely," he said matter-of-factly. "Cold. I've been told the life went out of the castle when my mother died. Some say that's when it left my father, too, and he became the dictator that he was."

"He loved her a great deal?"

"Too much, by all accounts."

Beauty and the Beast. She tipped her head to the side. "Was he really the man he was portrayed as?"

"A tyrant, you mean?" His mouth twisted. "It depended on which iteration of him you encountered. He was charming, charismatic and warm when he wanted to be, self-centered, compassionless and sadistic during his dark moods. A chameleon. A compulsive liar—to himself and others."

Sadistic. *Thee mou.* A chill went through her. "And to you, his son, what was he like?"

"I was his protégé from age five on. It was about learning the role, following in his footsteps. It was never a father-and-son relationship."

And what about the childhood, the *innocence*, he should have been allowed? She recalled a photo she'd seen in one of the hallways of the castle of Kostas and his father inspecting a military guard when the prince must have been just five or six, surrounded by hundreds of thousands of people. He had looked so lost…so bewildered.

The only man who could stand alone in the middle of a crowd. Kostas had been built that way, *conditioned* to stand alone, created by a man notorious for his lack of humanity. Her chest tightened. "Did he discipline you?"

"Beat me, you mean? Yes. It was part of his modus operandi. Fear and intimidation—the devices he used to control everyone around him. Sometimes it was physical, sometimes mental. He was a master at both."

"Please tell me you had someone, a grandmother, a *godmother*, someone you could go to?"

"My *yaya.* My grandmother on my father's side, Queen Cliantha. She died when I was twelve. But by then I was in school. It was an escape for me, a break from the brainwashing, the conditioning. I was lucky my father felt it necessary to present a civilized front to the world."

It may have been a break from the conditioning, but Kostas hadn't made many friends in school. By Athamos's account, he had always been the loner in the British boarding school they'd attended, the aloof presence that had been hard to get close to even though the Constantinides boys had tried to befriend him, having their own painful knowledge of a larger-than-life father.

Where had he drawn his strength? His belief in his vision? From some unshakable core inside of him?

She sank her teeth into her lip. "What happened when you developed a mind of your own? When it became apparent your philosophies differed from your father's?"

"I tried to keep them inside in the beginning. My grandmother said it was better that way. But eventually, as I gained in confidence, as I acquired external validation of my ideas, they came out. I was considered a threat then. A competitor. Anyone who questioned my father's practices was, and was suitably disposed of, but I, of course, posed the biggest threat of all—the blood heir who wanted a different way for his country. I wasn't so easy to contain."

"How could you coexist like that?"

"Uneasily. I made it clear to my father I would bide my time until it was my turn. In the meantime, I did the official engagements he couldn't manage, presented a civilized facade to the world, attempted to keep the internal workings of the country moving while he obsessed about taking Akathinia. But with the onset of his dementia, with his increasingly erratic behavior, it became harder and harder to talk sense into him—to stand back and do nothing."

Given how passionate Kostas had always been about

his beliefs, it must have been crippling for him. A gnawing feeling took root in her stomach. A feeling that she had been vastly unfair. "Things escalated before you left."

"Yes. There were those who wanted my father replaced, those who supported me and my democratic ideas and those who fought any decentralization of power that would strip them of theirs. It was a…tenuous situation threatening to implode at any minute."

With him squarely in the middle of it—loathe to turn on his own flesh and blood no matter how wrong his father's actions. Surrounded on all sides. The man in the middle of the storm.

The uneasy sensation in her gut intensified. She lifted her gaze to his. "Was that why you raced Athamos that night? Because you were frustrated? Because you weren't in your right head?

"It was…complicated."

Clearly, from the myriad of emotions consuming those dark eyes of his. The pieces of what had happened the night she'd lost her brother started to come together, beyond what Kostas had told her. She didn't like the doubt that invaded her head as they did. The gray zone it put her in with the man she needed to have zero feelings for.

Confused was not how she needed to enter this evening.

Kostas straightened away from the dresser. "I should get dressed." He handed her the sheaf of papers he was holding. "The final guest list. You should look it over."

She curled her fingers around the papers, glad for something to do rather than *feel* things for this man she shouldn't be feeling. "Anyone interesting coming out to play?"

"General Houlis and his two key lieutenants. You will stay away from them."

"Why?"

"Because they are dangerous men. You may think you are a dragon slayer, Stella, and no doubt you are, but this side of things you will not involve yourself in. Devote yourself to getting to know the people I've highlighted. They are key social, business and political figures who will be valuable to you."

She nodded. She would do that *and* get to know General Houlis, Kostas's biggest foe, because he would be her enemy, too.

Kostas headed for the door. Halfway there, he turned. "What are you wearing, by the way?"

"That will be a surprise."

His mouth tipped up at one corner. "I'm quite sure there will be enough of those tonight, but have it your way."

He left. Page returned to finish her hair. Stella immersed herself in the guest list, going over each key name and title, committing them to memory. Thank goodness hers was photographic.

When she'd made it to the *L*'s, her eyes widened. *Cassandra Liatos is attending?* The guest of Captain Mena, one of General Houlis's disciples, according to the list.

The woman Athamos had lost his life over. The woman her fiancé had most likely bedded.

Her pulse picked up into a steady thrum, blood pounding in her ears. *An unimportant detail Kostas had forgotten to mention?*

CHAPTER FOUR

"WE ARE *LATE*, Your Highness."

Kostas was well aware of that fact as he waited for Stella in the foyer of the castle, the arrival of their first guests imminent. The crowds, he had been told, were in the tens of thousands in the courtyard, all of them waiting for a glimpse of their king and future queen.

The global media was also impatiently waiting for them, three rows deep behind the red stanchions, cameras at the ready. The need to greet both the people and the media before their guests began arriving weighed heavily on his mind, along with the speech he was about to give, perhaps the most important of his career. He did not have time for a recalcitrant princess making yet another expression of protest.

A flash of blue caught his eye on the stairwell. As if her ears were burning, his future queen appeared. The hem of her ankle-length sapphire-blue gown in her hand, she made her way carefully down the steps. The look of focus on her face, the determined tilt of her chin, the fire that blazed in her electric-blue eyes, stopped his breath in his chest. She was out to conquer. He could read it in every stubborn line of her body…in the sheer force of will she was projecting. He'd never seen anything sexier in his life.

He drew in a deep breath so he could enjoy, *absorb*

the rest of the picture, for she was something to see. The gown that perfectly matched her incredible eyes wrapped itself around her slender curves in a seductive embrace that begged a man to do the same. Her hair, caught up in curls atop her head, revealed the long, slender sweep of her neck, the diamonds that glittered at her ears and throat reflecting the incandescent glow that blazed from inside of her, reaching out and wrapping itself around him.

Not for the first time in his life he found himself consumed by her. *Intrigued* by her. When Stella was in a room, everything else paled in comparison.

She stopped on the last step, eyes on his. Those sapphire-blue orbs widened imperceptivity as he made no effort to hide the effect she had on him—the way she owned him in that moment. The air between them was charged, heated. He left it like that, waiting to see what she would do. Mouth tightening, she lowered her chin, adopting that cool, blasé look he was beginning to recognize was her first line of defense.

"I'm sorry I'm late," she said crisply. "My hair was not right."

He studied the perfect curls. "There isn't a hair out of place."

"Now." She glanced toward the antique glass doors that led to the entrance of the castle. "There are thousands out there. I saw them from my window."

"Tens of thousands. And we are late. Are you ready?"

She nodded. He offered her his hand to help her down the last step. She took it, the fission of energy that passed between them as he wrapped his fingers around hers a living, breathing entity. Stella stared down at their clasped hands, then looked straight ahead as they walked to the doors.

He brought his mouth to her ear. "You look astonishingly beautiful. But where is the *back* of your dress?"

Her lips curved. "I thought we needed to shake things up a bit."

That she would do so had never been in question.

The flash of exploding camera bulbs was blinding as they stepped out onto the portico of the castle, a roar going up in the crowd that filled the courtyard. The electric excitement, the sense of anticipation that blanketed the night, sent a chill up his spine; brought his heart to a stuttering halt. The crowds assembled for his father had been coordinated, manufactured photo ops meant to send a message to the world of the power of his rule—the people paying lip service to the dictator for fear of reprisal should they not.

This was spontaneous. No one had been forced to come and yet…they had. Packed into the courtyard, the crowd spilled out onto the avenue beyond, confirming the rise in his approval ratings since the announcement of the coming elections and the news of his engagement to Stella. Proof that hope had taken root in his country.

A piece of him he had kept buried for months, *years*, a part of him that had survived the darkness, the self-doubt his father had instilled in him with every derisory remark about the fallibility of democracy, about his own inadequacies, throbbed in his chest. It was, he realized, his own hope. Somehow it had survived the hell he had endured.

If he continued to earn the people's trust, he could rebuild this nation. He could make everything that had been wrong *right.*

Stella squeezed his hand. He hadn't realized he'd stopped dead in his tracks. Looking down at her, their eyes held for a long, emotion-filled moment. *Go on*, hers seemed to say. *Seize the moment.*

They stepped forward and smiled and waved to the throng. The press was hungry for them, too. They gave them a photo before they took their place at the top of the stairs beside the Constantinides family as the first limousine rolled up.

A fully recovered, if fragile-looking, King Gregorios stood by Queen Amara, flanked by Nikandros, his wife, Sofía, Aleksandra and her husband, Aristos. That he was alone, yet again, struck him at the same moment as Stella's presence at his side filled that space inside of him. She was the strongest woman he knew.

Confident and utterly at ease, she greeted every guest with the perfect poise he had known she possessed, but it was her ability to connect with each one of the arrivals that blew him away. She found something in each brief greeting to make every encounter memorable, transforming like the chameleon she was—but it was always genuine. The skill was born of her royal heritage, yes, but it went deeper than that—to who she was, how she *cared.*

By the time they'd made their way through the first three flights of royalty, politicians and Carnelian high society deemed important enough for a personal greeting, he had had more than enough.

He pressed a hand to his fiancée's sexy bare back as the PR person gave the contingent the cue to go in.

Stella glanced at the crowd, who were still waving and calling their names. "We can't leave them like this."

"We need to. The agenda is tight."

She turned a vibrant blue beam of stubborn defiance on him. "If you want to *win* the people, Kostas, you have to *know* the people." And with that, she picked up her skirt and made her way toward the stairs.

He cursed under his breath and started after her. His bodyguard stepped forward. "You can't go into that crowd, Your Highness. You know the—"

"Threat," he said grimly. He was well aware he was a target for assassins. That there were many who would like to see him dead. But his future queen had now cleared the stairs and was accepting flowers from a young girl, the stubborn curve of her back *daring* him to follow.

He did. This time it was his bodyguard who cursed, rifled off a series of instructions to his security team, then followed him into the crowd. Stella gave him a sweet-as-pie smile as he made his way to her side, curving an arm around her waist. "This is Berdina from the west coast. Your father once shook her hand."

He shook Berdina's hand. Then the hand of the elderly lady beside her that Stella had just finished hugging. *Hugging.* They worked their way through the front row, comprised of everything from those elderly ladies to children wishing to greet the royals to people anxious to confirm change was coming.

A man whose lined face had seen a great deal of life stepped forward and clasped his hands. "Will the elections really happen? We have waited so long for this."

"Yes," Kostas told him, "you have my word."

"But will they *mean* anything?" the man asked, doubt in his eyes.

"They will not be shadow appointments," he promised him. "The people will have real power. We are going to change this nation together."

By the time they were called back to the stairs by his frantic PR person, his throat felt as if it was lined with glass. He wrapped a firm hand around Stella's waist and directed her toward the stairs.

She aimed a satisfied look at him. "Glad you did it?"

"Yes," he said. "My security, however, is not."

"Why? Our bodyguards were with us."

"I am an assassination target, Stella."

Her mouth fell open. Staring at him, she missed her step and would have fallen had he not snared an arm around her waist and hauled her into him.

"Assassination target," she gasped. "Oh, my God, I didn't—"

"Think," he said, finishing her thought. "You were too busy making a point."

Her face went bright red.

"I know you're living to be a thorn in my side at the moment," he said as he directed her up the stairs and into the castle, "but could I please ask that you think before you act, particularly where protocol is concerned?"

Thee mou. Stella's head spun, blood pounding in her veins, as she matched Kostas's long strides through the doors of the castle and down the stone hallway toward the ballroom. She had not considered such a horrific thing and yet she should have. Kostas had detailed his enemies to her, outlined their hostility toward his rule. It only made sense he would be a target.

But *assassins*? Fear coated her mouth, gritty and dark. What she had been *trying* to do was shake Kostas out of that aloofness he protected himself with in a crowd. The stiff formality he had clearly learned from his father. She had felt his tension as soon as they'd emerged outside, and yet the emotion emanating from him had been anything but removed. He had been caught off guard by the people's response to him. By the joy they had displayed. Moved by it. He just didn't know how to show it.

"Lypamai," she murmured as they halted in front of the massive, gold-plated doors to the ballroom. *I'm sorry.*

Kostas looked down at her. “How about a little less wave-making and a little more obedience?”

Her jaw dropped. “As if I—”

He pressed a finger to her mouth, a brilliant smile lighting up his somber face. “I was just getting you going… You will need your fire in there tonight, *yineka mou*.”

Her mouth burned where he touched her, the casual endearment throwing her completely off balance. She didn’t want to feel this pulsing, inescapable connection to him that had burned between them ever since she’d walked down those stairs tonight. Ever since she’d first laid eyes on him.

As if he didn’t look spectacular enough in full military dress, the severe black uniform adorned with gold buttons and a red sash playing up his hawk-like, brutal good looks. It made him appear larger than life—the weakness she’d always had for him.

She lowered her chin, the infinitesimal movement making him drop his fingers away from her mouth. “No need to worry about me. I’ve got this.”

“That is the one thing I do not doubt.”

A booming voice announced their arrival to the buzzing ballroom. She took Kostas’s arm as they made their way through the crowd of almost five hundred guests toward the front of the room, where Nik stood waiting. The cacophony of sound as the guests applauded echoed off the hundreds of stained-glass windows that lined the room, highlighted to dramatic effect by the golden-hued arches that framed them.

The dark, seductive ambience lent by the stunning purple, gold and orange light from the glass windows highlighted by a dozen antique candelabra chandeliers scattered throughout the room seemed to set the tone for the evening as she and Kostas took their place beside Nik on a low balcony. Goose bumps unearthed themselves on her skin as she took in the packed ballroom, a glittering, privileged crowd who would decide the king's fate. *Her fate*, she corrected herself, for it was hers now, too.

Silence fell as Kostas greeted their guests. If he was aloof in a crowd, he was compelling as an orator, his even, measured tone underpinned by the passion he held for his vision of a new Carnelia founded on the self-determination of its people and the modernization of his country to bring it into an "enlightened" age. If he knew he was making enemies with some even as he attempted to build trust with others, he was undeterred. He was daring his people to accept his challenge, daring them to dream of a brighter future.

"I'm ready to sign up," she murmured under her breath as he finished and stepped back beside her to allow Nik to take center stage.

He bent his head, his breath a warm caress at her ear. "*Efharisto.* Perhaps in time you will be ready to sign on to…*other* pieces of our partnership as things become illuminated."

She lifted her chin, cheeks burning. "In your dreams, Kostas."

"You already are, Stella."

She kept her gaze averted from his, looked at the crowd as Nik began speaking, refusing to engage. Except every part of her body *was* engaging with that seductive comment that had her excruciatingly aware of him long after Nik had delivered an eloquent speech of peace and friendship, and they had stepped off the balcony to mingle with their guests. It was not helped by the firm hand Kostas kept at her bare back, his big paw burning into her skin.

She hadn't thought about that aspect of the dress when she'd chosen it and really should have, because it made it difficult to concentrate on the important introductions being made with his splayed fingers declaring an ownership over her. A reminder of how strong and overwhelmingly male he was.

Firming her jaw, she forced herself to focus, attaching faces to the names Kostas had given her, familiarizing herself with each and every one of the VIPs as they engaged in polite, easy bites of small talk. She was laying the groundwork for relationships she would later build on, some of which would be a challenge she discovered because Carnelia seemed to be as closed an inner circle as Akathinia was. But others were open and curious, welcoming.

It was exhausting, the mental effort it took to absorb all that information about so many people, despite her razor-sharp memory. She was craving a break when Kostas stiffened by her side, his hand tightening around hers.

She followed his gaze to the couple directly in their path. The tall, dark-haired, middle-aged male wore a military uniform with enough stripes on the shoulder to indicate he was very senior. Not quite handsome, with his clearly defined, masculine features, but his piercing dark eyes held her attention. Her *yaya* had always said the eyes were the measure of a person and this man's dark stare held nothing good.

General Houlis.

Kostas drew her toward the couple, his hand at her waist. "General Houlis, I'm pleased to present my fiancée, Stella Constantinides. Stella, General Houlis is the commander of the Carnelian navy and a member of my executive council."

Stella held her hand out to the general, who took it

and bent lightly over it, the mocking significance of the gesture not lost on her. “A pleasure, Your Highness,” he said, straightening. “Your presence here in Carnelia has been highly…*anticipated*.”

The general made the introductions to his wife, then turned his attention back to Stella. “That was quite a reception for you two out there tonight.”

She tilted her head. “It was wonderful. I am looking forward to restoring the close bonds Carnelia and Akathinia once shared. My childhood is full of those happy memories. It was also,” she said deliberately, “lovely to see the excitement of the people about the forthcoming elections. Their belief a better future is ahead…”

“Indeed,” said the general. “But are they ready for such widespread change? That is the real question.”

“They’ve been ready for a long time now.” Kostas set a deliberate gaze on the general. “Fear and intimidation have kept them silenced. Change is always hard, but for those who seek a better way, the short-term pain of the unknown will bring long-term gain. It is the faith we must all have. Those who resist change do so because it’s in their own self-interest. They fear what they have to lose.”

The general’s eyes glittered. “Or they don’t want the change that’s being shoved down their throat. How many examples can we count of nations who’ve signed on to regional and global lovefests only to find the old ways were better?”

“Old ways as in the suppression of their rights? As in the fear for their own safety if they refuse to toe the line? I am sure you would agree that can hardly be called *better*.”

“Sometimes,” the general countered, “the people

aren't equipped to make such important decisions for themselves. Sometimes they don't have the vision required. It could all go to hell in a handbasket if not handled correctly."

"Which is why the transition time will be used to smooth the way." Kostas's tone was frigid now. "My belief in the Carnelian people is absolute. There is only one way forward for this country."

General Houlis lifted a shoulder. "Time will tell, won't it?"

Stella drew in a breath. The general turned to her. "You will certainly have a front-row seat to pursue your vision from your position on the executive council if the rumors are to be believed..."

She opened her mouth to respond. Kostas tightened his fingers around her waist. "We still have elections to carry out," the king said. "Many details to consider before the new council takes shape."

"But she will have a place on it?"

The disdain in the general's voice snapped her back straight.

"Her Highness," Kostas intoned, "will play a significant role in governing this country, yes."

"Don't you think," Stella interjected, "that it's time the council reflected a woman's perspective? The addition of some empathy, some *compassion*, to even out the testosterone-laden mistakes of the past? After all," she said, tilting her head to the side, "we aren't stuck in the Dark Ages anymore, are we?"

"No," said the general, "we aren't. It's when emotions get in the way of lawmaking that the mix gets murky."

Her gaze locked on his. "I *promise* you, General Houlis, my emotions will not obscure my clear thinking. I've found empathy, attempting to understand each other, *communicating*, has the power to solve some of the world's greatest conflicts. It can only be a powerful force when it comes to ruling a nation."

"And you bring a great deal of popularity with you to spread that message. Your work around the world has brought you much acclaim." He raised a brow. "The next Eva Perón, perhaps?"

"I would hardly make that comparison."

"Ah, but it's an intriguing one to consider. Some say that Eva, in fact, had all the power."

Kostas went dangerously still beside her. "Accumulating *power* is not the goal, General Houlis—putting it in the hands of the people is."

The other man lifted a shoulder. "I'm merely making the point that your future wife will be a force to be reckoned with."

A shiver went down her spine. Was there an underlying message there?

Kostas announced the need to move on. His hand at her elbow, he bid General Houlis and his wife farewell and propelled Stella through the crowd. He was practically vibrating with fury.

"When I *ask* you to refrain from adding fuel to the fire, you will do it. Your appointment to the council is a delicate move that requires much finessing. There is no point in making waves before the time comes."

"Perhaps you've changed your mind?"

He set his furious gaze on her. "I never go back on a promise—that you will learn, as well. But you need to be patient. We must take this in baby steps."

"I get that, Kostas, but I will not be *muzzled*. You will not tell me what I can and cannot say."

His gaze turned incendiary. "I may be giving you power, but I am still the king of this country, Stella. You *will* listen to me when I give you a direct order. *Obey* me when I ask for your cooperation."

Her skin stung as if he'd slapped her. "I have not agreed to the *obey* part yet. You might take that into consideration as you throw your weight around or you might find yourself minus a wife."

"Stella—"

"I need a break."

She shrugged her elbow free and stalked away, picking out Alex and Sofía in the crowd. Jaw clenched, she headed for them.

Alex eyed her as she approached. "What happened? You look positively combustible."

"Three guesses."

"Kostas, Kostas and Kostas." Her sister plucked a glass of champagne off a passing waiter's tray. "You clearly haven't had enough of this."

Clearly not. She took a sip of the bubbly. "I might kill him before this is over."

"What did he do now?"

"He told me I have to *obey* him."

Alex's mouth curved. "What did you say back?"

"That I haven't signed on to the *obey* part yet." She took a deep, calming breath. "How has your night been?"

Alex flicked a glance at Sofía. "Oh, *you know*, the usual chitchat. It's a bit disconcerting that these people were our enemies last year and now we're socializing with them."

"Not the people," Stella amended, "the leadership. And why do you have such a funny look on your face? What's going on?"

Alex directed another of those sideways looks at their sister-in-law. "Nothing, I—"

"Alex."

"Cassandra Liatos is here. The woman who—"

"I know who she is." Her heart thudded against her chest. "Where is she?"

"She's standing beside the chocolate fountain…with the man in the gray suit."

She turned in a subtle movement, locating the couple Alex had described. It must be Captain Mena in his sharply pressed military uniform standing beside Cassandra, but it was the woman herself who caught and held her attention. Of medium height, with the perfect, voluptuous figure she herself had always craved, Cassandra was astonishingly beautiful. As dark as Stella was fair, with long silky hair and exotic eyes, she was the kind of woman who stopped traffic.

The kind of woman men lost their heads over.

For a moment, she was unable to speak, unable to do anything but stare at the person who had turned her life upside down. "Does Nik know she's here?"

"Yes." It was Sofía who answered. "He elected not to speak to her."

She couldn't do it. She could not exercise that type of self-restraint. She didn't have it in her.

"I need to talk to her."

"I don't think that's a good idea." Alex put a hand on her arm. "Let it go, Stella."

But she was already walking toward the fountain. Cassandra looked up, eyes widening as she approached. Stella greeted Captain Mena first, then the woman at his side. "May I have a moment of your time?"

The other woman nodded, the tempest in her dark eyes the only sign that this was anything other than a polite social interaction. Stella led the way out of the ballroom and onto one of the outdoor terraces. Face-to-face with the woman who had dogged her thoughts for weeks, she took a deep breath.

"Efharisto," she murmured. "I'm sorry to pull you away."

Cassandra shook her head. "When I saw Nikandros, I wanted to speak to him. My fiancé persuaded me not to. He said it was better left alone."

"Everyone seems to think that." Stella wrapped her arms around herself, resting her champagne glass against her chest. "I need to know if you loved my brother. If he loved you. It's the only rational explanation I can find for him to do something so out of character. Yes, the competition between him and Kostas has always been the height of stupidity, but it had to have been more."

Cassandra put her glass on the railing, taking a moment, as if to gather her thoughts. "I cared about both of them," she said, lifting her gaze to Stella's. "You need to know that. I felt as if I was in an impossible situation. I knew the history behind them. It made it very…difficult."

"But you must have had stronger feelings for one than the other?"

"I was in love with Kostas," Cassandra said quietly. "I adored Athamos, but it was Kostas I wanted."

She was unprepared for the sharp claws of jealousy that climbed inside her and dug deep into her soft recesses. For the jagged pain that raked itself over top of it on behalf of her brother's ill-fated gamble. Athamos had not loved easily, as had been the case with all her siblings after her parents' disastrous example of a marriage, but when he'd fallen, he'd fallen hard.

"Did he know?"

"I don't know. I told them both I needed time to think. I was trying to work out how to tell Athamos it wasn't him I wanted. It was—" Cassandra pressed her hands to her cheeks. "It was done before I even knew what was happening. The first thing I knew of it was when I opened the newspaper the next day and saw the news of the crash."

When Athamos was dead. "Do you wonder," she asked, unable to stop herself, "if you'd said something sooner…?"

Cassandra paled, her deep olive skin assuming a gray cast. "Every day. Every day since it happened. But at some point I had to forgive myself. Move on. Punishing myself wasn't going to bring Athamos back. It wasn't going to change what happened."

Stella bit hard into her lip, the metallic taste of blood filling her mouth. She should tell Cassandra it wasn't her fault, that she couldn't have predicted what would have happened, but a tiny part of her couldn't forgive the woman for not sharing the truth with Athamos before things got out of hand. And because she suspected Cassandra had been hedging her bets. If the crown prince of Carnelia had fallen through as a potential mate, she could have picked up the pieces with Athamos and still become queen.

She studied the woman across from her. "Have you found happiness now, with your fiancé?"

Cassandra's gaze dropped away from hers, but not before she caught the myriad of emotion that ran through those dark eyes. *The sadness.* "I have found…peace."

"With a man who wants to take the potential for that away from this country?"

The other woman lifted her chin. "It isn't wise to judge others until you've walked in their shoes."

But the deep, searing flare of jealousy invading Stella didn't care about fairness. Athamos was dead. Cassandra Liatos was still clearly in love with Kostas. Perhaps their relationship, made impossible according to her fiancé, had never really finished. Perhaps Kostas still loved her. It made her feel ill in a way she'd never experienced before.

And that, she told herself, was ridiculous. Her and Kostas's marriage was not a love match. It was a partnership. It was, however, a potent reminder of what it would cost her to allow her old feelings for her fiancé to resurface. To allow them to rule her.

She lifted her gaze to Cassandra's. "I wish you and Captain Mena the best of luck. I hope you find the peace you are looking for. I really do."

Turning on her heel, she strode inside. Alex had been right. That had been no kind of closure.

"How many High Court justices will you appoint?"

Kostas attempted to concentrate on his conversation with a high-ranking Carnelian judge, but the sight of his fiancée in the arms of Aristos Nicolades had unearthed a strange, combustible force inside of him that felt a great deal like jealousy. A foreign emotion he had little experience with. If he wanted a woman, he pursued her and enjoyed her. If she played games, one of those ineffectual exercises designed to inspire him to think seriously about her, she was gone within the hour.

But right now, watching Stella enclosed in the casino magnate's arms on the dance floor, an intense conversation going on between the two of them, he was not unaffected. He wanted to walk over there and end it.

Exhaling a long breath, he pushed his attention back to the woman in front of him, a powerful figure who was a key supporter and would be an ally in the justice system. "I'm not sure yet. Rest assured, you will be among them."

He concluded his conversation with the judge, making his way toward the dance floor, attempting to corral his temper while he was at it. It was tradition that the engaged couple kicked off the dancing, but since his fiancée had been out on the terrace with Cassandra Liatos, a collision he hadn't been able to prevent, then taken to the dance floor with Aristos, he'd had to cool his heels while his event planner continued to look as if she might burst a blood vessel.

He was also feeling as if he might burst a blood vessel at his fiancée's latest rebellion. He caught her hand as she walked off the dance floor with Aristos and the look of careless disregard on her face sent his blood pressure up another ten points.

"That line I was talking about earlier," he murmured in her ear as he directed her to the side of the dance floor. "We're fast approaching it."

She turned near violet eyes on him. "What happens when we do? Will you *discipline* me?"

"The thought is vastly appealing."

Her eyes widened. "You wouldn't lay a hand on me."

"No, I wouldn't. Not in anger. There are many forms of discipline, *yineka mou.* I would find an appropriate one for you."

A layer of heat stained her perfect skin. Dropping her chin, she leveled a heated glance at him. "You *knew* she would be here and you didn't tell me."

"Cassandra?"

"Yes."

"She was on the guest list. I knew you'd see it. I didn't see the point in rehashing the whole subject again."

"Rehashing it?" She stared at him. "My brother died when that car plunged off the cliffs. Excuse me for wanting the whole story."

"I've apologized. I've told you the story, Stella. It needs to be finished."

She set her hands on her hips. "Were you afraid I would discover she's still in love with you? Are *you* still in love with *her*, Kostas? I'd like to know the lay of the land before I walk into this marriage. Will there be three of us in it?"

"No," he said flatly. "I am not in love with her. I told you it ended at the time. But I am happy to see you care. Maybe there's hope for us yet."

"I don't *care*," she growled. "I am more concerned with being humiliated."

But she did. He could see it in the green-eyed jealousy consuming her. It filled him with a supreme sense of satisfaction as the bandleader gave them the signal to take to the dance floor. Wrapping his fingers around hers, he led her to the center of the space that had been cleared for them. "Perhaps you should concern yourself instead with the fact that it is Carnelian tradition that we kiss during the first dance, and since everyone will be waiting for it, we'd better do a convincing job."

Her eyes flew to his as he curved an arm around her waist and laced his fingers through hers to pull her close. "Why didn't you tell me about this?"

"Ask yourself that, *paidi mou*, and I'm sure you'll come up with the answer."

Her skin paled. "Stop using those ridiculous endearments. They hardly suit us."

"I beg to differ." He directed her through the first steps of the dance. "I think they are perfect."

She was stiff, but there was undeniable fire beneath his fingers. He could feel the pulse of her fury, sense the scattered direction of her thoughts as she looked for a way out of the inevitability to come.

"Perhaps you should just enjoy it."

"Perhaps I should close my eyes and channel a former lover. Think about someone I actually *want* to kiss. It would provide far more inspiration than the thought of kissing you."

Heat flared under his skin, jealousy rocking him hard. A tight smile twisted his lips as he closed his fingers around hers and drew her closer. "Refuse me, Stella, deny how you feel, but don't ever, *ever*, tell me lies."

Fury drove him as he clasped his fingers around her jaw and brought his mouth down on hers in a kiss that stamped his possession all over her. That made it clear to anyone in the room, to *her*, that he was the only one who would touch her this way. To expose her lies for what they were.

Stiff at first, she yielded only enough to cover up the animosity swirling between them. But then the kiss morphed, changed into something entirely different. Her soft, tempting mouth beneath his threw him back ten years to another kiss, another time, when her belief in him had been a shining light in the darkness that had consumed him. Reminded him who she was. The woman who had stood on those stairs outside with him tonight and prompted him to seize the moment. The woman who had agreed to take a massive leap with him with the ending yet unknown.

Gentling the kiss, he exercised a more persuasive possession. His thumb at her jaw stroked its way across her satiny skin, his hand at her waist drew her into the heat they generated. A tiny, animalistic sound emerged from her throat as he angled his mouth across hers, lips sliding over lush, sacred territory, caressing her with a reverential touch that demonstrated her potent effect on him.

A sigh left her lips as she gave in, mouth softening,

parting for him. He claimed her then with a kiss that was pure in its origins, both of them giving of themselves without reservation, hot and sweet all at the same time. A shudder went through her, vibrating its way along his nerve endings. It caught him off guard. Tapped something deep and latent in him, claimed *him* in a way he hadn't expected.

For a brief moment in time, oblivious to the hundreds of people in the room, the truth existed between them. That this…*this* had always been right.

CHAPTER FIVE

STELLA BLINKED AS Kostas lifted his head from hers, the blinding spotlights on the dance floor flickering in her eyes as she attempted to focus. Her palms were damp, her knees weak, and her heart thrummed in her chest as the undeniable affects of his kiss reverberated through her.

That had been a full-on, five-star Robert Doisneau kiss right there, rolled up in some Mary Poppins magic. The kind she couldn't have fought no matter how hard she'd tried, because this was Kostas delivering it, the man whose kiss she'd measured all others against. Jessie had been right about that.

Her fluttering heart plummeted to the toes of her Christian Louboutin shoes. She'd been fooling herself all these years hoping she could find that magic with someone else because it had only ever been Kostas who could inspire it.

The stomach-churning realization settled over her as she unlocked her gaze from the man throwing her into confusion and attempted to wrestle her composure back as catcalls and applause broke out around them.

"Pulling out the big guns, Kostas?"

"If I was pulling out the big *guns*, we certainly wouldn't be standing on the dance floor," he returned with a velvety soft composure that made her crazy. "I'll save that for when you finally admit how you feel."

She had no smart comeback for that because she was quite sure her feelings were still plastered across her face. She focused on Nik and Sofía instead. They had joined them on the dance floor, along with a dozen other couples. She moved her gaze elsewhere when her brother's amused expression sent another wave of heat to her cheeks.

She and Kostas had been dancing the night of her mother's birthday party all those years ago, the night she'd made her big mistake with him. Her dream of becoming a lawyer in tatters, the fury and frustration she'd been trying to hold in all night overcoming her, and Kostas had seemed to be the only one to recognize her misery.

He'd pulled her off the dance floor and out to the library so she could collect herself. Except alone in the library, their attraction toward each other had caught fire after a summer spent dancing around it. Kostas had just arrived home, fresh from flight school in California with Athamos, taking his place as a captain in the Carnelian navy, a *man* when all the others had been boys. A man with an edge that turned her heart and hormones upside down.

Even among all the female adulation he'd engendered with his aloof, unattainable air, he'd always made time for her. Had always *listened* to her. When he'd kissed her in the library, she'd been sure she'd met her soul mate. Everything in her miserable, lonely existence had felt better, the pain of having her self-determination stripped away replaced by the heart-pounding excitement of being in Kostas's arms.

For a brief moment in that painful adolescence, she

had felt whole, as if she hadn't been missing some crucial piece that made her so unlovable. So defective she could never seem to do anything right. She'd waited for Kostas in his bed, thinking he'd be thrilled to find her there after the kiss they'd shared that had felt like a revelation. Instead, he'd shattered her heart with the callous, mortifying dismissal he'd administered.

Her eyelids squeezing closed, she banished the memory to the recycle bin of her mind and this time she *would* empty it. She was no longer that hopelessly naive, vulnerable girl looking for a fairy tale that didn't exist. For a man who didn't exist. So Kostas had caught her off guard with that kiss… She just needed to try harder to channel the impenetrability she aspired to.

Her emotions too close to the surface, she stayed silent during the rest of the dance. Completed the remainder of her obligatory turns around the spotlighted floor in the same self-protective state until it was finally time to wish their guests farewell.

She stood by Kostas on the front steps of the castle and waved everyone off as the early hours ticked by on the clock. After a nightcap with Nik, Sofía, Alex, Aristos and her fiancé in the Gothic-inspired conservatory, she went to bed. Except as tired as she was, she kept staring at the ceiling of the creepy, dark room.

So it turned out the remnants of her old crush were actually a dangerous adult attraction toward a man she was realizing she may have vastly misjudged, a far more dangerous proposition than the first. Her defense strategy for this marriage remained the same. She needed to take her attraction to Kostas and banish it to the deep, dark place she harbored inside her for the heartbreak she'd accumulated more than her fair share of.

Kissing him in public had been an unforeseen, necessary diversion from the master plan. She wouldn't have to do it again until their wedding day and that was four whole weeks away. Lots of time to render herself immune to the king.

The week that followed saw both Stella and Kostas wrapped up in their own separate endeavors. Kostas worked insane hours planning the elections and meeting with foreign investors as he attempted to jump-start Carnelia's economy with an aggressive modernization plan, while Stella followed up with the contacts she'd made at the engagement party, booking meetings with various charities and organizations she wanted to get involved with.

She wanted to dig in, to discover the issues Carnelians faced after decades of King Idas's totalitarian rule. What she found was disheartening. The people were suffering both emotionally and economically, leaving them bruised and battered, cynical and distrustful. It was going to take a great deal of time and hard work to heal them and put this country back together.

On Friday, she returned home from a meeting with the head of the largest social services charity to find Kostas walking in the door at the same time. Powerful and compelling in a dark navy suit and red tie, the lines bracketing his eyes and mouth revealed the pressure he was under to repair this broken country with so many opposing forces in play. The dark, intense aura somehow managed to make him even more dangerously attractive.

They'd been like two ships passing in the night, but when they did manage to sit down together for a quick meal there was an ever-present and unresolved tension between them. Neither of them had forgotten that kiss. They were simply choosing to avoid it.

"Long day?" She attempted a polite, even interaction.

He set down his briefcase, raked a hand through his thick, dark hair and focused his tawny gaze on her. "Exceedingly long. I thought I'd unearth a bottle of good burgundy from the cellar, since we're staying in tonight. We can sit down to a civilized dinner for once. A date if you like."

Her nerve endings tingled. "Aren't we a bit past that?"

His catlike eyes hardened. "We are getting married in three weeks, Stella. We need to spend some time together, learn how to interact, get to know each other better. So no, I don't think we're past it. I think it's perfect timing."

The rebuke rippled across her skin. "All right," she said, lifting a hand to slide her bag off her shoulder. "I will go and get changed. A power suit puts me in a particular frame of mind."

An amused glint entered his gaze. "So what will you change into, *yineka mou*? Your agreeable, soft, feminine side? If so, I'm all for it."

"I'm not sure I have that."

"Oh, you do, Stella." His sleek, sensual rejoinder slid down her spine like silk. "All it takes is the right mood to bring it out."

With that kiss that had brought her to her knees far too fresh in her mind still, she cocked her chin at a defiant angle. "Is that your specialty, Kostas, with all those women you collected? Wining and dining them so you unearthed their *soft, agreeable sides*?"

He lifted a shoulder. "Sometimes it required dinner, sometimes not. But since you are my fiancée, your presence at dinner is *my* pleasure."

Thee mou, but he was arrogant. It didn't stop her head from going to that story Athamos had told her—of Kostas setting his attention on a particular woman in a bar near the base where they'd trained at Miramar. The rumor went that he'd had her outside against the back of the bar—no dinner needed there. The woman, according to Athamos, had returned to the bar with a very satisfied look on her face.

"Stella?"

She blinked. "Sorry?"

"I'll meet you in the dining room."

Mouth tight, she climbed the stairs to her room. Deliberately picking out the furthest thing from what could be considered sexy attire, she dressed in black leggings and a loose-fitting, gypsy-style blouse she loved. Kostas's gaggle of women might have been easy targets, but she was *not*.

Kostas registered Stella's reappearance with amusement. If she thought the outfit she had on less than *agreeable*, she was mistaken. The leggings emphasized the long sweep of her elegant legs to perfection, providing a tantalizing glimpse of firm, toned thighs and smooth hips, just enough to fill a man's hands. The turquoise blouse, while covering her fully, was sheer enough to hint at the delectable curves beneath.

Blood headed south fast, something that hadn't happened since before he'd left for Tibet. In his quest to find himself, his guru had preached abstinence as the path to clarity. Having had no desire to have a woman, it had been an easy practice to follow. But not now. Not with his sexy fiancée baiting him at every turn.

Right now, with the frustration and tension of the day throbbing through him, finding an empty room, backing her up against a wall, wrapping Stella's beautiful legs around his waist and solving this friction between them exactly as she'd suggested that night in her suite held great appeal. *Hot, hard and fast.*

Unfortunately, he conceded, as he picked up his fiancée's wineglass and filled it as she sat down beside him, he couldn't do that. Ensuring his fiancée thawed enough to make this partnership of theirs a viable proposition was his goal tonight. Figuring out what had made her so cynical, so *brittle*, was a big part of that. Hot sex was not.

"So," he said as she gave him a wary look, "tell me about your day."

She took a sip of her wine. Cradled the glass in her palms. "Almost all of the RSVPs for the wedding are in. I'm shocked at how many can make it, almost three-quarters of those we invited."

"They are curious. Curious to see if this Camelot they have invoked is the real thing."

Her mouth twisted in that sexy, slightly crooked smile that had always fascinated him. *Turned him on.* "Now to live up to such an ideal."

"Not possible—that's why it's a myth."

She lifted a shoulder. "This afternoon I met with Theda Demarchis. She offered to give me a tour of the various charities her organization runs. We saw two of them this afternoon."

"The system is not in good shape, I know. My father drove the country into the ground before he died. Used far too much of the public funds to tighten the reins on the people, for his security, rather than to help them prosper. I've been returning what I can to organizations like Theda's, but the funds we receive from the foreign investment will be the real key."

Her mouth pursed. "It was sad, to see how this once proud country has diminished. There are so many who need help, so many who have suffered so greatly."

A knot formed in his gut. At his failure to stop his father. At allowing it to get this far. “It is painful to see,” he agreed. “But slowly it will get better. The foreign investment, the hotel developments, will also create jobs. Unemployment is a big problem.”

“Speaking of which.” She pressed her wineglass to her chin. “I had a cappuccino in town after my meeting. The proprietor of the café sat down at my table, worried the hotels are going to obstruct his view and take away business.”

He shrugged. “They might. This isn’t about one store owner’s view, it’s about revitalizing the nation’s economy.”

“Yes, but he isn’t *just* one person. He’s an influential voice in the community. He sees the townspeople every day, talks to them, tells them what he thinks.”

“So what did *you* tell him?”

“That more tourists means more business for him.”

“Exactly how he needs to view it.” He shook his head. “I think, somehow, the people are looking for roses and sunshine from me, when what they really need is actual solutions to their problems.”

She frowned. “Three generations of that man’s family have run that café, Kostas. It’s the best view in town. I’m not saying there are easy answers, I’m not saying change is going to come easily for people or that you can accommodate all of their requests, but perhaps you can accommodate some. In this instance, perhaps, keep the buildings low-rise like we have in Akathinia.” She lifted her glass to her lips and took a sip. “I told him to write you a letter.”

“A *letter*?”

“Yes. And you will answer it. You saw the night of our engagement party how much distrust and cynicism exists among the people. The only way you are going to win your people back is to show them the empathy and care your father never did. Prove to them they can trust you."

His mouth flattened. "They also need to trust *me*. Let me do my job. If I get mired down in what every café owner thinks, I'll never get anything accomplished."

She shook her head. "You need to choose your key influencers carefully. Those closest to the people. That café owner is one of them. You need to listen to him."

Stella watched Kostas over the rim of her wineglass as the salad was served. She was pushing him, but he needed it. His default mode was to know everything, to fix Carnelia's problems the most efficient way he knew, but that wasn't going to work here. He couldn't be a one-man show.

However, a man like Kostas, so utterly sure in his opinions, needed to find his own way to the truth.

They managed to pass the meal in a distinctly civilized fashion. By the time it was through, the excellent wine and the chance to relax had her feeling distinctly mellow.

Kostas picked up the bottle of wine. "Let's finish it in the conservatory."

She followed him there. He sprawled out on the small sofa, long legs splayed in front of him. She headed for one of the wing-backed chairs beside it.

"Sit here." His command pulled her to a halt. She turned to look at him. "You may have decided our intimate relationship will be conducted on an as-needed basis," he drawled softly, "but that doesn't mean you have to sit a mile away."

The glimmer of challenge in his dark perusal was too much to resist. Curling up on the other end of the sofa, she discovered she had little room, as his big frame hogged the space and a hard thigh pressed against hers.

She pulled in a breath only to find *him* in her lungs. Spicy aftershave with a rich, dark undertone that was all Kostas, pure carnal male.

She handed him her glass to refill. The brush of his fingers against hers transferred his masculine heat, amplifying her awareness of him.

Seriously, Stella. She searched for an innocuous subject. "I had the interior designer come by this morning. I can't live in this mausoleum one minute longer. He's going to have some plans to us next week."

"Good." He handed the glass back to her. "Can he start in the master suite? Perhaps he could have it finished by the wedding?"

When she would move in there with him, *share his bed*, sometimes in an intimate fashion. Her stomach curled in on itself. "Might be possible." She chewed on her lip. "He was wondering about a nursery. Do we want it connected to our suite?"

"Yes. I want our children to be close in case they have a nightmare or they need us."

Children—*plural.* She swallowed. "How many children are you planning for us to have?"

"More than one. Maybe three? Four?"

"Four?" That would require much *baby-making*, particularly if it didn't happen right away.

His mouth kicked up at one corner. "I want lots of kids, Stella. And not because I want to turn you into a *broodmare.* Because I never had siblings...because I never want our children to feel the isolation I once did."

A vise closed around her chest. She couldn't get his pain out of her head—the childhood he'd led, how destructive it must have been to his soul... It had haunted her as she'd stared at the damn creepy shadows at night trying to sleep.

"How did you cope?" she asked huskily. "I keep thinking about you by yourself. You were only twelve when your grandmother died. How did the world even make sense?"

He cradled his glass against his chest. "I retreated into myself. I lived in my own little world. My grandmother kept pulling me out, engaging me, forcing me to find a sense of self. She knew I would need that strength when she was gone."

She wrapped her arms around herself and hugged tight. "She was a popular queen from what I remember."

"Both her and my grandfather, King Pelias, were very popular, benevolent monarchs of the people—not the ambitious, controlling rulers of the past. Unfortunately, my grandfather's ill health took him very young and my father became king perhaps sooner than he should have. It was up to my grandmother to guide my father then, but after my mother died, he became unreachable. She began coaching me instead. Every night when I went to visit her, she taught me the principles of what she believed in, what being a good ruler meant—that they were *of* the people, not *over* the people."

"And what you learned at school, during your time in the West, the philosophies you developed, were grounded in what she had taught you."

"Yes."

She pressed her palms to her cheeks, remembering the loneliness she'd felt. Imagining it ten times worse because there would also be *fear*. Her gaze rested on him; so stoic, resolute, like he *always* was. "It was so much for a child to absorb. To *understand*."

A hint of emotion flickered in his dark eyes. "She told me whenever I lost my way, when I harbored doubts about which direction to go, to always remember to be a force of good. That I would be afforded great power, but with that came the responsibility to use it wisely. That if I was strong and followed my heart, I would not fail."

A wave of emotion swept over her, tightening her throat, spurring a wet heat at the back of her eyes. To be so brave, to carry his grandmother's wisdom with him throughout his life and somehow manage not to be consumed by the force his father had been, struck her as remarkable. *Extraordinary.* But it also illuminated her own shortcomings. Whereas Kostas had been defined by his duty, she had spurned hers, acting out in her need to have someone acknowledge the pain and isolation she had felt. But that acknowledgment had never come—not from the place she'd needed it most.

His dark lashes lowered. "Your childhood was also difficult. You never said much, but I could see how painful it was for you. Athamos and Nik were better at hiding it."

She lifted a shoulder. "You know what my father is like. He doesn't have it in him to love anyone. My mother was too broken by his affairs to want to be anywhere near us. I was raised instead by three very conscientious nannies who tried to hide the fact that they felt very, very sorry for me. And even they didn't last long because of the toxic atmosphere."

"It could not have been easy for you to watch your mother go through that. To see your family torn apart."

All the while in the glare of the media spotlight. Never a moment of escape… "My life was supposed to be perfect," she said, a brittle edge to her voice. "To everyone else it was perfect—to me it was hell. My mother was a tragic figure stripped of her self-worth and pride, forced to carry on a facade. I, in turn, was supposed to act the fairy-tale princess, living my fairy-tale life, when in reality it was anything but."

He took a sip of his wine, his intense scrutiny remaining on her. "Instead, you rebelled. You skipped out on boarding school, you partied, you dated all the wrong men…"

She narrowed her gaze. "Is that a statement or a question?"

"I'm simply trying to understand you, Stella. The woman you've become. Just like you just were with me."

"I'm not that rebel anymore."

"But it goes to what shaped you. I'm curious, though, about where all the cynicism is coming from…about what you said in Barbados—that relationships *just aren't worth it.*"

"Life," she said flatly. "That's where it's coming from. Life."

He lifted a brow.

"And what were all the men about? Choosing the most unavailable ones who'd never commit so you'd never know the hurt your mother did?"

She blinked. "Which men are you referring to?"

"The captain of the English national football squad—the most notorious womanizer in Europe—the South African mining magnate with his third divorce behind him, the American rancher with two women on the go…"

She could tell by his face he thought she'd slept with them all. That he believed the tabloids when, in fact, most of them had been lies. It made her blood heat. *He*, of all people, should know better.

She lifted her chin. "What's wrong with having some fun? You have surely had your share. You're the poster child of no-strings-attached, meaningless relationships."

"I am not you. You wanted more. You told me you wanted more. What happened to the Stella I knew?"

Her blood fizzled hotter. "What do you want to know about them, Kostas? Why I was with them? Why I slept with them?" She put her fingers to her mouth. "Well, let's see, I gave my virginity to Tony Morris after you turned me down. It was after his big game in Prague and can I tell you what a long, hot ride that was? Maybe I should be thanking you for that one. Then I dated Angelo Adamidis, whose ego was even bigger than Tony's, which didn't really appeal to me, followed by—"

"Stamata." He put his wineglass down, liquid sloshing up the sides. "That's enough."

"What's the matter?" She directed a defiant look at him, heart pounding at his flared nostrils, the sizzling heat in those whiskey-colored eyes. "You *asked* for the details... Does it *antagonize* you to hear that about your future wife? Or perhaps you're miffed because you missed out? That you misjudged me... That all I wanted was a hot roll between the sheets and some other male enjoyed the privilege?"

A silence passed, so long, so extended, she had to fight the urge not to fidget, to look away from the intensity of his laser-like expression as it branded her skin. "If I'd known all along that was what you were after," he finally said quietly, "I would have taken you up on your offer. But I don't think that's what it was, was it?"

Her gaze fell away from his. Her initiation into sex with Tony had been awful, his ego rendering him utterly insensitive to a woman's pleasure. She had stumbled away from that horrific experience vowing never to do it again and almost hadn't. There had always been something missing for her in the sexual act—an emotional bond, something beyond the physical.

She lifted a shoulder, deflecting the need to go more than surface-deep because that was where she liked to stay these days. "What does it matter?"

"It matters. Look at me, Stella."

She did, then wished she hadn't because he saw right through her. Always had.

"That kiss," he stated, "was the truth of us. You know it and I know it. You vibrate every time we're within ten feet of each other, yet you refuse to admit it. You fight me at every turn because you don't know how to handle this thing we have. But at some point it's going to have to stop. You are going to need to learn that I am not your father. I will not hurt you like he hurt your mother. I am the man who has always respected you enough to treat you the way you deserve."

She caught her bottom lip between her teeth, fighting for impassivity. "So now that I've agreed to become your wife, now that you're about to bestow upon me the lauded title of Mrs. Kostas Laskos, I should fall into your bed and count my lucky stars I'm the *chosen* one? I don't think so, Kostas. I've given you the agreed-upon parameters of this relationship. That's how it's going to work."

"I'm not disputing that. What needs to end is this standoff, this mistrust you have of me, the tension between us. We need to have a *relationship* if this partnership is going to work."

She considered him over her glass. "What exactly is it you're suggesting? Sex as intimacy? A mutual understanding based on our pheromones so we can produce that heir you need? Because the last time I checked, you were still the most emotionally unavailable man I know, Kostas. That little boy you talked about? He grew up into a big, life-size version of himself. You let people in so far, then you shut them down."

His olive skin stretched taut across his aristocratic face. "We will have to find a way to work through our failings. There is no other option."

Because his children were a task he had to tick off his list, as was *she*. He would fix his personal life as he was fixing the legacy that had been left on his doorstep. All he knew was to eye the end goal and attack the obstacles in between.

She set her jaw. "We'll make this work. We both have too much at stake for any other outcome. As for the rest, the *trust*, it's earned. You can't snap your fingers and order it to be so."

The glitter in his eyes said he thought he could. "We have a mutual respect for each other, we *appreciate* one other. We can have something good, we can be different than the relationships we've experienced in the past, if you will stop throwing every advance I make in my face."

She put down her wineglass. The wine was making her head too hazy, too *unclear*. She needed to put some distance between herself and this man who stirred far too much emotion in her, who liked to push every wish of his through like a steamroller, running over everything in between.

She knew they couldn't sustain this tension between them. Knew they had to make this work. But investing herself in something with Kostas that was halfway between hate and love—the gray area he was asking for? Was that even possible while keeping her emotions under wraps?

"I need some sleep."

"I have more work to do. I'll walk you up."

She thought that was a bad idea, but she couldn't refuse given his study was down the hall from her room. Silently she climbed the massive staircase beside him to the third floor, where the royal wing was located. Defenses not as solid as they should be, she crossed her arms over her chest and stared up at him as they stopped outside her bedroom door.

"Thank you for dinner."

His mouth twisted. "We almost remained civilized."

Almost being the operative word. She wasn't sure she and Kostas were ever going to get to civilized.

He bent toward her, his delicious, dark scent invading her senses. Heart hammering in her chest, she froze, debating whether to accept or reject his kiss. His mouth landed on her cheek instead. Firm and undeniably male, his lips made a slow, sensual journey up to her ear, her skin firing beneath his touch.

"*Kalinihxta*, Stella." His low voice raked across her insides. "Sweet dreams."

Straightening away from her, he walked toward his study. She let herself into her suite and leaned back against the door, her insides a mass of confusion.

Only Kostas could ever make her shake over a *non*-kiss.

Kostas worked for another couple of hours, then gave up, his head too cloudy to accomplish anything. In the master suite, dominated by the dark colors and fabrics Stella hated, but which had great bones with its exposed stone walls, he stripped off his clothes and immersed himself in the steam shower, one of the few modern amenities his father had added in deference to his bad lower back.

Sitting down on the bench, he let the water pour over him and eat away at the tension bunching his muscles. Negotiating foreign investment with a dozen different countries, spearheading the country's first elections and dealing with a recalcitrant executive council seemed like child's play compared to understanding the woman Stella had become. She wasn't the innocent, vulnerable girl he'd once known, wasn't the rebel she'd spent years as, but was something else entirely.

Philanthropist, cynic, hardened veteran of life at twenty-seven. Moving out of the hot, hard spray, he sat back against the tile, sluicing the water out of his face. He'd always known Stella's life had scarred her badly, but tonight he'd gotten a glimpse at how wounded she really was.

Closing his eyes, he recalled their conversation. *Trust is earned.* His fiancée's rebuttal to his request they develop some sort of manageable, doable relationship between them. He would do it, had to do it, but Stella was right—his ability to be in a relationship, to be emotionally available, had always been in question.

He had been conditioned to never show emotion, never feel it, or allow himself that luxury. Designed to be impenetrable. Other than his grandmother's affection, he'd never had love, didn't know what it was, nor did he want it. Maybe it had been watching his father fall down a rabbit hole when his mother had died, one from which he hadn't emerged whole. He just knew it wasn't for him, wouldn't ever be.

Which, he thought, wiping a layer of perspiration from his brow, shouldn't be an issue given Stella's pronouncement she wasn't interested in love, wanted to make herself as impenetrable as he was. It was just that he wasn't sure she had meant it, wasn't sure a lot of the Stella he'd seen today wasn't just tough packaging over the real thing and that woman *was* exceedingly vulnerable, had always wanted more.

And therein lay the problem. He couldn't ever offer her that, even if she decided she did want it. Not only was he incapable of it, but he also *couldn't* allow his relationship with Stella to ever become any more than the partnership he'd promised her because there were parts of him she didn't know. Deep, flawed parts of him he would never admit to anyone—pieces of him that would destroy Stella if she knew.

He pushed aside the guilt that knotted in his chest. He had forgiven himself that particular sin because he and his country needed Stella. It was necessary. Which meant he had to earn that trust his fiancée was demanding, prove to her they could make this work, while never making promises he couldn't keep.

Considering the fact that in three weeks the eyes of the world would be upon this country as he and Stella cemented ties between Akathinia and Carnelia, he had his work cut out for him.

CHAPTER SIX

KOSTAS STOOD LEANING against the blacked-out windows of the Bentley, jacket discarded, a dusk-driven breeze stealing across his skin. His oxygen-deprived brain had craved fresh air as he waited for Stella to appear for their dinner engagement, too many weeks of conference rooms and endless bickering about election minutiae clouding his brain. That and the seemingly endless pushback he was receiving on the hotel developments he was negotiating for the east coast of Carnelia.

It was enough to make a man question his sanity for attempting to take on this almost impossible job.

Tonight, however, would be enjoyable. With his wedding just a week away, he and Stella were joining Tassos Andropoulos, his best friend and best man, for dinner at a tiny, low-key restaurant in the city to discuss last-minute details. It was an establishment he knew well, whose proprietor would keep their presence hush-hush, a necessity considering the anticipation for his nuptials had reached a fever pitch. The madness descending over Carnelia was something he would be happy to see the back of.

The foreign media, scheduled to arrive this week to cover the lead-up to the wedding, were salivating over the celebrity-packed guest list, as were the people of Carnelia, who hadn't seen such an influx of famous visitors since the wedding of his grandmother Queen Cliantha. Their enthusiasm was heightened by the weeklong festivities scheduled around the ceremony, which included two days of national holidays to celebrate. He thanked the high heavens the only thing he had to do was show up.

Pulling in another deep breath of the clean, quiet air, he focused his attention on the entrance to the castle and his fiancée's imminent appearance, rather than the insanity to come. Punctuality was not one of Stella's virtues, but since she had so many others, he was willing to overlook it.

She had been picture-perfect in an appearance at the annual fig festival, winning over the farmers with her wit and charm as they served as the judges of the cake-baking competition featuring the star fruit, then doing the same at an official state dinner for the Italian prime minister as Carnelia officially reopened relations with that country.

Unfortunately, for his goal of creating a manageable stasis for his own relationship, the cool, composed Stella who had presented herself on those public occasions had been the same one to greet him every morning in the two weeks since their confrontation in the conservatory. He seemed to be an object of suspicion, to be avoided, while she wrapped her head around their relationship. He hoped the tiny but noticeable thawing in her manner toward him meant they were headed in the right direction.

His introspection came to a halt as Stella exited the front doors and came down the stairs in a cloud of exotic, sophisticated perfume. He was a fan of the scent as well as the dress she wore—a formfitting, knee-length cocktail number embroidered with some type of flower he couldn't identify.

"Sorry," she murmured, coming to a halt in front of

him, the careful smile that seemed to be her de facto response to him of late pasted on her lips.

"No, you aren't," he said easily, shifting away from the car, "or you'd be on time."

Oh. Those blue eyes sharpened. *It's going to be that kind of night?*

It's been that kind of fortnight.

Her lashes lowered in that reining in of emotion he was coming to hate.

"We should go," he murmured, sliding his fingers around the handle of the car door and opening it. She walked past him, sinking her bottom into the seat, then swinging those incredible legs of hers inside. His palm grazed the curve of her hip as he bent to tuck her in, the brief touch of his fingertips to her firm, delectable bottom eliciting the full stare of its owner.

He shut the door on her pensive face because there were some things a man simply couldn't resist and that had been one of them. Nodding at the driver, who was perched by the front of the car along with Darius and his own bodyguard, he walked around to the other side and slid in.

She eyed him from a safe distance away. "You are exhausted. You need sleep."

He rested his head against the back of the seat and closed his eyes. "Clone me. That would help."

"At least you'll be able to relax this evening with Tassos. I like him."

"All woman like Tassos. He's good-looking and he flies fast, dangerous planes."

"His occupation certainly doesn't hurt." Amusement laced her voice. "How did you two meet?"

"In military training. First here, then in England and

California. We were on the same path and we clicked. Then we were deployed together in the navy."

"He's the light to your dark," she said. "You are good foils for one another."

"Perhaps."

A silence. "You're upset about the editorial."

"*Frustrated* is a better description." The scathing piece by the business editor of the Carnelian daily newspaper this morning had felt like a betrayal. He'd unleashed the stranglehold his father had kept on the media as one of his first actions as king.

The editor had paid him back by describing him as an "unyielding force determined to push through modernization plans the people weren't ready for." "The new king," the piece had gone on to say, "is showing shades of his father."

"Why don't you meet with him?" Stella suggested. "It would be good to establish that relationship. Another key influencer."

He opened his eyes. "What's the point? He clearly doesn't comprehend or care about the facts."

"Kostas." She shook her head. "There's been significant pushback on your plans from more than one group. You need to educate, but more than that, you need to *listen*. The more you push forward without doing that, the angrier they are going to become. If you don't want to lose the goodwill you've built up, you need to create some bridges."

He trained his gaze on her. "He accused me of having my father's *dictatorial tendencies*."

"Then prove him wrong." She shook her head. "He is not entirely incorrect in that portrayal. You *are* dogmatic. You see the world in black-and-white. You need to acknowledge the gray, find a middle ground."

Antagonism stiffened his shoulders. "It's the people who need to wake up. They all want the gain and no pain. *I* am trying to give them a future. If they are too shortsighted to recognize it, that's not my problem, it's theirs."

"It will be yours if they turn their backs on you."

Blood throbbed against his temples. Pushing his head back against the seat, he stared straight ahead. "I'm getting enough on all sides, Stella. I don't need it from you."

"Then why marry me? You said you wanted a partner, so here I am, telling you what you need to hear rather than what you want to hear."

His lashes fluttered closed. He had asked for that, yes. He just didn't need it right *now.* Nor did he need his fiancée agreeing with that damn editor. He couldn't believe she'd *gone* there, knowing who he was. What he was.

Stella considered her combustible fiancé as the car pulled up in front of the restaurant. Darius and Kostas's bodyguard got out first to scan the area. So much for her stress-free, enjoyable evening getting to know Tassos better. He was the one person, it seemed, who knew the king beyond a superficial level.

Kostas was like an explosive device, primed and ready to go off. Clearly the insane amount of pressure he was under was taking a toll, and how could it not? Still, she knew her role was to help guide him and she wasn't about to pull any punches for both their sakes. Not with General Houlis continuing to amass support behind the scenes, the frustrated public a perfect target for his efforts.

She let him cool off as their security declared the area secure and they were welcomed into the cozy little restaurant off a main avenue by the proprietor, who led them to an out-of-the-way table at the back, where the handsome, dark-haired, green-eyed Tassos sat waiting for them. He was, of course, busily engaged with their beautiful blonde waitress.

"Attempting to find a suitable bottle of wine," he informed them as he stood and gave Kostas a clap on the shoulder and Stella a kiss on both cheeks. "Any preferences?"

"Anything with alcohol in it," Kostas suggested, holding out Stella's chair and tucking her into the table.

Tassos gave him a mocking look. "I thought you gave that up with the monks?"

A half smile broke through her fiancé's stiffness. "There were certain habits I wasn't willing to give up."

Tassos asked the waitress to bring them a bottle of Chianti. "It's the sex I couldn't do without," he said, offering the departing blonde a smile full of promise. "That's where I derive my *tranquillity* from."

"Clearly you must be very tranquil, then," Kostas returned mockingly. "Have you decided who the lucky recipient will be for the wedding? We're seven days out."

"It's an issue," said Tassos, face deadpan. "There is an implicit assumption among women if you bring them to a wedding that it's serious. On the other hand," he said, a contemplative look on his face, "when the champagne is flowing, it's sure to be enjoyable. Maybe I should just take the waitress."

Stella shook her head at his arrogance. Tassos was good-looking and charming enough to get away with it. The blonde would likely trip over herself in her haste to say yes. It turned her thoughts to her current problem—her very arrogant fiancé's request for calmer waters in their relationship.

She had to let go of her antagonism toward him, she knew. Of the history that prevented them from moving forward and truly realizing this partnership because she knew in her heart they could be different if they had a fresh start, that they did have a strong mutual respect for each other. Perhaps it had been the reality of what she'd committed herself to that had been driving her aggression, the radical changes in her life, the loneliness she had felt without her siblings at her side, the tenuous situation she and Kostas were in. Not to mention her own conflicting feelings toward him.

But with her introspection had come clarity. She wanted this partnership to work; knew that together she and Kostas were more powerful than the sum of their parts. It was painful, hard work they were doing, but it was so worth it—she knew she could make a difference in this country's future. Felt she *had* a purpose. With her and Kostas's biggest challenges yet unscaled, he was right—a resolution was necessary. Some sort of relationship was necessary between them.

It had also been impossible not to admire the strong, powerful force of good her fiancé had been for his wounded country. He was still the larger-than-life figure she'd always thought he was, but she'd now accepted that he also made mistakes, as everyone did. Could they manage a real relationship together where she let down her guard and let him in while keeping love firmly out of the picture? She thought maybe they could.

She'd always considered Kostas incapable of opening up emotionally, but he had changed since his time in Tibet. He had talked to her about his past—yes, because he'd wanted her acquiescence, but still he had done it. Maybe he was capable of investing in a relationship—maybe he was capable of more. Maybe she had to take a risk and trust him as he'd suggested.

Tucking that away for future thought, she returned her attention to the conversation at hand. Her fiancé gradually lost his combustive edge in the presence of the ever-entertaining Tassos, who clearly knew how to handle him. She took mental notes. By the time their dinner plates were removed and a bottle of wine had been consumed, with liqueurs on the way, Kostas was almost human again. Then his phone rang.

"I have to take it," he apologized. "It may be a few minutes."

"Go." Tassos waved a hand at him. "Your sexy, intelligent fiancée is in safe hands."

Kostas slanted him a look that said that was debatable, then disappeared onto the terrace. Tassos sat back in his chair, cradling his wineglass in his hands. "He's agitated tonight."

"It's the editorial. I keep telling him communication is a two-way street, but you know what he's like. He thinks he knows best. Which he does… It's how he's executing that needs finessing."

"He struggles with his father's legacy." Tassos's gaze was frank. "More than anyone knows. He feels the pressure because of the duty that's so deeply ingrained in him—the responsibility for his father's misdirection. He ends up caring too much and internalizing the stress."

She nodded. "I know. I'm just not sure how to help him."

"I think you are. You aren't afraid of him, afraid to give him a different perspective. That's what he needs, that and someone who will stand by him and give him the unconditional love and support he's never had. Who lets him know he isn't alone."

"You have," she pointed out.

"Yes. But I'm not engaged to be married to him. That kind of bond is different." Resting his glass against his chin, he gave her a contemplative look. "He needs to see the light again. He needs to remember the world is a good place beyond everything he's been through."

A knot formed in her stomach, pulling her insides tight. Shame was its origin. The shame of being so horribly oblivious to the truth an apparently far-deeper-than-she'd-thought Tassos had just voiced.

"Yes," she said in a low voice, edged with emotion. "I agree."

He eyed her. "It must be complicated for you two. With what happened with Athamos…"

That might be the understatement of the year.

"*They* were complicated," he continued with a frown. "At each other's throats one minute, tight the next. Always the competition. But to have what happened happen? Kostas went off the rails. I've never seen him like that."

The knot in her stomach tightened. "What do you mean 'off the rails'?"

"I mean I didn't know if he was coming back from Tibet, mentally or physically. He wasn't communicating with anyone, not me, nor his father. He literally disappeared. When everyone was asking where Kostas was, why he wasn't intervening with Akathinia, not even the king knew where he was. When Idas fell ill, he had no idea if his son was going to assume the crown or not. The wolves were circling."

Thee mou. She bit her lip, a feeling of disbelief spreading through her. Had Kostas seriously been thinking of not coming back? Of *not* becoming king? It was so far from the man she knew and the duty he had lived by that it blew a hole in her brain.

"I can't even conceive of that."

Tassos swallowed his last sip of wine, then put down

the glass. "He hasn't flown since Athamos's death. Hasn't gone near a plane. Flying is his peace, his serenity."

She stared at him. "You think he isn't flying because of Athamos?"

"I think maybe he thinks he doesn't deserve to be happy."

"It was an *accident*."

His gaze probed hers. "Is that how *you* saw it in the beginning?"

No. Her heartbeat thickened in her chest. But then again she had been so wrong about so many things when it came to Kostas, too caught up in her own anguish to consider what he might be going through, that she'd made a million assumptions.

A weight descended over her, a thick blanket of culpability she wasn't sure how to handle. "Like you said," she murmured, "it's complicated."

The pretty waitress arrived to deliver their liqueurs. Tassos waited until she disappeared before he spoke again. "Did Athamos ever tell you what happened between him and Kostas in flight school? The day they flew their first solo cross-country flight?"

She shook her head.

"It's an exercise all of us had to do as part of our flight school training. You fly the route first with an instructor, who takes you through the checkpoints and familiarizes you with the route. Then you fly it the next day by yourself. Kostas and Athamos were up there together, vying for best-pilot status. They were neck and neck at the time.

"Kostas was about half an hour ahead. Unfortunately for them, the weather deteriorated as the day went on. It was difficult to see the checkpoints and Athamos got lost. So lost he was dangerously low on fuel. He panicked and radioed for help. Kostas heard his calls, flew back, found him, took his wing and guided him back to the base."

She felt the blood drain from her face. "If he had run out of fuel…"

"They were both critically low on fuel by the time they touched down, Kostas worse than Athamos because he'd flown farther. He was flying on fumes by the end."

She set her glass down, hands shaking. "What happened afterward?"

"They were given a chance to refly the route. Athamos didn't want to. He was shaken up, crushed by his failure, frightened by what happened. He wanted to quit. Kostas talked him out of it."

She pressed her hand to her mouth, fighting to hold back the emotion welling up inside of her. "What did he say to him?"

"That every pilot makes mistakes and those mistakes define their career. That he had to dig down deep and go back up there—that he would be by his side the whole way but to quit was not an option."

"And he did."

"Yes."

Liquid fire burned the backs of her eyes. She blinked furiously, but this time she didn't manage to hold back as she had so many other times. Tears slid down her cheeks like silent bandits.

Tassos closed a hand over hers. "I didn't mean to make you sad. I'm telling you this so you understand…so you can understand Kostas better. It kills me every time I hear that damn story about the race because it's only one piece of what he and Athamos were. Only those two men know the truth of what happened that night and it's far more complicated than anyone knows."

And she had been the biggest judge of all. Anger at herself dueled with the need to make this right.

“Thank you,” she murmured, “for telling me this. I needed to hear it.”

If it wasn’t a sign she needed to let go, then nothing ever would be. She needed to let go of *all of it.*

CHAPTER SEVEN

HAVING BEEN EFFECTIVELY blown off by her fiancé, who'd gone off to work as soon as they'd returned to the castle with that dark cloud around him again after the phone call he'd received, Stella elected to go to bed. She was too emotionally wrung-out from her evening to contemplate anything else.

She took a long soak in a bath in the rather garish, outdated purple-and-gold marble bathroom that adjoined her suite—any renovations would have to wait until the key rooms were finished. Stella slipped into a nightgown, picked up a book and took it to bed. But the more she thought about her conversation with Tassos, the more she didn't understand. Confusion mixed with frustration in a caustic brew. Why hadn't Kostas told her about his and Athamos's history? Why had he never attempted to defend himself? How was she supposed to have a real relationship with a man *she didn't even know*?

Throwing back the covers, she strode to the door, flung it open and headed for Kostas's study. The light that streamed across the stone floor from underneath the door told her he was still working.

Fingers curling around the handle, she let herself inside. Kostas looked up from behind his desk, the hard lines of his face haggard, his beautiful catlike eyes a vivid beacon in the dim light. Dropping his gaze down over her, he made her suddenly aware of how see-through the ivory nightie she had on must be in the pool of light she stood in.

"This isn't a social visit," she snapped, rounding the desk to put herself in shadow. "I've come to talk."

"Pity," he murmured, his gaze eating her up. "I thought you might finally have come around."

She crossed her arms over her chest. "That would entail both of us entering this so-called relationship on equal footing, and since that isn't the case, we have work to do."

He threw down his pen and leaned back in the chair. "I'm assuming you're going to tell me why that isn't the case."

"Tassos told me about your cross-country test in flight school. About what you did for Athamos."

His mouth tightened. "So."

"So you saved his career, might have saved his life if he hadn't found his way out of that mess before he ran out of fuel, and you chose *not* to tell me?"

"He would have."

"No, Kostas, that isn't a given." She clenched her hands at her sides. "Why did you allow me to paint you the bad guy, to *damn you*, when there was so much more to the two of you?"

"Because it didn't make any difference. I needed to own my mistake."

"It *does* make a difference. It goes to who you are. The kind of man you are. The man I've always known you are."

A glimmer entered those dark, inscrutable eyes. "Don't go painting me a hero, Stella. I've already crushed your illusions once. I did what any pilot would have done in my position. As for not providing explanations, you didn't want to hear them."

"Because you waited a year and a half to tell me. Because my grief has been ruling me." She blew out a breath. "I owe you an apology."

"Just like that?"

"No, not *just like that.*" She dropped her hands onto her hips. "Are you punishing yourself? Is that it? By pressing forward and not giving a damn what anyone thinks?"

His expression hardened. "Now who's psychoanalyzing?"

"Yes. It's my turn now. And you know what I've determined so far? You were always closed, Kostas, your focus was always on the endgame. The women you collected, your top gun status, your summa cum laude superiority—nothing was allowed to interfere with your vision, with *winning.* But with everything that's happened, you've locked yourself up and thrown away the key. You've decided you will save this country, come hell or high water, and that is your *penance*. You've given up your idealism for the very cynicism you accuse me of, when that is exactly what this country needs most."

His dark lashes lowered to half-mast. "What do you propose I do? Let the country wither away and die while we all hold on to our outdated, fatal visions of what we want to be?"

"No. You compromise. You dream *together.* I *see* you wanting to connect with the people, desperate to make them understand your vision, but in order to do that you have to show them you are one of them, just like your grandmother said. Right now, they aren't sure about that."

His gaze fell away from hers, a silence filling the room. He dropped his head into his hands, fingertips massaging his temples. She could feel the storm emanating from him, the loneliness, the frustration, the drive to make everything right. The need to never again be that five-year-old boy standing beside his father inspecting a military guard, bewildered and lost. It tore the heart right out of her.

Taking the last steps between them, she bent and framed his face in her hands, making him look at her. "I am willing to be all-in with this partnership with you, Kostas. I think we can be that unstoppable team you spoke of, that we can *do* this together. But if we're going to make this a real relationship, you need to give of yourself as much as you're asking of me. You have to show you're *capable* of being in a relationship for me to invest in you. For me to trust you. I need to know we are in this together."

His gaze darkened. "I've shared things with you. Things about my past."

"Yes," she agreed, "and I need you to keep doing that, to prove to me this is the right decision I'm making, because you were right about me—my past means I don't trust easily, I never have. But I do believe you are right, I do believe we can be different. I believe the respect we have for each other means something."

He rubbed a hand over the stubble on his jaw. "Being emotionally available isn't my forte, Stella. It never has been. But I will do my best. I am committed to making this work."

She straightened, hands falling away from his face. "Trust, transparency and complete honesty between us are the rules."

A play of emotion flickered in those dark eyes. She wondered which of the three things she'd listed had caused it, because they needed all of them if this was going to work.

“All right,” he said. “Agreed.”

She blew out a breath. “Okay, then.”

His gaze slid over her. Settled on the thrust of her breasts under the thin material of the silk negligee. Electricity sparkled across her skin like white lightning, heat pooling low in her abdomen at his blatant perusal. She bit her lip as her nipples betrayed her and hardened to tight peaks.

“You want to come here and seal the deal with a kiss?”

A part of her knew it would be a big mistake. Another part knew it was inevitable. An intimate relationship between them was a given with the need to produce an heir. She couldn’t deny she didn’t want him, hadn’t always wanted him. Perhaps a test run would be a good idea to see how hard it was going to be to keep a handle on her feelings for him. And it was just one kiss…

Kostas hooked an arm around her waist and tugged her down onto his lap. She sucked in a breath, pressing a hand to his ripped, rock-hard chest. His big, hard body underneath her was a hot brand she couldn’t ignore, leashed, pure masculine power that told her she was playing with fire, that perhaps this hadn’t been a very good idea at all.

He curved a palm around her neck and brought her head down to his. His mouth took hers in an exquisitely soft, gentle kiss, butterfly-light, easy to extract herself from. Except she didn’t because it destroyed some of the connections in her brain.

She allowed herself to sink into it, to discover whether the kiss on the dance floor had really been that magical, exactly *how* dangerous he was to her. Angling his mouth over hers, he deepened the pressure, turned it into a soul-destroying exploration that sent more of those little quakes through her.

So it had been magical. She should have ended it there,

should have called the experiment done, but then he slid his tongue along the crease of her mouth and demanded entry. Too caught up in the sensual web he was weaving to object, she opened for him and the kiss turned breathtakingly intimate; a relearning of each other on a deeper level.

Not hungry, but staking a claim instead. *Sealing the deal.* Her stomach muscles coiled as the smooth, hot length of his tongue slid against hers. Stroked her languidly, provocatively, like a bit cat on the prowl. The hand he held at the small of her back drew her closer until she was plastered against him, breasts crushed against his chest.

He trailed his lips along her cheek, along the line of her jaw, working his way toward the sensitive spot just below her ear. She gasped as he brought his tongue into play in an erotic caress that made her shiver. Fingers clutching the fabric of his shirt, she arched her neck back as he licked his way higher to take possession of her lobe, sucking it into the heat of his mouth.

Thee mou, but he knew what he was doing. A low moan escaped her as he closed his teeth around the tender skin, scored her vulnerable flesh, her insides contracting with her reaction to him. He could take her now and she'd be ready for him.

She was fairly sure he knew it as he lifted his mouth from her and brushed a thumb across her cheek. "One kiss as promised, *glykeia mou*. The next move is up to you."

She blinked. "What do you mean?"

"It means I'm not touching you again until you ask me to."

A bizarre sense of disappointment sliced through her. "What about the heir you so urgently require?"

"It can wait."

"And if I never come to you?"

He set her on her feet. "That doesn't even rank on the scale of probability."

Kostas watched his fiancée walk out of the room, an emotional tsunami that had hit, then departed. She had been ready to crawl into his bones. He had been ready for it, too. His erection pounded with every beat of his heart, craving satisfaction, but since his fiancée had finally agreed to commit to this partnership in every way, he would gladly suffer through it.

With their wedding happening in a week, madness about to descend around them, they needed this consensus. Having Stella share his bed, and he had no doubt she would after the response she'd just given him, would allow both of them to get this chemistry out of their system. Produce the heir his country so desperately needed. Allow him to return a singular focus to the job at hand—right-siding Carnelia.

It would have been better, however, for that story of him and Athamos to have never come out. Stella insisted on seeing him as a hero—as the ideal she had always wanted, *needed* him to be, when in fact, he was far from it. He'd gone so far as to deliberately hurt her all those years ago to dissuade her of that vision and still she had persisted with it.

Guilt clawed through him, sinking into his insides. He pushed it aside with ruthless precision. He had been careful what he'd promised her. Trust, transparency and complete honesty—*those things* he could offer. With his one necessary sin of omission.

Restlessness drove him to his feet. Crossing to the bar, he poured himself the nightcap he'd missed at the restaurant. Turning, he leaned against the sideboard and took a long gulp. Today's high-profile, public lashing had flattened him…stung him with its betrayal. Made him wonder about his country's will to pull itself from the ashes.

He had spent his life nurturing a dream of democracy for Carnelia. Was five weeks away from attaining it. Yet, history was full of examples of the offspring of dictators who had set out to be different, with bright visions for their country, only to be defeated by the forces stacked against them. As if they'd never stood a chance. He was not going to be one of them.

Backtracking on his plans would poke holes in his leadership, holes General Houlis could exploit. The general was a man who wanted to hang him before the elections ever happened.

He lifted the glass to his mouth and took another sip of the whiskey. His father's voice filled his head, as clear as if he'd been standing in this room, one he'd once presided over, delivering one of his sermons.

A great vision is one that must be believed in without reservation, preserved at all costs. Any show of weakness means it all falls apart.

His mouth twisted. His father might have been driven by misguided and, at times, warped ideas, but he had been right about that particular one. Any show of weakness by him would allow his enemies to pounce. He was never going to let that happen.

CHAPTER EIGHT

THE ANCIENT CHURCH bells rang in Carnelia as they would on the quarter hour until the royal wedding took place in the Marcariokastro chapel in just under sixty minutes. With each deep, resonant gong of the bells, Stella's stomach pulled tighter, a rock-hard fist she couldn't unclench.

Not because of the five hundred guests preparing to attend her wedding. Not because of the vow she was about to make to king and country. Not even because General Houlis and his dangerous group of disciples would be in the audience. Instead, her nerves stemmed from the fact that in just over an hour she would not only pledge to stand by Kostas's side forever, but she would also share his bed.

"Right." Satisfied with the job she'd done, the makeup artist fussing over her face declared her a masterpiece. "I'm leaving tiny backups," she said, gesturing to the dresser. "Smudge-proof lipstick and powder. Your mascara is waterproof so crying shouldn't be a problem."

She smiled her thanks. She was fairly certain that wouldn't be an issue. She felt frozen, as if she'd been carved out of marble. Wondering if she'd made a huge mistake agreeing to embark on a real marriage with Kostas, to have an intimate relationship with a man she was still sure had the ability to tear her heart out.

She had, however, made a promise to Kostas and she intended on following through on it. Intended on putting everything she had into making this partnership—their relationship—a success. Part of that commitment included providing Kostas with an heir, and since that electric kiss in his study had proved chemistry wasn't going to be a problem, she had decided to simply get it out of the way.

It made sense, after all, to consummate their relationship on their wedding night. Symbolically it was a fresh start for them. All she had to do was ensure her complex, reemerging feelings for her fiancé never went past the mutual respect and partnership they had promised each other.

A rock lodged itself in her throat. Simpler said than done. She wondered what it was going to be like to set this thing loose between her and Kostas. The thought was equally soul-shifting and terrifying.

Sofía bustled through the door with her dress, having made a tiny, last-minute alteration, with Alex close on her heels. "All done," her sister-in-law announced breathlessly.

Discarding her robe, Stella stood and lifted her arms to allow Sofía to settle the dress down over her in a rustle of satin. An unexpected wave of emotion swept over her. It was gorgeous. Her dream dress on the odd day she'd ever imagined herself getting married.

"Oh, Sofía," Alex breathed. "It's perfect. You are a genius."

It *was* genius. The romantic, off-the-shoulder, fit-and-flare satin gown made the most of her slim figure, the lace overlay softening an otherwise sleek, unadorned silhouette. "You don't need any more with your strong look," Sofía had said earlier. Which had meant, in reality, the square line of her jaw and her prominent nose, but she'd been okay with that assessment. She was aware she wasn't beautiful in the traditional sense and was more frequently labeled *striking* by the tabloids.

She gave Sofía a hug. "It's amazing. *Efharisto.*"

"*You* are amazing." Her sister-in-law squeezed her tight. "Carnelia is lucky to have you."

"As is Akathinia to have you." She kissed Sofía on the cheek.

And then, all too soon, the moments had flown by. With her delicate sparkly gold heels on, jewelry in place, including a heavy sapphire-and-diamond necklace Kostas had given her last night that had been Queen Cliantha's, Stella had an awkward last moment with her mother that didn't end up being so bad because Queen Amara looked so truly happy for her.

It was *time.*

Kostas waited for his bride under the fresco-emblazoned dome of the eighteenth-century Marcariokastro royal chapel, Tassos at his side. Beyond the stunning centerpiece of the Venetian-inspired chapel, the guests sat in the main gallery, presided over by a massive gold filigree chandelier that bathed the room in a muted glow.

Every manner of politician, royalty, aristocrat and celebrity was in attendance. They had come, according to the international press, to see the dawn of a new age in Carnelia, the coming of Camelot. He wasn't sure how long that label was going to stick after that damning editorial and the increasing public discontent that had risen in the wake of it over his modernization plans, but he was determined to stay the course. The future of his country depended on it.

A flash of white appeared at the entrance to the chapel

as the strains of Vivaldi's *Four Seasons* began. Jessie's three-year-old daughter, in a beautiful white dress with a red bow, started down the aisle and was followed by her mother in an elegant bloodred gown Sofía had designed. Next came the designer herself, vivacious and stunning in a red gown of a different style, followed by Aleksandra.

"All married..." Tassos sighed. "You could have allowed me just one."

"You don't need the help," Kostas countered, appreciating the comic relief. "You acquired your blonde waitress."

"She's a short-term rental." Tassos, sharp in a black tux and red bow tie, flicked him a glance. "If I had one like the one you're marrying today, I would happily trade her in as a permanent addition."

A message. *Appreciate what you have.* It was unnecessary. He had no doubts he was making the right choice today. In his duty and the woman he'd chosen. Stella was his match in every way. Fearless, passionate and strong enough to accomplish the most impossible dream with him.

Duty, however, didn't explain how his heart rose to his throat as a ripple went through the crowd. Stella had appeared at the entrance to the chapel on Nikandros's arm, the train of her dress flowing behind her. Her hair was caught up in a sophisticated twist that illuminated the arresting lines of face, her dress an elegant, perfect foil for her beautiful body, the necklace he'd given her glittering around her neck.

All he could do was stare. The desire to possess her, to mark her as his, moved through him as an inescapable force. To claim what he hadn't taken ten years ago but had desired above all else.

He wasn't sure what he'd expected in return, which

Stella might show up today as she walked down the aisle: the fiery, combative version who had greeted him in Barbados, or the cool, aloof creature who had driven him crazy for weeks, or the warm Stella he'd witnessed of late, intent on making them work. But as she and Nikandros walked down the aisle, Stella's features distant, untouchable, the smile on her face perfect, but more a mask than a real form of expression, he knew exactly what he'd gotten.

She could have been attending a coronation, any official occasion other than her own wedding, she was just that removed. A wave of infuriated heat spread through him, despite his own doubts about his ability to give her what she needed. *They were not going backward, not now.*

The music at a crescendo, the pair reached him. Stella's beautiful eyes, as electric a Constantinides blue as her brother's, were cool blue sapphires as they came to rest on him, about a dozen layers of that ice he despised painted over her. Transferring his attention to Nikandros, he shook his hand as the king gave his sister away. Enfolding Stella's slim fingers in his, the slight tremor he found there threw him yet again.

"Nervous about devoting your life to me?" he murmured in her ear.

"Hardly."

"Then why is your hand trembling?"

"It's a big day."

He pondered that comment as they turned to the priest, the guests sat and the service began. The joining of the hands, which they'd already accomplished, was followed by the service of betrothal, in which they exchanged their rings, and the procession of the crowns.

He spoke his vows to Stella in a clear, unwavering

tone that spoke of his confidence in them. Her icy, cool demeanor slipped slightly, her eyes turning a deep violet blue as she spoke her vows to him, her elocution perfect in the cavernous chapel.

The priest completed the benediction of their union, declaring them man and wife. Kostas curved an arm around his bride's waist and drew her to him. His touch, as he cupped her jaw in his fingers, was light, but firm, staking his claim in that way that was irresistible to him, his kiss as he captured her satiny soft lips a demonstration of how very good this was going to be between them—in every way.

Stella needed time to recover from that calamitous kiss Kostas had given her that had promised so much. She got it as they exited the chapel to applause and cheers amid a contemporary, hauntingly beautiful version of "Hallelujah."

After being saluted with handfuls of rice and good wishes, they headed to the gardens for the official photographs. They seemed to take forever in the bright sunshine, pushing the throb in her head to a full-on ache. Jessie produced some aspirin from her bridal emergency kit that Stella downed with a bottle of water, as opposed to the champagne that was already flowing among the others. By the time they'd returned to the ballroom for dinner and she had eaten a few bites of the roasted lamb and her favorite, the spinach-and-feta pies, she was feeling better. Now if only she could diminish her ever-present awareness of the man sitting beside her.

Speeches were held throughout the courses, by family and dignitaries alike. It wasn't until dessert was served that she and Kostas stood to deliver their toasts to each other. Kostas, devastating in military dress, went first, a glass of champagne in his hand. His eyes on her, he praised his choice of bride—for her duty to country, her valuable philanthropic work, her beauty, wit and intelligence.

Warmed by what she knew to be genuine appreciation on his part, she stood to do her toast, unsure if she could match Kostas's brilliant endeavor with anything better. But she had a story to tell.

"When I was six," she said, focusing on the crowd, "I met a boy named Kostas. It was a hot summer day and I was climbing a tree in the gardens of the Akathinian palace, mad at my parents for something I can't remember now. I, along with my brothers, were supposed to be entertaining the children of some visiting guests, but I was too angry and couldn't make myself do it.

"I was halfway up the tree when this voice, this little boy's voice, reached me. He asked me what I, a girl, was doing climbing a tree. I sat down on a branch, secured my perch and told him that I was going to do great things one day, so why not climb a tree? This look passed over his face, this thoughtful look. Then he climbed up the tree, sat down beside me and told me his name."

Tears, unexpected and disconcerting, stung her eyes. Swallowing, she blinked them back. "He told me he, too, was going to do great things someday. He was going to become king, like his father, except maybe he would be a little bit nicer to the people. I agreed with him that that would be a good thing and we sat there, sometimes talking, sometimes not, for a long time until our parents came to flush us out.

"And you know, as children, we sometimes have dreams that fade with time. We realize we want to be a doctor instead of a football player, a lawyer instead of a ballerina, but the little boy I met turned into a young man and then a man and those dreams never died. I was awed by his ability to focus—to never forget he wanted to make the world a better place. It has inspired me in so many ways with my own life."

She turned to her husband. "To watch Kostas carry out his dreams, to witness his passion for Carnelia, to *see* this country shine with a brilliant future because of it, only solidifies what I always knew because of him. If you allow yourself to hope, to *believe* this world can be a better place, anything is possible.

"And so tonight," she said, swallowing past the lump in her throat and lifting her glass to the man who affected her on such a profound level, "I give a toast to my husband and say thank you. I and Carnelia are very lucky to have you."

Kostas stood as applause swept the room, the crowd rising with him. His eyes were dark, full of emotion for a man who claimed to feel little and suspiciously bright as he held his glass up to hers. It made her wonder if she would give the waterproof mascara a run for its money.

He bent his head to hers. "Always trying to make me the hero, Stella?"

She shook her head. "Always trying to put words in my mouth, Kostas? I called you an inspiration because you are that to me."

He pressed his lips to her cheek. Dragged his mouth to her ear. "I can't believe you remember that story. You forgot, however, the part where I offered you half of my lollipop. It goes to the gentleman in me."

She smiled. "I didn't. But to be honest, Kostas, I never was much interested in the gentleman part."

A pause. "Is that a request, Mrs. Laskos?"

"Why don't you try it and find out?"

Her stomach dissolved into complete chaos after that.

They took to the dance floor for their first dance, her fingers enfolded in his, his hand at her waist. Then there was only heat between them, a slow, languorous, deadly conflagration that turned her bones to mush.

When the others joined them, the dance floor packed with bodies, Kostas's hand dropped lower on her hip, pulling her into the muscular length of him. It was just barely an appropriate hold, one that telegraphed exactly where this night was headed.

Her breath trapped in her chest, she joined the riotous dancing—the Orea Pou Enai H Nifi Mas, which the wedding party danced in a circle in honor of her, the Kalamatiano, which Stella led, and the Hasapiko, her favorite.

Her headache thankfully receded. She got herself a glass of champagne and then another in an attempt to quiet the anticipation fizzing in her blood. Tassos turned out to be a demon on the dance floor, of course. She danced the night away with him, Alex, Sofía, Jessie and Aristos, aware of her husband's dark stare when she did so with the latter. A feeling of satisfaction spread through her. A little jealousy never hurt, not when it came to a man like Kostas, who was used to having everything he desired.

The clock struck midnight. It was as if an invisible line had been crossed. Kostas murmured something to the wedding planner, retrieved her from the dance floor and led her to the exit. The room was still boisterous and loud, but all she could hear was the pounding of her heart.

CHAPTER NINE

Why wasn't there air in this room?

Stella kicked her shoes off in the newly renovated master suite that had been transformed into a sumptuous, warm retreat by their genius of a designer, retaining the room's exposed stone walls and medieval ambience.

Plush, comfortable chairs formed a sitting area overlooking the tall windows. A mahogany canopy bed with intricately crafted pillars draped in gold brocade overlooked it, with a separate area at the far end of the room for dressing.

It was dreamy, gorgeous, but right now it seemed *claustrophobic.*

She walked to the French doors and threw them open. The cool, crisp air floating down off the mountains kissed her overheated skin. Drawing in a deep breath, she stood, looking out at the rugged, forbidding landscape, so harsh compared to Akathinia's sparkling, gilded beauty. It only underscored the different world she now lived in; how that world was shifting beneath her feet.

Her pulse ticked at an elevated rate she couldn't seem to regulate, a heat consumed her cheeks and her knees felt weak. Crazy, because she'd had sex before, she knew how this worked. But she was also aware it was going to be different, very different with Kostas. He touched an elemental part of her no one else ever had.

A skitter across her skin was the only notice she had before strong arms slid around her waist and pulled her back against a warm male body, one big enough to secure her compliance with anything he chose to do to her. But she knew Kostas would never have to resort to that with a woman. His strength would be used only for pleasure. *Hers.*

His lips found the sensitive skin below her ear. Her swift intake of breath was all too revealing.

"Why are you so nervous?"

Because the last time she'd put herself in this position he'd cruelly rejected her. *A decade ago, Stella. Time to get over it.* And yet still it hurt.

She gave him a half truth. "Sex is an intimate thing. It's hard for me to remain unaffected by it."

"Despite your determination to do so." He set his mouth to her shoulder, teeth scraping over her sensitive skin. "Is that what today was all about? Remaining unaffected by me?"

A shudder raked through her. "What do you mean?"

He sank his teeth into her skin, a tiny nip meant to punish. "I mean the return of the aloof, distant Stella I dislike. She disappears tonight, *yineka mou*. Those layers of ice you like to hide behind? *Gone.*"

She struggled to regulate her pounding heart as his tongue laved the tiny bite he'd administered. "So I can take care of those *needs* you talked about?"

"No," he said throatily, "so I can take care of *yours*. You want this so badly you can taste it, *moro mou*, but you aren't sure how to engage."

So utterly true. Her stomach hollowed out, a shiver rippling across her skin. She took a deep breath, attempting to regain control. "I bought some lingerie…I should go put it on."

"We don't need lingerie, Stella." His mouth scored her other shoulder, sending another wave of shivers dancing across her skin. "The chemistry we share is more than enough."

Apparently so. "I bought it especially for you," she protested, her voice raspy. "You don't want to see it?"

"What color is it?"

"*Not* red."

"Pity." He reached up and unzipped her dress, pulling the metal slide down past the small of her back to her hips, where a tiny hook held the dress together. Undoing that, too, he ran a possessive hand up her spine, his caress a clear declaration of ownership. "Go. Put your armor on if you need to."

Finding refuge from her exploding pulse in the luxurious dressing area she and the designer had fashioned with deep walk-in closets, she lifted the dress over her head, hung it up like the precious piece that it was, then exchanged her nondescript, line-minimizing underwear for a beautiful sapphire silk baby doll and its matching panties.

The nightie came just to the top of her thighs, the lace cutouts at the sides hinting at the curves of her breasts and hips. It might be the armor Kostas had so astutely described it as, but it made her feel sexy and desirable, gave her the confidence she needed right now.

Pulling the dozens of pins out of her hair and running her fingers through it, she removed her jewelry and gave her still perfect makeup a once-over. She was ready. Of course, *ready* was a relative term. How could she ever really be *ready*?

Anticipation sizzling in her veins, she returned to the

bedroom. Kostas had taken off his tie, leaving him in a crisp white shirt he'd partially unbuttoned and dark trousers. His gaze shifted from the cuff links he was removing to her. Setting the gold pieces on the dresser, he turned and leaned back against the wood, the heat in his catlike eyes licking at her skin like a flame.

"Come here."

Her legs continued to evade full functionality—she felt vastly incompetent as she moved toward him. When she was within striking distance, he snaked an arm around her waist and pulled her into him with a swiftness that stole her breath.

Setting his big hands on the back of her bare thighs, he swept them up over the curve of her bottom to her waist. Fingers tightening, he lifted her onto the dresser, perching her on the edge while he cleared its contents with his free hand. Coins, cuff links and various other paraphernalia scattered to the floor, metal skimming across stone. Her heart hammered in her ears as she stared up at him. He was all dominant, aggressive male.

She had asked for this.

A slow burn worked its way across his olive-skinned cheeks. He was just as caught up in the moment as she was, she realized, just before he captured a chunk of her hair, tilted her head back and took her mouth in a kiss that was surprising in its gentle edge. Breathing into him, she rested her hands on his waist and returned it. Kiss for kiss, they exchanged intimacies until her entire body was pliant, melting, utterly his to command.

Opening to the heat of his tongue, her palm slid up to brace against his chest as he invaded, stroking deep inside her, forecasting how intimately he wanted to know her body. Dark and heady, the erotically charged essence of him made her toes curl.

Mouths separating, they sought air. Kostas rested his forehead against hers, his breathing rough. “Do you understand how badly I wanted you that night? How hard it was for me to put you on the other side of that door? I felt like I’d walked into the Garden of Eden and been told to keep my hands to myself.”

“I didn’t tell you that.”

“I was wiser than you.”

No, you weren’t. It should have been with you. She kept that thought to herself as she leaned forward to kiss him again.

“No.” He pushed her back until her hands braced themselves on the wood. *Utterly at his mercy.* “Stay put.”

Her heart roared in her ears. His gaze settled on the rise and fall of her chest. The peaks of her breasts were hard, betraying points beneath the transparent silk. Bending, he took a hard peak into the heat of his mouth, sucking her deep inside. Alternating that excruciatingly delicious caress with gentle nips of his teeth, then soothing laves of his tongue, he sent liquid heat pooling between her thighs.

A low moan escaped her throat. He switched his attention to her other nipple, engorged and waiting for him now, administering the same exquisite torment until her low whimpers became an urgent plea.

Lifting his mouth from her breast, he clasped her hips and dragged her forward. His long fingers left a searing imprint on that sensitive, smooth, most intimate flesh. He took her mouth as he traced the inside edges of her panties with his thumbs. It was close, but not close enough to where she wanted him to touch her. A low mewl left her throat.

Abandoning the kiss, he took hold of the sides of her panties and stripped them off her, Stella lifting her hips to help him. His big hand cupped her hot, aching flesh in the most possessive of caresses. She gasped as a lightning bolt of sensation tore through her.

Sliding his other palm beneath her hips, his eyes held hers as he parted her slick, smooth flesh and filled her with one of his big, long fingers. She was wet, took him easily, her muscles clenching around him. It was good. *Too good.* She closed her eyes, a shudder raking through her.

He withdrew and filled her again, setting up a smooth rhythm that had her hips chasing his hand. The pressure inside her built fast and hard, her nails digging into the wood.

"I'm big," he murmured in her ear, his breath a heated caress. "You have to be ready for me. Would you like to come like this for me first?"

The last question was part purr, part tease, the animal in him in full evidence. Her cheeks flamed, her tongue struggling to find itself as the pleasure washed over her.

"I need an answer."

"Yes." Thee mou, yes. Her gaze found his. "Do you always talk like this?"

"Always. It's how I know I'm giving a woman pleasure."

Oh, my.

"There is another condition."

"What?"

"You have to watch. That part is for me."

She opened her eyes. He rewarded her with deeper, harder strokes. It was like getting lost in a storm, watching her pleasure written across his beautiful amber eyes, every moan, every whimper she let go reflected back at her. Her insides tightened as he worked her, pushing her toward orgasm, but every time she got close, he slowed it down and teased her with shallower strokes, keeping her release maddeningly out of reach.

"Is that good?" he asked, leaning forward to kiss her.

"So good."

"You want me to let you come?"

"Yes."

Drawing back, he withdrew his finger, then came inside of her with two. Thick and powerful, his fingers stretched her, filled her, tearing an animal-like moan from her throat. *So insanely good.*

"Please."

He was intent on pulling her apart. Intent on dismantling every single one of her defenses. She saw it in his eyes. He must have decided he'd accomplished his goal because he increased his rhythm then. She felt feverish, consumed by the sensations he was lavishing on her, her hips matching him stroke for stroke. When he slipped his thumb over the tight bundle of nerves at the core of her, his eyes darkening with purpose, and stroked her with a single, deliberate movement, she screamed.

The room blacked out around her.

Kostas carried a limp, sated Stella to the bed, setting her down beside it. Satisfaction pulsed through him at her explosive release. He had intended on breaking down every one of her walls, shattering that ice-cold composure she'd been wearing all day. Instead, her beautifully uninhibited response had taken him apart.

That she *affected* him was an understatement. Stella's impact on him had always been like a critical blood transfusion, injecting a life—a *need*—in him that escaped the boundaries of the rigidly held control he prized and made him want more. Made him want to *be* more; to be a flesh-and-blood man, capable of all the human emotion he'd never allowed himself.

She had been the only thing making him feel alive these past few weeks when taking on this rebellious, wounded country had seemed beyond any one man's ability, a constant, determined presence who had grounded him with the power of her tenacity. But thinking he could ever be the man Stella needed or wanted beyond the respect and affection he'd promised her was a recipe for disaster. Better to be realistic about what this relationship was—a partnership with intense, sexual chemistry.

Pushing his mind firmly back into realistic territory, he swept his gaze over her. All long limbs and slim curves, her golden skin gleaming in the light, hair mussed from his hands, she reminded him of an ancient Greek goddess: strong, brave, fearless. *Almost* fearless.

The flush darkening her cheeks drew his eye. Raising his hand, he trailed the back of his knuckles across the stain of color. "What?"

"Your body is a work of art. I want to see you."

Need clawed at his insides, swift and hard. "It's yours now, *glykeia mou*," he said huskily, capturing her hand and carrying it to the erection that swelled the front placket of his trousers. "For use immediately, *urgently*, in fact."

Heat blazed in her beautiful blue eyes. Spreading her palm wide, she traced the size and shape of him as he moved her fingers over his heat. A low, rough word escaped him as he arched into her touch. "Undress me."

She moved her fingers to the top button of his shirt, working her way down, the brush of her fingertips against his skin setting him on fire. Grasping hold of the collar of his shirt, she pushed it off his shoulders and let it drop to the floor. Feminine appreciation lit her gaze as it traveled over him. "You are insanely beautiful."

His mouth curved. "Should a man take that as a compliment?"

"Yes." The rasp in her voice made his heart thump against his chest.

Her fingers moved to his belt. She unbuckled it, then undid the button of his pants and slid down the zipper. His erection throbbed with every beat of his heart, hard and painfully ready to have her. He hadn't had a woman in over a year—since everything had fallen apart—but he knew it was the woman touching him that elicited his need, awakened his hunger, not the time that had passed.

She sank her fingers into the waistband of his trousers and worked them over his hips and to the floor. He stepped out of them, adding his close-fitting black boxers to the pile. Her eyes were riveted to the jutting erection that skimmed his abdomen, fascination warring with… *apprehension*?

Curving an arm around her waist, he caught her against him. "You saw me that night in my bed."

Long, golden-tipped lashes hid her gaze from him, but not before he saw a flash of something in all that blue fire. The remnant of the wound from that night? A part of him knew it was better if he left it alone. *Safer.* But he couldn't stand to watch her hurt.

Cupping her bottom, he brought her closer, until the length of his erection pressed against her belly, imprinting her with his need. "I've never wanted a woman more than I wanted you that night, *yineka mou*, not since and not now."

Her gaze darkened to a deep, indigo blue. "Never?"

He knew exactly who she was thinking about—the jealousy staining her eyes was crystal clear. Cassandra, however, as stunning as she was, had never touched him like this woman did.

"Never," he said, sliding his hands up the backs of her thighs and over her bottom, lifting the wispy, sexy piece of silk as he went, up and over her head. Tossing it to the floor, he rested his hands on her hips and drank her in. Her breasts were beautiful, high and taut, with rose-colored peaks, her hips delicately curved atop long, sexy legs he had pictured wrapped around him so many times he was aching with the thought of it. *She* was the work of art.

Lowering his mouth to hers, he brushed a single, hot caress across her lips, the palm he held at her bottom bringing her closer, getting her used to the press and slide of his body against hers. Skin-to-skin contact, the most intimate foreplay there was. When her lips clung to his, his name slipping softly from her lips, he picked her up and deposited her on the bed. Coming down over her, he ran a finger from breast to hip, her stomach muscles contracting beneath his touch. She was tense, edgy, despite the release he'd given her.

Closing his palm around her thigh, he spread her wide. Her eyes were liquid blue fire as she stared up at him. Dropping his gaze, he took her in. Beautifully open to him, she made his mouth go dry.

"Kostas." Her gaze willed his back up to hers.

"I like looking at you. *All* of you, Stella." He circled her wet, pliable flesh with his thumb, coming to rest on her core. Pressing down, he played her in sensual circles that made her hips arch up to meet his touch. "You're like a perfect, pink shell waiting to be discovered," he murmured, a raspy edge to his voice. "I'd use my mouth on you if I didn't need to be inside you so badly."

The sharp hiss of air she took in pleased him. Cupping

the back of her thigh, he wrapped one of her beautiful, elegant legs around his waist. Exposed to him, *ready* for him in a way that made his blood heat, he palmed himself and brought the flared head of his erection to her most intimate flesh. With more control than he thought he had left in him, he slid inside, giving her body time to adjust to the size and breadth of him. She exhaled, fingers clutching the velvet coverlet.

"Easy," he murmured. "We take it slow."

She took a deep breath, then another. Her body softened, melted around him. He eased forward another inch, then another. Arching her hips, she struggled to accommodate him, her tight channel clutching and rejecting him all at the same time. Hanging on by a thread, his pulsing body begging for release, he leaned forward and brushed his lips over hers. "You're so tight, *yineka mou*. So good. So sweet."

She nipped at his lip. Allowing her the distraction, he slid his hand between their bodies and rubbed his thumb over the swollen center of her. Caressed her as he whispered earthy, sexy words in her ear. Burying her fingers in his hair, she gave beneath him, her body relaxing. Finally, he was buried deep inside her.

Unsheathed by a condom for the first time with a woman, he absorbed the hot, wet velvet encasing him. She was like a tight, silken glove, the lush clenching of her muscles around him as her body expanded to take him the most erotic sensation he'd ever experienced.

Her eyes fluttered open. "Kostas," she gasped, "you're so big. I can feel you everywhere."

"I can feel *you* everywhere, *moro mou*." His gaze tangled with hers. "So strong, so passionate, you make me so hot for you, Stella."

She bit her lip. The overload of emotion he read in her

reverberated through him, touched him in a deep place he'd thought unreachable, because he felt it, too.

"Slowly," she whispered. "I want to feel every inch of you."

The huskily issued command was nearly the end of him, but somehow he managed to move in brutally restrained strokes; teasing, caressing movements that made her writhe against him. "You like that?" he rasped, rotating his hips. "You like that I fill you up?"

"So good," she moaned. "Don't stop."

He brought his mouth to hers, nipping at the plush curves as he pushed deeper, harder, inside her, giving her all he had. Her body rippled around him; tempted his self-control. Still he held back, his palm sliding beneath her buttock to lift her higher so he could find the spot that would give her the deepest, most intense orgasm.

"Right there," he breathed in her ear. "I can feel you tightening around me, Stella *mou*. Come for me."

A low moan ripped from her throat. "Kostas…"

He gripped her hips tighter, penetrating her body with deliberate, forceful thrusts that had her contracting around him. Digging her nails into his buttocks, she threw her head back, a sharp cry leaving her throat as her body clenched his in a long, hot pull that shattered him. Bracing his hands on either side of her, he let go, spilling himself inside of her.

The intimacy of it blew every emotion he'd ever had to smithereens—the giving of his life force to this woman, who in turn gave hers to him.

Long minutes later as his wife lay sleeping in his arms, the same state of being remained elusive for Kostas. Sleep had once come easily to him, a gift as his *yaya* had called it, an escape from the complexities of his life, but as the years had passed and his father's manic phases had escalated, plunging the country into disarray, a solid night's rest had eluded him. How could he rest when he was torn in a dozen different directions? When his father was a madman terrorizing his neighboring countries? When his people were suffering?

When no decision had ever seemed like the right one.

He would have woken Stella and lost himself in her addictive warmth again, but a part of him needed distance, the distance he had always craved when people got too close. When his life seemed too complex to manage any other way.

Sliding out of bed, he dressed and went down the hall to his office, where he read the latest security report that had come in on General Houlis's activity. The man who had just wished he and Stella the best of luck for their future happiness in an award-worthy performance was growing increasingly desperate as the elections loomed and his window of opportunity diminished.

If he was going to make a play for control of Carnelia, he would need to do it soon. When that might be was unclear according to Kostas's eyes and ears on the ground.

Grimacing, he tossed the report aside. He was hoping it would never come to pass; that Houlis would realize the time for change had come to this country. But his security team was preparing contingency plans in case the general did elect to go for the jugular.

He leaned back in his chair, rubbing a palm over the coarse stubble on his chin. He should be focusing on the threat to his country, to his own personal safety. Instead, his head remained on the woman who lay sleeping in his bed—his wife, whose armor had come off tonight, proving she was every bit the vulnerable, passionate woman he'd known existed underneath all those protective layers.

Watching her walk down that aisle today, deliver that emotional toast, had touched a piece of him he hadn't even known existed. Taking her to bed, unleashing the passion that blazed between them, had only intensified those feelings; deep, uncharted ones he knew he should smother, the very ones he could never have for his wife. He had been so intent on scaling Stella's defenses, revealing the woman he knew, obliterating this chemistry between them, that he had ignored the potential consequences.

He felt for her, he always had. Perhaps too much. Her speech tonight had touched him but had also left him deeply conflicted, more aware than ever that he was not the man she thought him to be.

His chest tightened, the guilt in his stomach a heavy weight he'd been carrying so long he was shocked it even registered. He could not afford to play emotional roulette with his wife, not now when he was so close to replacing his father's legacy with a brighter future for Carnelia.

A throb pulsed at his temples. He massaged it with his fingers, attempting to ease the pressure. Allowing this thing between him and his wife to run any deeper couldn't happen. Better to cut off these feelings at the source, stick to the rules they had agreed on.

Stella was already digging holes in his armor, making him question what he was, what he wanted to be. And although she'd been an unquestionably integral presence by his side and would continue to be so, he needed to keep her at an emotional distance. His father was too stark an example of what happened when emotion clouded rational thinking.

Sitting forward, he reached for yet another report he hadn't had time to read. He and his wife were on the same page when it came to this marriage. Deep emotion, love, didn't belong in it.

* * *

Stella awoke alone in the big, luxurious bed, the bright dial on the clock telling her it was far too early to be awake. Three in the morning, in fact. But her husband was.

She sat up and reached for a drink of water. Setting down the glass, she hugged her arms around her knees, a hollow feeling invading her. It didn't surprise her Kostas wasn't there. He never slept well. But the fact that he had taken her apart tonight, then left their wedding bed to work, turned the key on a long-seated feeling of rejection she couldn't quite shake.

I've never wanted a woman more than I wanted you that night, yineka mou*, not since and not now.*

Her stomach clenched, curling into a tight ball. It had been just as beguiling as she'd imagined it would be to discover Kostas wanted her as much as she wanted him. To wipe away his rejection of the past. But on the heels of his expert seduction had also been the knowledge she was exposing herself to new vulnerabilities, *scarier* ones, because now she would have to guard against the adult version of falling in love with him, which could be oh, so much more painful than its predecessor.

Which she would never do. Firming her mouth, she got out of bed, slipped on a robe and went to find her husband rather than ruminate. Ensconced behind the handsome cedar desk in his study, he looked as if what he needed was sleep—days of it.

Fatigue-darkened eyes regarded her as he put down his pen. "You should be sleeping. The send-off breakfast is in a few hours."

"I was thirsty. You were gone." She walked around the desk and perched on the edge closest to him. "Have you always been this way? Not able to sleep?"

"Most of my life, yes."

Because he'd never had any grounding influence to make him feel secure after his grandmother had died. Because the fear and intimidation his father had practiced had likely chased him everywhere, even in his sleep. Her chest grew tight, the soul-deep wound she felt for him growing with every day they spent together. She couldn't change the past, but she could help him now.

She absorbed the lines creasing his brow and mouth, deeper it seemed, in the hours since he'd left her. "What's keeping you up tonight?"

He waved a hand toward the desk. "Half a dozen things."

"But something is making you extra stressed."

He reached out and scooped her off the desk and into his lap. "The election is less than a month away. I have a million things on my mind. I am preoccupied. But now that you are awake," he murmured, gaze dropping to the curves of her breasts the gaping neckline of her robe revealed, "I'd prefer to enjoy you."

Heat invaded her bones, warming her insides, her body recalling the pleasure he could give her. Fighting the hedonistic pull, she curled her fingers around the thick muscle of his biceps. "You promised to share things with me. Let me help."

"I will. Just not tonight." His fingers traced the line of her jaw.

"Did you miss him today? Your father?" So many people had spoken of the late king, some with a reverence that had blown her away.

"No," he said evenly, "I did not."

She could only imagine the complex feelings Kostas held for his father that must have been unearthed by today. "Your mother's sister was lovely. She seemed to find it bittersweet."

His fingers dropped away from her face. "She didn't want her sister to marry my father. She considered him far too power hungry, too ruthless, but my mother was in love with him."

"It sounded as if she softened him—made him less so."

He nodded. "She was the balancing effect on his personality, the thing that held him in check. When she died, it set off something in his brain, turned loose the controlling side of his psyche, his near psychopathic need for power."

"Too much pain," she said softly.

His eyes turned bleak. "Shortly afterward, his aide found my father in his study with a gun pressed to his head. I think he might have killed himself if the aide hadn't stopped him, made sure my father saw a doctor and received medication for his manic depression. It wasn't a commonly recognized thing then—being a manic depressive—but he clearly was one."

Her heart dipped. "Love can be destructive in so many ways."

"Yes, it can." Amber eyes speared hers. "It's why this arrangement of ours will work—because we based it on our mutual respect for each other, not some illusionary emotion."

She nodded. She was going to keep her feelings out of this. She *was*.

He traced the line of her throat with his fingers. "And very hot sexual chemistry. That we have, too, *moro mou*."

A wave of heat suffused her skin. Nudging the lapel of her robe aside, he closed his fingers over her breast in a possessive movement that stole her breath. She inhaled as his thumb nudged her soft, sensitive areola, sliding over its peak.

"We should go to bed," she said huskily. *Before he obliterated her again.*

"Or not." He covered her mouth with his and bit lightly into her lower lip. "It is our wedding night after all. Creating an heir is...necessary."

Her head spun as his mouth hovered over hers, their breath mingling. *Waiting. Anticipating.* Her insides fisted tight with need. The urge to walk away, to extricate herself before he destroyed more of her defenses, dissolved in a sea of lust.

This *was* her wedding night. Rational thought could come tomorrow.

Gripping her hips, he lifted her, bringing her down so her knees straddled his lap. Eyes on hers, he settled her against his erection covered by the thin pajama bottoms he wore, no barrier to the thick heat that parted her most intimate flesh with possessive intent.

Her gasp split the air. *"Kostas—"*

He rocked against her, sliding his staff against her. Every sensual movement stoked the inferno rising inside of her.

The whisper of his big hand sliding along the sensitive skin of her inner thigh. A stroke of his fingertips against the crease where hip met leg. She squirmed against his touch, flesh on fire.

"Get on me," he murmured in her ear. "I want to take you like this."

Excitement pounding through her veins, she reached down, freed him from the silk that covered him and guided his rigid shaft to her slick flesh. Lowering herself on him, the wide tip of his body pressing against her, a harsh breath escaped her. She froze, absorbing the power of him inside her still tender flesh. Centimeter by centimeter she took him inside her until his big body stretched her muscles so tight she was at the very edge of how much pleasure she could take. Until he touched things that had never been touched before.

Never had she felt so full, so taken, so *possessed.*

"You have all of me now," Kostas said huskily, his voice a hot burn in her ear. "Is that good, *yineka mou*?"

She nodded, past speech. Opening her eyes, she set her hands on the muscular bulk of his shoulders. There was emotion radiating from those fiery, dark eyes as he watched her. He felt *something* for her. But his caution rang in her ear, underlining her own promises to herself. He wasn't ever going to let himself be his father, nor was she ever going to become her mother.

She closed her eyes and focused on the sea of pleasure washing over her. Kostas lifted her off him, then filled her with a delectably slow movement, his erection tantalizing every inch of her. He did it again and again until she dropped her head back and moaned with the pleasure of it.

Cupping her bottom tighter in his palms, he increased his pace, thrusting into her with a deep, intensely erotic focus that sent starbursts of blinding pleasure exploding behind her eyes. He was so big, so hard, he pushed her pleasure beyond anything she'd ever felt, winding her tighter and tighter with each controlled thrust.

"Kostas—" Hot, white lightning radiated out from her center, stiffening her limbs, toes. Whispering hot, heated words in her ear, he pressed his thumb to the tight bundle of nerves at her center, drawing out her orgasm. Another wave of pleasure washed over her, shattering her. Taking her mouth with his, Kostas filled her with deep, deliberate strokes, a low growl escaping his throat as he came.

When the tremors in both of them had subsided, Kostas picked her up and carried her back to bed. This time, as the crisp night air flowed in through the windows, he slept. Head on his chest, she absorbed the tiny victory, then let unconsciousness take her, too.

CHAPTER TEN

A LAVISH WEDDING breakfast had been laid out in the newly renovated dining room of the Marcariokastro for close friends and family leaving Carnelia that day. The warm, charismatic room was a feast for the eye, its recent renovations retaining the original frescos on the walls and ceiling as well as its large, cathedral windows and stunning, intricate dark woodwork.

A massive harvest banquet table ran down the center of the room, the focal point of the space. Dressed this morning with the finest Laskos crystal and china, it was full of fresh flowers and the animated discussion of its occupants, a lively, happy destination. Except for the preoccupation of the bride.

Sitting at one end of the table with Alex, Sofía and Jessie while her new husband was immersed in conversation with her brother at the other end, she had woken up alone in bed again at seven, full of so many conflicting emotions about the night before she could have painted the Akathinian Independence Day parade in about fifty colors of them.

Confusion about her feelings for Kostas. Concern about the pressure he was under. Worry she felt more for him than she'd ever let herself admit.

He had looked as preoccupied as he had the night before when he'd entered the dining room this morning, greeting her with a quick kiss before sitting down with Nik. She knew in her bones something was going on he wasn't telling her.

"So," Alex said archly as Sofía and Jessie went off to find more of the figs and fresh waffles, "how was last night?"

Stella eyed her. "Are you asking me to give you details about my wedding night?"

"Yes." Alex looked unrepentant. "I want to know if that hunk of a man is as good as he looks."

She took a sip of her coffee. Reined in her emotions. "Yes. He is."

Alex's mouth turned down. "That's *all* you're giving me?"

"Yes."

Her sister did not need to know her night with Kostas had been mind-blowingly good. That it had exceeded her expectations in every way. That she was sore in places she'd never been sore before. Because he had also annihilated her defenses, stripped her bare, left her skin feeling too sensitive, her vulnerabilities wide-open.

Alex eyed her. "You okay?"

"Tired."

Her sister chewed on her lip. "Can I say something brutally honest?"

"That depends on what it is."

Alex took a sip of her coffee. Set it down. "Any fool could see you and Kostas have deep feelings for each other. There wasn't a dry eye in the room last night. Try not," she said quietly, eyes on hers, "to sabotage this relationship as you've done every other."

Antagonism lanced through her. "I don't do that."

"Yes, you do."

She put down her cup and shoved it away. "This is a partnership, Alex. I'm too far gone to ever find love. I don't have it in me and neither does Kostas. In that, we are a perfect pair."

Alex frowned. "Don't you think you and Kostas can be different? That you can build on what you have? Aristos is different, *changed*, since us, you've seen that."

"Aristos was crazy about you from the beginning." She sat back in her chair, her gaze flitting over her husband. "Kostas has been molded with so much fear and discipline, taught to keep his emotions inside of him at all costs or he will pay the price. I'm not sure he's ever going to let himself feel. I would be crazy to think I can be the one to change him."

"You don't think I felt the same about Aristos? The press were putting bets on how long our relationship would last, Stella—*bets*—and I was falling in love with him. It was like walking on quicksand."

An apt analogy. "It's not the same," she said with finality. "I believe Kostas cares about me. I believe we can do great things for this country. But that's as far as it goes."

She moved the conversation on to when they would all next get together as her sister-in-law and Jessie came back, plates laden. Better to keep her expectations where they should be and focus instead on what was making her husband so edgy.

The last guest left in the late afternoon. Her husband retreated to his office, murmuring something about a pressing phone call. Missing her family already, Stella sat in the conservatory reading a book.

Her mood disintegrated as the hours went by and her husband remained chained to his desk. She'd signed on to a *partnership*, not to be shunted off to the sidelines while Kostas looked ready to self-destruct.

By nine o'clock she decided enough was enough. Heading upstairs to his study, she knocked, then entered. Kostas looked up from the document he was reviewing, a dark shadow on his jaw, his eyes weary.

"Lypamai." I'm sorry. "I didn't mean to be in here all night."

She fixed her gaze on his. "What's going on, Kostas? What can I help with?"

An unblinking dark stare back. "Election mechanics. Boring but necessary."

"Bore me, then."

"I have to take another call in a few minutes. I'll join you after that."

Heat streaked through her veins at being stonewalled yet again. She turned on her heel and left. In their suite, she undressed and slipped on a more modest ivory negligee than her armor of the night before. Standing in front of the mirror, she brushed her hair with jerky, violent strokes, sending a cloud of electricity up in the air.

Her husband walked in minutes later, tawny gaze fixed on her.

"I thought you had a call."

"I made it quick."

She kept brushing.

"Stella—"

She threw the brush on the dresser and turned to face him. "Talk to me, Kostas, or go back to work."

He folded his arms across his chest. "It's nothing you need to be concerned about."

"I think it is. You're distracted. Your conversation with Nik looked intense."

A weighted silence. "It's Houlis," he said, raking a hand through his hair. "I didn't want to say anything until I had something substantial. I'm receiving intelligence reports he is getting desperate, that he may act before the elections. That phone call was with my security chief putting contingency plans in place."

Ice swept her veins. "He stood there and wished us well yesterday."

"Civility for civility's sake."

She pressed her lips together, a chill chasing up her spine. "Do we have enough support to repel him if he does act?"

"I believe so, but we won't know for sure until the time comes."

Until the times comes. Thee mou. "The pushback you're receiving on your modernization plans... Is that giving Houlis an opening he can exploit?"

That cast-iron look of defiance he'd been wearing for weeks passed across his face. "Perhaps. But it's the right thing to do. Backing down on my plans would only cast my leadership into question. Give Houlis an excuse to pounce."

"Heading into the last weeks of the election with an unhappy public will also do that."

"I am not negotiating this point." Spoken with an iron core.

Diavole, but he was impossible. She gave up. "What are the security plans if something does happen?"

"The plan is to have Houlis and his supporters in jail before a coup can take place. As for you, Nik and I have an extraction plan."

"An *extraction plan*?" Her hands clenched by her sides. "I am the queen of this country, Kostas. I'm not going anywhere if something happens. We are a team. I knew this was a possibility when I signed on."

His expression hardened. "If your life is in danger, you go."

"No."

"Yes."

"We agree to disagree." She held his gaze, a belligerent tilt to her jaw. "I'm tough—as tough as you."

"Yes," he agreed, mouth curving. "You are."

She rested her hands on the edge of the dresser. "You can't carry this alone, Kostas. *You* aren't alone anymore. I am here with you."

Something flickered in his impassive gaze. "All right," he said quietly. "I promise you will know everything I know. But there's nothing more we can do at the moment. We've taken every precaution we can."

She studied the stoic, unfazed look on his strong, *infinitely strong* face. He had a bounty on his head and yet he was unfazed. As if it was just one more obstacle he had to surmount. But this was the man, she reminded herself, whose own father had considered him a threat—to be managed or eliminated. She wondered what kind of an iron interior you would need to have to deal with that. Likely the one that made her husband close himself off when any kind of threat, emotional or physical, put his existence in peril.

She walked over to the bed and sat down. Understanding him, getting through to those locked-away places she needed to know, meant finding out more about how that iron interior had been shaped.

"What was your life like?" she asked. "Being your father's protégé? I can't even conceive of it."

He blinked at the change in subject. "You want to make this relationship work," she said quietly, "let me in, Kostas. I'm trying to understand *you*."

He leaned back against the dresser, long legs splayed out in front of him. "I didn't know any different a life. My studies came first, my grandmother insisted on that.

When I wasn't with her or my tutor, I was with my father, shadowing his steps. Which, in reality, meant I was in the care of his bodyguards and security team."

"You didn't have a nanny?"

"My father didn't believe in them. He said they made you soft."

Of course he had. "What about friends? Were you allowed to have them?"

"The question was did they want to be friends with me. I was the dictator's son, my father was the man who would throw one of their parents in jail one day, or exile another the next. I didn't have a lot of friends as a result of it. Sometimes the children of the palace staff were ordered to play with me when no one else would."

Christe mou. Her heart contracted into a tight ball.

"When my father did spend time with me," he continued, "he was focused on the propaganda—maintaining our legacy. I was his most important disciple. It was all about control and power—over the people and the military junta who backed us. We needed to be impenetrable, stronger than all the rest. Emotion was anathema, a weakness never to be shown."

"Emotion is not a weakness," she countered. "It's a strength. It's how you become a balanced ruler, how you connect with the people. Your grandmother knew that."

"Yes, but she and my grandfather were the exception to the Laskos dynasty. The rest of my ancestors governed with the same fear and intimidation my father did, perhaps to a slightly more moderate degree."

She wrapped her arms around herself, asking the question she wasn't sure she wanted the answer to. "The physical and mental controls he used on you…what were they?"

"It depended on the mood he was in. When he was

on a dark, depressive swing and I'd displeased him, he would ignore me for days, lock me in my room. Sometimes he'd have his henchmen administer whatever punishment they thought fit.

"When he was in his manic phases, he would teach me the skills he thought I needed to master. I was a good shot for my age, for instance, but he wanted me to be the expert marksman he was. If I didn't hit all the targets the first day we went shooting, we'd go back the next until my hands were bruised, my shoulder and arm numb from holding the gun. By the end of that second day I would be hitting those targets. I was so good I rivaled the sniper's shots in the military."

Her insides recoiled. "But not worth the price you paid, surely. No child should have to live up to those unreasonable standards of perfection."

"No," he agreed, with a nod. "I'm merely telling you how I was conditioned. It's not a *way* I choose to be, it's who I am."

She shook her head. "You *feel*, Kostas, just like you've never lost your sense of right and wrong. Just like you never let that monster claim your soul. The passion you have for your people, how overwhelmed with emotion you get every time you see those big crowds that show up for you, the pain you have felt over Athamos's death…it speaks to the depth of feeling you are capable of experiencing. You may *choose* not to allow yourself to feel, but that is another thing entirely."

His mouth twisted. "I feel, but only so far, Stella. Whether it's because I'm not capable of it, or I don't allow it, the end result is the same. Don't expect miracles from me."

"I'm not looking for miracles," she said quietly, "I'm

looking for *you*, Kostas. I know you are in there somewhere."

His face transformed into a blank, unyielding canvas. "Be careful what you wish for. You might not like what you find. You have unrealistic views of me, Stella."

"No." She shook her head. "Perhaps I once did, but not now. Now I realize it was unfair of me to hold you to the standards I did. Unfair of *everyone* to do it. All of us have our human failings—I, more than anyone—but you need to forgive yourself for yours, truly forgive yourself so you can rule with a clear head."

His cheekbones hardened into sharp blades. "I *have* forgiven myself."

She studied the tense set of his big body; how everything seemed to be locked away behind metal bars. "Have you?"

A frozen silence passed. She watched him retreat back into that impenetrable facade of his. "I have more work to do," he said, levering himself away from the dresser. "Don't wait up for me."

Her skin felt too tight and her chest knotted as he walked out of the room. He had needed to hear that, she told herself. He still wasn't thinking clearly about the impact of his aggressive plans on his people and the irreparable harm he was doing himself in the process.

She crawled into bed, physically and mentally exhausted. Kostas's words echoed in her head. *Be careful what you wish for. You might not like what you find. You have unrealistic views of me, Stella.*

Frustration curled her toes. She did *not* have unrealistic expectations of him. Hadn't she just told him that had been unfair of her? Or had Tassos been right? Had Kostas shut down just now because he felt he didn't deserve to be forgiven? That the mistakes he'd made had been unforgivable? Or were there other demons plaguing her husband she would never be privy to?

Curled up in the massive bed with its luxuriously soft silk sheets, she felt chilled, apprehensive and alone—more alone than she'd ever felt in her life. And that was saying something. She'd thought it couldn't get any worse. Perhaps it was because last night with Kostas she'd felt that elusive emotional connection she'd been searching for her entire life.

Where once it had seemed unobtainable, it had been organic with her husband, as if it had just taken the right connection to slot into place—the connection she'd always known was special. Dangerous to her.

The irony of it was undeniable. She'd found that bond with Kostas, the one man she could never explore it with because he wanted no part of it.

An ache wound itself around her heart. What he had told her about his childhood had chilled her, had given her so much more insight into what made him tick. But it had also made her wonder if it wasn't so much that Kostas didn't *want* love, but that he didn't know *what* it was. That he'd been taught it was a weakness, *any* emotion was a weakness, a vulnerability to be exploited.

He was *afraid* of it. If he let someone in, if he admitted his master plan was wrong, if he became anything less than impenetrable, it might all fall apart.

She bit her lip, the salty tang of blood filling her mouth. It might all fall apart anyway if he kept this up; if he refused to bend. But what more could she do than she'd already done? She could only stand by his side, be that unconditional support she knew he needed, ignore the fact that with every day that passed, her true feelings for him were bubbling closer and closer to the surface, threatening to complicate an already too-complicated scenario, the very thing she'd said she'd never do.

CHAPTER ELEVEN

KOSTAS SAT IN his office finishing up work, knowing Stella was likely back from her meeting with the charity, but he elected to push on until dinner. Avoiding his wife was easier than talking about forgiveness and absolution, something he couldn't stomach.

He sat back in his seat and rubbed a hand across his brow. It had been like this since their confrontation in the bedroom. Better to withdraw now and save his wife more pain in the long run, than continue to let her uncover too much of him. Ask for the things he'd warned her he could never give.

A knot tied itself down low. He was hurting Stella with his withdrawal, could see it in her eyes when that tough facade slipped for just a second. Knew it was the last thing he should do to a woman who'd been marginalized by the people she'd loved, who'd experienced enough rejection for a lifetime. But what choice did he have?

He'd tried to make it up to her by allowing her to attend an executive council meeting yesterday as the council prepared to transition to its postelection membership. It had been good to see her light up, to see her brain working frantically as she scribbled notes, had assuaged his guilt just the slightest little bit. But she was looking for more than that from him—she always had been.

Pushing his attention back to his schedule for tomorrow, he perpetuated his avoidance strategy; how that knot twisted itself into a dozen more tangled iterations.

Takis knocked on the door and entered for their final debrief of the day. Working through a few urgent items, they finished with his latest approval ratings that had just come in. The hairs on the back of his neck stood up at the look on his aide's face. Dipping his head, he scanned the numbers. *They were disastrous.* "You're sure these are accurate?"

Takis nodded. "We expanded the poll. The numbers came back the same."

He threw the report on the desk, his heart plummeting. The goodwill he'd amassed since becoming king had vaporized in the wake of that damning editorial and the increasing public discontent that had followed. In fact, he was back to where he'd started. Given they were three and a half weeks away from the elections, it was a disaster.

A disaster his wife had warned him about when he'd shut her down in the bedroom.

"I need time to absorb these." He looked up at his aide. "We'll pick this up in the morning. Discuss a strategy to counter them."

Takis nodded and left. A low, rough word escaped him. How could he have been so shortsighted? Have so vastly misjudged public sentiment as to allow this to happen?

A buzzing feeling settled over him as he attempted to absorb the disaster he'd created. Stella had been right all along. He should have listened to the people, should have compromised, should have found a middle ground. Instead, in his need to be right, to correct his mistakes, to prove to his father, a *dead man*, that he had been wrong about him, that he *would* lead this country to its freedom and self-determination, he had sewn the seeds of his own demise. Given the military an opportunity to hang him.

Rising to his feet, he walked to the bar stored in a hidden cabinet and poured himself a drink. Carrying it to the window, he took a long sip of the smoky, aged whiskey as he looked out at the dark mass of the Ionian Sea spread out below the rugged cliffs that bounded Carnelia.

It was his people's voice he had been fighting for. *Their* voice that needed to be heard. But somewhere along the way he'd forgotten that, the principle swept aside by his blind ambition to save this country.

He took another sip of the whiskey, welcoming its fiery burn down his throat. He struggled with his father's legacy, he knew. Always had. His father had drilled his propaganda into him with such force and regularity, it had been impossible for him to escape his legacy completely.

Confused, caught between what his grandmother was teaching him and what his father was drilling into his head, he had kept his developing thoughts to himself. Closed himself down. Shaped himself into that impenetrable force his father had been. Made himself *unbreakable* in order to survive.

The knot in his gut expanded. His arrogance, his need to become impregnable, had become an obsession, defined his existence. Usually, he managed to keep it under control, rein himself in when he knew he was swinging too far to the other end of the pendulum, but that self-awareness had disintegrated the night Athamos's car had plunged over that cliff on a hot Carnelian night borne of temporary insanity. Then nothing had made sense anymore.

Are you punishing yourself? Stella's words floated

back to him on a quiet mental whisper. *Was he?* He thought he'd put Athamos's death behind him, forgiven himself for his own self-preservation so he could accomplish what he needed to do. But now, as he stared out at the sea from which they had pulled the crown prince's car, the sky as solid a black as it had been the night he and his rival had raced, lit by a sea of stars, he wondered if he had. If Stella was right—that he had made this country his penance… If the one thing he'd never told anyone was the one thing he could never forgive himself for…

A darkness rose up inside of him, an all too familiar, corrosive guilt that had once threatened to eat him alive. He'd been operating on autopilot ever since Athamos's death, determined to lift this country from the ashes, to salvage *something* from the wreck of his life, his wife the only thing that came close to jolting him out of it.

He *had* lost his passion. His idealism. Stella was right. He didn't even recognize himself anymore.

The sight of Athamos's car careening off the road ahead of him filled his head. The squeal of brakes as his rival attempted to steer away from the deadly drop to the cliffs below. The heart-pounding silence that had followed.

His heart pounded in his chest at the memory, so violently he thought his ribs might bruise it. That night was a hell he would never fully escape, a stain on his soul that would forever mark him. But somehow, he knew, he had to find the lessons his guru had preached. Some he knew he'd learned. Others he was sure were yet to come.

It occurred to him as he looked out into the dark, star-strewn night that perhaps part of truly moving on was not becoming what he had been, but what he would *become.* Something better than before. Something worthy of the second chance he'd been given. *Something that would make up for all of it.*

He would make this right.

Stella regarded her husband over the very old, very good bottle of Bordeaux he'd unearthed from the castle's wine cellar, the agony he was clearly in threatening to crush her heart, steal her breath. The emotional knives that had been turning inside of her the entire meal, making it impossible to eat, forced her to finally lay down her fork and knife.

Her husband, who had consumed only a few bites of his meal himself, finally spoke. "Aren't you going to say, 'I told you so'?"

She shook her head. "I think you've punished yourself enough already."

He took a sip of his wine. Pushed the glass back onto the table. "I called Aristos before dinner and asked his advice on how he's dealt with public opposition to his properties."

She nodded, hiding her surprise. A good idea given Aristos had built hotels and casinos all around the world.

"What did he say?"

"He took me through the key interest groups. Told me which ones are key to get onside, which ones we need to court to neutralize the negative factions. He said to make them a part of the decision-making process."

Exactly as she'd counseled. "Good advice. But that will take time. You need something you can execute immediately, something that will turn the tide of public opinion before the elections."

His expression was bleak. "I'm not sure that exists."

"What about a town council?" She voiced the idea that had been percolating ever since that editorial had run. "Get everyone out and let them have their say. Once they've had a chance to offer their opinions, you choose some of those key influencers Aristos was talking about to join your advisory council. Nothing will *happen* before the elections in terms of results, but at least the people will see the promise you are making to listen."

He gave her a skeptical look. "That could end up being a zoo. They will ask for the moon."

"You don't make any promises you can't keep. You agree to compromise."

Kostas was quiet for a long moment, swirling the wine in his glass. "It could," he said finally, "be positioned as me being an empathetic, inclusive leader rather than my backtracking on my plans."

"Yes," she said quietly. "There are worse things than being seen as an empathetic leader."

His gaze sharpened at the gibe. "The people are right to be frustrated. It should never have been allowed to get to this point. *I* should have done something sooner."

Finally, an insight into what was going on in his head. "It took decades of your father's misrule to get the country to this point. You yourself told me how complicated the political situation was before you left. You can't second-guess your decisions."

"It's impossible not to wonder how much damage I could have prevented."

Her heart squeezed. "But it won't solve your problem. You need to leave the past in the past."

He was silent for a long time. When he looked up at her, there was a myriad of emotions blazing in his dark eyes. "Do you really believe that's possible?"

"Yes," she said. "I do. I have these past few weeks and you need to do it, too, Kostas. You're spending so much time trying to prove yourself right, to prove you aren't your father, you've lost the vision that's always guided you, the one your people are looking to you for."

His mouth thinned. "Sometimes I swing too far to the wrong end of the pendulum, I know that. I have a lot of my father in me. In this case I know I have."

"So do the town hall. Open yourself up, show everyone who you are, *prove* to them you are on their side." She shook her head, her voice softening. "I signed up for the man who gave that speech at our engagement party about the self-determination of his people. For *that* man, not *this* one. For the Kostas who sat in that tree and told me he was going to be a more empathetic king."

His gaze fell away from hers. He picked up his wine and took a sip, staring into the flickering candlelight.

"What are you afraid they're going to see?" Her quiet voice brought his head up. "What are you afraid *I'm* going to see, Kostas? Why did you shut down on me the other night?"

He lifted a shoulder. "It would take a psychologist years to get to the bottom of it."

She bit her lip. "And that's it, is it?" she murmured. "Your job is done. Wife secured, wife deconstructed, wife in her appropriate box, the work toward an heir under way? No need to put in any additional effort toward this so-called relationship you wanted?"

The skin across his cheekbones went blade-sharp. "You know it isn't like that."

"Tell me how it *is*, Kostas, because I have no clue."

"We are good together." His amber eyes blazed. "We are making a great team. I *have* made an effort with you. I have told you things I've never told another human being. But you need to know when to pick your battles, when to push and when to stop."

"So you can walk away when it gets hot in a room?

'Be careful what you wish for, Stella, you might not like what you see.' What does that even mean?"

"You're reading too much into it."

"I think I'm not." She fixed her gaze on his. "You asked me to trust you at the beginning of all of this and I have. I've let you in. Now you need to play by the same rules. You are capable of opening up, you've shown that. This marriage hinges on you doing it, because we left the old rules behind us a long time ago. And if you think I can't take it, this is me, Kostas, saving a country with you while a madman waits in the wings."

He gave her a long look. "I know you can take it, Stella, but tonight is not the night." He pushed his chair back, the screech of wood across stone making her wince.

She watched him walk away *again*, her heart dropping. She could only hope she'd given him a potential solution to think through.

Getting to her feet, she went to bed because clearly he needed to process. Pacing their beautiful exposed-stone bedroom, she couldn't settle. The distance between her and Kostas seemed like a million miles apart tonight. Her tumultuous relationship, the tenuous situation they were in coated her mouth with fear.

She should have kept to their original agreement, should never have allowed Kostas to convince her to turn this into a real relationship because exactly what she'd feared would happen was happening. She had allowed her emotions to get involved and Kostas was shutting down, as emotionally unavailable a man as her father ever was.

Her insides twisted into a tight, protective ball. The silence, the palpable strain of dinners in the formal dining room of the palace as her parents had forced her and her siblings to suffer through mandated family dinners, had been toxic, thick with her mother's hurt and anger, her father's ambivalence. Nik used to come up with every excuse in the book to miss them, the atmosphere had been so tense, inventing a stomachache one day, a sprained ankle the next.

When she couldn't stand the empty room one minute longer, she picked up the phone and called Alex. They talked about the latest news, the gossip at home, about the jazz concert Alex was putting on in the spring with the Akathinian legend Nina Karvelas for the youth charity she chaired.

Her sister was over the moon about it, clearly in her element. Stella grew quieter and quieter as the conversation went on.

Alex paused. "You okay?"

She brushed away the tears sliding silently down her cheeks. "Alex," she whispered, "I feel like I'm walking on quicksand."

CHAPTER TWELVE

THE BENTLEY SLID through the night, following the king's town council, the driver taking a complicated series of roads back to the castle as part of the heightened security measures in place given the ongoing threat from the military junta.

Stella rested her head against the seat, heart full to bursting. Her husband had been amazing. With the weight of the world on his shoulders, he had opened himself up to the packed crowd that had filled the auditorium, showing himself as the Kostas she knew, the man who had nurtured infinite dreams, who had enough strength to hold a country together, to build a future for it. The man she had always known he was.

It had not been an easy ride. Frustration, fear and mistrust reigned among Carnelians. They wanted to know they had been heard. Kostas listened to every one of their questions, answered with an insight and compassion that floored her, then took her suggestion and promised to put a handful of representatives on his advisory council so their voices would be heard going forward.

A swell of hope, of rightness, filled her. The café owner had been there. These were her people, too, now. No longer did this country feel foreign and cold to her, devoid of the gilded brightness of her homeland. Instead, she found herself surrounded by a resilience of spirit, a warmth that came from deep within the people's hearts, a courage and fortitude that Carnelians would not see themselves bowed again.

"You were incredible," she told Kostas, breaking the silence. "I think you turned the tide tonight. I think you earned their trust."

He looked over at her, tawny eyes glimmering in the dim light. "It was your idea. Perhaps General Houlis was right. Perhaps you will become the power behind the man."

She searched his face for sarcasm, for some clue to his mood, but there was only the same intensity he'd been wearing all night, dark, unreadable.

"It's you they believe in," she said quietly. "You they needed to see and tonight they did."

Another silence. Kostas looked out the window, the hard lines of his perfect bone structure set in shadow. "I need to thank you," he said finally, looking back at her, "for tonight, for standing by my side. I know it hasn't been easy. I know *I* haven't been easy."

Her heart was a rock in her throat. "You're welcome," she said huskily, past the giant lump. "You aren't the only one who keeps your promises, Kostas. I do. I always do."

He rubbed a palm against the stubble on his jaw, eyes contemplative. "You were right," he said, "about everything that night in my office. I had lost my idealism, my passion, *myself*." His gaze held hers. "You wondered how I dealt with being who I am. How I made sense of it all. I made myself into that impenetrable force my father conditioned me to be. That need to succeed, to win, as you pointed out, translated to every part of my life. It was my defense mechanism when my life became too complicated, when who I *was* became too much. It worked for me, it made sense to me, until," he said quietly, "the night Athamos died. Then nothing made sense anymore."

She bit hard into her lip. "No one can be impenetrable. It's a coping strategy bound to self-destruct."

He nodded. "I did. I walked away. I shattered. But that only made the guilt worse because I had deserted my country. I had *left* them to my father's aggression. My spiritual adviser in Tibet helped me to recover. He taught me my endless drive was destroying me, and it was, clearly. I was determined to learn that lesson, but when I came back, when my father died, the pressure was immense. I shut down. I went on autopilot. The only thing I could see was saving this country, making amends for what I'd done. I didn't see the drive to help my people was becoming as blind an obsession as all the others had been."

"The good intention was there."

"Badly misguided." His gaze darkened. "I *have* been treating this country as my penance, my punishment. Because I haven't truly forgiven myself."

Her throat felt raw. "And have you now?"

"I'm not sure I ever will." A blunt, honest answer. "What I have realized is I've been given a second chance, a chance I plan to make myself worthy of."

Her chest tightened, so tight, it was hard to draw a breath. *The chance Athamos hadn't been given.* It should have ravaged her to hear the consequences of the night put that way, yet instead her emotion for this man and the journey he had been on superseded it.

Reaching out, she laced her fingers through the hand he had resting on the seat. "I think that's a very good plan."

He tightened his fingers around hers. His eyes blazed hot as they met hers. "You are a warrior, Stella, but you are also infinitely wise. You have pushed me when I needed to be pushed and supported me when I refused to listen. I owe you a great deal for that."

"We're a team," she said, eyes stinging with a wet heat. "And don't forget, we made a promise in the tree that day. We said we were going to make this a better world."

"Yes," he said. "So we did."

Kostas returned a couple of calls when they arrived back at the Marcariokastro, then sat back in his seat at his desk in his office, his adrenaline levels slowly easing. He thought maybe Stella was right, that he had turned the tide tonight. But it was his wife's unflinching belief in him that filled his head.

For the first time, he wondered if it was possible to truly forgive himself—for all of it. To leave the past behind. Could he be the flesh-and-blood man he'd never thought himself capable of, love when he'd never known the meaning of the word other than his *yaya*'s affection for a fleeting few years of his life? Be the man Stella needed him to be?

He had married her, he realized, because he'd wanted her, not just because she had been a valuable political tool. Because he'd always wanted her—had walked away from her because he'd feared he wasn't good enough, that he would never live up to her ideals of him.

His wife was right—the point of no return had passed, they had committed themselves to this relationship. He had to make it work. Could she be a part of the second chance he'd been given?

He rubbed his hands over his eyes. Even if he was able to forgive himself for his mistakes, could he ever give Stella what she was asking for? Could he open himself up, or did his conditioning go too deep?

He stared at the pile of work on his desk. Urgent things—things he should attend to. Instead, he turned off the light and stood. Headed toward the irresistible force of nature he no longer had the will to resist.

Stella was brushing her hair in front of the antique mirror when he walked in. She was dressed in a slip of ivory silk, arms raised above her head, her slim body, with its just-enough feminine curves, making his blood heat.

He stood there for a moment, watching her, his body vibrating with need. The blood pounding through his veins flowed into his sex, hardening him with painful precision. Only Stella had ever had this instantaneous, undeniable effect on him. As if by having her, he found his humanity lodged somewhere deep inside him.

She watched him as he walked up behind her and slid his arms around her.

"Kostas..."

He raised one arm up and put a finger to her lips as he pulled her into his pulsing body. "No more talking. Not tonight."

Removing his finger, he set his mouth to the curve of her neck and took a long, deep taste. Her breath hitched, the hand holding the brush dropping to her side. Brushing the tips of his fingers over her nipples, he stroked her into hard peaks. The light imprint he made with his teeth at the pleasure point between her neck and shoulder sent the hairbrush clattering to the dresser.

Watching the pleasure rise over her face in the mirror sent heat to every inch of his skin. He ached to taste, to *devour* the delicate, rosy red peaks that pushed through the translucent silk, so perfectly made, but that wasn't the only part of her he wanted to sample.

Dropping his palm to the shadowed intersection of her

thighs, he pressed the heel of it against her, rotating with sensual, deliberate movements that made her eyes darken.

"I haven't tasted you yet," he murmured in her ear. "I'll bet you're sweet, like honey, Stella."

A red stain moved across her high-boned cheeks. Sliding an arm beneath her knees, he picked her up and carried her to the bed. Depositing her on the rich, dark fabric, he followed her down, pushing up the sexy, transparent fabric she wore to reveal her creamy, golden skin.

Drawing a berry-red nipple into his mouth, he sucked hard, then transferred his attention to the other, until deep, sensual, feminine sounds of pleasure escaped her throat. Sliding down her body, he inhaled her lush, decadent scent, her musky arousal consuming his head.

She watched him as he shackled one of her ankles and bent it back. It left her beautifully, delectably, open to him. The flush in her cheeks deepening, she stayed where she was, motionless, her throat convulsing. Nudging her other thigh outward, he lowered his head and pressed a kiss to the inside of one knee. Continuing the open-mouthed kisses, he worked his way up the silky soft skin of her thigh, feeling the tremors that snaked through her.

When he reached the heart of her, she was rigid, hands buried in his hair, urging him on. But instead of giving her what she wanted, he set his mouth to the back of her other knee and worked his way back up again.

Drunk on the scent of her, he lingered over the aroused heart of her. She arched her hips up in a silent beg. Lowering his head, he swept his tongue over her slick crease. A sharp pant escaped her, her fingers tightening in his hair. *"More."*

"More what?"

"Stop teasing me. *Please.*"

He dipped his head and repeated the tantalizing caress

until she begged in a soft, broken whisper that turned his insides out. Pressing a palm to her stomach, he consumed her in long laps. Her feminine taste was intoxicating, exotic, sinfully good. It made his erection lengthen, thicken.

When she was too close, too soon, he changed strategy, applying a whisper-soft nudge against the tight bundle of nerves at the heart of her. She dug her nails into the sheets, her body so taut she was the perfect, delectable instrument for him to play.

He lifted his head, eyes on hers. "You taste sweet, Stella, as good as I knew you would. Like sweet, hot honey."

She closed her eyes. Clutching the back of his head, she returned him to her. His low growl of approval of her greed sent a shudder through her as it reverberated against her flesh. He picked up speed then, licking her with short, hard strokes designed to take her to the edge. When she begged for him to make her come, he slid one of his fingers inside of her and caressed her deeply. Two. Then he closed his mouth around her and sucked hard. She came with a sharp cry that destroyed the remainder of his self-control.

Rolling off the bed, he stripped his clothes from his body. Coming back to her, he pressed a kiss against her lips, letting her taste the musky, sweet smell of herself on him while he settled himself between her thighs. She wrapped her legs around him, her greed inflaming him with the need to possess her.

She was wet and ready, but she was also tight and delicately feminine. Taking his time, he stroked inside of her, her body easing around him as he went.

A sigh left her lips when he filled her to the hilt. *"Kostas."*

He cupped her jaw in his fingers, pinning his gaze on

hers. “I feel for you, *yineka mou*. More than I should. I always have.”

Her gaze deepened to a sparkling amethyst, more violet than blue. Mouth on hers, he thrust inside her, her hips rising to meet his deep, hard strokes. Sliding his tongue against hers, he made love to her mouth as erotically as he took her body, wanting to blow her mind as much as she unbalanced him, took him apart and put him back together again.

She started to shake, come apart beneath him, her sensual response taking him apart. Their lips came together in a darkly sensual connection that destroyed his control. Bowing to the demands of his body, he pumped himself inside of her, taking her faster, harder. She convulsed around him, his name on her lips as her silken flesh gripped him, goaded him into a release that shook his body.

The deep shadows of night swept the bedroom as he curled his wife against him and stroked her silky blond hair. She fell asleep almost instantaneously, the events of the past week having taken a toll, but as exhausted as he was, living on fumes, sleep would not come.

Moonlight sliced across the room, a triangular patch of light shifting on the stone floor as the minutes slid by. His wife wrapped in his arms, the perfection with which they fit together impossible to ignore, he knew he had crossed a line tonight, a line from which he couldn’t return.

He wanted everything he’d never had. If there was danger in that leap of faith, if fear fisted his stomach with cold, hard fingers at allowing Stella into a place he’d never allowed anyone, he was willing to risk it.

CHAPTER THIRTEEN

STELLA WALKED OUT of the executive council meeting with Kostas at her side. It had been the final meeting of the council before the body was dissolved and replaced by members selected from the new legislative assembly chosen in tomorrow's elections.

A chance for the current members to earmark issues of importance for the new council to address, it had been a spirited and vocal meeting. Whereas she had sat back and listened in her first meeting, discussing it afterward with Kostas, this time she had spoken up with her ideas about the future, about the injustices Carnelians had suffered and the programs she felt necessary to help them thrive.

Some of what she said was a clear reprimand to those who had managed such portfolios. It sent a ripple through the male-dominated council, but Kostas had backed her up, agreeing the programs she had proposed were necessary.

Hand at her elbow, he helped her into the car, then slid in beside her and shut the door. Her mouth curved as she sat back against the seat. "Your chief of security called me a loose cannon."

"You are."

She flicked him a glance. "Are you angry with me?"

"Obeying protocol is not one of your strong points,

agapi mou. Fortunately," he drawled, a sensual heat in the gaze he swept over her, "you know how to obey when it counts."

Her breath hitched in her throat, her pulse beating a jagged rhythm. He had enjoyed giving her orders when he'd taken her to bed last night. Stark, sexually explicit orders that had made it more exciting than it had ever been before. Caught up in the pleasure he was giving her, she'd obeyed every single one of them.

With the swiftness of a cat, he caught an arm around her waist and pulled her onto his lap.

"Kostas," she breathed, "we're in the car."

"Which has blacked-out windows and a privacy screen." His fingers curved around her neck to bring her mouth down to his. "You in power mode puts me in an indecent frame of mind."

His kiss was hard, hot and possessive. She sighed and melted into him, returning the kiss with the responsiveness he demanded. Flicking his tongue over the seam of her lips, he insisted on entry, deepening the kiss with slow, sweet strokes.

Her fingers curled into his shirt. Every touch, every stroke, every lick, carnal and earthy, pulled her deeper and deeper into the vortex that was Kostas. Somewhere along the way, she realized hazily, her desire to be impenetrable had been exposed as the front it was, for what she really wanted—the love of this man.

It stole her breath as she broke the kiss and leaned back, studying the harsh set of his jaw, how he was hard lines and strength everywhere except in his eyes at that moment. His feelings for her were written across them. She just had no idea how deep they ran.

Perhaps he might come to love her in time. Maybe it was possible. Maybe they could learn to do this together. Or maybe she was the biggest fool on the planet for thinking such self-destructive thoughts when he'd clearly warned her off.

"What?" Kostas smoothed a thumb over her jaw.

She breathed deep. Attempted to stem the panic crawling up her spine for this wasn't the only thing she had to face today.

"Later," she murmured, sliding off his lap.

When they arrived at the castle, Stella went directly upstairs to her bedroom while Kostas headed to his office to work. The purchase Page had made was tucked away in the drawer as requested. Her heart was a hammer in her chest as she pulled the two pregnancy tests out of the bag. Two—just to make sure—although she already knew the answer.

Her breasts were tender, her mood even more jumbled this past week, her psyche somehow more fragile. Kostas was so damn virile, she'd *expected* it, but nothing could really have prepared her for the two plus signs that stared back at her a few moments later.

An heir for Carnelia. What the country had been waiting for… Head buzzing, she tossed the evidence into the trash can and sat down on the antique stool. It had been the goal, of course, to conceive Kostas's heir. With Kostas's approval ratings having risen dramatically since the town hall, it was the last piece of the puzzle to slide into place.

Her hands clenched so tight she could feel her nails digging into her skin. She knew it was good—*wonderful*—news. Fear still clamped her chest like a vise. Could she be a good mother after her own childhood? Could she and Kostas give their children the unconditional love and acceptance they'd never had? Ensure they never knew the loneliness and isolation that had marked both their early years? Would her relationship with Kostas continue to flourish so they could be those parents they'd never had?

She dropped her head into her hands as the room spun around her. Giving that last piece of herself to Kostas, making a leap of faith that he could someday learn to love, meant letting go of the painful experiences that had shaped her life and trusting the future could be different.

Alex had been right. She'd sabotaged every relationship she'd been in because she'd been afraid of getting hurt. Perhaps it was time to stop letting the past rule her. Hadn't she preached the same to her husband? Shouldn't she be brave enough to do it, too? Or was she setting herself up to repeat history in the most painful of ways?

"There is a lieutenant from the navy here to see you, Your Highness."

Kostas looked up from the report he'd been scanning. Frowned. The navy was Houlis's domain. "He's been screened?"

"Yes. He said it was a personal matter. He wouldn't discuss it with me."

A personal matter? Curiosity pulled at his insides. "*Kala.* Send him in."

A young man in his late twenties walked in, his short, buzzed haircut instantly marking him military. He introduced himself as Lieutenant Miles Colonomos. Kostas returned his greeting and waved him into the chair opposite his.

"How can I help you?"

The lieutenant reached into his pocket and withdrew a box. He set it on the desk and pushed it toward Kostas. "One of my men was doing a routine check on the western perimeter when he found these caught on a rock at the base of the cliffs."

Kostas's heart was a knot in his throat and he didn't know why. Athamos's car had gone over the cliffs on the western side of the island, but the crown prince's car had been the only thing they'd ever been able to find, Athamos's body swept away by the strong currents.

He pulled the box toward him and closed his fingers over the cover. Lifting it, he saw two oblong, flat aluminum discs attached to a chain of the same material. His brain flatlined. *Dog tags.* The piece of identification pilots wore in case they were lost in combat.

They all bore a soldier's first and last names, their social security number, blood type and religion. Came in twos so that one could be removed from a dead man's body to notify his family of his death should the body need to remain behind.

The tags in the box were wrong side up. His gaze blurred and his hand trembled as he flipped one over, an unnecessary action because he knew whose they were.

Athamos Constantinides
102300
Blood Type: O
Religion: Greek Orthodox

He sat there, motionless, staring at the two pieces of metal, jagged glass lining his throat. "Anything else?" he asked, his voice a sharp rasp. "Did your diver find anything else?"

The officer shook his head. "The tags must have been ripped from the prince's body during the fall. They were lodged in a crevice. The only reason we found them was the rock had shifted."

He nodded. They had scoured the waters for days, *weeks*, looking for Athamos's body to give his family closure, but they'd never been able to provide it. Now, he thought, his gut twisting, they would have it.

"Efharisto." Thank you. He nodded at the officer. "Please keep the information to yourself. The family must be notified."

The other man nodded and took his leave. Rising from his chair, Kostas walked to the window and attempted to breathe past the tightness in his chest. He couldn't bring Athamos back, he had accepted that, but giving his dog tags to Stella was something else entirely.

Spreading his palm wide against the glass, he absorbed the shame that flooded through him. For his recklessness that night. For his weakness in not going to Athamos's family immediately and telling the story. For thinking he could hide the truth from his wife as to who he was.

For he had to tell her. This was a sign, a reminder that the last piece of the truth still lay between them. It had been foolish of him to think he could keep it from her, he realized, heart sinking. It would lie there forever, festering, rearing its ugly head whenever his demons got the better of him, and that couldn't happen, not when he was sure he loved his wife. That he had always loved Stella.

She had transformed from willful princess to a powerful, empathetic queen in front of his eyes. She had slain every dragon alongside him. Now he had to hope they were strong enough to weather this storm together or he would lose the one woman who meant everything to him.

Stella paced the floor of the conservatory, waiting for Kostas's meeting to end.

Takis finally appeared in the doorway after she'd nearly worn out the floor. "His Highness's guest is gone."

"Efharisto."

Making her way down the stone corridor that led across the castle to the visitor's wing, she walked into the king's offices. Tapping lightly on the door, she opened it at her husband's command to enter. The minute she looked at Kostas's face she knew something was wrong. *Something was very, very wrong.*

Her news fell to the wayside as she came to a halt in front of his desk. "What is it?"

He held out a hand. "Come here."

She skirted her way around the desk and slid onto his lap. Taking her hand, he pressed a kiss to her palm. "I need to show you something."

Her heart was a drumbeat in her throat. "Is it the military?"

"No. Everything's fine."

Letting go of her hand, he reached for the small, black box sitting on his desk and handed it to her. "A navy diver found this today."

"A navy diver?" She frowned. "What is it?"

"Open the box."

The edge to his voice turned her blood to ice. Hands shaking, she opened the box. Knew immediately what was inside because she'd seen Athamos wearing them. *Dog tags.* Her gaze flew over the two pieces of metal, fingers clenching the box so tight her knuckles went white.

Athamos. *They were Athamos's dog tags.* Her hand flew to her mouth. "You found him?"

"No." He shook his head. "I'm sorry, *agapimeni*, we didn't find him. These must have been torn from him when the car went over the cliff."

Her heart convulsed. Picking up the two pieces of metal, she cradled them in her palm. They were cold. *Final.*

Heat stung the back of her eyes, the truth washing over her like an undeniable force. This…*this* was all she was ever going to have of her brother.

She looked up at her husband. “He’s never coming back.”

Such dark, dark emotion reflected back at her. “No.”

Moisture streaked down her cheeks. Kostas rested his chin on her head and held her as she cried, tears soaking his shirt. It seemed as if she cried for a very long time.

“Thank you,” she murmured when the tears had slowed to a crawl. “At least we have a piece of him. It’s more than we ever thought we’d have.”

Kostas was silent. The tenseness enveloping him straightened her spine. “What?” she whispered. “What is it?”

“I need to tell you something.”

The hairs on the back of her neck rose. Somehow she knew another blow was coming and she wasn’t sure if she could take it.

His gaze captured hers. “The night Athamos and I raced, I was furious with my father for his behavior, worried about what damage he would do before I could take control, antagonized I could do nothing about it, tortured by the decisions in front of me.

“Cassandra,” he continued, “is a beautiful woman. Both Athamos and I wanted her. Athamos fell hard, though, harder than I’d ever seen him fall for a woman. He was in love with her, but I knew Cassandra was interested in me, maybe even in love with me. I should have let the two of them be, but my need to blow off some steam, my need to *win*, was stronger.”

She pressed a hand to her mouth, bile stinging the back of her throat. “Kostas, no—”

"Yes." His voice was a harsh whip against her skin. "You need to know the truth. You need to know all of it."

She shoved a hand against his chest, needing him to stop, needing not to hear this right now because everything—*everything*—depended on them making this marriage work. He held her there, his arm an iron band around her waist.

"It was a game for me, Stella. To prove I could have her." His words were like grenades, blowing up in her face. "Athamos had become my friend and yet I didn't care. I goaded him, ensured he would take the challenge. *I* was responsible for his death."

She put her hands up to shield herself from the blows, from *more*, but he was done, staring at her with jagged pain in his eyes.

"Why?" she whispered. "Why are you telling me this now?"

"Because keeping this from you would have destroyed me. Because *we* need to have a future free of the past."

"Destroyed *you*?" She shoved a hand at his chest. This time she caught him unaware and managed to scramble off his lap before he caught her. She stood in front of him, limbs shaking. "You challenged my brother to a race when you *knew* he was in love with the woman you were playing with. You stole his life from me, Kostas."

Naked pain crawled across his face. "Don't you think I wish I had been the one to have gone over that cliff? Don't you think this hasn't nearly driven me mad, Stella? But I can't do that. I can't take his place. I can't bring back the dead. I can only forgive myself as you yourself said and do the best I can to make something out of all of this. Something good."

She closed her eyes because rational speech wasn't

penetrating the grief surrounding her. All she could feel was the spear of ice he'd shoved through her heart.

Kostas walked around the desk, stopping a step away from her. "We have something special, Stella, something rare. We always have. Our marriage was a key alliance, yes, but you know it was because I wanted you. I've always wanted you."

Red rose in front of her eyes. *"Wanted?"* She spat the word at him. "The game has never ended, has it? It never will. It's the only thing you know."

He shook his head. "It's not a game. This thing between us is real, you know it is."

The pain lancing her heart dug deeper. "I gave you so many opportunities to tell me the truth. I was *begging* for it and still you said nothing. How can I believe anything you say?"

"Because I love you."

She recoiled, feeling as if she'd been sucker punched. "You don't know how to love anyone, Kostas. You said so yourself."

His gaze was steady. "I do love you. I have always loved you."

She shook her head. "You just decimated that."

"Stella—"

Turning on her heel, she flew out of the room and headed for the hallway to the other wing, footsteps echoing a solitary tread on the stone floor.

Tears rolling down her face, she dashed them away with her fist as she sidestepped a maid and took the stairs to the royal wing. Staff dotted the hallways as they went about their afternoon tasks, so she changed direction and took the back stairwell to the top of the castle. Climbing the extremely old, dank set of stone steps, she emerged on the palace ramparts, a sweeping view of the mountains to her right, the cliffs and coastline to her left.

She wasn't sure how long she sat on the stone bench, knees to her chest, arms wrapped around them as the high sun of midafternoon faded into a dusky pink-and-orange sunset. It was the type the tourists went gaga over, one that would bring them here in droves when Kostas's developments came to fruition, but it barely penetrated the ice that surrounded her heart.

There were no more puzzles now, no more mysteries. Her brother, who had never loved easily, had been mad about Cassandra Liatos, and in typical, stubborn Athamos fashion had refused to give up. Perhaps he had known Cassandra was in love with Kostas and pursued her anyway, perhaps he hadn't. The only thing that was certain was that the two people who could have put a stop to the madness—Cassandra and Kostas—had not.

She stared out at the foam-capped waves as they crashed against the cliffs where her brother's car had gone over the edge. It was true, Athamos had also been responsible for his actions that night, but Kostas, however, bore the biggest blame of all because his actions had been premeditated. He had wanted to win and to hell with the consequences.

She understood he could never have predicted what would have happened that night, understood the frustration that had driven his rash behavior, *believed* his grief over it had nearly shattered him. But how could she be sure, given her husband's ruthless determination to save this country, that she was not simply the pawn she'd always feared she was? That that was all she was to him?

Because, a tiny mental whisper said, *he didn't have to tell you.* He could have carried the truth of that night to his grave and no one would have been the wiser. No one would have gotten hurt. But he hadn't.

Be careful what you wish for. You might not like what you find.

He had been agonizing over this. Tortured by it. Suddenly, it all made sense. He had been doing exactly what she'd asked for just now, telling her the whole truth—the deepest, darkest part of him. Because he wanted them to work.

In her heart she knew he'd meant everything he'd said, that this had been the thing holding him back all along. But could she trust what he had said? That the man who'd professed he wasn't capable of love had discovered he could?

CHAPTER FOURTEEN

KOSTAS SLEPT EVEN less than usual. The pink fingers of dawn were creeping across the sky when he got out of bed and dressed, his movements slow and deliberate as he donned a dark suit and a silver-gray tie.

Today his future would be decided in the first elections in Carnelia's history. His *and* Stella's future.

His wife had chosen to sleep in one of the adjoining bedrooms last night after telling him she needed space. Relieved she had not walked out, left him, he had given her the space she needed, resisting his urge to *fix*.

His heart beat a thick rhythm in his chest as he did up his cuff links, fingers feeling too clumsy for the task. He'd thought he'd been done with the big, life-changing mistakes, but not telling Stella the full truth about Athamos, not taking the opportunities she'd given him, was going to haunt him for a very long time.

For a man who'd always thought himself incapable of love, it had been a sin of omission he could live with. But for one who'd realized he could, it was blind stupidity of the highest order.

He drank an espresso as he went through his day with Takis, stomach pacing like a tiger in a cage. He was scheduled to meet with the chief administrator of the elections first thing this morning before visiting key polling stations to greet Carnelians as they came to the polls. His wife had still not appeared when he left the castle at eight thirty. Dust in his mouth, gravel in his throat, his heart in no way right, he got into the Bentley and made the drive into town.

He was exiting the government building after his meeting with the administrator when gunfire cracked around him.

Stella rose after a long, sleepless night. Her mind, however, was clear. She loved Kostas. She wasn't going to let him stand alone today, not after everything they'd been through.

She dressed in dark pants, a white blouse and a scarf done in vivid blues and reds. Unwilling to wait the whole day until her husband's return, she found Darius and asked him to drive her into town. She'd do some of the polling station visits with him.

Darius brought the car to a halt at the base of the front steps. The crowds from the night of her engagement party flashed through her head. The night had been full of such hope. Would today be the culmination of it all? The realization of her husband's dreams? Or would his mistakes prove fatal?

Darius was talking into that eternally present wireless headset of his, a bud in his ear and a microphone embedded in his shirt. Rather than sit in the car, she waited, foot tapping, hand against the car. It was a beautiful day. A day for new beginnings.

Her bodyguard had his serious look on now, one that put her senses on alert. Moving closer, she listened as he spoke rapidly into the mouthpiece. She caught only every second or third word, but she heard enough to make her blood turn to ice.

Gunfire. Junta. Not secure.

Firing off a couple of rapid-fire sentences, her bodyguard cut off the call. "You need to get inside *now*."

"Why? What—" A shout from the palace gates stole her attention. They were closing them, the thick, iron doors swinging shut.

"Darius—what's going on?"

"The military. They're attempting to seize control."

Her heart jumped into her mouth. "Kostas?"

"He was exiting the building when it happened. I can't get Henri on the phone. Everything's on lockdown."

Cold fingers clamped down on her spine. She headed around the car to the passenger seat. "We need to go there."

Darius came after her. "You need to follow protocol and get inside *now*."

She glared at him. "I don't give a damn about protocol. We are going there."

Darius, now toe to toe with her, shook his head. "I have an extraction plan to follow. Get inside."

She reached for his car keys, heart pounding, perspiration breaking out on her forehead. He evaded her, a dark look on his face as he pocketed his keys.

"Darius," she yelled, "something could have happened to him. Take me there."

He caught hold of her like the precision machine he was and slung her over his shoulder. She pounded on his shoulders, fury raging through her.

"I am the queen of this country. *Christe mou*, Darius. Put me down."

He didn't put her down until they were inside the castle, doors locked behind them. Takis met them in the entrance hall.

"Any news on Kostas?" Darius asked.

The old man shook his head.

Darius got on his phone again. The words *extraction* and *bird* filtered through her consciousness, but she wasn't really listening. *What if Kostas had been shot? Why wasn't Henri answering his phone?*

Her bodyguard ended the call and turned to her. "The helicopter will be here in minutes. Get your stuff."

Her knees felt weak. "I told you, I'm not going anywhere."

"Your husband and brother gave me orders, Stella. If I don't get you out of here *now*, our window of opportunity closes."

"Then let it." She crossed her arms over her chest. "I'm not going. Kostas was prepared for this. Our troops will come through. It will be fine."

Darius turned the air blue. Pulling out her mobile, she punched in Nik's number. He answered on the second ring. "You okay?"

She nodded, then realized he couldn't see her. "Yes. They've attacked the government building."

"I know. I'm on the other line with my contact on the ground. The chopper is minutes away."

"I'm not leaving him, Nik." Her hand clutched her mobile so tight it nearly cut off her circulation.

"Stella." Her brother's voice hardened. "Kostas and I agreed on this. Anarchy could ensue if Houlis takes control. Get on the helicopter and come home."

"Listen. To. Me." She said the words slowly, with control. "I am not leaving him. I love him. So tell me what to do."

"Stella." Nik used his most persuasive voice. "I know you love him. You still need to get the hell out of there and let Kostas straighten this out."

"No."

A harsh sigh in her ear. "If anything happens to you…"

"Nothing is going to happen to me *or* Kostas," she said fiercely. "I told him I was going to stay by his side and I will. Sofía wouldn't leave you in the same position, you know she wouldn't."

Silence. "*Kala.* We've sent in commandos to help Kostas and his men. I'll keep you updated as I know anything. Keep your damn phone on and make sure I know you're okay."

"Okay."

She hung up. Felt herself die a little more as the minutes and hours stretched by with no news. Finally, just after noon, a call came in from Kostas's chief of security. The king was fine, his security forces had apprehended General Houlis and the rest of the insurgents and placed them in jail. According to the security chief, key factions allied to Houlis had deserted him in the final hours.

Stella's knees nearly gave way. Page made her sit and eat something. It was four o'clock before her husband walked in the door, dark-shadowed and hollow-eyed. She stood, so relieved to see him in the flesh, unharmed, her knees did give way. A curse on his lips, Kostas ate up the distance between them and caught her in his arms.

"You should have left." Sliding an arm beneath her knees, he picked her up.

"I promised you I wouldn't. We're a team." She buried her mouth in his throat, drinking in the dark, masculine scent of him, ensuring herself he really was in one piece.

Kostas muttered something to Takis, then carried her into the conservatory. Sitting down on one of the sofas, he cradled her in his arms.

She pulled back so she could see him. "I love you. I was coming to tell you that when Darius picked me up and locked me inside."

"It's the only way to control you. You still can't follow protocol." His low, raspy voice was filled with emotion as he smoothed his thumbs across her face.

"Did you hear what I said? I love you."

"Yes." His gaze darkened. "Does that mean you forgive me?"

"If you promise me there are no other secrets. That we can move on with a blank slate. That you will *talk* to me. Always, about anything."

He nodded, pressing a long, hard kiss to her lips. When he drew back, the pain in his eyes tore at her heart. "What happened that night with Athamos is a stain on my soul, Stella. I didn't think I deserved to be forgiven, not by myself and certainly not by you. I thought I could protect both of us by suggesting we have a marriage of convenience, one that involved only sex and affection, that never went too deep, because then I would never have to hurt you. What I didn't factor into the equation was the fact that my feelings for you have always run too deep. It was never going to work."

"You should have told me. On this we were clear, Kostas. Trust, transparency and complete honesty were what we agreed on."

"I was afraid you would walk away." He shook his head. "You're right, I know, but I never thought it would be a problem. I thought it would never go that far. Then you started shooting sparks, forcing me to feel alive, forcing me to acknowledge my past and my emotions. Then I fell in love with you and I couldn't risk telling you because I knew you would hate me."

She bit her lip. "Is that it? Is that all I need to know? I can do this, Kostas, but there can't be any more land mines to blow us apart."

A bleak cast entered his gaze. "I can't promise the

pieces of me that emerge—*who* I am—will be pretty. There is too much ugliness in my past. But that was the whole truth I told you. There are no more secrets."

"Then we can do this." She curved her fingers around his nape and brought his mouth down to hers in a long, promise-filled kiss. It lasted for what seemed like forever, but not nearly long enough.

"You make me want to be things I never thought I could be," Kostas said huskily, resting his forehead against hers. "You make me want things I thought I could never have. You always have."

Her heart fell apart. "Speaking of which," she whispered, "I have something to tell you."

His face went silent, still. "You're pregnant?"

Her brows drew together. "How do you know?"

"I suspected when you didn't drink wine at dinner the other night, but you didn't say anything, so I figured I was wrong."

"I hadn't done the test. I did two, actually. Both came back positive."

"And you stayed here today?" His stillness dissolved in a blaze of pure emotion. "Stella, *Christe mou*, what were you thinking?"

"That we are doing this together, you and I, like we promised." She lifted her chin. "And we will, as soon as the election results come in."

He smiled. "Confident as always, *yineka mou*."

"I believe in you." She brushed a kiss against his mouth. "When did you know you loved me?"

"The day I saw you in that tree."

Stella stood with Kostas on the steps of the new government building that evening, her hand in his as the election results were confirmed. A roar went up in the crowd assembled. The monarchy would remain in Carnelia, with Kostas as head of the new government, leading an elected national assembly. A new age had begun, ending the darkest period in the tiny Mediterranean country's history.

Stella stood on tiptoe and kissed her king. "Whoops," she said when she was done, lips against his. "Was that a break in protocol?"

"As if you care." Cupping the back of her head, Kostas gave the crowd a kiss to remember.

The rebel princess had become a queen. This time her wings would not be clipped. Not with this man at her side.

* * * * *

HIS DRAKON RUNAWAY BRIDE

TARA PAMMI

CHAPTER ONE

"IS THIS A coup to overthrow me?" Crown Prince Andreas Drakos of Drakon joked as he walked into his study to find his family staring at him with a spectrum of emotions—concern in his sister Eleni's eyes, stubborn resolve in Mia's, something he couldn't define in his brother Nikandros's and pure frost in Gabriel's.

"None of us want your job, your popularity rating or your life, Andreas," replied Nikandros, the financial genius who had set Drakon on its path of recovery after the mess their father had made in the last decade.

Nik was right. The state of his life currently—utter chaos with the Crown Council breathing down his neck for the announcement of his choice for the next Queen of Drakon, the questions the media was raising about his mental health, his frequent disappearances from Drakon in the last year, sometimes even his sexuality—would have usually had the effect of fire ants crawling all over his skin.

But he didn't have any mental energy left beyond the hunt he'd been on for two years now. He was getting close, he knew it in his blood.

He settled down next to Mia. The smell of baby powder drifting from her was strangely calming. "How are you, Mia?"

Mia took his hands in hers. He tried not to flinch. Physical contact made him twitchy and now Mia knew it. But somewhere in the last few months, his sister-in-law and he had become strangely close.

"You didn't come to see the twins, Andreas. After all the hullabaloo you raised about heirs for Drakon, I'm feeling neglected."

He smiled. "I have just this hour returned to Drakon."

"Which nicely segues to why we are all here. Andreas, what is going on?"

"You let her leave Tia and Alexio's side to ask me this question?" Nik glared at him in response. Dark shadows bruised Mia's eyes. "You look awful."

"Stop posturing, Nik. You know he's just trying to get a rise out of you." She smiled and her eyes lit up with that same incandescent joy he'd seen in Nik's of late. "I have two very good reasons for *my* ghoulish look, Your Highness," she said, her gaze tracing the angles of his face. "You however do not.

"You look like hell," she said with that forthrightness he'd come to expect from her, "and whether Nik and Gabriel will agree to put it like that or not, we're all…very worried about you."

He frowned, looked up and, with a strange knot in his gut, realized it was true. "It's not necessary."

"There's talk from the Crown Council about asking you to step down. Your popularity level is at its lowest," Nik said in a deceptively calm voice. "Some political pundits have dared say Father's madness has already begun to manifest in you. You leave Drakon for days, not one of your aides knows your schedule, you refuse to see even Ellie and me…"

"That's why you're all worried?" Andreas asked with a laugh. "That Theos gave me his madness in addition to everything else?"

Eleni spoke up. "Of course not. But we do think you've been acting strange. Andreas, the House of Tharius is waiting for your word to release news of your engagement. The coronation is in two months and you—"

His phone pinged and every nerve in him went on high alert. He knew even before he switched on his phone's screen what the news was going to be. His fingers shook when he swiped the screen.

Found the target. Sending location specs now.

His breath balled up in his chest, and he had to force himself to exhale.

Anticipation bubbled in his blood, coupled with savage satisfaction. “Let the House of Tharius know it’s off.”

The shock that spread through the huge room made the hairs on his neck rise. Nik and Eleni looked at him with such concern in their eyes that for the first time in months Andreas felt a little guilt. “I apologize for leaving you both in the lurch these past few months. I needed—”

“*Thee mou*, Andreas!” Nik burst out. “We don’t care that for the first time in thirty-six years, you took a few months for yourself.”

“Not the first time,” he said automatically. “I took a free year just when your health improved. Almost ten years ago.”

Nikandros frowned. “When Theos tried to make me his leashed dog?”

“A few months before that happened, yes.” When Andreas had, in a fit of madness, threatened Theo that he would walk out on Drakon if he didn’t give him some time off.

“Andreas.” Eleni reached him, her voice wavering. “You can’t be crowned King without a wife. That’s one of the oldest Drakonite laws. No member of the Crown Council will let you defy it. Are you…are you giving up the crown?”

Nikandros cursed so filthily that he had to laugh.

Andreas patted his sister’s hand awkwardly. “I’m not doing any such thing, Eleni. I will be crowned as scheduled.”

“You need a wife for that.” Nik again. Only Gabriel

stood silent, staring at him from those steel-grey eyes. Gabriel, his brother-in-law, who had figured out the truth.

"Whatever you're considering—" Eleni was close to tears now "—please tell us. Nik and I would never judge you for what—"

"I can't marry Maria Tharius because I already have a wife. For two years, I've been trying to locate her."

You are like me, Andreas, in every way. The same taste for power and control runs in your blood. Why do you think your little wife ran?

Those words had haunted him for two years now. But he didn't give a damn.

He would willingly be a monster if that meant she was back in his life.

"You're married? To whom? When? Why didn't you ever..." Eleni faintly shook with the force of her questions, until Gabriel put his hands on her shoulders and absorbed her petite form into his.

"She was Father's ward. I married her during that sabbatical year in a secret civil ceremony."

"Father had a ward?" Another curse from Nikandros, for he knew that meant another life his father would have played games with.

"Your pity is wasted on her, Nik," Andreas said stonily. "Turns out Father and she understood each other perfectly well."

"Ariana Sakis." Eleni pronounced the name that had become so much a part of his own makeup that Andreas couldn't remember a day before her life tangled with his. "She was shy of eighteen by a few months."

Utter shock was etched on their faces now.

He'd been twenty-six and he'd married a barely legal eighteen-year-old in a secret ceremony... He could have grown two horns and a tail and it would have been less shocking.

"Her parents…died in a car accident. There were rumors that they'd been arguing, that her mother had driven it into the tree on purpose," Eleni explained to Nik. "Her father…was a military general, a close friend of Father.

"There was a lot of talk about what an abusive husband he was and Father immediately severed the connection between the House of Drakos and him.

"Only a handful of people knew he had her custody and he sent her off to…no one knew where. I don't think she even set foot in the palace."

"To a fishing village off the coast," Andreas finished. "Having met Father a couple of times, she'd been more than willing to go."

"That's where you met her?" asked Nikandros.

Andreas nodded. "I… I demanded Father give me a year to do as I wanted, to research a book I wanted to write. He agreed, after a lot of ranting.

"Little did he know that I would end up at the same little village that summer."

Crisp mountain air, blue ponds surrounded by lush woods, a remote cabin, a single coffee shop…and a girl with copper-colored hair and a wide, impish smile.

Andreas swayed as the past reached into him with a clawed hand. Those months in that village with Ariana had been the most glorious of his life.

Too good to last, he realized now with a bitterness that choked him.

"If you married her, how come none of us met her? We didn't even know."

"Father and I decided to wait for a more opportune time to announce that I had wed. For the three months of our marriage, she stayed in an apartment ten miles from the palace."

"You've been looking for her…since Father's decline began." Eleni jerked her chin up. All the pieces were beginning to fall into place. "Where was she all these years, Andreas?"

"Father told me she died in a boating accident after I returned from that oil summit in the Middle East that year."

"Instead?" Nik asked the question, tension filling his shoulders.

"Instead, she took the ten million he offered, faked her death and disappeared under a new identity."

"That's…horrible." Eleni, always loyal to her brothers, had formed her opinion. "How could she make you think she was dead?"

Mia frowned. "You've found this woman now, haven't you?" Something almost like fear glittered in her tired gaze. "Andreas, what is it that you intend to do? Clearly, the woman has made her choice. All of Drakon's eyes will be on her."

It was an edict he'd heard since before he'd even hit puberty. All of the media's eyes would be on him and the woman he chose, Theos had whispered continuously.

She must bring either incomparable wealth—Gabriel's sister had met the first condition—or good breeding in her own blood—Maria Tharius had met both—or be a woman with powerful connections who would agree to become the perfectly ornamental Queen.

Ariana had been none of the above.

"You could divorce her." Gabriel spoke for the first time.

"Drakonite law mandates the couple wait for eighteen months after they file for divorce," Eleni supplied, frowning. "With the coronation in two months, he can't file for a divorce now."

Andreas smiled, uncaring what they all saw in his face. "Father, in his Machiavellian masterminding, assumed that her being officially dead was enough to terminate our marriage. But she's alive. So, even if I wanted, I could not marry Maria Tharius now.

"Ariana will be the next Queen of Drakon." The declaration fell from his mouth, resonated in the very air that filled the King's Palace.

He found he liked the sound of it. An additional bonus was that his father would be rolling in his grave.

Ariana stared at the white stone building of the small, beautiful church in downtown Fort Collins and shivered from head to toe. The frigid October wind that stole through her flimsy wedding dress had nothing to do with it.

The past would not leave her alone today. Didn't matter that it was over ten years since she had married Andreas Drakos, the Crown Prince of Drakon, in a little forgotten church in a backwater fishing village near the mountains.

Didn't matter that in a few hours she was to marry Magnus.

A vein of utter misery ran through her day and night.

She was Anna to her friends, to her colleagues at the legal aid agency where she worked, and to the little community she belonged to amidst the Rocky Mountains in Colorado.

Anna was not an impulsive, reckless woman that self-destructed in the name of love. Anna was not a woman who gave in to the dangerous passion for a man who didn't know how to love.

Instead Anna was supposed to be married this evening to a nice, understanding man. Her friends must be thinking she'd lost her mind. But she had needed to get away from the madness of it all. She'd barely eaten a morsel of food yesterday and nothing at the dinner their friends had arranged for her and Magnus.

Against every better instinct, she pulled her phone out of her coat jacket and compulsively opened a browser. The page was still open to the same article she'd been reading for the last month.

She perused it greedily, as if reading it for the hundredth time would somehow change the gist of it.

Crown Prince Andreas Drakos of Drakon was to announce his choice for his Queen, before his coronation as the King of Drakon, a tiny principality in the Mediterranean again making its mark in the financial world.

A woman who was regal and educated, a doyenne of charities, born to wealth and perfect bloodlines. A woman who would be soft and womanly, a perfect complement to his brooding, controlling masculinity.

She had known that Andreas would one day take another woman, a woman far more suitable than her, to be his wife, to be the Queen of Drakon. That he had waited this long at all, when she knew of his devotion to Drakon, was a shock in itself.

And yet, from the moment she'd seen the little article, her world had tilted on its axis.

Was Anna really any better than the impulsive hothead she had been then? Was there any other reason except that her heart had broken a little again when she'd seen news of Andreas's coronation and it had prompted her to accept Magnus's proposal?

Thee mou, was she willing to destroy Magnus's life, too?

Whatever sun had been shining this morning had receded under dark clouds, the weather resonating her own dark thoughts. She had to break it off. Before she hurt Magnus, before…

The smooth swish of a finely tuned engine broke her focus.

She looked up and froze, wishing with every cell inside of her that she could truly freeze, become invisible, blend into the gray, leaf-bare trees around her. Could become one of the statues that littered the lovely town.

The pounding of her heart in her ears said she was far too alive.

For she recognized the little black-and-gold flag fluttering in the harsh wind on the hood of the European luxury car idling not two steps away. She knew the symbol of the golden dragon with fires spewing out of its wide jaws. She knew the man inside and his body and he knew hers, better than she did her own.

Legs quaking under her, she stumbled away from the curving stone wall that led to the steps of the church. Wrapped her arm around a tall tree for support.

Every primal instinct she possessed screamed at her to run, to flee. And yet not a single cell obeyed. Not a single muscle moved even as she heard the click of the car door, even as she saw polished black shoes step out of the car, even as the tall angular form straightened.

He'd found her.

Dear God, after ten years, he'd caught up to her. Just as she had always known he would, in the deep dark of the night when she couldn't hold the memories at bay.

Crown Prince Andreas Drakos, soon to be King of Drakon, was here.

A long black coat fluttered around his ankles, wavy hair the color of a raven's wing carelessly combed away from a high forehead. Power stamped across those high cheekbones, the patrician nose, the thin-lipped mouth. Arrogant entitlement and self-confidence dripped from him with every movement of his body.

Jet-black eyes, hard and flinty like glittering opals, eyes that reflected nothing back, eyes that had sometimes felt as if there was nothing behind them, swept over her shivering body and came to rest on her face. "*Kalimera*, Ariana."

Their eyes collided and held, sending a tsunami of emotions racing through her body. God, those eyes…she had drowned in them once. She had reveled in making them glow with humor, in making them darken in passion, in trying to break through that opaque shield.

She pressed her bare hands against the rough bark of the tree, hoping to jerk some kind of self-preservation instinct into life, for some kind of rationality to master the sheer emotional assault she was under.

Hands tucked into the pockets of his trousers, clad in all black, he looked like a dark angel come to serve swift justice. "It does not seem like a good day to be getting married. Does it, *pethi mou*?"

So he knew.

Ariana licked her dry lips, swallowing away the knowledge that she'd been about to call it off. Her gut instinct had been right. "What…what are you doing here?"

"Here on this side of the pond, in Colorado, in this little wonderful town that you've been hiding in?" He didn't move, nor did a muscle flicker in his face. In that deep, gravelly voice of his, he could have been inquiring after the bitter weather.

They could have been a couple of friends discussing trivialities. No anger or emotion fractured his cool expression. Only a faint thread of sarcasm bled through.

"Or here in front of this beautiful little church on this bleary afternoon where you're waiting for the man you're supposed to marry in a few hours? Should I answer the general or the specific?"

Ariana closed her eyes. Didn't help one bit. His presence was a hum of power in the air, making something in her vibrate in tune. Dragging cold air deep into her lungs, she flicked her eyes open. Feeling was beginning to come back into her muscles. And along with it memories and an unholy amount of panic.

How had she forgotten that the smoother Andreas's voice got, the hotter his rage? The deeper the fracture in his self-control, the colder and calmer his actions? It was his shutdown mode, where neither reason nor begging would filter through. Fresh wind made her eyes water. It had to be the wind. "I don't have your magic with words, Andreas."

He inclined his head in a regal nod. "I am to be King soon. I thought now would be a wise time to take care of the little business between us. After all, you ran out on me without a word, and who knows when you will decide you want to come back to me?"

Shivers raced down her spine. "Go back to your precious Drakon." She couldn't help the bitterness in her voice, even as she cautioned herself against it. "You have nothing to worry about with me. You and I—" her voice caught, and still, nothing changed in his expression "—were an episode from a different life. The media will never catch hold of our little story, neither will I claim even an acquaintance.

"Ariana Sakis, for all intents and purposes, is dead."

She glanced up and her breath seized in her lungs.

Suddenly, he was there in front of her, blocking everything else from her vision. Blocking the entire world from her. Sandalwood, flared by his body's heat, taunted her nostrils. Filled her with sensations and memories. Such an interestingly warm scent for a man whose blood was decidedly cold. But then his passion had been just as contrasting to the ruthless lack of his heart.

"Ariana Drakos," he corrected with the faintest trace of warning. "Do not forget you belong to me."

Nothing so tacky as a raised voice or a teetering temper from the House of Drakos.

"You might be King of your bloody palace, Andreas—" panic rushed reckless words to her mouth "—but not of me. Magnus will be here any minute and I won't—"

"Your fiancé has been made aware of the situation and is not coming."

So polite even as he stood there, playing havoc with her life. So infuriatingly calm. Her hands itched to muss up that perfectly placid expression of his. The devil in her burned to unsettle him as he did her. That urge was dangerous. Just being near Andreas was like throwing herself off a cliff—exhilarating and terrifying. And she had stopped doing that to herself a long time ago.

"What the hell did you tell Magnus?"

"That he should call it quits while his life is still under his control."

"Is this what you have sunk to? Chasing away the man in my life? Have you become as low and manipulative as your father then, Andreas?"

His jaw tightened. "I didn't have to chase him, Ariana. Like any sensible man, Magnus seemed uninclined toward being the other party in bigamy. In fact, he sounded angry at your deception."

"Bigamy?" She covered the distance between them without caring. Her heart seemed to slow down in her chest, a dreadful cold filling her. "What do you mean, bigamy?"

His mouth relaxed, he stood waiting against the same tree as if he had all the time in the world. As if there was nothing that would give him more pleasure than to watch the ground being pulled away from under her. As if he'd planned and lived this moment a thousand times and he couldn't let his enjoyment end.

She shook her grip on his coat but he didn't budge. "What do you mean?"

A smile curved his mouth. Rendering him starkly beautiful. "My father and you missed one small detail in your plan. If I had never discovered you were alive, it wouldn't have mattered so much.

"But I did."

"What detail?" she was shouting now, her voice lost in the gray bleakness around her. Everything about those few days was still jumbled in her head. She'd been acting on pure animal instincts—fear the overriding one—and listening to King Theos had been the worst kind of mistake.

All she'd wanted was to escape Drakon before Andreas came back from his summit. Before she was caught in the web of her own love for him.

She'd been so naive that she had played right into Theos's manipulative hands. But Andreas wouldn't believe her now.

Her leaving him had been a betrayal to a man who didn't break rules for anyone, an unforgivable mistake to a man whose word meant everything to him.

She clasped his jaw, forcing him to look at her. "What detail, Andreas?"

He still didn't hold her. Didn't touch her in any way. Those eyes trapped her again, until even breathing was a chore. Those eyes betrayed all his emotions—fury, shock and the cold enjoyment of her fate now. "The papers you signed for Theos, dissolving our marriage, he never presented them to me.

"Your supposed death bought him time and then… I don't know what he and you planned. I never saw those papers until a few months ago. The motion didn't even get filed in court.

"You are still my wife."

CHAPTER TWO

SHEER TERROR FILLED her eyes as she stared at him. "Your wife?" she repeated, as if she couldn't think past those two words.

Andreas studied her greedily, his skin prickling with that sensation only Ariana could arouse.

Her lips were dry, trembling. Her copper gold hair, her crowning glory, was tied into that messy knot she'd always put it in, complaining that it was too much. Her cheekbones were sharp and high, forever giving her that malnourished look. Her skin was still that golden shade though it looked alarmingly pale just then.

"You and I are still married, Ariana. Ten years and going strong. Except for the little problem of you wanting to marry another man."

Her fingers became lax around his coat, her body trembling with tension. "Ariana is dead," she kept repeating through pale lips.

Words that had haunted him for eight years.

He had imagined her death a hundred different ways, a million different times. He had hated himself for leaving her with his father. He had been through hell and back because he thought he hadn't protected her.

He fisted his hands by his sides, fighting the urge to wrap his hands around her. Fighting the overwhelming impulse to push her against the tree and crush her mouth with his.

Because to see Ariana was to want Ariana. He didn't remember a time he hadn't wanted to possess her with that raw longing.

And yet lust was only a pale shadow behind the need to

ensure that she was alive and not a figment of his imagination, a flimsy shadow from his feverish nightmares.

Outwardly, she hadn't changed at all.

Thin, angular body built with lean muscle. Wide, brown-ringed eyes too big for her gamine face. Sharp, bladelike nose followed by a mouth so lushly pillowy, so poutingly full, that no man could see it and not think dirty, lustful thoughts.

It was as if all the austerity that had been executed in her face had to be made up for in that mouth.

She looked just as common and nondescript as Theos had called her back then.

Only her eyes had changed.

That twinkle that had made them glow, as if she held the glorious flicker of life itself inside her, it was gone. Wariness filled them now. He wanted to shove her away from him, stop her from touching him like she used to do.

But the damage to his system was already done.

His body roared to life at the soft imprint she left with hers. Long, toned legs tangled with his, her body trembling faintly against his. The scent of her—just her skin and the lavender soap she apparently still used—invaded his bloodstream. Like Pavlov's dog, every cell inside him stood to attention. Memories and sensations of pleasure and something else, a sense of being utterly alive, poured into his skin, making him heated.

"This is your petty revenge on me," she finally whispered, her mouth only inches apart from his. A loud thrum began under his skin. "Your way of playing with my life while you announce your own marriage to the world. You will let me dangle at your fingertips, holding this ridiculous threat over my head.

"Because I had the temerity to walk away from the controlling, arrogant, ruthless man you are, Andreas."

He scowled. "You think it was my pride that was dented by your betrayal, by your lies?"

"Yes," she said defiantly. "For you're not capable of feeling anything else."

Andreas flinched, her words landing like barbed fists on his flesh. *Thee mou*, it seemed even now, when she was utterly in the wrong, she dared to challenge him, dared to call him out for her mistakes.

"You could have done this through your lawyers. You could have sent me the divorce papers through one of your lackeys. But no…you had to do it personally because you couldn't forego the pleasure of ruining my life before you go back to rule your bloody kingdom."

"You're mistaken again, Ariana. I did not come simply to ruin your engagement."

"Then why are you here?"

"For two years, since Father let it slip that you were alive, I've been waiting for this moment.

"I will be crowned King of Drakon soon and I need my wife by my side. I have come to take you home to Drakon."

Her gaze searched his, desperate. What little fight had been there seemed to deflate out of her. As if she was shrinking right in front of his eyes. "You've got to be kidding me."

He touched her then, tracing the delicate line of her jaw with the tip of his forefinger. Her skin was silky smooth to his touch, a faint tremor running through it. "But you already know I have no sense of humor."

"You…can't…" her breath came in little gasps "…do… this."

Her thin body going slack against him, his wife did what she'd always forced him to do. She fainted and forced him to catch her. Forced him to hold her fragile body in his, before he was ready for any such contact. Feeling fear, and panic and a hundred other emotions that he'd never had encountered otherwise.

Her gown's bodice was so tight that Andreas drew his pocket knife out of his coat and cut the front off. The blue tinge around her mouth began to recede, his own panic fading with it.

He easily lifted her slender form and made his way to the waiting car, icy anger thawing and giving way to shock.

She might not have changed outwardly but there was something different about her. Something fragile and fractured. Almost as if there was a piece missing.

He'd expected a radiant, carefree bride, ready to ride into another adventure with another man she'd sucked in with her effervescent personality, with her vivacity and wit. He'd expected her to be living it up in some party town with the money she'd taken from his father.

He hadn't expected this…this *waif*, with bruises under her eyes, working away all hours at a nonprofit legal agency. She made barely any money. She shared a one-bedroom apartment, the size of his closet, with another woman. He'd have never believed that silly, rebellious girl would have the interest to study law much less the grit to get a degree and practice.

Barely out of breath, he slowly lowered her into the seat and slid into place next to her.

Every savage promise he'd made himself that he'd make her suffer crumbled as he gathered her body into his.

Once again, all his plans turned to dust by the infuriating woman.

Just as she had been able to make him laugh, make him long for something he had never known back then. Make him lose his mind in the desperate need to possess her.

All through that summer, Ariana had wielded some kind of magic over him.

That laughing, reckless girl had shattered through to

his core, given him a taste of an unparalleled joy he'd never known.

And so he'd done the unthinkable and married her when it had been time to leave. Possessing Ariana had equaled holding that joy in the palm of his hand. It had meant being something more than the Crown Prince, something he hadn't even realized he'd needed to be until then.

He had forgotten who and what he was, he had clung desperately to that feeling, had thought it enough to have her in his life.

Except it hadn't been enough for her.

With that same recklessness that had lured him to her, she had destroyed their lives. It was that same girl he had expected to find today.

But she was right.

This was not the Ariana he had met that summer, the Ariana he had married.

And yet, letting her go was not an option.

Ariana came awake slowly, her throat parched, her mind blank. Air filled her in quick, choppy bursts.

"Drink this."

Ignoring the questions buzzing through her head, she took the bottle and drank the water. It was cold and crisp, what she desperately needed.

"Iedas Mountain Springs," the label on the water bottle said, with a small sketch of the majestic mountain range in Drakon… *Drakon!*

She jerked upright. Cream leather walls greeted her, understated luxury permeating the ambience. Soft lights from the ceiling cast a golden glow around the cabin.

Cabin… She was in the rear cabin of a private jet—a jet that belonged to the blasted House of Drakos.

The events of the afternoon came back in a fast reel.

Andreas had said they were still married.

Andreas had said he was going to take her back to Drakon.

Andreas had caught her when she'd fainted.

The panic felt like ants crawling all over her skin. She pushed her legs out and stood up. The cabin tilted but she had to get out of here.

The slither of her dress, her wedding dress, alerted her. She looked down, found the corset cut neatly down in the middle. The beaded bodice hung open through the center, gaping open to reveal her slip and the shadow of her breasts.

Ariana held it up with both hands and forced her Jell-O legs to move.

Before she took another step, he was before her.

A man as hard as the rock on which his palace sat. Yet, as she looked at him now, there were white lines around his mouth, and he was not so solid.

"Why am I here? What is that sound?"

"They're readying for takeoff."

"No!"

"Sit down, Ariana."

"Get out of my way."

"You're in no shape to go anywhere."

"I swear, Andreas, if you don't move out of my way—"

His fingers gripped her arms, exerting pressure backward. "Calm down before you faint again!"

"How dare you? You bastard!" Ariana let her hand fly.

The crack of her palm against his cheek was like a pop of thunder, leaving an utter silence behind. She clutched her wrist with her left hand, shock jarring it. Breathing hard, she looked up.

He hadn't even touched his jaw. Except for the tight clench of it, the little jerk of his head, he showed no reaction to what she'd done. He still supported her.

"Does that conclude this episode to your satisfaction, Ari?"

Her shortened name made her breath catch. "I will not apologize."

He shrugged.

That casual gesture was like fuel to her rage.

"You're kidnapping me. Really?" She fisted her hands and went at him, lost to all reason. "After all the propriety and decorum and a hundred other rules you demand of everyone, you're actually kidnapping me?"

Of course it was exactly what he had planned. And Ariana had so nicely played into his hands, by literally fainting at his feet.

Damn it, Ari.

"You will not like it if I subdue you on the bed, Ari. Or maybe you will, since we both know what will happen the moment I lie on top of you." The cold matter-of-factness of his threat made everything still in her.

Ariana turned and met his inscrutable gaze, wrapping her mind around this.

"Should we put my theory to the test or shall you calm down?"

"Let me go."

He did instantly. With an urgency that made her flush.

Her legs simply gave out and Ariana slid into a graceless heap on the bed.

This had been coming, Ari, a nauseating voice whispered. *You just buried your head in the sand. You knew he was going to catch up with you one day.*

She didn't know how long they sat like that. She on the bed, trying to catch her breath, trying to quell the panic, and he sitting in the one armchair in the corner, watching her.

A lion crouching in silence, waiting for his prey to show weakness.

The long coat and jacket were gone. Replaced by a white designer dress shirt with a white undershirt—nothing so scandalous as going without one for the uptight Crown

Prince of Drakon—and black custom-made trousers for his six-four height. Dark olive skin at his throat beckoned to her. She followed the trail of the chain around his neck with her eyes.

His dog tags from his time in the Drakonite Army, where he'd trained from fifteen to eighteen, would be under that undershirt. Platinum cufflinks. A platinum-plated watch glinted on his left wrist. Black Italian handmade shoes gleamed where he'd folded one foot on top of his thigh.

The soft lightning of the cabin wreathed his face in shadows, showing the sharp planes and hollows of his face to perfection.

He was leaner than she remembered and it made him look even more distant and withdrawn. There were lines on his face now, especially around that thinly sculpted mouth. At twenty-six he'd been gorgeous in an uptight, starchy kind of way.

Ten years later now, he seemed even more comfortable in his skin. Even more arrogant and ruthless about his place in the world.

Every small thing she noticed brought back a memory thudding into her conscious, as physical as a blow to her solar plexus. Her throat dried promptly again, her heart forever in that lurching rhythm when he was near.

Slowly the impact of this, *of him*, hit her in its completion. She wasn't running away from this, not yet at least.

No, there was no running away at all from this, she corrected herself. Not unless she wanted him to give her chase for the rest of their lives.

Realizing she'd been gaping at him, she pulled her gaze up. Chin propped against his fist, he raised a brow. He didn't tease her for gawking at him like a teenager.

He didn't need the validation to his masculinity, to his ego.

Power was second skin to him, women flocked to him

like buzzing bees. Actresses and models, CEOs and princesses, women had been falling at his feet since puberty. If he'd been merely one more vacant, lazy royal out to have a good time, maybe he wouldn't have so much pull.

But no, Andreas Drakos was smart as a whip. A historian, an army veteran, a weaver of words. *Christos*, there wasn't anything he didn't excel at.

And yet he'd chosen her.

She frowned, the question had tormented her for years, struggled into a comfortable position and took stock of her body. A leaf fluttering in a harsh gale would have more strength than her at the moment.

Of all the stupid, moronic things to do in front of this man... She pressed a hand to her temple.

She felt the heat of his body instantly in the air around the bed. Whatever reprieve she'd gotten was over.

In silent scrutiny, he fluffed the pillows and propped them against the wall, and then pulled her into a sitting position. With economic movements, his fingers barely touching her, he arranged the duvet around her. Gave her another bottle of water that she emptied within seconds.

Hysteria began to bubble up through her throat and she laughed. Water spurted out of her nose and mouth inelegantly, and he promptly wiped her nose and mouth with a napkin. On and on went her near manic laughter until tears streamed out from her eyes. Until the ball of tension that had lodged in her chest since she'd seen him standing in front of the church slowly deflated.

He raised a brow again.

"How many women can claim Crown Prince Andreas Drakos waited on them like a lowly member of staff?" she quipped, perfectly understanding his question.

A sudden tightness gripped her chest. Wordless communication had been so their thing.

"So you still possess that ridiculous sense of humor."

She tensed as he sat down at the edge of the bed. Not near enough to touch, yet tantalizingly close. Her body couldn't take this much heightened awareness after what had been a drought of ten years. Not for long, not without combusting with need.

"What the hell was that?"

"Be glad I didn't scratch that perfect face. Or maybe I should have. A little imperfection would have at least made you look human."

A jagged sigh. An echo of all the times Ari had pushed his buttons. "I speak of your fainting."

"You showed up after ten years and I fainted." She sighed. *Regression much, Ari?*

"Continue like that and it will only confirm my belief that you're still that reckless, juvenile, rebellious brat I knew back then."

"What can I say? You bring out the worst in me, Your Highness."

Their eyes sought each other instantly.

Are you my watchdog, Your Highness?

Crack a smile, Your Highness.

It's called a vodka shot, Your Highness.

Had she been that naive, that foolish to have teased this man like that? Had he actually let her?

"Ariana, focus." It wasn't even a warning. Just a smidgen of his impatience leaking. "If I hadn't been there, you would have been on the grass, in the cold, for God knows how long. Is this your new thing now, fainting?"

"New thing?"

"Yes. Pot brownies, vodka shots, fasting for days to lose weight… *Christos*, do I need to go on? You were always ridiculously reckless about your well-being."

Ari massaged her temples with her fingers. He was right. She had thrown herself into her sudden, boundless freedom, as naively as jumping off a cliff. Guilt over her parents' deaths had stolen reason from her. The need to experience life to the fullest after seventeen years of being trapped in a golden cage…it had consumed her.

He'd thought her ditzy, willful, reckless and any number of even less complimentary things. She had been all those and more. But not in the past ten years, not anymore.

Her hands settled on her belly, corrosive grief scratching her throat.

The freedom she'd finally got, the need to make something of her life, it had come at such a high price. But it had helped her find herself, helped her achieve control over those impulses that would destroy her.

Until this past month when his impending announcement had undone her again. And that made fear whisper through her bones. It was the same circle of self-abuse her mother had been stuck in with her father.

"Ariana?"

"I…had a salad for lunch yesterday and nothing since then. It has been a stressful week—the caseload at the firm is crazy right now and then a doubly stressful morning. I've never fainted before." Except that one time after she had left Drakon and him behind. Because in her recklessness, the same that he accused her of right now, it had taken a fainting spell to realize she'd been three months pregnant.

His instant control of the situation, his interrogation of her as if she were a child, grated like nothing else. But to be fair, that's what she had been then. "Because of the elevation above sea level of this town, I sometimes find it hard to breathe."

"Mountain air makes your asthma worse. I checked your little purse and you didn't have your inhaler on you."

She looked up then and swallowed. She'd thought he would delete anything related to their time together from his life, from his mind. At least after learning of the biggest lie she'd ever told.

Apparently, like her, Andreas had forgotten nothing of their time together. Of their short-lived marriage. Of how they made each other burn up in flames when they touched, and ruined each other when they didn't.

"It does flare it up from time to time. But it makes up with everything else."

A little frown appeared between his brows. "Makes up?"

"The fact that it flares my asthma is a little inconvenience to what I have found here. I…found a community here, Andreas. My life has meaning here. There are women who count on me." She held his gaze, air ballooning up in her chest, smothering her lungs. Time to face the facts. "You can't really mean what you said earlier."

"Have you ever known me to say anything I didn't mean?"

No. He'd never once said that he loved her, even in the throes of passion, even when he'd let his control slip. And it was something to watch the iron-control-clad, emotionless, uptight Crown Prince lose it in the sheets.

She swung her legs out of the bed and stood up slowly. When he neared her to offer assistance with clear reluctance—because of course every touch and look had to be calculated in that steel trap that was his mind—she held him off with her hand.

The cut corset of her wedding dress hung limply around her waist but Ariana didn't care. She didn't care one bit what her sheer slip showed.

She didn't care that his gaze traveled all over her, noted her defiant pose, and yet didn't betray anything.

He had unraveled her life all over again and she was not going to hide and feel shame about it. She had to face Andreas and whatever came now, if she ever wanted to move forward in her life.

"Think about what you're proposing, Andreas. Your father was right in one thing—I hardly possess the bloodlines. I was never brought up to be the next Queen of Drakon.

"You…completely agreed with him." It took no small amount of effort to put this forward rationally. "You… The moment we left the village…"

"What about it, Ariana?"

He had regretted what he'd done, she knew. But the past was done, useless. "Do you think I would be any more malleable this time around?" She lifted her chin. "The last ten years have only made me realize how right I was. We would have destroyed each other if I'd stayed."

He reached her then. Breath serrated her throat as he lifted his hand and softly clasped her jaw. For one sheer, indefinable moment, a wealth of emotion danced in his jet-black gaze. Pure rage and something else. A bleakness?

"Silly Ari. Do you think I give a damn about what you want or need right now?

"Your death tormented me for eight years.

"The little slip from Theos's mouth that you were not only alive, but that you took money from him to disappear—" tight lines emerged around his mouth, a small fracture in his control "—that news has tortured me for the last two years."

Ariana stared, stunned. A dent to his ego, she'd expected. But for Andreas to admit that losing her had tormented him…it was akin to the sun revolving around the earth. The pithy declaration raged through her, kindling feelings she couldn't handle.

Had he truly felt something for her then?

"This is exactly what your father wanted you to become."

"Theos is dead, *agapita*," he said softly, a wicked gleam in his eyes. "It has been years since his will, his word, has had the power to move me. The power to persuade me. The power to control me.

"I have become my own man, Ari. Isn't that what you wanted long ago?"

She'd have given anything to hear that ten years ago. But not anymore. "The moment we land in Drakon, I'll yell what you've done through the rooftops. Your image can't survive a scandal."

He bared his teeth in a feral smile. "So you have kept tabs on me."

The sound that fell from her mouth was half growl, half screech. "I know my place even in the illustrious world that you're the unrivaled lord of. One word from me will plunge the House of Drakos into a horrible scandal."

"Do you really want to threaten me?"

Panic bloomed, making her voice rise. "My entire life is here. Even more importantly, my clients are here."

"Your fiancé fell over himself in his haste to accept my conditions. He gets to keep the legal agency running and keeps quiet about your secret identity for the rest of his life."

"I built that agency with my blood and tears." The one good thing that had come out of the loss she'd suffered.

"You built it with the dirty payoff you took from my father. Even your education was paid for by the House of Drakos. And since we're still married—"

"Half of everything I own is yours," she finished. Her mind whirled. "And you need Magnus to keep quiet about where I've been and what I've been doing."

His jaw clenched and Ariana exhaled roughly. Finally, there was one point she could negotiate with. But he didn't give her even that chance.

"Your clients, what do you think will happen if the media gets hold of who you truly are? That you've been living a lie for ten years."

"It's not a lie. I busted my ass to earn my law degree. I opened that nonprofit legal aid agency because I wanted to help those women."

"And when the world finds out that you're not Anna Harris but Ariana Drakos, wife of the King of Drakon—"

"My clients will be dragged into the limelight along with me." She exhaled roughly. "Those are women who have already been abused by men they trusted. Which will keep me quiet. Am I getting close, Andreas?"

He smiled then—a jagged mockery that made her chest ache. "You know what I find truly hard to believe in this new, peachy life you've made for yourself?"

"What?" She snarled the question at him.

"Am I to believe that you have found your true, deep purpose in your scattered life finally? That you truly devote yourself tirelessly to those women and their plight?"

If there was a moment that Ariana truly wanted to sink her nails into that perfect, arrogant, condescending face and scratch it, it was then. Ten years of striving to make something of herself, to give meaning to what she'd lost, to make a meaningful path for herself, and his careless disdain crushed it all.

And he knew it. He was all but challenging her to launch herself at him again, to go back to that lowest denominator of herself she'd once thrived on.

She would attack him and he would subdue her…and it would lead to only one conclusion. The knowledge suffused the very air around them with a dense heat.

Every time they had fought in those horrible three months of their marriage, they'd ended up in bed. Or against the wall. Or on the chaise longue with the Crown Prince on his knees, with his arrogant head between her thighs.

The memory shimmered like a bright glitter in his coal-black eyes.

With the sheer will that had helped her survive through the darkest night of her life, Ari looked away. Air rushed into her lungs, clearing the haze.

Her biggest defense against Andreas was to show leaving him hadn't been a whim. That she wasn't a car crash in the making anymore. That she had come into her own strength these last ten years. That she'd proactively made something of her life.

"I care about my clients, about their privacy, about not turning everything Magnus and I worked for into a lie. So, yes, you win my silence. But nothing else."

"How refreshing that you're capable of loyalty, even if it's toward another man, *pethi mou*. I told him, soon enough you'd have found a reason to run out on him. That your precious freedom would have come calling.

"Is it not your pattern?"

Ariana flinched, the softly delivered statement even more painful for she'd been about to do exactly the same thing to Magnus. Not for some kind of femme fatale reason but because she'd realized Magnus deserved much better than her.

"I didn't think you of all people would be crass enough to typecast me as some kind of vacant-headed, freewheeling slut. If for no other reason than that it would taint your own pristine image, your own association with me."

"What does that mean?"

"I was eighteen, Andreas. I… I was bowled over by you. I threw myself at you. I was…messed up after my parents' deaths, and you were a high unlike anything I'd ever known.

"You were—you *are* unlike any other man I've ever known.

"Jesus, did you know what your attention, your reluctant interest, meant to me? You…who didn't show interest in princesses, and models and CEOs.

"You looked at me. *Me*—messed-up, frightened, guilty Ariana.

"You married me knowing who and what I was. So, if

we have to call out someone for the…*twisted* mess that was our marriage, it's you."

"Was that the justification when you let me think you had died in a horrible drowning accident," he bit out and she flinched. "Maybe I will let you go, Ariana. Maybe one of these days I will find that little bit of decency within myself again. Maybe you can go back to being Anna Harris and the savior of those women in your little town again."

And in those statements of his, Ariana saw his shredded control for what it was. Saw his loathing that she was still an obsession with him. He despised himself, and her, because he couldn't give her up.

Any hopes she had of convincing him perished in that moment. After all, she did know him better than anyone.

"So this is about revenge?"

"Call it whatever the hell you want to." His gaze tracked her face and her torn clothes. He fisted his hand so tight by his side that the knuckles were white.

For the first time that day, Ariana realized how tremendous his self-control was.

"You need food and rest. Do not force me to manhandle you into that, too. We both know whether it will be pleasure or punishment."

Ariana fell onto the bed with a soft thud, the recrimination in his eyes burning through her like acid. Her skin still prickling, for the first time since she'd known him, she was grateful for his iron-clad self-control.

Because, even after all these years, she had none when it came to resisting the Crown Prince of Drakon.

CHAPTER THREE

"MRS. DRAKOS? YOUR HIGHNESS?"

For the second time in a few hours, Ariana jerked upright so suddenly that her neck gave a painful twinge. She looked at the stewardess patiently waiting for her to wake up.

So the cat was out of the bag.

Instead of the panic she braced herself for, all she felt was a…quiet resignation. Not the give-up-and-become-his-wife kind. But the guilty-as-hell kind.

Whatever he had done to her, however much she had despised him at the end of their marriage, it was clear that she had miscalculated the effect of her supposed death on Andreas. On hearing of his swift engagement to a real estate mogul's sister, her own guilt had been alleviated.

She didn't belong in the Crown Prince's world and that he'd replaced her so fast had been proof enough.

Of course, that miscalculation had been aided by his father.

If Andreas had grieved her loss, who knew how Theos had twisted that to his advantage?

King Theos, she had realized within a week of meeting her guardian as her father-in-law, had possessed an unhealthy hold on his heir. He'd seen her as nothing but a weakness to eliminate from his son's life.

What had been painful was from the moment he had presented her to King Theos, even Andreas had begun to see her as that—a weakness to be hidden away.

The stewardess's eyes traveled over Ari's hair, which could rival the Amazon forest for its wildness right now, to the torn dress she had fallen asleep in.

Ari cringed. She stood up from the bed, and pushed the dress off her shoulders and hips.

Ill-concealed curiosity scampered across the woman's face. "I will take care of the dress, Your Highness. Have it mended. I'm sure you'd want to—"

"No, that's not necessary," Ari replied, pulling the slip off her shoulders. Her strapless bra stuck to the underside of her breasts uncomfortably, thanks to her habit of smothering herself under the covers. She stepped out of the slip seconds before the woman took it, almost dislodging Ari off her feet.

"Have it burned," a soft voice commanded from the entrance.

The need to cover herself was instinctive, self-preservation at its primal. Shaking, Ariana covered her midriff with her arms.

The stewardess had that look again, switching between her and Andreas, as if she could figure out the secret as to how this average-looking, falling-apart-at-the-seams waif had snared the most powerful, gorgeous man in Drakon.

It was a question the whole world was going to ask this time, not just King Theos, if Andreas had his way.

His gaze dipped past Ari's face this time—as if he'd given himself permission to look, to linger—moved to the pulse beating wildly at her neck, betraying the sudden tension that suffused her every cell, to the curves of her breasts rising and falling. A languorous ache settled low in her belly, her nipples hard against the flimsy bra.

"Checking up on me already?" Fear of how just one look from him turned her on destroyed the need for discretion in front of a member of the staff. "There's no way to escape, unless you're willing to provide me with a parachute. You can see me plummet to death, at least."

He closed his eyes, his chest barely lifted and fell with his exhale, and then leveled that black gaze at her again.

Military precision to every single breath. "I came in to see if you were awake. Petra needs your prescription for your inhaler. I will not have you fainting everywhere."

"Petra?"

"Yes, my secretary." He looked down at his phone, frowned, typed a message and looked up again.

Tall, blonde, with a voluptuous body, armed with a master's from a renowned university in Drakon, and hailing from a highly connected Drakonite family. Andreas's oldest friend and shadow. Theos's spy. If Ariana could give a form to all her self-doubts and insecurities back then, it would be Petra Cozakis. "I know Petra runs your life. And for the last time, it was the stress of the last week and that dress that did it today.

"Do not treat me as if I am still an imbecile, Andreas."

He raised a brow. Confirmation enough that that was exactly how she was acting. "Petra is on this flight. Let her know if you need anything."

"No," she said loudly.

His gaze pinned her. "Precisely what are you saying no to?"

"If you're dragging me to the King's Palace, it will be different this time. I will not be hidden away like some stain on the great House of Drakos. I will not let your uptight, snobbish staff run circles around me. I will not communicate through your minions, will not let you pawn me off on them as if I was a thing to be managed." Maybe what Andreas needed was a dose of reality. For his staff and his family and the world to realize who he had chosen and how unsuitable she was.

Lines formed between his brows. "Leave us," he said to the stewardess without moving his gaze from Ariana.

The woman froze in the process of folding the damned dress. She thought Ariana and Andreas had gotten married in that dress, Ariana realized.

"Burn. That. Dress," he repeated. The stewardess nodded and scurried out.

Arms still around her waist, Ariana turned, grabbed the duvet and pulled it around her like a shroud. However she tried, the choice was to either cover her chest or her midriff.

She covered her midriff. Her bra was enough for her meager breasts. It wasn't like he hadn't seen the little she had to offer before.

The small scar she bore above her pubic bone might not be visible in the soft light, but she couldn't take the chance. Closing her eyes, she willed the grief down. The situation with Andreas was explosive enough without adding her discovery *after* she had left him that she'd been pregnant.

That she had lost her precious little baby boy was an unbearable, ever-present weight on her soul. For Andreas, it would only mean more betrayal. Worse, the loss of a *potential heir*, a figurehead to represent the House of Drakos's future.

Ariana couldn't bear to hear his dismissal of that tiny life. The guilt of it, the grief of it was all her own.

At least, it served as a reminder that she couldn't chance a pregnancy again.

Because there was no point in denying that she was going to end up in his bed. The attraction between them, it seemed, had survived despite everything.

She took a Post-it note and pen from the small bedstead and scribbled the name and number of her GP. Shards of glass seemed to be stuck in her throat when she turned. "I also need the prescription for my birth control pills filled."

The memory of their last fight, the bitterest and dirtiest of them all, sculpted sharp grooves in his already gaunt cheeks. His hesitation was like handing her a live grenade. Bulky duvet and all, she reached him, her heart threatening to rip out of her chest. "Have something to say, Andreas?"

As if pulled from the past, he slowly looked down at her. "No. Even I'm not cruel enough to bring a child into this. At least not anymore."

"Does that mean you intend to let me go at some point?"

This time, his answer was more thoughtful than driven by fury. "No."

"But isn't my only duty as your wife to produce as many healthy heirs as soon as humanly possible? My purpose, to be your broodmare?"

Deep grooves etched on the sides of his mouth as he responded without inflection. "Nikandros's twins will be heirs."

"Of course," she said, swallowing away the ache. She had no idea why she was pushing him like this. Only that she wanted to hurt him as she was hurting. "How does the timeline look then? Do I have enough time to find a new GP in Drakon and get my pills without Petra and the entire palace knowing my business?"

His chin tilted down. "What?"

"The sex, Andreas? You and me and the humiliating sex that we're going to have, you have a timeline for that, right?

"Sex is your weapon in this revenge scheme, *ne*? The thing I could never refuse you, the thing that you threatened to hold against—" Her voice broke, and he…his features paled. "So, yeah, if your schedule allows me to wait, then you don't have to ask your secretary to fill your wife's birth control prescription."

When she'd have turned away from him, he gripped her arms so tightly that Ari knew she'd have bruises tomorrow. But the pain was worth the satisfaction that she had finally, finally ruffled him. "Humiliating sex? Punishment sex?" He turned her until she was facing him, her duvet forgotten, her stomach tying itself in knots. "Have you convinced yourself that with my power and prestige, I somehow forced you?

"Have you conveniently twisted the truth in that too, *agapita*? That you gave your innocence unwillingly?"

Laughter fell from her mouth, serrated and strange. "No, it was never that, whatever it was." Her nose rubbed against his biceps, her mouth curving into a smile against the fabric of his shirt. Faint tension emanated from him, making Ari throw caution to the wind. "Even in this we disagree, *ne*, Andreas?"

He looked at her as though he was afraid she was going mad. She was a little afraid of that herself. "How?"

"To this day, I'm convinced that I seduced you and you're convinced that you seduced me. Even in this, we have a power struggle."

He didn't outright laugh. The rigid, sculpted curve of his thin lips didn't even move. But his grip on her arms eased. Something softened in his black eyes. A flash of that dry humor she had seen back then. Only she.

He lifted a finger and touched the tip of her nose. Her breath suspended in her throat, for Ari had a feeling he had been about to touch her mouth and changed his mind at the last second.

He'd been tempted. And it filled her with a heady power she didn't want.

"It was not so much a power struggle as it was you defying me. Defying everything I stood for—Drakon, the Palace, the House of Drakos, my father and me." His tone became far off, as if he too was reliving those first heady months when they had met.

Memories permeated the very air around them.

The first day he'd arrived at the café, he'd introduced himself as simply Andreas. As if he could ever be just that. But, of course, she'd known who he was. Ariana had only laughed at his imperious command to let him or his team know if she needed anything. Until she realized he'd been in earnest. That he meant to keep an eye on his father's ward.

Keep an eye, he had.

He would come to the café where she had worked every night, two huge tomes, and newspaper cuttings and reams of paperwork spread out on his table. Not a word, not a greeting after that first one. No chatting with any other customers. Just that dark gaze tracking her all over the café, until the early hours of morning, as if he found her endlessly fascinating. After the first day, he'd walked her home to the apartment, again with nary a word exchanged between them.

Ariana had never found herself so thoroughly captivated.

He had done that for a whole month before Ari had lost her patience and approached him.

Are you my very own watchdog, Your Highness?

She cringed, remembering how outrageous she'd been.

His reply: *You should not be drinking with strange men, Ms. Sakis.*

And then he'd followed her to the party where she'd proceeded to get drunk. Taken her home to her little apartment she'd shared with three other girls.

No more exchanges except her increasingly reckless taunts to break his self-assurance over the next month.

Until the afternoon the verdict had come out about her parents' deaths. There had been no doubt that her mother had deliberately caused the accident.

She'd taken her life and her husband's, a day after he'd struck Ariana.

She'd been mindless with grief, desperate to run away from her own life. Andreas hadn't asked her a single question that day, nor left her side. Like a shadow, he'd been at her back throughout the day and night as she'd flitted from the café to a party, from the party to a walk along the coast and then back to her apartment.

Finally, she had broken down into anguished sobs, finally, she had realized that she was now forever alone, a fate she'd wished for for so long. At her apartment, he had sat by her on the couch—not even their shadows touching, always so careful to not touch her even by accident—and he had started talking, uncaring of whether she was listening.

In that deep, gravelly voice of his that had been just a tether to hold on to at first.

He'd started with the reason for his stay in the little village, a question she'd asked of him countless times. Told her of how his trail had led him there.

It was the first time she'd heard of the story of the dragon and the warriors. For hours, he'd told her of his fascination with the history of Drakon and its centuries-old lore since he'd been a little boy. Of the painstaking years of research he'd put together in his free time, which was far too little and rare. Of his fierce determination to pin down the real truth behind the war the warriors had waged on the dragon.

And in the passion in his words that had been a revelation—when she'd relentlessly taunted him for being an uptight, dutiful, one-dimensional prince puffed up with his own privilege and power—Ariana had seen the man beneath the Crown Prince's mantle. A historian, a weaver of words, a dreamer; a man that struggled to survive within the constraints of his birth and his position of power without even knowing it. A man who liked her, her company, her laughter, yet wouldn't, or couldn't put it in a simple sentence.

A man who could have the world at his feet and yet saw something worthwhile in her.

The realization that somehow the Crown Prince of Drakon, powerful and gorgeous, needed her just as much as she needed him, had reverberated through her.

As dawn had painted the sky a myriad of purples and pinks, his voice had slowly guided Ariana back to the world, to the life waiting for her.

Through her death, her mother had given her a gift. She had given Ariana her own life back.

With a fiercely alive feeling coursing through her veins, she had done what she'd been dying, but had been terrified, to do, until then. She had wiped her tears away roughly, kneeled between his long legs and pressed her mouth to his.

Her first kiss, she had decided so full of herself, would be the Crown Prince's.

Of course, he hadn't kissed her back as she'd mashed her lips against his. Tenderly, he'd clasped her jaw and pushed her back while she'd been burning with humiliation and thwarted desire, had guided her to her room, tucked her in, waited until she fell into a dreamless sleep.

The next morning, she'd woken up, brimming with a renewed verve for life and determined to have him, in whatever form she could.

Thee mou, she'd been playing with fire. Was it any wonder she'd been burned?

He'd made her feel so secure that night—a feeling she'd never known. Like she could survive the bitterest grief if only she had his words, *him* by her side.

Except she hadn't foreseen that what had attracted him to her would be what he would despise in the end.

"Challenging everything I had ever believed in," Andreas said, pulling her back into the now, a strange glitter in those dark eyes, "about myself, about the world, about my place in the world.

"You were this skinny, reckless seventeen-year-old and the first person I had ever met in my life who…"

"Who what?" she whispered, desperate for more. Even knowing that this self-indulgence would only lead to pain.

"Who didn't care how powerful, educated, or accomplished I was. With you, I was…" she'd never seen him lost for words, yet right then, she was sure he was choosing them carefully "…just Andreas for the first time."

They were words Ariana had never heard him say before. Almost regretful. A little wistful. They gouged open a longing she'd shut away.

Tears filled her throat. She wanted to pound at him for never saying those things to her then, for never telling her… No. Ruthlessly, she pulled herself to the present. They would have never survived, she needed to hold on to that.

He slowly disentangled himself from her, pushed away a lock of hair that had fallen onto her jaw. Small touches. Calculated touches. Her skin prickled. "I will make you a promise, Ari."

She scowled, more angry with herself than with him. "It won't be without some hidden motive."

And this time, he really smiled. The flash of his even white teeth against his darkly olive skin was breathtaking.

Unlike him, patience had never been her strong suit. "What is it, your promise?"

"I will not touch you until you come to me. I will not take you, *agape mou*, until you beg me to take you. Until you crawl into my bed and ask me to be inside you.

"Taking you when you can't breathe for wanting me… it is unlike any high I've known."

Ariana jerked away from him, slumberous warmth pooling low in her belly. A throbbing between her legs. "Like I did the last time."

A flare of heat darkened those impossible black eyes. It was all there in them—the log cabin at the foot of the mountains, the storm that had been raging outside for a week, the huge king bed with soft-as-sin sheets and Andreas and she stuck inside, with their supplies dwindling every day and the fire between them raging higher with every moment.

The knowledge that she had turned eighteen four weeks earlier was explosive in that silent cabin; that they had both been ignoring King Theos's summons; the knowledge that her dare in trapping the Crown Prince, who seemed to be made of stone and rock like the mountains around them, far too dangerous when she'd seen the evidence of his attraction to her finally in those first few days in the cabin.

Until the day he had decided that he was going to give in.

Sparks filled her body at the memory of that decadent night. It was the night she had begun to understand the uptight, arrogant Crown Prince, to realize what she'd thrown herself into. But it had been too late.

She'd already fallen in love with him.

Her fingers shaking to hold the duvet, Ariana pushed out the breath lodged in her chest. Barely a few hours with him and she was on fire. She cleared her hoarse throat. "Why?"

He shrugged. "To level the field a little."

"This is exactly what you wanted when you kidnapped me—me at your mercy."

"Yes, but having you at my mercy when you have no fight in you…" he made a bored sound "…that is not the Ariana I want. What fun is tormenting you when you have no say in it?

"This way, I will know that when I'm inside you this time, you have surrendered despite the little self-preservation it seems you have developed."

Thee mou, it was impossible. The man she had married would have never been open to a challenge like that, much less taunt her with it. He would have never given the reins of anything to her hands. Much less his revenge scheme. Or the simple matter of when they'd have sex.

Had he changed or was it just a game?

He leaned a hip against the wall, all lean masculinity and hungry eyes. "Since you've always blamed me for wanting to control everything, I will leave this in your hands. We will have sex only when you want it."

"Don't you get it? I'm not self-destructive anymore, Andreas. The last time burned me enough for an entire lifetime."

Sudden stillness seemed to come over him. His gaze probed hers, as if he wanted to plumb the depths of her. "Did I burn you, Ariana?"

The question was not a taunt or even a rebuke. It rang with curiosity that made her stomach twist. Tears pricked behind her eyelids, making him a shimmery vision.

Say no, Ari. Let the guilt be your own.

"Yes," she whispered. "I still have scars from it."

He nodded, a thoughtful look shuttering away his thoughts. "Then I owe you this, *ne*? This little game of ours can proceed as you want it or it could end as soon as you desire."

She trusted this reasonable Andreas even less than the controlling one. "End?"

"You could get naked and invite me to join you in the bed right now." Their gazes flicked to the bed and back. The soft duvet seemed to burn her skin. "I could give you the wedding night you'd have had tonight with your adorable little fiancé." His eyes hardened to dark chips, his mouth edging into that cruelly ruthless curve. "The longer you hold me off, the longer this whole thing will take."

The bastard! He had nicely trapped her. She was damned to stay with him the longer she denied this thing between them, and she was damned if she gave in. Because it had been apparent within two minutes of seeing him again, within seconds of breathing that scent of him, that she was into the special brand of masculinity that was only Andreas Drakos.

"You will be waiting a long time, Andreas. And we both know being denied what you want is a foreign concept you, *ne*?

"Also, from what I remember, celibacy makes you extra cranky."

"True, but after dealing with your deceit, my tolerance for everything has changed, Ari. You have no idea what or who I've become anymore." He turned and left the room, closing the door behind him.

Ariana buried her face in her hands, panicking over the lack of panic. Did she believe him? Would he truly give her a choice now that he had her close? And even if she did somehow resist not falling into the old patterns, she scoffed at herself, what was the point if it meant being his wife again?

A groan erupted from her mouth.

He was right in one thing, though.

Just because he had her where he wanted didn't mean she was going to roll over and let him do as he pleased. The image that her overactive mind supplied at that made the rub of her thighs excruciating.

This time, she knew what came of playing with fire. What came of tangling with Andreas Drakos.

First things first, she needed to take a shower, wash off the grime and doubts from the day she'd had so far. Ari made a note to thank the stewardess for the new set of underwear and designer jeans with their tags still intact, all in several sizes. Several shirts and blouses, too.

Why Andreas's private jet had a supply of women's underwear and clothes was something she was not going to dwell on. Not her business.

Shedding her underwear with a grimace, she grabbed a towel and walked into the small, but luxuriously decadent shower.

The jet head of steaming hot water on her tense muscles was glorious. She scrunched her nose at the row of high-end perfumed shampoos and gels, and found a bar of soap with minimum ingredients.

Running away was not an option. Avoiding him was not an option. Staying married to a man who thrived on control like it was air—even without the history between them—was not an option.

Being the Queen of Drakon…a hysterical laugh hurtled past her throat, was not at all an option.

Her only option, she stilled with her hands in her hair, was the truth. Andreas would not let her go until he figured out why she'd deceived him, until he understood how any woman, much less Ari, could walk away from him.

But the truth was a jagged, thorny, twisted mass. Her hand moved to the scar on her lower belly.

There were other things she could make him see. She could convince him, for one thing, that it hadn't been a juvenile game to her. That she had been foolish, naive, not willfully destructive. That leaving him had been a point of survival.

She had to convince him that she could never be that Ari again. That she would never put him or his precious Drakon or his duties to the Crown before her life. That she would never love him, never put her obsession for him before her happiness.

That she had learned how destructive love could be.

CHAPTER FOUR

I STILL HAVE SCARS.

What had he done to hurt her so much?

Andreas had hated her for two years, had dreamed of ways he would ruin her when he got his hands on her.

And now that he had her…now that he had found her on the eve of her wedding to another man, the rage and betrayal simmered down, morphed into something much more insidious.

All his energy in the last hour had gone into burying the urge to stalk back into the rear cabin and demand what the hell she had meant by it.

The sight of her—the globes of her breasts falling up and down, the expanse of golden flesh, the pulse beating violently at her neck, the defiant tilt of her chin… No, right now, he wanted her more than he wanted answers. His fingers itched to run through the silky mass of her hair, to reach that sensitive spot above the nape of her neck and see if she'd respond with a moan.

He could have spanned that tiny waist with his hand, brought her up to him until those breasts crushed against his chest, could have kissed away the dare in her eyes. Within seconds, he could have had her panting for him.

Could have pressed her down onto that bed, torn out her underwear and buried himself inside her. The images his thoughts painted made him shift uncomfortably in his seat.

Thee mou, that's all he needed, to give his staff a view of his inconvenient arousal. But instead of satisfying his body's craving, he'd made that ridiculous promise desperate to banish those shadows from her eyes.

There had been something so fragile about her in that

moment. As if a single wrong word about the pills could forever shatter her.

Damn his arrogance for forgetting that anything that involved Ariana could never be simple.

"Your Highness? Andreas?" Petra repeated, a little impatience slipping into her tone.

He met her silent accusation and shrugged apologetically. He could hardly blame her. After all, he'd heard nothing of what she'd said in the past fifteen minutes. Tilting his head up, he found Ariana.

Tension filled his shoulders and neck.

A white dress shirt, custom made for him, hung loose on her slender frame and was tucked into a pair of tight jeans that seemed to have been poured onto her lithe body.

The denim hugged the long muscles of her thighs and the flare of her hips. A moment's relief filled him. She did not look as unhealthy as he'd assumed earlier. Her wavy hair, she had tied into a messy knot at the back of her head. A knot he had reveled in undoing, as many times as he'd wanted.

She wore no jewelry except for a thin gold chain.

Her gaze flicked to each member of his team, an array of expressions passing through her face. When she saw Petra, a little frown appeared between her brows. When she saw Thomas, one of his oldest security guards, she threw herself at him with a grin.

A grin that turned her from that wary, resentful woman he'd kidnapped to that smiling girl he'd known long ago. Not that it was news that Ariana had always found more in common with the staff than him.

And then her eyes found him. With a regal nod that would have made the starchiest of his royal ancestors proud, she took a seat on the opposite side of the cabin. When the steward inquired if she wanted to eat, she rattled off food enough for his entire team.

All vegetarian, he remembered. At least, his private chef was more equipped than Andreas himself had been to feed her.

Andreas continued to listen to his team's updates with one ear while he watched her polish off most of the food she'd ordered. A little color returned to her cheeks and her hair glittered like drying copper left out in the sun for too long as it began falling from her knot.

He went back to discussing the security arrangements for the upcoming coronation, the details of the new trade deal he would be signing with their neighbor courtesy of Nikandros and Gabriel. "Petra?" He was about to ask her to bring him the proposal the Crown Council wanted him to push to the cabinet when he saw Ariana standing before him.

"Do you intend to work the entire flight?"

He lowered his head back to his work. "Yes. My coronation is in two months and I have let my duties slide in the last few months. Nikandros has been carrying the brunt of them."

She sat down in front of him, and raised her brows when he silently stared at her. Her skin had that freshly scrubbed look. Her body, lithe and toned, he fought the urge to give in.

"You…ditched work? Had hell frozen over?"

He frowned, remembering the number of times after they had returned to Drakon that she had pled with him to take the day off. Or to spend the evening with her. Or at the least, to eat dinner with her every day.

And he remembered his answers very well, too.

No.

He'd always said no, pushed her every request off as juvenile or attention-seeking. He'd been far too busy trying to prove to his father that his lapse in judgment was limited to marrying her. That he was still capable of representing

Drakon at the oil summit that year. That he could shoulder the tremendous task of digging Drakon out of the financial pit it had fallen into.

And then one day, she…had stopped asking.

How hadn't he noticed that until now?

"I had other things on my mind."

She flicked her gaze to his face and then back to her hands on the table. "I'm sure losing your father must have been very hard."

He laughed. Maybe he could tell her how terrified Theos had been that Andreas would kill him with his bare hands. That would discourage the sympathy in her eyes. "I was obsessed with finding you."

"Oh."

Petra stood silently by them. Waiting for him to dismiss Ariana, he slowly realized. It was not an incorrect presumption. Nor out of place.

Andreas did not let work slide for anyone. Even when he'd been searching for Ariana the last year, Petra had accompanied him most of the time. He'd done as much as he could to stop Nik from drowning under the weight of Drakon. Petra had been with him since he'd returned from the navy at eighteen and his father had chosen her to be his secretary. She knew him, knew his priorities. Maybe even came closest to a friend, though the simple art of making friends had never been allowed to him.

Petra knew him enough to come to the conclusion that whatever he was doing with Ariana, which bordered on the insane, would not affect his other functions.

The words to dismiss Ariana hovered over his lips when he noticed the edge in her smile, the whiteness of her knuckles gripping the table.

"Petra, we will continue later."

Petra hovered, her shock clear in the air. Andreas frowned and let her see it. *Christos*, his entire team had been with him for too long if Petra was questioning his orders.

Ariana crossed her legs in a casual gesture but the tension didn't leave her mouth. The flash of vulnerability reminded him again of how young she'd been then.

The cabin was now mostly empty for his look had dispersed his team. He let the silence build.

She had come with an agenda.

He waited patiently. And with a thrum of anticipation. She had always been full of crazy schemes. Like when she'd suggested they run away to the States for a couple of years and leave Drakon behind. When he had looked astonished at that, she'd modified it to say she'd wanted to backpack through Europe for a couple of months while he sorted out Drakon and its myriad problems, since their marriage hadn't been publicized.

The thought of reckless Ariana wandering through the hostels in Europe while he stayed back in Drakon…he had shot her down quite harshly.

Only now, however, he began to see the pattern. Crazy or not, he had denied her everything she had asked for. He'd given her over to his father, returning to the apartment when he'd needed sex. When he couldn't go without touching her for another minute. When he'd made some headway through the myriad of issues on his desk and she was his reward for it.

As if he'd ration his quota of her.

And every time he'd gone to see her, he'd found her to be increasingly restless, coming up with crazier plans.

He had given her the most coveted role in his life, in all of Drakon and it had been utterly lost on Ariana.

How had he forgotten those months of their marriage? It had been hell, the direct contrast of the months they'd spent in the village.

"Did you ever sleep with her?"

His head jerked up at her soft whisper.

The filthy curse that had been about to fly from his mouth arrested when he saw that her question was in earnest. The wariness in her expression, as if she were bracing for the answer, the way she seemed to retreat into herself… It galled him that even when she was in the wrong, Ariana made the most primal, possessive, protective urges come out in him.

"You lost the right to ask me that." But her question rankled. "Are you asking me if I cheated on you when we were together?"

"No." Her immediate denial seemed to surprise her just as much as it did him. "I don't think so."

He leaned back and wrapped his arm around the seat. Wanting to touch her became secondary to the questions building up in his head. "I'm beginning to realize you did not think much of me when we were together."

"No. I thought the world of you, actually," she replied in that honest way she used to have. So where had it all gone wrong? "I knew…" Her gaze was serious when she met his. "I know that you wouldn't have cheated on me.

"I meant before…before we met. Or maybe after." She sighed. "But like you said, I've no right to ask that question."

Just as easily as she provoked his ire, she mollified it. "Petra is my employee. A woman who depends on me for her livelihood. You're aware that my sister, Eleni, was born of an affair between Theos and my nanny. Do you think anything could provoke me into repeating his scandalous, abusive behavior?"

Ariana looked away. There could be a hundred women ready to fall at his feet among his employees like Petra, a hundred more who adored the very ground their Crown Prince walked on. He didn't notice the women as anything but staff members.

Petra was no more than his three aides, who were thankfully all men, no more than his security guard Thomas, no more than his tailor, or his fitness instructor or his chef.

Another cog in the complex machinery that made his life run smoothly.

And yet… "You worshipped your father."

From the moment they had returned to the capital city, Ariana had seen the frightening truth. The man she had married was really no different from the cold, ruthless King Theos who had looked at her just as her father had done—as if she were a failure. A stain that had to be hidden far away from the gilded brightness of his palace.

"There were days when you were frighteningly similar to him." As if the world and the people in it were accessories to his own life. They were present only to provide his life with certain value.

Even Ariana had been another cog, just a pleasurable one.

His self-imposed isolation at the village, she'd made the mistake of thinking that was his life. Instead it had been a stolen pocket of time.

He laid his head back now and rubbed his jaw with the base of his palm. A bristly stubble had come in since this afternoon. Coupled with the dark shadows under his eyes, he looked a mess. Tired and almost imperfect.

A twinge of ache settled in Ari's chest. It was that same ferocious protectiveness for a man who owned the world, who didn't need it that had led her into following him into fire. Had she gained no sense in ten years?

"Because at the height of his regime my father had been a magnificent statesman. Nik had a better measure of him far before I did. He hated that Theos alienated him from me." The regret in his words stunned Ariana. "All I saw in Theos was the man who equipped me to rule Drakon. A man who'd worked tirelessly for years to make me perfect. A man who only wanted me to have the world and rule it.

"Only later did I realize that in his personal life, Theos was a manipulative monster."

Ariana bit her lip. She didn't have much time. Not if she wanted to stop him from parading her next to him come coronation day in front of all of Drakon. "I would have given anything for you to see that side of King Theos back then, Andreas."

"It must be so tempting to put this all on him, but he only aided you, Ariana."

She caught his hands on the table and laced her fingers through his. To anchor him to her, to not lose him to the memory of a cruel old man. "That's not true. He knew everything that was going on between us. Every fight, every disagreement. Petra relayed everything to him."

"He was a ruthless bastard, yes, but do not put your faults on him."

When he jerked his hand away, she held fast. For a man who spent hours at his desk signing treaties, he'd always had such rough hands.

"Andreas, it was never my idea to fake… I never agreed to pretend that I was dead. I only signed the papers dissolving our marriage. I took the money your father offered, yes, but I…"

He pulled his hand away from her as if she was poison.

Ariana stood up and blocked him. "If you're determined to make us walk through this hell again, at least listen to my side."

His hands fisted. "How did you realize what he had done if you didn't even look back?"

"I received all the paperwork through a lawyer. God, I didn't even completely understand the ramifications for a month. I panicked and called Giannis who told me what Theos had done behind my back."

Such bleak rage emanated in his black eyes that Ariana stepped back. "Of course, you kept in touch with your little security guard friend."

The insinuation in his tone cut bone deep. "Giannis was my friend. He understood what I was going through. He..."

"What happened when Giannis told you of Theos's convoluted lies? Why didn't you call me then?"

"It was too late."

"Too late to tell me that you were alive?"

"Your engagement had been announced. I was not in a good—"

"What, Ari?" His voice caught, his words clipped like hard gravel. "You thought I deserved to continue believing that my young wife was dead. Probably at my own father's hands or because of my own negligence, of which you'd been complaining for months."

"You thought he killed me?"

"Yes." The haunted look she'd thought she'd imagined was back in his eyes. The pain there...it was a knife in her chest. "He didn't hide his satisfaction that you were out of my life for good. After all his rages for weeks because I had ruined our legacy—because I had..." He ran a hand through his hair roughly. "It was the first time I saw Theos for what he could be.

"But it was only a suspicion. I threw myself into my work, I alienated Nik, I hurt Eleni. I thought I was going mad, suspecting my own father of a terrible thing.

"Theos hated the thought of you as my wife. It was as much a shock to him as it was to me that I...married you. That I could make such an unprecedented, uncharacteristic decision with my life."

"Then why did you, Andreas?" The question burst from her lips. A question she should have asked instead of running away. "You could have had me for as long as you wanted and walked away. I wouldn't have made a peep."

"I told you. You were a virgin that night and I didn't use protection."

"We could have waited to see if there were any consequences."

"I seduced you!"

"You took me to bed after I threw myself at you for months. Repeatedly."

"Still, you were eighteen, my father's neglected ward. You had no one in the world to look after your interests. What I did was—"

"Don't you dare take that away from me. I wanted you, God, I needed you just as much you needed me that night.

"But after, you…could have walked away. You could have paid me off. You could have… Why marry the shallow, ditzy, reckless failure that I was? Why marry me when you knew what your real life was like, when you knew how wrong I was for you?"

His breath was rough, his eyes blazing with an unholy light. "Because I got used to it."

Her heart thumped so hard against her rib cage, Ari could hardly breathe. "Used to what?"

"Used to being adored by you. Used to being loved by you." Shoulders tense, he rubbed his nape. For a man who exuded arrogant self-confidence out of every pore, the gesture was disconcertingly hesitant. "I was the center of your universe and it made me lose sight of who I was and who you were.

"Thanks to Theos, I had tasted every kind of power that was to be had in the world. But you, Ariana…your adoration for me even as you mocked everything I was in this world, it was a drug I couldn't give up on.

"I thought I could keep that, keep you for myself. One selfish indulgence that I would allow myself.

"It was the biggest mistake of my life. In that, Theos was right."

Ariana wound her arms around her trembling body, something deflating out of her. Hope, after all this time. Hope that he would admit that he'd married her because he'd loved her, too. That he had been shattered at the loss of her not because he felt responsible or guilty but something else.

"Then put a stop to that mistake. Don't continue the farce of our marriage."

"What do you suggest? That I marry another woman, make her my Queen and keep you on the side?

"Should I give you the place you're so determined to prove is yours, Ari? Should I visit you in the dark as if you were a paid whore, a kept mistress my father encouraged me to make of you?

"Would you have me become the monster Theos and you made me out to be? Because nothing has changed, *pethi mou*. I still want you with that same madness.

"You're still a weakness—the only one that I can't overcome."

Her hands boldly reached for his face, the scent of her skin a familiar twining in his blood.

With his fingers on her wrist, he stayed her movements. He could not bear to be touched by her. Not yet, and not like this. Not when he felt like a cauldron of volatile emotions, not when all he wanted was to push her into the bed, and bury himself in her.

"I shouldn't have run away like that, not with his help. But...but it was not a bid for freedom because I got bored with you or because I was shallow enough to fall in love with another man who was nothing but my friend. It was not a fickle game."

"No?"

"No. I...loved you. You. But loving you... I realized, slowly began to kill me and in the end, I chose survival."

Her words pinged through his mind like a bullet ricocheting through a closed room. Puncturing and tearing, scraping and scorching the walls of his mind.

He wanted to hate her as he had done for two years. He'd opened the Pandora's box of their relationship willingly and it seemed there was no end to the things that could come crawling out.

Things Andreas wasn't sure he wanted to face. "How was I killing you?"

Utter helplessness filled her face. And it was seeing that in her eyes, when Ariana never stopped fighting, that made him believe everything she'd said.

"It doesn't matter anymore," she whispered.

The pilot broke the tense silence with an update that they were landing soon.

Between mourning her death for eight years and the discovery of her treachery, he had forgotten that he was at the root of this.

The enormity of his marrying Ariana had only sunk through when his father had confronted him. Had shown him the hopeless state of the treasury of Drakon, the mounting national debt. The alliance that Theos had carefully cultivated with Gabriel Marquez, to make his sister the Queen of Drakon, crumbling to dust.

So he'd immediately tried to right his world.

He'd been prepared to do anything for Drakon but not give her up. She was only a small part of his life, he'd told his father. After all, the Queen's role was only titular in Drakon.

For the first month, it had worked. She became his escape from the weight of his nation's problems. From his father's spiraling moods and sudden rages. Then slowly, things had changed.

It was as if he'd lived in two different realities, one as

the Crown Prince and one as the man obsessed with his young wife.

As long as they didn't merge, he'd convinced himself his world would be all right.

As long as he didn't let her take over his life, as long as she meant nothing more to him than physical relief at the end of a hard day, a pleasure he looked forward to at night, as long as he didn't let her disrupt his duties ever again… *Thee mou*, he'd made so many promises to Theos just to keep her.

I chose survival.

Like a bone-deep bruise, those words lingered.

Was he prepared to face what he'd done to make his bright, cheerful, eighteen-year-old wife flee the moment his back had been turned, to learn that he was the one responsible for putting those shadows in Ari's eyes?

Suddenly, he questioned the sanity of everything he'd been doing since he'd found she was alive.

CHAPTER FIVE

Miles of neatly manicured land greeted Ariana as the jet taxied into the private airstrip and they disembarked. The same airstrip where King Theos's staff had seen her into a jet that left Drakon ten years ago.

It wasn't as bitterly cold as it had been in Colorado. But the air was just as crisp and fresh. In the distance, the outline of the mountain range made the perfect horizon. Tall palm trees dotted a neat perimeter around the airstrip.

As Ari stood there, a strange thread of homecoming rang through her. She hadn't thought she'd missed Drakon but she had. Or maybe it was the sense of purpose that she'd found in herself that changed her view.

She wasn't swinging from guilt over her mother's death to the sudden, terrifying taste of freedom. Not running away from the fear that maybe her father had been right and she was good for nothing.

Suddenly, she was glad she was here. If only she could throw every derogatory word her father had called her about being a failure in his face, if only her mother were here to see that Ari had made something of herself, that Ari was utterly happy…

But you've not been utterly happy. Focused, dedicated, busy to the point of exhaustion and restless. But not happy, never happy.

That girl who'd laughed recklessly, who'd loved so generously, she'd just stifled her, desperate to avoid that heartbreak again. As if to punish herself for losing her baby boy.

But had it been anything more than a half-life?

Had it been anything but penance?

Three bulletproof cars arrived on the curb, the black-

and-gold flags whipping in the wind. Three separate teams waited for Andreas's attention, their curiosity evident in their scrutiny of her.

Her every action was going to be scrutinized and sanitized, her every word dissected to ensure it measured up against Andreas's image. But no one was going to intimidate her this time.

Andreas stood before her, his eyes holding hers captive.

She shivered and was immediately covered in a warm, long coat that fell past her knees.

Sandalwood and his body heat combined to make a potent drug emanating from the thick wool. The familiarly comforting scent curled through her.

His hand around her shoulders caught them up in their own little world. So close, she could see the tiny golden flecks in his eyes. Feel the wiry strength of his lean body.

She stood mutely as he settled the coat around her shoulders and buttoned up the first couple buttons so that her chest was adequately protected.

Her heart thudded when he lifted the ring finger of her left hand. The tiny point-one-carat diamond struggled to throw off even a spark. With gentle movements that suggested he loathed putting her through any discomfort, a startling contrast as he ripped the fabric of her very life apart, he pulled the ring off her finger.

His jet-black gaze held hers in a possessive dare as he threw the ring into the acreage behind them.

Ariana jerked but his hand around her nape arrested her. Even for her five-nine height, he had to bend down. "Welcome home, Ariana," he said, in a silky voice at her ear, before touching his mouth to the corner of hers.

His lips were warm against her skin, sending pockets of heat through her. Her entire body trembled at the searing contact, her hands rising to his chest automatically. To hold him close, to soak in his warmth.

She let her hands fall to her sides, heat swamping her face.

Andreas would always have this power over her, this… ability to turn her inside out. Accepting that was strangely calming.

She needed closure just as much as Andreas did.

She needed to figure out if it would always be a half-life without him. And if it was, would the little Andreas was offering be enough this time?

Because there was one thing she knew.

Andreas Drakos could never love.

The drive back to the palace was long but thankfully not intimate. Three of his staff, including Petra, joined them in the expansive limo, leaving Ariana to sit opposite him.

His cuffs rolled back to reveal strong forearms. Ariana followed the column of his throat, his chest tapering to a lean waist and then to his legs stretched out. His trousers cleanly molded the length of his muscular thighs.

Needing a reprieve from that overwhelming masculinity, Ariana leaned back and closed her eyes.

His words, assertive and rapid-fire, assaulted her senses.

Andreas answered questions and asked his own. Matters that would have been over her head and, quite honestly, boring, made more sense to Ariana this time.

Now, instead of being told by everyone how rapier-sharp Andreas's mind was, she saw it in play. His memory was astounding, his attention to detail when he was mired in so many matters awe-inspiring. She listened in fascination as he took the first draft of a speech written by one of his press team and shredded it to pieces by calling out clichéd phrases and for not addressing any of the scare rhetoric that the media had been doling out about him following Theos's madness in the last few years.

For the first time in decades, the populace was questioning what the royal house was doing for the people.

It was his coronation speech, Ariana realized, with unwise curiosity.

Absolute conviction rocked in his every gesture. "Drakon enters a new era with me at the helm. We shall not rest on the past laurels of the House of Drakos anymore. The royal house will begin the process of decoupling from the cabinet in coming years."

Ariana scoffed. The sound was like an elephant blaring in the quiet interior.

"Do you have something to say, Ariana?"

"Nothing you would want said in company, Your Highness," she replied sweetly.

"We do not want my staff to believe you're afraid of me, do we?"

That put her spine up like nothing could. Even as she'd been utterly overwhelmed by him back then, she'd never let him intimidate her. There was a distinction, an important one they both knew.

She sat forward, looking him in the eye. "Decoupling the House of Drakos and the Drakon cabinet? Andreas Drakos walking away from power to rule the lives of millions? That's like a lion giving up its ability to hunt.

"That power is in your blood, your bones, your very skin. You will never do it."

"I'm not giving up power so much as I'm redistributing it into the right hands," he said surprisingly receptive to her criticism. "I want more checks and balances. The Crown Council was supposed to do that, but Theos controlled them with his power and wealth. Until there was no one to question his executive command of the cabinet.

"Nikandros already has the economy of Drakon in his hand. He's always been the financial genius.

"Eleni, if Gabriel lets her accept my proposal, will become the formal liaison between the palace and the hundreds of charities we support."

"Your brother and sister? That's your power distribution—other members of the House of Drakos? You think they will go against your wishes?"

"You would understand if you had..." He bit his accusation off, aware of the staff watching them with a hungry fascination. "My father hoarded power, until it drove him to madness. Until he began to think of even me as his enemy.

"I don't intend to let that happen to me.

"After all, I have a personal life now and I intend to enjoy it."

As much as she wanted to fight it, the truth of it shone in his eyes. "Control is everything to you."

In the intimacy of the dark night, even as he had shocked her with his demands and his carnality, he'd not once let her lead. Even as he'd lost himself in the pleasures of sex, it had still been very much calculated.

The very devil glinted in his eyes. "Is that another challenge then, *agapita*?"

She felt a collective hiss of exhale from the two women in the car. Not that she could blame them.

He's mine, she wanted to say, that wildness she'd tried to bury surfacing with a vengeance. Maybe it was the air of her homeland, maybe it was facing Andreas as the woman she was now, but restlessness slithered under her skin.

"Don't make promises—" she raised a brow, and almost pulled it off "—that you cannot keep, Your Highness."

His eyes shone with unholy mirth, deep grooves dug into his cheeks. His brows went all off-kilter. "Worried that you might not be able to resist me after all?"

A reluctant smile curved her lips and she looked out the window.

The outline of the mountain range became vague as the car entered the city, the white stone structure of the King's Palace sitting atop the small hill emerging ahead.

Was he serious about all these changes? What had brought it on?

The more she spent time with him, the more she was realizing that something had changed in him. But the very idea of revealing the last bit of truth she had hidden, the condemnation in his eyes if he learned of what she had lost… Fear skated over her spine.

They arrived at the King's Palace with very little fanfare.

The lack of his family's presence was conspicuous and Ariana was caught between relief and a bit of disappointment, if she were honest.

She had obsessively followed every bit of palace gossip over the last few years. The changes it seemed Andreas was determined to bring to Drakon. Even the rising sentiment against the once-beloved Crown Prince.

She knew that the Daredevil Prince, Nikandros, had returned to Drakon after a years-long rift between him and Andreas. That Nikandros had married the ex-soccer player Mia Rodriguez and had two infant children.

That Eleni Drakos, dubbed with the cheap moniker the Plain Princess of Drakon for years, had recently married Gabriel Marquez—Isabella Marquez's brother, the same woman Andreas had been engaged to after Ariana fled.

Were these changes Andreas had brought out too?

Two security guards accompanied her through the miles of corridors.

Barely a staff of five, Andreas's personal retinue greeted them. She was shown into a set of rooms done in elegant creams and mauves. A lounge, a bathroom that spanned the square footage of her legal aid agency, and a massive bed that was the pride of place in the bedroom.

"Do not even think of running, Ari," Andreas suddenly whispered at her ear and Ariana jerked.

Her hand fluttered to his chest and she kept it there now, loving the solid feel of him under it. Needing suddenly the reassurance of his presence before he was lost to her in the maze of the palace.

"Do not give me reason to, Your Highness," she quipped back, trying to hide her elation that he hadn't forgotten about her as soon as they had set foot in the palace. That, this time, he had actually brought her to the palace and not hidden her away.

God, but she was pathetic that even the smallest crumbs from him made her heart dance.

He didn't smile. But covered her hand with his, the long fingers tangling with hers. "Rest up for a couple of hours." His gaze caressed her face, as if looking for proof that she wouldn't faint again. "My family wishes to meet you."

"More people who hate me, yay," she said, a sudden panic seizing her chest. "Andreas, couldn't we—"

"No, Ariana. I have defied every tenet I had for my personal life and pushed every Crown Council member that hates me to the edge by bringing you here." A dark smile touched his eyes. "You're ten years late, *pethi mou*. Drakon wants its queen and I want my wife."

Ariana watched him leave, but instead of fear, a fierce determination filled her.

She had gone from a train wreck to something hopefully akin to a woman who knew her own mind.

Was it possible for the Crown Prince of Drakon to change, too?

CHAPTER SIX

"WELL, IS SHE HERE? What does she do? Where did she go after she left you?" Eleni demanded the moment Andreas walked into the Green Room at King's Palace.

His head was pounding after the quick report he'd had from his aides.

Nikandros had been right. The situation with his popularity ratings was much worse than even he'd anticipated.

Soon, he had to find a way to turn the sentiment that was rising against him. "Calm down, Eleni," Gabriel muttered. Andreas felt a flash of sympathy for his brother-in-law. It had to be hard to see Eleni continue like the little dynamo she was when she was pregnant.

"She's a lawyer," Andreas answered while accepting the drink Nik had poured him. "She set up a legal aid agency with the money she took from Father."

Gabriel whistled, a devilish light in his green eyes. "The controlling bastard that you are, I always thought you needed a woman with steel balls. A woman who could perhaps be your saving grace. She sounds like it."

"I didn't realize I needed saving."

The insufferable smile slid from Gabriel's mouth. "You do. Before you end up like your father."

Nothing fractured his self-control these days more than being compared to Theos. "I interfered in Eleni's life because I wanted her to be happy. Because I knew what Theos did to her and I wanted to do right by her."

"Leave it, Gabriel. It is his life," said Nik.

"Being a member of the illustrious House of Drakos doesn't mean you're above the law," Mia added, glaring at Nik.

"She gave him little choice when she decided to marry another man, Mia." Eleni's loyalty for her brothers had always been absolute. The scowl on Gabriel's face made Andreas grin despite the open bashing of his morals. "If it came out later that the King of Drakon's secret first wife had committed bigamy, it would—"

"It would have made the scandal of the century for the populace of Drakon," said that husky voice Andreas would know in the darkest of nights.

Ariana walked into the evening lounge where they had all gathered for predinner drinks with the aplomb of a queen. Every cell in him came to attention, his skin tight over his muscles. There was a bright glitter in her eyes.

"A headline that could rival even the stories about that first band of warriors conquering the dragon. And believe me, your people need new material. That dragon lore..." Ariana rolled her eyes when Eleni, a staunch believer in all myths, dragons and the superiority of the House of Drakos, gasped. "It gets boring as hell after a while. Not to mention, it isn't something to crow about to the world."

Stunned silence met her prosaic announcement.

Disbelief etched on his family's faces. Andreas flexed his fingers trying to forget the feel of her silky skin.

"Andreas," she said, "introduce your family. After all, I did answer your royal summons." She turned to the rest of them and smiled. "Apparently, ten years has only made Andreas's penchant for control worse."

Nikandros broke the ice. "We didn't give him a choice, Ms. Sakis." He took her hand in his and shook it. "Welcome to Drakon, I'm—"

"The Daredevil Prince," she said with that wide smile of hers. Andreas scowled. She leaned into Nik, her voice lowered to a whisper that wasn't quite one. "Come, Nikandros," she said with that easy familiarity that was second nature to her, that made Andreas want to pull her to his side, "you really don't expect me to believe that Andreas bowed to pressure from someone else, do you?"

Eleni bristled. "Is it hard to believe that we would want to meet our brother's wife?"

"As far as I remember, Andreas did not share a close relationship with you or Nikandros. I have mostly found that he is incapable of nurturing relationships."

Andreas stared into his drink, knowing that she was right. It was only in the last few years that he'd begun undoing the damage he'd done to his brother and sister.

He had still made mistakes, as Gabriel had pointed out.

"Maybe you do not," Eleni replied, sending Ariana a cool look, "know our brother as well as you think you do."

Her nostrils flared, her chin set in stubborn lines, Ariana looked like she wanted to argue. In the end, she shrugged.

"Point to the House of Drakos," she added, with a wink at Gabriel.

Gabriel took her outstretched hand into his while Mia walked over to Ariana's side and introduced herself.

Within minutes, Ariana had Mia and Gabriel roaring with laughter. Brows raised, Nik conveyed his own surprise about her with a twitching mouth.

Irate at his brother's humor, Andreas turned to watch her. Acknowledged the fact that physical possession of Ariana was never going to be enough.

The cap-sleeved floral knee-length dress in white and pink with a string of pearls jarred with the elegant ambience of the palace as he accompanied Ariana to dinner. Her hair was in a riotous knot at the back of her head, wavy tendrils already falling away from it and framing her gamine face. Bright red lipstick made her full-lipped mouth stand out even more than usual amidst her stark features.

Even for a man who rarely understood fashion, Andreas was immediately aware that the whole outfit and makeup and what he knew of Ariana just didn't gel.

When she moved to the other end, he forced her to sit on his right. Forced her to brush her body against his as she sat down. Still, she wouldn't spare him a look.

Nothing however could leave Ariana daunted for too long. The moment the first course was served, she said, "I know what you must all be thinking. Not only is she an almost bigamist, but she has the most atrocious sense of style, *ne*?"

Mia just stared back with a rueful glint in her eye while Eleni flushed.

"You see, Andreas's secretary—who very efficiently arranged these clothes for me because your brother kidnapped me in my torn wedding dress—and I have this cold war thing going on. From years back.

"Petra is making a point that everyone loyal to Andreas is dying to make right now. That I'm not fit to polish your brother's handmade Italian boots much less to be his wife. A fact that was drilled into me with a sledgehammer in Version One of our marriage."

"By our father," Nik finished for her.

She shrugged. "In your father's defense, King Theos already knew from my father what a failure I was. I got thrown out of three finishing schools, ran away from home three times, embarrassed and humiliated my father in a hundred different ways.

"For a military general whose sparkling reputation and pride were most important, I was a huge letdown. I had neither academic smarts, nor did I fit well with his friends' high-achieving children.

"I was an utter failure, a fact he constantly reminded me of."

Andreas stilled with his glass of water halfway to his mouth. The thought of Ariana running away sat like a boulder on his chest. *Christos*, he'd never known. He'd never even asked her about her life with her parents. "Why did you run away?"

"Whenever I… I defied him, my father locked me in my room." A vacant expression emanated in her eyes. "Probably not a huge thing. But he would cut me off completely for days. I would be given food and water. But nothing else. He thought it character-building.

"I found the silence…unbearable. All it did was make me resolute that I'd never be caught again.

"Anyway, when King Theos inherited my guardianship, I don't think he knew what to do with me.

"He sent me off to a corner of Drakon until I turned eighteen. Only a few months later, there I was, his worst nightmare.

"To find out what his dear heir had done…to see me stand at his doorstep as the future Queen…" A shiver went through her.

"Theos went ballistic," Nikandros finished for her.

Eleni asked, "What did Father do?"

For the first time since she had blown into the room like a summer storm, Ariana met his gaze. "I was installed in an apartment, away from the gilded walls of the palace, a stain to be hidden away. Theos's team put me on a diet of history lessons, etiquette lessons, posture training. I was cut off from the few friends I had. Petra and her team had nothing but contempt for me. I was not allowed to leave the apartment. I was not allowed to contact anyone for fear of leaking who I was to Andreas.

"I was in a cage again. And my jailer was the man I loved, the man I had trusted."

The clatter of his fork against the plate sounded like an explosion in the room.

Her chin tilted up boldly, taut lines carved around her mouth, she stared at him.

Nik's expression became haunted. "I'm aware of our father's routine to mold people, Ms. Sakis. His penchant to strip one of every good thing. Only Andreas could ever bear his rigorous requirements and stay standing." He turned an accusing look toward Andreas. "Where were you when this was happening?"

"If your father thought to mold me," Ariana answered with a glittering anger in her eyes, "it was only with Andreas's encouragement. Andreas visited me when he needed—" their eyes met, and he saw the dirty truth there "—a *diversion* from his busy life," she finished and looked away.

Why the hell hadn't she told him any of this back then?

Because he hadn't been available. Because he had never even asked.

Because from the moment Andreas had realized the magnitude of his mistake in marrying her, he'd tried to limit the damage. To the crown or to himself, he didn't know to this day.

"It was for your own good," he said, trying to fight the guilt that settled on him. For the first time in his life, trying to offer justification. "You had neither the education nor the background to survive in my world. You would have been shredded to pieces.

"I had to salvage the situation. I had to make you worthy of—"

Her chin reared down, her body tense. "Worthy of you, Andreas? I never pretended to be anything but what I am."

No, she hadn't. She hadn't even wanted to marry him. Only he had seduced her into it.

This was what he had done—clipped her wings, caged her, and for Ariana, for the girl who had defied her father's abusive edicts, for the girl who had loved so freely, freedom was everything. She had loved him and he had choked the life out of her.

His father had been right. Andreas only knew destruction.

He'd wanted answers and here they were. The rest of the dinner proceeded in a strained manner, Andreas unable to contribute anything more. Unable to see past the haunted look in Ariana's eyes.

Grappling with the magnitude of the mistake he'd made in marrying her and refusing to give her up, he'd retreated from her. He had given her over to his father to be molded into whatever the hell Theos thought she should be.

All he'd wanted was to get his life back to normal. Before he'd lost sight of what and who he was, and what he was not capable of.

He had delegated her to a small part in his life. The relief from the loneliness, a respite from the increasing demands of his father, an escape from the fact that Theos's dementia had begun to manifest even back then, making him feel the burden of Drakon on his shoulders.

"The dragon lore, Ms. Sakis?" Eleni piped up just as Ariana excused herself. "A band of warriors defeated the dragon and made its treasure their own. They provided land and riches to their community. What is there to not crow about?"

Ariana's gaze pinned him. "You never told anyone what we found in that old library?"

Andreas shook his head, a savage clamor inside him at how easily she had used *we*. At the light that came on in her eyes when she spoke of those months. At the connection that seemed to have survived between them despite the destruction wrought.

She moved toward him, unconscious of her own movements, he was sure. The weight of her brown gaze, the concern in them, pinned him. "You never finished your book?"

"No," he replied, shying away from the shock in her eyes.

"What book is this?" Nikandros asked, his gaze shifting between them.

Her fingers pulled his wrist. “You never shared it with anyone?”

Feeling as if his entire insides were being pulled up for display, Andreas stepped away from her. From the emotion ringing in her eyes. “No.” When he had returned and thought her dead, the last thing on his mind had been his research. And after a few years, everything relating to that time had become far too private and precious. A part of his life—*their life*—that he wasn’t willing to share with anyone.

“But it was your dream, Andreas,” she whispered. The loss of it shone in her eyes, in the tremble of her lips.

Had his dream meant that much to her then? *Thee mou*, he couldn’t tolerate this turmoil within. Couldn’t stand the weight of his guilt bearing down upon him. Anger had been so much better.

“Andreas came to that village,” she said turning toward his family, her voice pitched carefully, “because he’d found a trail to the warriors’ first settlement leading back hundreds of years there. We…” She colored under his gaze. “He found a manuscript that was written in one of the old Hellenic languages. He spent weeks trying to translate it.

“You know that Andreas can read and write in eight languages, right?”

Everybody in the room looked stunned. But she had eyes for no one else. Nor he for anyone but her. “There was a price to pay for defeating the dragon so easily. In fact, that manuscript suggested the leader of that band hadn’t so much defeated it as made a deal with it.”

“A deal?” Eleni asked.

“The dragon demanded a price. The warrior was to sacrifice his wife to its fiery jaws and it would relinquish the treasure.” Her brown eyes shone with a wet brilliance.

And suddenly Andreas realized why she was so emotional about the story. Why she looked as if she was about to break like a piece of glass.

She saw him as the head of that fierce band of warriors. The man who had so ruthlessly sacrificed his wife for duty and glory, a woman who had loved him completely.

"The warrior accepted," she finished. "And became the first King.

"He was given the name Drakos and when he married again, his family became the House of Drakos."

A long sigh left her, her body almost weaving at the spot. Finally, she lifted her gaze away from him. But the recriminations he had seen there had already latched on to him.

"There you are, Mrs. Marquez. That is why I don't think it is something to celebrate. But of course Drakonites must have their tales.

"And House of Drakos its fairy-tale reputation to live up to."

Her head held high, she left the room without looking back, leaving Andreas standing stunned.

He *had* sacrificed her, hadn't he? He had treated her as a possession to be used when he needed it, a toy he could wind up when he wanted to play.

He'd given no thought, ever, to her dreams, her fears. Even to her needs. *Christos*, he hadn't treated her any better than a staff member. Or a mistress, hired for his pleasure.

It had all been about what she could give him. About his desires and wants.

Gabriel was right. He had been, he still was, just like his father. Using people for his own means, hurting the ones closest to him. It had always been hard for him to see beyond his own needs, his privilege. To see anything that he didn't control as a weakness.

It had never been about Ariana. It had always been about what she made him feel. What she brought to his life.

Now he saw the distinction between what he had done

to her versus how Nikandros had been ready to sacrifice his own happiness for Mia's. Now he understood why Gabriel had been willing to love Eleni even knowing that she might not love him.

The thought of being that vulnerable felt like needles under his skin.

Had Theos destroyed his ability to care for anyone but himself?

Was he willing to do the same to Ariana again?

Ariana left the dining salon and stumbled into another vast room. She needed to catch her breath. She needed a reprieve from everything Andreas made her feel, despite her every effort to stay rational.

Pink Carrera marble as far as she could see, claw-toothed arm chairs, velvet-upholstered chaise longues, the luxury was unprecedented, understated.

Gilded portraits looked down from the walls, witness to every event. It seemed the walls themselves were seeped with the history of the House of Drakos. And yet, she knew that Andreas had had a quiet happiness in that small village that he had not found here.

Something reverberated in her at being inside the palace. She'd been denied this the last time. Because she had been deemed unfit for its hallowed halls. Denied her rightful place by his side.

Did she want it this time? Did she want to carve a place for herself in Drakon by his side?

Turning around, she saw Andreas, leaning against the high arch, his gaze studying her intently. Hands tucked into his pockets, dark shadow outlining his jawline, he was heartbreakingly gorgeous.

And determined to keep her in his life. The little fact weaved its own web around her.

"You look… I don't know what that look is, to be precise," she heard him say as she walked around the room, checking where the myriad doors led.

She stilled, stunned that he had recognized her…confusion.

Slowly, she turned around, ready to face him. "I thought you would be furious with me."

He didn't move, just raised a brow.

"I didn't mean to…wash our dirty linen in front of everyone."

"Then why did you?"

She ran a fingertip against the arm of a huge wingback chair. "Being here…unsettled me. Seeing your family look at me with accusing eyes…disconcerted me. I was ashamed of what I did and it just came pouring out.

"I… I've never been part of a big family and if they're going to be mine, I need them to understand that what I did was cowardly but not malicious."

"I'm not angry, Ariana. At least not with you."

Her head jerked up, their gazes colliding across the vast room. Was it that simple to give his forgiveness?

He shrugged, sensing her disbelief. "My family knows what Theos made me into. You've already turned them."

Only Andreas could ever bear his rigorous requirements and stay standing.

Nikandros's flyaway remark hit her hard.

"Nik? What did he mean by it? What did your father do to you?"

"It's irrelevant, Ari."

"It is not, Andreas. Our pasts have made us this. We hurt each other…because of what was done to us. Please…let me understand, too."

His face tightened, his gaze far away. "He isolated me from everyone else. I had no friends, no playmates. I was not even allowed a pet, because my father thought it would weaken me.

"He put me through rigorous physical routines, harsh enough to chill a grown man, much less a boy of ten, because he thought I was becoming a bookworm. He thought the Crown Prince could not be all brains and no brawn.

"He made me join a military unit at fifteen because he thought it would toughen me up.

"He sought to make me invincible."

And he had, in a way.

Ariana sat in the chair, stunned, the implications whirling through her head. That's why there had always been such a wall around him. In the beginning, she had thought it was his station in life, his privilege that made him oblivious to the world.

"No wonder you thrived on the isolation in that cabin." The words fell from her mouth without conscious thought.

"I do not thrive on solitude, as much as it is all I've ever known," he offered. "For years, I had no one for company except books and tutors and my father. I had no other role in life except being the Crown Prince. Not even a son to Theos. Not a brother, not a friend.

"I rarely even heard anyone call me by my name. It was always Your Highness.

"I learned to keep myself happy with my books or go crazy.

"I was not allowed to see Nik unless they were supervised visits. Anything that was assumed could be a weakness, anything that I could depend on, I was forced to get over it.

"Then slowly as I grew older, I began to chafe at Theos's restrictions. Drakon was still everything to me but Camille, Nik's mom, made me see that I could have a life outside it, too. Then Eleni, who was always there, who never asked for anything. I began to realize how different life could have been. But it was too late by then.

"Being alone became second nature.

"It became who I was."

She felt like crying. "How did you survive it?"

"How did you survive being locked up?"

Even having known the best part of him, she had so easily stereotyped Andreas into that uncaring role. In her naive stupidity, she had barely even tried to understand the pressure he must have faced from Theos, the duress of having to fix the gaping hole of Drakon's economy.

She had always blamed Andreas for knowing her so little. Had she been any better? But suddenly, it was as if she was seeing the true Andreas for the first time.

The man at the village, and the Crown Prince—it had always seemed like two polarizing opposites that she could never understand. She had struggled to fathom how she'd misjudged him so terribly.

He had wronged her, yes. But she had done just the same.

Suddenly, she wanted the past cleared between them. She wanted a fresh start. She walked back to him, purpose in every step. "Do you believe me? That it was never my intention to deceive you?"

His jet-black gaze held hers for what felt like an eternity. Something had changed in his perception of her, she realized now. The truth of their marriage? "Does it matter to you that I believe you?"

Frustration flared and she forgot to temper her response. "Of course it does."

Only when he smiled, a soft light in his eyes, did she realize that she had betrayed herself in the now.

What he thought of her had always mattered to her.

Still mattered, it seemed.

He traced her cheek with his knuckles. As if that small fracture in her resistance of him was a prize. As if he would give her the world if only she became that Ari again.

I got used to being loved by you.

What did that truly mean? she wondered now. For a man

who'd had everything, had her love meant something? Did he want that again?

His gaze searched hers, as if he wanted to see through to her soul. "Because it alleviates your guilt?"

Her hands rose to his chest. His heart thundered under her palm. She wanted to pull away the layers of clothes, feel the silk of warm skin tightly stretched over muscle. Emotions battered at her from all sides, and only this awareness of him was constant, this heat and hardness of his body the only real thing. "No, because I…never wanted to hurt you. Because I need you to know, even after all these years."

He didn't say she hadn't hurt him, and in his silence, in the things he said without saying anything, Ariana found a world of hope. The moment stretched between them, wanting and morphing, his heart thundering away under her palm, her own beating a thousand a minute.

A moment between the past and the future.

His fingers crawled to her nape, not pressing, not moving. Just touching. His other hand moved to her hip, the tips of those long fingers reaching the jut of her hip bones.

Her entire being wanted to melt in his arms. To curl up in his heat. God, this was it. This was exactly what had been missing from her life.

What her heart and soul had desperately needed.

She had needed him to understand the truth of what she had done. But given up all hope that he would look at her like this…like she still mattered.

"Andreas? Please, you have to—"

Gently, he pushed her back until he could see into her eyes. "Yes, *pethi mou*. I believe that all you did was run away the moment I turned my back," he replied, twisting her words.

She sensed his confusion and something more in that. A loss that she hadn't stood and fought for them? She waited for him to say more, to call her a coward even.

After all, she'd declared again and again that she loved him, hadn't she?

But no more came from him.

"Your father went through an elaborate scheme to make me unforgivable in your eyes. He couldn't have been worried that you would chase me. You'd have hated me too much."

Something glittered in his gaze. "Are you asking me or telling me?"

It was one of those moments that defined life. A door opening. Years of tightly suppressed hope unfurling. "I'm asking you," she whispered, hiding her face in his chest.

God, she was so tired of staying strong. Of…denying, even now, that he meant something to her, after all these years.

"I would have come after you, yes." A long sigh fell from his lips. "There's no moving forward without facing the past, is there?"

A rush of tenderness filled her. "No."

He did care. He cared that he had hurt her. He cared that he had driven her away. Too little, too late, but God, she hadn't been without culpability. She hadn't made it easy with her flights of rage and her sulks and that fear that she had fallen in love with a man so horribly wrong for her. So much a despot like her father.

"I'm sorry for what I let him do to you."

But what about what you did? she wanted to ask. *What about your incapability to love me? To see me as anything other than an obsession or a weakness. Incapable of giving me a tiny, tiny piece of your heart.*

But she wouldn't be, she *wasn't* that needy girl anymore.

She didn't need to be loved by him to know her worth. Maybe she'd even lost her own ability to love, to trust someone else with her happiness, the ability to share fully of herself.

Seeing her son's small, unmoving body had done something to her.

She had lost her ability to love and he'd given up his dream.

Sanitized and sterile, weren't they perfect for each other now? "You could have any woman in the world. Why me?"

He grinned, suddenly looking incredibly boyish. "Is this one of the reasons then? That I didn't compliment you enough?"

"Compliment me enough? Andreas, our entire dialogue was comprised of you usually warning me off something or the other. What we excelled in truly…" she raised her brows "…was nonverbal communication."

His chest rumbled with his quiet laughter while his fingers dipped into her hair. Prickling warmth spread down from that touch.

"I hate to diminish the impression you have of my power and influence," he added, and she snorted, which in turn made him grin, "but Drakonite law prevents me from divorcing you for at least eighteen months."

She didn't even panic anymore. "So I have eighteen months to bring you to heel then?" She traced the flat of his brow with the tip of her finger. "I'd better start taking inventory of the weapons I can use against you."

"You've become bolder, *pethi mou*." His fingers dug into her flesh, feral hunger blazing in his eyes. "I didn't think it possible."

Her skin prickled with answering need. How could she forget that the harsher his control, the deeper his need for her?

"You and I will celebrate a jubilee even as the only King and Queen of Drakon together in two hundred years because I intend to prove that Theos was wrong."

"You said he didn't control you anymore. And what do you mean jubilee?"

"For two hundred years, there hasn't been a jubilee celebration. And no, Theos does not control me," he said cryptically. She hated the harshness that came into his eyes every time they talked of his father. The patrician features tightened, the easy humor fell. "Giving you up, giving up on this marriage will mean he wins, *agapita.* And I could not let Theos win. I could not let him be right…"

"Revenge against your dead father is no more a better foundation for marriage than an inexplicable obsession is. It will never work."

"It will work because I refuse to give in.

"If you truly are dedicated to making a difference in the world, if you really care so much about the work you did at that legal aid agency, you could do it from here.

"You could have the prestige and power of the King's Palace behind you. Or lead the pampered life of a queen.

"Find your place in my world, Ariana. I do not care what it is. But stop running away from me and from yourself."

Ariana stared, tremors running through her.

Every time she thought she finally understood him, he went and did something like this. And yet, she was beginning to understand him, beginning to see how his mind worked.

Andreas didn't know how to handle guilt any more than he knew how to handle the little something he had felt for her back then. So this opening to her. Not because he thought it was important to her or because her happiness mattered to him.

Yet, here was the perfect way to know whether they could ever work, the chance to pit the Ariana she was now against the future King's personality. The chance to see if that connection that had brought them together years ago could mean anything.

The chance, as he said, to prove the great King Theos wrong when he had called her a curse upon his heir's life.

"You're on, Your Highness," she whispered.

Hands crawling up his chest, rising to her toes, she touched her mouth to his.

For a few seconds, he was stiff, shock tensing his entire body against her. But Ari didn't care. She needed a taste of him, she needed courage to see this thing between them through.

His mouth was hard and unyielding but this time, she knew. She knew what simmered beneath that stoic, unaffected exterior. She knew the raw passion that dwelled under the academic's soul.

Hands perched on his shoulders, she licked the seam of those sculpted lips. When he growled, when he roused out of that momentary freeze, she swiped her tongue inside his mouth. Nibbled at his lower lip.

Heat poured through her in liquid rivulets, pooling in her lower belly.

And just when his hands descended to her hips, just as he slammed her chest against his, Ari somehow managed to slip away from his hold.

Breaths harsh, dark pupils wide, he scowled at her. "Come back here, Ari." The tension that poured out of his lean frame was a balm to her soul.

Holding his gaze, she made a show of wiping her mouth with the back of her hand. As if it was that simple to erase the taste and feel of him from her being. "No."

"No?"

She smiled, feeling a freedom, a joy she hadn't known in years. "That was just a small test for myself, Your Highness."

A vein fluttered at his temple. "A test?"

She nodded, loving his frustration in that moment. "A test to see if I still had it in me to bring you to your knees."

"And?"

Andreas Drakos reduced to blank questions…was there

a sweeter victory? "Are you ready to fall to your knees, Your Highness?"

He said nothing. And yet the gleam in his eyes told her all she needed to know.

She still had it in her and this time, she was going to use it to design the life she wanted.

CHAPTER SEVEN

ARIANA SPENT THE first two weeks as Andreas's wife being swept up in the storm that was the King's Palace and the Crown Prince's life.

True to Andreas's warning, there had been no time to center herself before the news had been leaked that the Crown Prince had married in secret.

Had, against every popular opinion and to the shock of the populace of Drakon, fallen irrevocably in love.

A strategic leak by his own PR team, she'd learned later. A way to massage the truth.

All of Andreas's overseas trips now had a perfect explanation. Having accidentally met Ariana, a young beautiful lawyer, General Theseus Sakis's daughter, in the States, he had fallen violently in love with her and, due to some obscure legal obligations, had to marry immediately.

It was as if Drakon and its people had been hungry for some explanation like this about their Prince. The tale of their stoic Prince falling in love and marrying in secret seemed to fill a much-needed hole in the country's perception of him. Overnight, Andreas turned into a romantic figure, vulnerable as any of them.

The moment the formal press statement from him had hit the news cycle, Ariana was lost.

Invitations to balls, charity galas and state dinners began pouring in. Dress fittings, appearances by Andreas's side, private dinners with powerful members of the cabinet and Crown Council, Ariana held her own through it all.

Even as she realized that she was mostly ornamental on Andreas's arm, even as most of the times, the men—powerful traditionalists—talked as if she couldn't understand a word of import, even as she realized that the Queen's role was mostly titular, Ariana behaved with the perfect decorum.

And the shift in the perception about him, the picture his PR team painted of the Crown Prince's marriage enabled Andreas to make his own headway in the political zone.

Tax reforms that had been introduced temporarily passed through the cabinet. A host of new members were appointed to the Crown Council—most of them direct appointees handpicked by Andreas and Nikandros—small business owners, professors from universities, had been met with resistance but finally passed.

That he was serious about the changes he had spouted gave Ariana much to think about. She saw the power that rested in Andreas's hands, the duty of serving his country that he thought was inviolable. Saw the magic of it in Nikandros's round-the-clock efforts to make Drakon's economy sustainable, the pride and tears in Eleni's eyes as Andreas, against Gabriel's threats to kidnap her away from Drakon if she accepted, appointed her the executive chairwoman for the House of Drakos charities that involved millions of dollars.

More than once, she'd caught surprise, humor, even curiosity in Andreas's eyes as she acted the perfect hostess, the adoring spouse to the serious Prince. Almost as if he didn't believe the meek image she'd presented to the world.

Thanks to Eleni, she'd chosen a stylist that understood her personal style. Petra ran her life as smoothly as she did Andreas's and for now, Ariana relented control. Her first few public appearances with Andreas would define her future as the Queen and she toed the line. She might be a lawyer but she didn't know the intricacies of a political system like Drakon's so she listened and learned.

No one could find fault with her, not even the staunchest royal critics. Thanks to Eleni's constant advice and unrelenting support—once she'd learned that Ariana meant to stay—she'd sailed through those first two weeks. Even King Theos would have been surprised.

Everything went great except one thing.

All the time she'd spent with Andreas could be counted down to minutes. Their exchanges limited to discussing the weather, which had turned dismally cold.

Nothing personal touched their words. At the end of the day, they retired to separate chambers, even as tension seeped through the very air between them.

Ariana saw his desperate need for her in his restrained touches, in the hot, hungry look he leveled her way even in the midst of a crowd. Felt the answering shudder of her own body.

He wanted her, and yet he'd barely said two words to her since that evening. Barely shared the pressures of his life, the constant stress that he must be under. What he wanted, again, was relief and she was damned if she was going to be it. Damned if she was going to let him slot her again.

It suited her just fine, she told herself. She didn't need him to hold her hand through her new life. She definitely didn't feel deserted when he left on a trip to Asia without so much as a goodbye.

It was her own naïveté in not realizing how busy his life was. In not understanding that Andreas could never truly belong to anyone. After the storm of the first couple of weeks, she finally had a moment to breathe. And her own plans to make, so she shut up that internal voice that said nothing had changed and threw herself into her work.

Only it wasn't that simple. Going up against Andreas and his will, she should've known, would never be simple. She wanted to learn more of Drakon, she needed to be more than an accessorized, haute-couture figurehead.

The first wake-up call came in the third week, when she'd decided to visit a woman's shelter in the capital city.

Petra had relayed the answer. *His Highness feels that such a visit would not be wise in the current time.*

Somehow, Ariana had kept her cool.

Then, she had decided to scout for premises near the palace where she could set up her legal offices. Before she could set a foot out of the palace, security had waylaid her.

His Highness has ordered an apartment to be cleared for Mrs. Drakos's use in the South Wing of the palace.

A mansion of a wing, attached to a team of lawyers who would do the grunt work while bearing the stamp of her name.

Somehow, she had kept her temper.

Next, she'd been drafted, without her agreement, to an afternoon tea with a host of powerful patronesses of charities from Drakon. Ariana had managed to not choke on the tea.

Next, the interview she'd given to a press member about her background in law dealing with domestic disputes and her aspirations to start a legal aid agency in Drakon had been sanitized until Ariana had sounded like a mouthpiece for the palace and a colorful accessory that belonged on Andreas's arm.

The last straw came when she'd learned, through a slip by Petra, that all the calls she'd been receiving from her friend Rhonda, whose divorce case had been pulled up on the calendar, had been rerouted without a word to her.

Ariana had had enough.

It had taken him mere weeks to revert back to type. To relegate her to a small part of his life. To turn her into nothing but a figurehead. *Thee mou*, if all he'd wanted was a placeholder, why had he gone to the lengths of kidnapping her? Why make her those promises?

God, she was a fool to have ever believed him, a fool to hope that they could make this work, even without love complicating matters.

But this time, she would not run away, she told herself walking the perimeter back into the royal wing. If he wasn't going to come to her, she would go to him. She knew he'd returned from his trip almost a day ago. And she was done waiting.

She pushed her way through the small corridor off her lounge and barged into the other master suite that was connected to hers through it.

She snarled at a sleekly dressed bodyguard when he blocked her in front of the massive double doors. "His Highness does not let anyone enter his private suite." When she raised a brow, the guard shrugged. "Not even his brother or sister."

"Did the Crown Prince have a wife before?" Ariana demanded in a soft, utterly privileged voice that would have surprised even her father.

After what seemed an eternity, the guard nodded, threw open the massive doors and moved aside.

Ariana stepped inside, blinked and came to a still. A faint thread of sandalwood and something so intrinsically Andreas curled through her muscles.

From the wide French doors on the side to the huge high windows, everything was covered with light-blocking blinds. She rubbed her arms. The room was cool.

Dark mahogany wood, almost black furniture dotted around the vast semi-circular room. A wide desk sat next to the French doors, which would open to a view of the mountain range in the distance, she knew. Not a single pen or paper was out of place on the gleaming wood yet there were reams of paperwork on it.

In the center, the room retreated farther back. Darker and quieter than the rest. Did it lead to his bedroom?

Pulse zigzagging, Ariana forced herself to look away.

One whole wall behind her was floor-to-ceiling bookshelves. She didn't need to go close to see they would be books mostly on the history of Drakon, and the history of the world, neatly filed in alphabetical order.

Moving on feet that felt no reticence, she went to the bookshelf. Her fingers, she noted, were trembling as she ran them over the spines of some familiar titles. Warmth filled her limbs, the books greeting her like old friends.

They were, in a way. All the months he'd spent at the fishing village, these books had been in the library of the Drakos estate. She'd gotten so used to seeing him carry them around, she had one day asked him to talk about them.

A whole new side of the Crown Prince had been revealed to her when he spoke of history with passion, wonder, a love in his voice that she'd never thought him capable of.

She moved along the shelves, sometimes smiling at a familiar title, sometimes frowning. Until a title hit her like an invisible punch.

Dragon Captured: A New Look at the Ancient Lore of Drakon, by Andreas Titus Drakos.

Ariana plucked it from the shelf, heart thumping hard against her rib cage. The book he'd been writing when he'd taken the sabbatical.

Why had he lied?

The gilded spine, the crisply expensive paper told its own story. It was a customized collector's edition. It had been his dream to share his love for the history of his country with the world.

That rich, new-book scent stole into Ari's blood as she slowly flicked the thick jacket open. She traced the title and his name on the inside with shaking fingers. Turned another page and her heart jumped into her throat.

For the girl who loved me.

The book fell from Ari's hands and landed on the thick carpet with a muffled thump. She fell to her knees, tears making big splotches on the thick paper. A silent sob falling from her mouth, she picked up the picture that had fallen out of the book when it landed.

It was her. She didn't even remember when it was taken. Her body was turned away from the camera, her hands full with a tray of dark coffee and a slice of oozing baklava.

The same thing that Andreas had ordered every day for months in the café.

But her face was turned toward the camera, that big, goofy, wide grin curving her mouth. Her hip jutting out at a cocky angle, her entire body screamed a sultry invitation, and her eyes were warm and sparkling.

Thee mou, she'd been audacious, teasing and taunting the Crown Prince like that. She'd been bold and brave, grabbing what she wanted from life. Something she'd forgotten. She folded her legs under her and sat on the thick carpet, the picture in her hands, the book sprawled open in her lap.

She read a few pages here and there and smiled, hearing his passion in his words. She traced the lines of her own face in the picture, worn-out and fading, a startling contrast among the crisp, new pages of the book.

Had Andreas looked at that picture again and again? Her mind raced, aided by her heart, raring to jump to all sorts of conclusions.

Like a leaf in a storm, she sat there. Guilt and hope vied. There it was, the proof that maybe Andreas had cared. A little. At least after he'd thought she'd died, said a bitter voice, the voice that wanted to keep her safe.

No, this was proof that his heart had not been carved from the same rock on which his palace sat. Something that had hardened in her chest loosened. The guilt that she had carried along for so long…it thawed at the sight of that rumpled picture.

She replaced the picture in the book and the book on

the shelf. On legs that felt like jelly, she ventured deeper into the suite.

The room was cavernous, with soaring ceilings that seemed like they could touch the sky. The huge skylight had dark shades.

The king-sized bed with a cream upholstered headboard and pristine white sheets beckoned to her. Andreas slept on his stomach on one side of the bed, the sheets up to his waist. Leanly muscled, his bare back was strikingly dark against the white sheets.

A smile broke through her at the sight of his large feet peeping out of the sheets. No couch or bed or sheets were ever tall enough for Andreas. Her sheets had looked like a child's blankets on him.

Ariana moved to the head of the bed, pulled by an urge she couldn't understand, much less fight. He had left her to fume and he was sleeping?

Then it came to her. He was used to not sleeping for days, went into that intense focus mode when an important matter came up and then he would crash, sleep through the day and night.

His face was to the side on the pillow, his arms under it. Even in the dark, she could make out those distinctive features. Impossibly long lashes fanned toward the slope of his cheekbones. His mouth, a rigid, stiff line, was relaxed into a soft curve. She ran a finger over the impossibly sharp bridge of his nose, traced the wing of his eyebrows, the defined line of his jaw.

Something fluid and desperate, a twisted longing rose through her. For weeks now, she'd been racking her mind as to why she'd run away like that, why she'd had to take her guardian's help, whom she had never liked, to flee Andreas.

Why hadn't she just stayed and made him understand what he'd been doing to her?

Now she knew. A part of her was always going to be

weak when it came to him. A part of her was always going to be that eighteen-year-old who'd fallen in love with him. A part of her was always going to hope that maybe, just maybe, he would love her a little.

She needed to walk out of here and think, she—

Long fingers wrapped around her wrist, arresting her, half prostrate over him and the bed. She slapped a hand over her mouth, but it was too late. Black eyes, that shouldn't have been shining in the dark, stared at her, sleep diluting the usual forbidding expression.

"Ari? What's wrong?" His voice was husky and sleep-mussed. Like he had sounded after sex.

"Nothing…is wrong." The sheets slithered around him as he blinked and moved to his side, his eyes still adjusting to the darkness. "I…didn't mean to disturb you. Go back to sleep."

Desperate to escape, Ariana wiggled in his grip, but it tightened. She gasped when his arms went under her shoulders and tugged her onto the bed.

His dark face hovered over hers, his sleek, taut body propped on his elbows, his breath hitting her nose in soft strokes. Not even out of breath as he watched her like that, his body a heated canopy over hers.

"It is hard enough to sleep knowing you are in the next suite, *finally*, after all these months. You should know better than to taunt me in my own bed."

Her hands rose to his shoulders to push him off. Hard and tense, he was like velvet-covered rock under her questing fingers. Heat swirled and pooled in her lower belly and she shook from head to toe. Standing on the edge of the abyss. Waiting to fall.

That faded picture of her, hidden away in a book he hadn't showed to the world, beckoned like a beacon.

Their eyes met and held in the dense dark, that connection, always so strong between them, tangible again.

Oh, but with his legendary self-control in play, he did not kiss her. He would not break his promise. Would not give in until she asked. She could see the desire in his glowing eyes, in the flaring of his patrician nose.

"Ask me to kiss you." Clipped and serrated. On edge. Only the Crown Prince of Drakon could make a request sound like an arrogant command. His body was tense, his breath, because she knew him so well, a little shy of normal. "*Diavole*. Ask me to kiss you, Ari."

CHAPTER EIGHT

ARIANA LICKED HER LIPS, longing cleaving her in half.

This, him. This fire that he invoked with a single look. It was all she'd been missing in her life.

"Kiss me," she said simply, throwing herself off the cliff.

His arms on either side of her head, his fingers digging into her hair tight, he slanted his mouth over hers. Tiny, numerous frissons shook through her body at that first contact. Firm and supremely male, his lips touched her in a soft, silken, barely there caress that was nowhere near enough.

A taste of whiskey and him. Fingers tracing his collarbone, Ariana shook all over.

Another butterfly-soft brush, there and gone again.

A sweep of his tongue over the seam, and then nothing.

Slow kisses. Soft kisses. Testing the suppleness of her lips. Tempting to steal her breath. Again and again. Over and over.

Her body bucked off the bed, seeking more, needing more. "*Please*, Andreas," she whispered half sobbing, every nerve ending taut with hunger.

A taunting smile breaking out on his mouth, Andreas moved to his side, and threw a muscled leg over hers. Rock-hard thigh pressed hers into the bed, a languorous weight that her body craved. "I've forgotten how much it pleases me when you say please."

"I have forgotten how much I hated you in bed."

"I have had two years to imagine this, Ariana. You've had days." Pure devil glinted in his wide smile. "Now that you're here, I intend to take my time."

His arms sidled under her as if she were a featherweight, tugging her onto her side. A long finger traced a lazy trail along the neckline of her loose T-shirt. Her breasts were thrust up, the upper curves visible through the hanging neckline. Up and down, until the pulse at her neck throbbed violently.

Anticipation was fire in every muscle every time his finger skated the edge of one curve. *Thee mou*, he'd adored her breasts. Worshipped them. So much so that she had once orgasmed just with his mouth on them.

The memory slid over skin like a silky caress. Fired nerve endings.

His finger hovered over the upper curve of one breast, his breath a harsh whisper. "Your body has changed."

A profound ache twisted through her. All she could do was nod.. Even as fear whispered over her spine, she needed this intimacy. Craved it for so long. Here, in the dark, the world shut away, maybe she'd find the man she'd fallen in love with.

Jet-black eyes held hers, possessive and powerful. "It turns me on even more." She saw the edge of that hunger in his eyes, the deep grooves of need around his mouth. "Although, nothing could turn me on faster than seeing how eager you always were."

She lifted her hands to his face. With the pad of her thumb, she traced the long curve of his lower lip. A stern, stiff line until he smiled. Or kissed. "And you were never desperate enough."

He frowned, but Ariana had had enough of the power play. She needed to know if it was as magical as it had been back then. She needed to know if this heat between them was worth burning herself all over again.

Sending her seeking fingers into his hair, she tugged his arrogant head down. Breath rushing in and out, she licked that sensual lower lip with the tip of her tongue. His growl reverberated from his hard chest. Without waiting, she opened her mouth over his and dragged it from one end to the other. Another growl, a warning. She didn't heed it. She kissed him again and again, until heat sparked where their lips touched, until she was out of breath. Until her lips stung.

Until the need to shatter that control was a scream in her blood. She dragged that lower lip between her teeth and then flicked her tongue over it. The curse he spewed was a balm over her heated skin. In a fraction of a second, she was pushed onto her back and his mouth crushed hers.

Her upper lip banged against her teeth. Her scalp prickled at how tightly he gripped her with one hand, while the other clasped her jaw, holding her still for his assault.

Spotlights filled her vision as the taste of him exploded through her body. There were no more games, no more teasing. Angling his head, he deepened the pressure until the heat of their fused mouths was enough to scald them both.

With a stark groan, she opened her mouth. He swooped in. The slide of his tongue as it chased hers was so erotic that her toes dug into the sheets. Again and again, he devoured her mouth, his wicked tongue dipping in and out with a frenetic rhythm that her body recognized. Craved.

His hands gripped her hair tight, his mouth opening and closing over hers, sucking and nipping, until she was trembling with a fever beneath him.

Until the taste of him was forever embedded in her.

She had no control over herself, no will of her own. She was begging with her body, her hips thrusting into empty air. His hands moved down to her shoulders, between her heavy breasts and then down to her abdomen. Again and again, up and down, touching, marking, staking a claim, while he ravished her mouth. Stroking her body higher and higher, promising her that cataclysm, enslaving her will.

"Tell me you need more, little wife." His tongue traced the rim of her ear in a silken stroke that had her clutching her thighs tight. The tip of it moved behind her ear, before his teeth caught her lobe. “Tell me where you want my hands and my mouth.” A wicked, wild promise in a deep, husky voice she barely recognized as his.

His hand lay palm down on her chest, the tips of his long fingers touching her neck. Her heart thundered against this palm. Her breasts swelled, begging to be cupped in those powerful hands. Her nipples ached to be sucked into that mouth.

And he missed nothing.

His gaze flicked down toward the tight tips of her breasts visible through the thin fabric of her top, the trembling of her body, the tight clutch of her thighs. Naked satisfaction lined the angles of his gorgeous face. “Ask me to be inside you, Ari. *Dio*, my mouth, my hands, whatever you want, wherever you want.”

Her entire body was screaming her need for him, her desire evident in her shallow breaths. And yet, for the devil in him, it was not enough.

He moved his hand down her stomach, down her pelvis until it rested over her mound. Her hips jerked against his fingers resting against the covered lips of her sex. Wetness drenched her panties, a fact he knew. For a dark strip of color scoured his sharp cheekbones.

“Ask me, Ariana.” His voice fell to a whisper. His lashes fell and rose slowly. His breath a soft hiss in the dark. “I will do it with pleasure.”

How was it that he gave her the power and yet it was Ari that was falling?

His body next to her was a fortress of need, yet controlled with that ironclad will. Ariana pushed her hip into him. He jerked back, his fingers digging into her hips. Arresting her movements. But too late.

She had felt the evidence of his desire. Her breath slowed, the faint tremor in his powerful shoulders telling her how on edge he was.

Only his control was better. Over his body, over his mind, always. He would never let himself lose that will.

She hadn't seen that back then. She hadn't realized that it pervaded every part of his life. Hadn't understood that for the Crown Prince of Drakon losing control of himself in bed was akin to giving Ariana a real place in his life. That it would mean him needing Ariana and not just the other way around.

The more she'd asked him for his attention, his time, the more he'd distanced himself. As if he didn't know what to do with her. As if she didn't fit in the neat box he'd made for her.

Needing her meant giving her power over himself, over his emotions.

And he was doing it again. He was compartmentalizing her because she made him feel.

Why had King Theos been so worried about him? Andreas's heart was stone.

A laugh erupted from her mouth. Whereas she… Ten years hadn't made a dent on the wants of her foolish heart. Every inch of her body, every beat of her heart wanted to grab this chance with him again. Wanted to find that happiness, that sense of completeness she had had with him in that village.

But not on his terms. Not at the cost of losing herself.

"*Oxhi,* Andreas," she managed, her lips stinging from the heat of his lips. The sound of her denial, somehow given voice, filled up her lagging will.

His hand didn't move from her sex. For a few seconds, Ari wondered if he'd even heard her. He looked up. A flash of consternation in his eyes before he exhaled roughly and buried his face in the valley between her breasts.

The damp warmth of his mouth made her nipples poke through her T-shirt. Ariana shivered, unraveling over the strength it took to resist him.

"I said no, Andreas." Steady and almost assertive. "Possible you don't understand the word because you've never heard it. Especially from me."

His laughter, muffled against her body, sent tremors through her. Eyes glinting with humor, he stared at her. But the curiosity was there. He was taken aback by her refusal, she was sure. "You and I both know why you walked into my suite, Ariana." A sultry dare. "I have never held your desire for me against you."

So sure of her always. So sure of her devotion, of her hunger for him. Once he'd given in to their desire, she hadn't challenged him in any way. Wherever he had led with that arrogant confidence, she had blindly followed. When he'd decided they would marry, decided not asked, she'd happily forgotten all her dreams.

Because, of course, this worldly, powerful, sophisticated Crown Prince of Drakon, a man women lost their hearts to, had chosen her.

Her.

No wonder he'd thought she was another part in his privileged life. She jerked away from under him, his supreme arrogance lighting a fire in her. "You're an arrogant bastard, did I ever tell you that, Your Highness?"

"No." He pushed his hand through his hair roughly. Harsh and accented. She could have laughed at the irate expression on his face if her mind wasn't jumping from thought to thought. "You're right. For a minute there, I forgot that you hate me now.

"You'd never have ventured into my room without a reason. Not unless you were desperate."

"You're doing it again." She cringed at the anger in her voice.

"I don't understand."

"You ripped me from my life, brought me to this palace,

and you go on your merry way. *Again*." For the life of her, she couldn't stop the last word from tumbling out.

His stillness betrayed his shock. "Ari, help me understand."

He'd never used that tone with her. He had ordered her around, he'd dared her. He'd condescended to her. But never had he asked her in that tender voice. As if it really mattered to him.

"Ari, so help me God, if you don't explain yourself, I will—"

"What? You will lock me up?" she said on a laugh. "I can at least count on you to buck me back up." She sighed. "If all you wanted was a placeholder, why go to the trouble of kidnapping me? Why make promises to me?"

He truly looked so disconcerted that Ariana didn't know whether to laugh or cry. He pushed up on the bed. The sheet slithered to his waist, baring his torso. Lean, ropey muscle stretched tight over his abdomen when he sighed. "If this is about me not breaking down the door to your suite and ravishing you in your bed—"

"I'm not talking about sex. Is that all the use you see for me?"

"By your own admission, I needn't declare you Queen in front of the whole world if all I wanted was to screw you." The words were like tremors on the ground. So softly spoken but powerful enough to pull the ground from under her. He pushed a hand through his hair roughly.

Already trying to patch the little rip in his self-control. Already putting the veneer of civility over the confusion she saw in his eyes. The strain his desire for her put in his face.

Ari slowly got off the bed, every inch of her balking at walking away from sure pleasure. But she wouldn't be able to deny him or herself another time. And sleeping with Andreas when he saw no other use for her was like signing away her soul. Again.

And she couldn't do that.

Every cell in her wanted to grab this chance fate had given them both.

No, not fate. Andreas had done this. She didn't care that he called it payback for what she'd done to him.

He'd come for her. From what Nikandros had said, Andreas had scoured the world for her for two years, while Theos had clammed up. At the cost of risking his duties to the crown.

Of course, the man didn't know what it was to love. But to the best of his ability, Andreas had kept that commitment he had made to her. Was it his fault she wanted what he couldn't give?

"You promised me I could carve whatever role I want in your life, in this life, and yet you…you deny me every step of the way.

"I don't think you quite know what to do with me."

"What the hell does that mean?"

"You denied my visit to the women's shelter."

"It is not safe for you." His jaw tightened. "And damn it, Ari, you made the trip anyway. You drove the security staff nuts with your little stunt."

She tilted her chin up, raring to go at him. "You forced me to it. Just as you created office space for me in the palace. In a bloody wing of the palace, Andreas. My career is not a joke."

"As my wife and Queen, you will be far too busy to take up a full practice. This way—"

She pushed her face into his, her blood running hot now. "Did I let you down in any way? Did I not act as the perfect ornamental wife?"

His mouth twitched. Finally, he was catching on. "I couldn't believe my own eyes that it was you. So biddable and meek." He took a step forward. The predatory glint in his eyes sent sparks up her spine and she took a step backward. "All I could think of was whether I wanted you like that in bed."

"Andreas, I… I will do everything you need as your wife. But it doesn't mean I'll give up a single part of my life. It doesn't mean I'll let you or your staff decide how I live my life. I…can't…*we can't* make the same mistakes all over again."

"Kala," he said, almost conciliatory in his tone. "Tell me what you want from me to achieve that."

She straightened her spine. "For starters, I want my laptop, my personal belongings and my case files. I need to speak to Magnus. I want someone allotted to me, someone other than Petra, to see to my needs."

Every spark of humor disappeared. "No."

"What do you think I'll do over Skype, Andreas? Disappear like they do on spaceships? Have Skype sex with the man I lied to for ten years?"

"I do not like another man's name and the word *sex* together on your mouth, *agapi mou*. If you want to negotiate with me, you should know better than to provoke my ire."

"There are things I can do to help Magnus, until he finds a replacement. A couple of the cases, those two women are my friends. The law does very little to protect them from their powerful, abusive husbands. Too many people have already let them down. I refuse to be one.

"I can't just disappear off the face of earth and let them believe the worst.

"You have your commitments and I have mine."

The lines around his mouth deepened. His dark eyes became flat, all that emotion wiped away. But Ariana was beginning to learn his cues again. The harder something hit him, the more shuttered he became. As if he could only implode. As if showing that emotion meant actually feeling it.

As if it were handing a weapon to Theos to use against him.

He pressed his fingers to his temple, his jaw clenched

so tight that it might break. "Is that what I did to you, what motivated you to study law? Were you afraid of me, Ari?"

"What? No, of course not." The truth that she had left unsaid glimmered like a phantom around the room, sending a cold whisper through her. When his expression didn't budge, she hurried on. "For years, I was directionless. I hated my father for forcing things on me, so I never even discovered what I would enjoy, what I would be good at. I joined Magnus's legal aid agency as a clerk. Literally my job was to keep the filing in order.

"The more I saw the women that came through the agency's doors, the more I thought of my mother. My father never beat her, as some of those women were, but he… abused her just the same and I was powerless then.

"But I realized I could change that. I worked hard to get my law degree.

"I can still provide help to Magnus with the paperwork. And I want a couple of my friends to be flown here. Rhonda is going through a rough patch and Julia has no place to stay since her husband froze all their assets until the divorce proceedings finish."

Something like shock filled his eyes and Ariana felt a surge of satisfaction. Clearly, until this moment, he hadn't taken her seriously. "Here where?"

"To Drakon. To the King's Palace."

"You want me to provide sanctuary for two women who are running away from their husbands, and maybe even the law? To turn the palace into…some sort of pseudo-shelter?"

"I want to invite a couple of my good friends so that they can reassure themselves that the husband I have been hiding from for ten years is not a complete monster. And yes, they get a vacation.

"There have to be some perks to being the Crown Prince's precious wife, *ne*?"

"Kala," he said after a long gap. In a sudden move-

ment that sent her heart lurching to her throat, he caged her against the wall. He took her mouth in a furious kiss that was all tongue and teeth and left her clinging to him. A sob burst out of her when he buried his mouth in her neck.

"Any more demands?"

Oh, his mouth was such a sensuous trap. So harsh when he dealt out commands and yet so soft when he kissed. She licked her lips and he leaned in closer, until his breath was a whisper across her heated skin. "I want Giannis back."

"*Oxhi.* Next?"

She placed her hands on his chest and pushed, determined to win this battle. "I want *my* people around me. People who care about *me*, people who don't think I'm your downfall. People who will stop me from feeling as if I live in a vacuum.

"I'm not a toy you play with, dress up and then put back on the shelf. That was me stopping before I fell into old, harmful patterns. I came—"

"Harmful patterns?" A vein pulsed dangerously at his temple. "Toy I played with? After every lie you've told, after everything you've done, I am still prepared to give you a place as my wife. A position coveted and sought out by the most beautiful, most accomplished women in the world today."

She flinched but refused to back down. "But you chose me. Whatever it is that sits in the place of your heart, wanted me, Andreas. In my own naive way, I didn't appreciate the magnitude of how uncharacteristic your choice was. How far off the mark you had gone."

She pushed against his hold on her wrists until her upper body grazed his. The hiss of his breath drowned her own. Jaw set, fingers taut over her wrists, he searched her face. As if he was seeing her for the first time.

"You still want me. You wish you didn't. And not just for a quick screw, or you would have taken me on the flight and dumped me. You could never be that ruthless with me then, and you won't now.

"Andreas Drakos has a weakness and it is me."

He pressed into her, a feral curve to his mouth. Bare chest crushed her breasts, and Ari threw her head back. Mouth drifting over her neck to the pulse, he smiled against her skin. "Point to Ariana Drakos. So why the hell are you not letting me give us both what we desperately need?"

"Because I'm not that train wreck reeling from her parents' deaths anymore. My primary function in life is not to provide you with sex and relief from your duties. I'm not awed that you noticed me, much less chose me." If her breath caught at the lies she was spouting, she hoped he didn't notice.

She twisted her hands in his grip and he let go, as if she'd burned him. But Ariana was not through. A fire ran in her veins, a sense of rightness that she belonged with him. A new hope that she could live with Andreas without losing herself.

She clasped his face in her hands, determined to make him see her.

"I'm not that girl who thought the sun and moon rose out of your eyes, Andreas. I will not be another cog in the machine of your life like Petra or Thomas or your chauffeur.

"Unless you're prepared to meet me as an equal, unless you're prepared to share your life with me, I'll run away again.

"And believe me, if I know one thing, it is how to escape from situations. This time, when you catch me—" his eyes gleamed at her acknowledgment "—I will come with a scandal that will rock your precious House of Drakos.

"So decide, Your Highness, if you want me in your life or not."

CHAPTER NINE

ANDREAS FORCED HIMSELF to let Ariana go, stripped off his drawstring pants and walked into the cold shower. The mosaic tiles were startlingly cold against his overheated skin. He turned the jets to biting cold and still it took a few minutes for his arousal to abate, for his rational mind to grasp hold of the situation.

By the time he was out of the shower, he was shivering. He wrapped a towel around his waist and stood in front of the mirror.

His hair was overlong, falling past his ears. His eyes still had those dark shadows but had lost that bruised look he'd been walking around with for God knew how long. Gone too was that black void he'd carried inside of him for months.

And the black, biting, cold rage after Theos, in one of his mad rages, had spilled that Ariana was alive. It was as if his world was beginning to tilt back to normal again. He was beginning to understand that he had known nothing about her back then. Nothing of substance at least.

Even now, he knew there were things he still could not grasp. Things he knew he saw in her eyes when she had lain in bed next to him.

Things he struggled to put into words.

If you want me in your life, Your Highness...

Laughter, shocking even him, burst out of him at the audacity of the woman.

She had always been reckless and defiant, and yet there was something new to her. A self-possession that was as intoxicating as it forced him to pay attention.

She clearly thought he'd miss that adoration, and a part

of him did. But this woman, who challenged him even as she trembled with her desire for him, she couldn't hold a candle to that girl.

He had no doubt she meant every word of her threat. No doubt that she would bring scandal, if not ruin, to his feet if he didn't give her whatever it was she wanted.

The challenge, instead of riling him, made anticipation flow in his veins.

He wanted to argue and negotiate with her. He wanted to dominate that defiance until it turned into desire. He wanted her under him, writhing and screaming.

Once he dressed, he could not however give her chase, as desperately as he wanted to.

The moment he had stepped out of his suite, Petra and his three aides had been desperate for his time. A contract he was signing with the House of Tharius came up and his thoughts veered.

His life would be so much better if he divorced her and took Maria Tharius for his wife. A doyenne of charities, Maria had been groomed since birth for a role like that. She would be amenable to his every wish, would know her place, be a proper mother for any children they had.

Maria would be the perfect Queen of Drakon. Maria would not demand that he give sanctuary to women fleeing their lives. Maria would not demand that he locate a security guard who worked in the palace ten years ago, who clearly had broken protocol and befriended the Crown Prince's young wife. Much less order that he not only be reinstated but join her personal team, knowing that it made her husband…uncomfortable that his wife was…chummy with that man.

Face it, Andreas. You're insanely jealous.

A growl rose through his throat and his team froze around him.

Dio, was this what she reduced him to?

In his heart of hearts, he knew Ariana wouldn't have cheated on him. And yet he'd been insanely jealous of her friendship with that young guard.

And he still was, given that Ariana clearly still had affection for Giannis.

He, the future King, jealous of a small-time guard.

Yet the thought of sitting down to dinner with Maria for the next thirty years, the thought of seeing Maria's placid smile across a crowded ballroom, a woman who would always remain a stranger because he just knew she'd stick to her place, the thought of taking her to bed… Distaste filled his mouth.

Thee mou, now that he had found her again, only Ariana would do.

Ariana, who had already won over his family with her effervescent personality.

Ariana, who would not give a damn about protocol and etiquette when it came to their own children. No, she would be the first one to slide down the side of a snow-covered hill. The one who would encourage them to break as many rules as possible. The one who would…love them unconditionally, whether they were an academic like him or a sick child like Nik had been. Or a little girl craving acceptance, like Eleni had been.

The one who would give a new definition to the future reputation of the House of Drakos.

"I want a Giannis Petrakis located as soon as possible," he said to one of his aides. "He used to be a security guard with the palace. Have him report to Mrs. Drakos."

"Mrs. Drakos?"

His aide paled when Andreas pinned him with a look. "Yes, Mrs. Drakos, my wife."

In the following week, he chose to avoid her, chose to immerse himself in the most pressing state matters. Tried to lose himself in the riot almost brewing among the members of the Crown Council after he had passed the latest edict, relinquishing them of their powerful positions.

His opening their real estate to Gabriel's company, and Nikandros's risky financial ventures, had already caused waves.

The people didn't understand investment when their national debt was already in millions of dollars. But Andreas had persisted.

It had taken everything he'd had to trust Nikandros, but he had. And it was the best decision he had made, for Gabriel's company had already boosted the employment rates in the remote areas of Drakon.

There were a hundred matters for him to see to.

Yet all he felt was this raw, fierce need to possess her. To shatter the defiance he saw in her eyes, to own the fiercely strong woman she'd become.

To fix whatever she thought they had to fix between them so that he could drag her to bed and drive himself inside her.

She would be unlike any Queen Drakon had seen, yes. But at least she would not let him descend into that kind of megalomania that Theos had fallen into over the last few years. She would not let Andreas complete the transformation into becoming that hard man who, despite having all the riches and power in his hands, would forever remain alone in the end.

The man his father had forced him to become.

A man who would always be feared but never liked. Never loved.

He'd give her everything she asked for, this time. Everything that was in his power to give.

It was late evening almost a week later when Andreas was finally free. He'd had Petra invite Ariana to dine with him in his private suite. He was determined to be civil tonight, and not slide down the slippery path to their disturbing past.

They needed a fresh start and for that, he needed to believe Ariana. He needed to understand, as much as it burned him, that Ariana had left him because he'd made living with him unbearable.

He had barely time to shower after his long day and put on fresh clothes when Ariana walked into his suite.

A panorama of expressions crossed her face as her gaze fell on the intimate table set out on the veranda, overlooking the courtyard, with a spectacular view of the horizon. He tried to see it from her point of view. Crystalware twinkled in the orange glow of the setting sun. A bottle of champagne sat in an ice bucket. Their food was already sitting on the table since he'd dismissed the staff already.

"*Kalispera*, Ariana."

He saw her head come up but she didn't turn.

So easily she snagged at his temper. Until he saw the tense line of her shoulders. Until he remembered that this was Ariana and emotional control didn't come to her easily.

In fact, it was the opposite of her nature. Which had been what had attracted him to her in the first place.

His amazement that anyone could live with such free rein given to their emotions.

Knowing what he did now about her background, it amazed him even more how fearlessly she had lived then. How generously she had given of herself to anyone who had come into the sphere of her life.

She slowly turned toward him, as if she needed the extra minute to compose herself. Something caught in his chest, a twinge of regret maybe, for how things had been once. The wariness in her eyes…he was determined to push through it.

He wanted the old Ariana back. The Ariana who had

worshipped him. The Ariana who would have never filtered anything that had come to her mouth, especially with him.

The Ariana that had made him feel that he was, finally, not alone. That he need not be alone.

"*Kalispera*, Andreas," she replied back softly. The wariness didn't abate but neither could she stop her gaze from devouring his face nor from sweeping down his body and back up. As if she had been starving for the sight of him.

Just as he'd been for her.

He felt no such compunction about showing his own interest, however. He had had a week from hell and all that had kept him going was that he would come back to this.

To her.

That tension that had become second skin flickered over his muscles as he swept his gaze over her.

She was dressed differently today, like the Ariana he remembered.

Sexy, confident, yet with a thread of vulnerability beneath.

A simple beige sheath dress that barely touched her knees, that made her golden skin glow with a burnished sheen. It showed off her toned arms and lithe figure with its simplicity. Black pumps made the most of her long, long legs, bringing her face almost to his chin.

Thee mou, he'd always loved how well she had fit against him. But now, that angular look was replaced by soft curves. Curves he wanted to feel beneath his body, softness he wanted to surround himself in.

She left her hair to fall softly around her shoulders. It softened that stubborn jaw of hers.

When their gazes met, he smiled and raised a brow. "You look gorgeous."

She flushed but held his gaze. "*Efharisto*. You look—" her mouth twitched, and so did his entire body in response "—very…dashing."

"Can I assume that the cold war between you and Petra reached its conclusion?"

"Let's just say we reached a mutually satisfactory agreement."

"What is that?"

"To stay out of each other's way. And now that I have my own people, her attitude doesn't bother me at all."

He frowned, remembering all the small tidbits she'd thrown out during the dinner with his family. The near panic he'd seen in her eyes as she'd stood by his bed.

"I have appointed Giannis as my aide and I've been interviewing candidates for an administrative assistant and a PR person. Eleni's miffed, I think, that I chose someone Mia recommended."

He half nodded, his mind still on the previous issue.

Knowing Petra's loyalty, and even her bit of possessiveness when it came to him, he didn't doubt the veracity of Ari's words. Regret, piling up as high as his guilt, made his voice harsh. "Petra is invaluable to me, *ne*. But not indispensable, Ariana.

"I will have her moved to another department instantly."

"Oxhi," she replied instantly but with such shock in her eyes that Andreas momentarily stilled. "Not necessary."

Christos, did she really think he would put a staff member before her, even now? After everything she'd told him about how isolated she'd felt then? About how Petra and her team had taken their lead from Theos's treatment of her, even from Andreas's own retreat as he'd struggled with his own emotions?

He reached her, refusing to let her shy away from him. "Why not?"

"Because it would mean that I'm still that insecure girl. It sends a message that I'm helpless and I hide behind your power." She lifted her chin. "I mean to hold my own, against you and against everyone in your world this time, Andreas."

He nodded, pride filling his very veins. She had come a long way from that girl and he needed to see that. "I think you've already proved that."

"I could not believe it when Petra told me you wanted to dine with me. Now I'm astonished that you went to this much trouble."

"Why?"

"For one thing, I know how busy you are. And for another, I didn't think you would take my ultimatum seriously. But I guess that's the one chink in your armor, *ne*? That I might somehow go to the media. In the current sentiment the people have with you, a woman crying kidnapping is the last thing you need."

He poured them both a glass of the champagne and handed it to her. "So let me get this straight." A thread of chill filled his tone and her head jerked up. "The only reason I'd want to spend time with you is for damage control."

Her white knuckles around the champagne flute were the only sign that she wasn't as breezy as she sounded. "Is it not?"

"No, Ariana." He put his glass on the table with not quite a steady hand, and then took hers. Then he went and stood in front of her. He plucked the small velvet box he'd had his aide retrieve from the royal treasury and held it out.

She didn't look up but her chest fell and rose with her shallow breaths. He waited, knowing in that moment how much he had crushed her tender heart ten years ago.

How he'd done exactly what he'd feared he would do.

"Ari, look at me." When she didn't, his patience finally unraveled its last thread. Clasping her chin with both his hands, he tilted it up.

Whatever he meant to say fluttered away at the sight of

her lush lips. Angling his head, he took her mouth with a hunger that punched through him.

Thee mou, he'd forgotten how sweet, how perfect she tasted. Lust surged through him as she swept her tongue over his lower lip.

No reluctance, no hesitation.

No lies, no dares.

Pure Ariana, pouring every inch of her emotion into the kiss, right down to the hoarse chuckle when their teeth banged in their hurry to get at each other.

But Andreas was not in a laughing mood today.

He was in a devouring mood. *Dios*, he'd waited so long for the taste of her. So long to feel like he would combust if he didn't slide inside her wet warmth.

Her hands moved to his chest, her body arching like a bow toward him.

The more he took of her mouth, the more he needed. Wrapping his hand around her neck, holding her still, he licked and stroked with his tongue, bit and suckled with his teeth, until she was whimpering against him. Trembling with need.

The kiss flared higher and hotter. The dinner was forgotten. Promises he'd made misting in the heat of their passion.

The press of her breasts against his chest, her long thighs straddled by his own, that scent of her skin…it was like striking a match to hot cinders.

He moved his hands to her hips and then to the curve of her buttocks. Roughly, he pulled her until she was plastered to his lower body.

His erection lengthened.

She moaned and arched into his touch, always so responsive. Always pushing Andreas toward a bit more madness.

He lifted her on the next breath and arranged her on the table. The ice bucket clattered to the ground with an almighty thud, the slide of ice cubes on the concrete a hiss in the silence.

She was breathing hard, her eyes heavy lidded, a protest on her lips, he knew. She meant to talk, throw up another one of her demands. Or dares.

He didn't let her get the words out. Instead, he stole them from her lips in another kiss that had them both growling against each other.

Thee mou, he wanted her like this—spread out on the table on a veranda of the King's Palace where sky and the stars would know that she was his. Her dress had already bunched up her thighs, giving him easy access to soft, silky skin. One hand sliding up her thighs, he buried the other in her hair and tugged her up.

Eyes glossed over, mouth trembling, she was utterly beautiful.

"I'm going to touch you, *glykia mou*," he whispered at her ear. "I'm going to see if you're wet for me already or not."

He held her against his chest while his fingers found the dampness through the thin fabric of her panties. Fire spewed in his muscles, his erection pressing persistently against his trousers. *Christos*, she was so ready, so wet for him. Burying his mouth in her temple, he pushed a finger into her sex and she jerked against him.

"Andreas, *parakalo…*" Head thrown back, she pushed her hips against his hand when he pressed his thumb against her swollen clit. A sob fell from her lips. The setting sun made her flushed skin shimmer like pure gold. His fingers had made a mess of her hair. Beads of sweat dotted above her lip. He licked that lush lip. The scent of her arousal spread through his blood like a drug.

He tugged the neckline of the forgiving sheath and growled at the sight of her bare breast. He gave the brown puckered tip a lick and her spine arched hungrily.

Her fingers moved to his hair and he complied. He rubbed his jaw against the wet tip before he closed his mouth and sucked.

She was close now. He could feel her body swelling around his fingers. The muscles in her pelvis tightening against the very pleasure she craved.

"You did not wear a bra," he whispered against her skin before he laved the plump nipple again. "Tell me, Ariana, that it was for me. Tell me that was because you knew how mindless I go at the sight of your breasts."

Her eyes flew open, unfocused, sluggish, before they settled on him. Desire made them glitter like the finest gems. An impish smile curved her mouth. "The material… it shows straps. Not for you."

Even now, she denied him that satisfaction.

He hooked his finger inside her tight entrance and waited, breath punching through him like bellows. She shuddered against him, and let out a slew of curses that had laughter thunder through him.

Her hands clutched his wrists, and her lithe body pushed against him. "Yes, okay. I went without a bra for you, *kala*. *Parakalo*, Andreas. More."

Fierce satisfaction raging through him, he pumped his fingers into that fast rhythm her body loved. He intended to dismantle all the defenses she had built. He intended to have that Ari of old again.

Her body tensed and bucked, like a boat flung against the waves. Sounds ripped from her throat, needy and raw. Bending his mouth, he nuzzled at her breast and like Independence Day fireworks, she fell apart around him with a keening moan.

Her thighs trapped his hand between them, her breath still harsh for several seconds.

She fell into his chest like someone had removed the bones from her body. Andreas pulled the dress up to cover her breasts, his own body screaming for release. And yet, utterly satisfied on another level. He swept his gaze over her, that possessive instinct she always brought out in him in full riot.

Long, quivering limbs, golden skin flushed, a smile hovering about her lips, her sensual repose was just as arousing as her uninhibited response.

On a deep level he didn't even try to understand, he felt as if his world was finally being righted.

From the moment he'd seen her standing in front of the city hall, her face pale, a stricken look in her eyes, he'd needed this.

He had needed to see her splinter with pleasure, pleasure he gave.

He had needed to know that Ariana was still his.

She opened her mouth and pressed a kiss to his chest, creating a damp patch. "I…" Her sigh whispered over his skin, his shirt no barrier to sensations. Another open-mouthed kiss against his abdomen. Which clenched like a steel wall. Her hands moved over him, stroking, touching, questing with a possessive flair that was more revelatory of Ariana than anything else. "What was that about?"

He tilted her chin up. "If you're asking me questions, clearly it was not that good."

Ripples of her laughter shook her slender frame. "Oh, believe me, it was an earthquake. But I still want to know… what—"

"That was about the present."

She looked up, and frowned. "What?"

He couldn't help himself. He dipped his head and kissed her swollen lips again. "Neither the past, nor the future. It was about now." He tucked a defiant curl behind her ear and stared into her eyes. The words came so easily to his lips. So clearly. "I wanted to kiss you, Ari. I wanted to see you shatter in my arms and I followed that urge."

The most beautiful smile spread over her face, something almost incandescent flickering in her eyes. That quality that defined Ariana. That quality that he wanted pervading his own life.

She nodded, clasped his jaw and kissed him softly. Slowly. As if she never wanted the moment to end.

A feeling he was coming to recognize within himself.

"Going with that urge was good. Andreas Drakos giving in to urges is *very* good. Provoking you to that urge—man, I feel on top of the world." She ran a finger over his lips, tracing them over and over. "I…have an urge, too." He held his breath as her hands traveled down his chest, past his trousers and slowly came to rest on his groin. He became still, arousal spiking through him as she traced his shape. "We can't go to bed yet, but your wife has other means to satisfy you."

How he managed to hold her fingers from wreaking havoc on him, he had no idea. Even he was impressed by his willpower. His erection throbbed in rhythm with his heart, his breath serrated. "Why can't we go to bed, exactly?" he asked softly. He hadn't planned any of this. He hadn't even meant to touch her until things between them had reached a new stage. But, of course, in his relationship with Ariana, passion had been one of the things that had always been right.

But now that she denied him, he wanted to know why.

A shadow passed across her face, though she tried to cover it up. "I started my pills again just the other day. So we won't be protected."

"Protected against what? I'm clean."

"Against pregnancy," she answered in a soft voice.

The moment stretched through awkwardness and fell directly into something altogether painful.

When he waited with a raised brow, she moved back

from him. An edge to her movements, she straightened her dress, careful not to meet his gaze.

A shiver snaked up his spine. "There is something called a condom."

She shrugged and ran a hand through her hair. Straightened her already perfect dress a little more. Buying time. "You hate condoms. More importantly, condoms are not foolproof. Nothing, actually, is foolproof."

Déjà vu hit him like a strike to his solar plexus. "Ariana…" he said but arrested anything that wanted to come out.

He ran a hand over his face, tension corkscrewing through him.

They had been through this once before. Their biggest, dirtiest fight when he'd asked her to get off the birth control pills.

The closest he'd ever come to losing his self-control because of course, she had absolutely refused to do so. And then his threat that he would not sleep with her unless she did.

Dios, he had been like a wounded beast.

Of course, Ariana could never take a dare lying down. They had ended up in a heap in front of the fireplace, clinging to each other after the stormy sex and having realized that something had been broken irrevocably between them.

The only time, the single time, sex had been something other than a source of joy between them.

He had left for the oil summit three days after that without a word to her. And when he'd returned, she'd disappeared from his life.

He had used sex against her, corrupted the only pure thing between them.

Desperation, he realized now, had clouded reason, good judgment. And *Thee mou*, he recognized only now how desperate he'd been back then to stop her retreating from him. His desperation to keep the one good thing in his life amidst the mounting pressure from Theos and the crown. And his own inability to fix the situation between him and Ari. His own inability to handle what she did to him.

He cursed at the color leaching from her face. In a second, the moment turned from sensual languor to a minefield.

Frustration made his voice rise. "Ariana, you need to share what you're thinking with me."

She nodded, but the wariness was in full force. Her hands around her midriff signaling untouchability. Barriers that he wanted to break but didn't know how. "I just don't want us to chance it. We're not ready."

"Not ready for what?"

"For children, Andreas."

The more she denied him something, the more he wanted to dig in. Andreas wanted to break that harmful pattern of their relationship. Yet something didn't feel right. Something goaded him to provoke her into a reaction. Into an answer. "Sooner or later, we will come to this point."

"It will be later then." Her spine straightened, a combative look in her eyes. "Andreas, we've barely made it through one evening, one, without going at each other's throats.

"I just don't want to bring children into this. At least not yet."

"Why not?"

"Because…between us I don't trust us to get this right."

"You mean, you don't trust me." Frustration coiled up inside him. After everything he had granted her, she still wouldn't give him everything.

Would she ever?

She came to stand in front of him. Lacing her fingers through his, willing him to listen. "It's not that I don't trust you, as much as I…am afraid.

"Please do not force this issue, Andreas."

Again.

The unsaid word hung in the air, morphing and growing like an impenetrable, invisible wall. A thread of disquiet ran through him. A feeling that if he didn't do something, anything, it would always stand between them.

"I want a family. I have always wanted children, you know that."

"You wanted heirs. There's a distinction." Her reply was instant, her eyes saying so much she didn't give voice to.

Feeling as if he was walking through a dark maze blindfolded, an experience his father had forced him through when he'd been eight and confided that he was scared of the dark, he formed and discarded several answers. "The requirement for an heir to the crown is always going to be there, Ariana. Our first child, a boy or a girl, will inherit everything.

"When the Crown Council and Theos put pressure on me to marry these last few years, I considered never doing so. I kept postponing coming to an agreement with Maria's father."

Listening to the other woman's name on his lips sent a shiver through Ariana. "Because of me?"

He shrugged. "I just was not eager to repeat the experience when I thought you were dead. After I found out you were alive..." Ariana had never wished more that she could understand what was going on in his mind. "Nikandros and his children were more than good enough for continuing the House of Drakos.

"So, yes, the heir to the House of Drakos is always going to be a question that will be raised.

"But what I want is...to be a father to my children. To give them the..." She saw him swallow. "The kind of life that I never had."

"What is that?"

"A normal, happy, carefree childhood."

Ariana stood transfixed as emotions buffeted her from all directions.

Guilt and grief choked her breath. Here was the proof that he had truly changed. Just as she had.

Could they make it work this time?

Could she trust that gut instinct of hers that said he cared at least?

She took his hands when he would have moved away. When the small distance she was insisting on could become a chasm neither of them could cross. "I need time. I need it to be just us first. That is, just you and me and Drakon at least."

His gaze probed hers, as if he wanted to know all of her secrets. He lifted their joined hands and kissed her knuckles. The tenderness of the gesture melted her from within.

Lifting his gaze, he held hers. "You've changed," he said finally, his thoughts running parallel to hers.

"I have stopped throwing myself headlong into everything, yes."

He nodded, a set to his jaw. "But I want that old Ariana back. The Ariana that was quick to laugh. The Ariana that loved so generously. The Ariana that lived life to the fullest.

"I assure you, *pethi mou*, I will have that old Ariana back."

CHAPTER TEN

OVER THE NEXT couple of weeks, Ariana found herself more and more captivated by her husband. It was as if he had mounted a campaign to conquer her—mind, body and soul.

And he was winning.

One evening had been a leisurely two hours where they had discussed the red tape she was having to muddle through for her legal agency; one dinner had lasted only an hour and had to be shared with two of his political aides who'd discussed his agenda on his upcoming trip to Asia; once with his PR team and hers, coordinating their schedules and events over the next few months, which had, of course, resulted in a fierce argument between her and Andreas, concerning her duties as the Queen and her increasing devotion to establishing her own career.

Neither of them packed their punches. Neither of them had won.

Ariana had loved every minute of it.

She loved pitting herself against his considerable will. While she never came out the victor, neither did she let him run roughshod over her.

If dinner could not be possible and there had been days when all she caught was a passing glance of him at a party they were both attending, she found him drifting into the small sitting lounge at precisely ten thirty every night, where she watched an American political satire show, a longstanding favorite of hers.

He would settle down next to her, his hard thigh pressed up against her. Sometimes they laughed at the comedy, sometimes they hotly debated the politics. Sometimes, when they were both far too exhausted, they just fell into a comfortable silence.

But whatever the scenario, a persistent thread of awareness flared between them over the most innocent of contact. Contact, she realized with heat flushing her as she waited for him, she seemed to initiate.

It was she who couldn't keep her hands to herself, who had undone his tie knot one evening when he'd looked utterly flattened after another meeting with the Crown Council, she who had quickly buttoned his shirt, covering that defined chest, when he hadn't quite finished dressing when she and Petra had arrived at the same time one evening, she who had pressed her mouth to his when he had given her his mother's ring.

All he did was watch her from those eyes, the epitome of patience and inscrutability. But Ari knew him as well as she knew herself. Knew that he was waiting for her to make the first move. Knew that it was his kind of foreplay.

He thrived on waiting her out, thrived on pushing them to the edge until every single touch was a fire that could sear.

She didn't know what she was waiting for. She didn't know why she couldn't take that last step in their new relationship. The last time she had jumped into a physical relationship with him, not knowing what was at stake. This time…this time, she knew the value of it.

She knew that when she took Andreas inside her, she would irrevocably lose a part of herself again.

Was it losing her will to his that terrified her?

Or was it the last bit of truth she still held on to?

She wanted nothing between them when he made love to her this time, nothing but want and need.

Except telling Andreas about their son that she had lost terrified her to her core.

They were finally getting to know each other. Finally

coming to understand what had gone so terribly wrong the last time. Finally realizing that something akin to magic existed between them. Even out of bed.

"You look utterly serious."

Andreas stood at the entrance to her bedroom. His suit jacket was gone and his white shirt was unbuttoned. The dark shadow of his chest held her attention, her lower body instantly tightening.

She blinked and tried to rearrange her face. "I'm just tired tonight," she replied, realizing it was true. All week, she'd been on conference calls with Magnus and Rhonda and her new lawyer.

He reached the sofa she was sitting on and took a seat without touching her. The tension in his frame radiated out in waves, dismissing her concerns. "Then you need to dial back on the amount of work you're taking on. Petra couldn't find a spare moment from you all of last week."

"Petra needs to stop spying for you," she countered with a smile. Even as his overbearing attitude toward her well-being grated, it also warmed a part of her. For years, she had looked after herself, with no complaints.

But now, she liked that Andreas worried about her. Now she could see his concern for her beneath his arrogant commands.

"Also, will you do the same with your work?" she asked and he grunted. "Very macho, Andreas. Your attitude is beginning to match your communication style."

A long exhale left his lips and he looked at her, a glimmer of a smile around his lips. "You keep up your duties as the Crown Prince's wife, you work all hours setting up your office and dealing with your friends' problems. And yet..."

That he was trying to put this into words rather than railroad her made joy bloom in her chest. "But I'm not being a real wife, am I?" she answered, covering the distance between them.

Dark desire made his eyes glitter. He fingered a wayward curl of her hair and tugged, his mouth a languid curve. "No. One of these days, *agapita*, my patience is going to run out and I'll be inside you and you cannot claim I seduced you.

"I have given you time, Ari." Gravelly and low, his voice pinged over her skin.

Suddenly, she was ready. Just like that.

Before he could blink, she straddled his legs and kissed him.

A long growl erupted from his mouth as he took over the kiss in an instant. Hands on her hips kept her pelvis ground against his, spiking her temperature.

His tongue caressed her with a silky slide, his fingers curling tightly around the nape of her neck.

Ariana moaned loudly when he took her lower lip between his teeth. Threw her head back in a wanton invitation when his hand covered her breast. Drifting her hands down his chest, she covered his groin.

Felt the jolt of his arousal against her palm.

She would have let him take her on the couch right there, if not for the loud peal of her cell phone.

"Ignore it," he growled against her breast.

And it was the command in his voice that made her realize the significance of that ringtone. She slid off him and picked up her phone. And her heart sank.

Andreas somehow managed to dig his senses out of the haze of arousal. Or maybe it was the fast leaching of color from Ari's face that did it.

Ignoring the distress that emanated from her, he wrapped his arms around her while she was still on the call. The lush roundness of her bottom incensed his deprived body a little more. But he liked holding her like that. Even if it was torture.

Somehow, urging his body to calm down, he kneaded the tense jut of her shoulders just as she ended the call.

He knew he wasn't going to like it the second she faced him.

"I have to go," she whispered.

The words sank like stones through his gut. He frowned. Tried to keep his voice even. "Go where?"

"To the States. To Colorado," she said absently, walking circles around the vast room.

"You're not going anywhere," he burst out.

Her awareness jerked back into the room. "Rhonda's divorce came through." Anguish painted her face deathly pale. "Her husband was so pissed off that he hit her. She needs me, Andreas."

Andreas reached for his own phone and called Petra. "I'll have Petra arrange for round-the-clock care for her. And security. That husband of hers won't touch her again."

She was still pale, her body tense. "I should have been there. She was…there for me when I had no one. When it mattered, Andreas," Ariana whispered, as if she hadn't heard a word he'd said.

The very idea made goose bumps rise on his skin. "If you had been there, then you'd have been hurt. *Christos*, Ariana, how could you not share how dangerous your cases are? What if you had been there and he had hit you instead?" Panic made his voice rise, made it harsh. He'd never felt panic like this. He didn't know how to handle it.

Thee mou, was this what came of caring about her?

He never wanted to imagine Ari hurt or worse. "If you want, we'll fly her here as soon as she's able to travel. And first thing tomorrow morning, you'll give over all your case files to Giannis.

"I want a security team vetting every case you take on in the future. You'll be a target as it is without taking on unnecessary—"

Ariana covered his mouth with her hand, her arm going around his body. He stiffened, rejecting her caress, wishing he could reject the answering thrum of his heart as she looked into his eyes.

When had she gained this power over him?

"If you curtail my career, if you do anything to change even the course of it, you'll lose me." Her words were a whisper, an entreaty. As if she understood what she did to him. As if she was willing him to trust this thing between them. Willing him to trust this strange coiling of his own emotions that he was feeling for the first time in his life.

When, suddenly, all he wanted to do was to fight the choke hold of it.

When all he wanted was to have his sterile, uncaring self back.

"It's the same as asking you to walk away from Drakon. Could you do it, Andreas? Could you do it for anything in the world?"

He pulled her hand away from his mouth, his pulse violently ringing in his entire body. "No."

She clasped his cheeks, forcing him to look into her eyes. Forcing him, again, to face what he didn't want to. "Then please trust me. Trust me to do what I need to do. Trust me to keep myself safe. Trust me to come back to you."

Pressing his mouth to the inside of her wrist, he took a deep breath. Letting her go was akin to tearing out a part of him.

But he needed to do it. For both their sakes. To keep a modicum of control over his own emotions.

Whatever madness had consumed his father and whatever manipulations he had run through his children's lives, Theos had been right in one thing.

Emotion was dangerous to men like them, men who held the fates of thousands in the palms of their hands. Men who could abuse that power so easily to rearrange the lives of people closest to them.

Even now, the urge to do something, to ruin her career, her case files, her associations, so that he could keep her safe, so that he could keep her to himself, was so rampant.

My jailer, this time, was the man I loved.

Never again. *Thee mou*, he couldn't do that to her again. He couldn't be the one who killed the spirit inside her.

He let her hand go, and turned away. "Fine, go. I'll give you a week before I'll drag you back here, by your hair if that's what it takes."

He felt her at his back, her arms vined around him, her laughter sending tremors through his frame. "I can't decide if I like you as an academic or a warrior." A wet kiss fluttered near his spine. "I think I like both." Her hands circled to his chest, moved sinuously lower until she was palming his arousal. "I want both."

A deep shudder went through him. Need shook him to the core. "You're a witch." He turned and took her mouth in a punishing kiss. He had to do it. He had to let her go, yet he hated the weakness in his gut. Hated the sweat that gathered at the thought of her not returning.

He poured everything he couldn't say into his kiss. Lifting her off the floor, he plastered her body to his, until even air couldn't separate them. Until she could have little doubt that she was his.

Longing rushed through Ariana, sending little tremors through her body. A haze descended on her and Ari struggled to keep her breathing even.

"Ari? What is it? Ari, are you having an attack?"

"No…" Ari whispered. She could hardly tell him that she was having one of those moments where you realized there was no hope for you.

That something in her was programmed to forever do

what was not good for her. It was like trying to straighten a dog's tail.

"Shh...*agapi mou*. Tell me what I can do, Ari. In this moment, just tell me what you want of me."

"Just..."

Just tell me you love me, please. Tell me so that I can say it back. Tell me so that I can scream it to the world. Tell me so that this time I can truly love you, knowing who you are and knowing who I am.

"You're mine, Ariana. I won't let you go. Anything except that."

Her laughter burst through the tears in her eyes. She had to give him points for constancy. "Just...hold me."

Silently, he tightened his arms around her. His skin was so warm around her, his body lean and yet somehow hard. His heart thundered under her ear as she placed her cheek against his chest. Nothing could equal being held by Andreas. Being dwarfed in his arms, being hit with that sensation of the world righting itself.

At the back of her mind, she was aware everything was changing. She was sinking, falling, and yet she could not stop. She could not be in his life and fight it. She could not be near him and resist what he meant to her. What he'd always meant to her.

She hid her face in his chest, afraid he would see everything in her eyes. "Never let me go," she whispered, shivering.

Three weeks later, coronation day dawned bright and sunny.

Her stomach twisting into a painful knot, her nerves stretched taut, Ariana stared at her reflection in the floor-length mirror in her suite.

The silence was startling after hours of hubbub with designers, hair stylists, her assistants running all over the palace and the palace jeweler, for God's sake.

Only a few minutes before she walked down those curving stairs to a waiting Andreas.

Only a few minutes before the world saw Ariana Drakos.

Only a few minutes before the ceremony that crowned Andreas as King and her Queen.

The gold-edged, oval, floor-length mirror made her dress shimmer as if it had been spun from pure gold.

The bright bulbs overhead made the diamonds in her combs—she'd had to draw the line at the tiara, which had looked more like a crown, and an old, tacky design at that—glitter. The tiny combs, nestled in the complicated up-do she'd twisted her hair into, winked as if there were stars in her hair.

Only now in the first minutes of what seemed like privacy, after hours and hours of makeup artists and stylists and her own secretary hovering over her, did Ariana admit the existence of the football-stadium-sized butterflies in her tummy. Admit to herself that this mattered to her. Far too much.

Of course it did.

It was the moment she had partly run away from. Andreas had given her a reason, yes, but he had also been right.

All Ariana had known then was to run away from difficult situations.

Her father, King Theos, Andreas—they had all been so sure that she'd amount to nothing. Until a few months ago, Ariana had thought she'd never measure up, either.

Had never believed in herself. Had never believed herself worthy of Andreas and everything he had thrust on her in that little fishing village.

Tonight was the culmination of years of sticking to her chosen path, the culmination of the heartache she had suffered, the doubts that had filled her in the darkest moments that her father may have been right, that she was bound to be a train wreck her entire life.

The added layer was that tonight the outer surface matched what she finally believed herself to be inside.

She looked bold, fearless, stylish, a woman who had seduced the ruthless Crown Prince into love. Even she, who had never been into clothes much, had to admit that there was something to be said for the confidence the right designer duds gave.

Her gold ball gown had been a bold choice. Her choice, since Petra and her own secretary likewise thought it unnecessarily defiant. Far too radical.

Ariana didn't give a hoot.

The gold silk was so soft that the soft corset naturally clung to her torso, drawing attention to the meager curves of her breasts. Baring her shoulders, it had a straight neckline and sleeves that fell off her shoulders. At her waist, it flared into a wide skirt.

As she ran a hand over her tummy to calm the butterflies fluttering there, she stilled, stunned by something she hadn't realized until now.

For weeks now, she had tried to shrug off the sinking tentacles of Drakon and all its centuries of glory. Had pretended to scorn the import of today, of her reception by the population of Drakon, to anyone who'd tried to lecture her on the importance of it.

Which meant Eleni, Petra, Andreas's PR team, her own PR team, Nikandros, who thought it hilarious and particularly revelatory when she'd asked him to honestly tell her about the women who'd been running contestants for the coveted role of the future Queen and how she compared against them.

Only Andreas hadn't put that pressure on her since she'd returned—later than the week he'd allotted but in time for the madness that was coronation day.

Only Andreas hadn't filled her head with well-intentioned advice, or warnings, or phrases to be memorized.

Only Andreas had just let her be.

He had not once told her what he expected of her. No questions about if she'd familiarized herself with the Who's Who of the guest list for the ball after, no questions about if she had memorized her statement on her husband's policies about his new directive for the Crown Council.

No comments about sanitizing the reality of the cases she'd dealt with in her everyday life. Cases like Julia's and Rhonda's, cases that rattled some of the most powerful men in the world.

Not even a teasing question about her dress.

Only now, away from the breath-stealing intensity of his gaze, away from that sizzling awareness between them, did she realize that Andreas had showed trust in her abilities, her judgment.

Had he kept his doubts quiet because of their history, or because he actually trusted her to see this through?

Whichever it was, Ariana found she didn't actually care. Did he know what a gift it was that he did not think her unequal to tonight's celebration and fanfare?

Dare she take the risk and tell him the last piece of the past that shimmered between them like a ghost?

The longer she waited to tell him, the harder it was getting. She saw the question in his eyes sometimes. Knew that he didn't like her answer about starting a family. That her lack of trust in him, in them, bothered him.

She did trust him, didn't she? She trusted that he'd changed just as much as she had. That they were both different people now. That any child they might have would be loved by him. In his own way.

Tonight she would tell him. After the coronation, when the frenzy of these few months came to an end. When they could just be Andreas and Ariana again in the intimacy of their bedroom.

She would tell him about the boy they had lost. She would tell him how much she loved him. She had never wanted to so desperately believe her gut instinct. And yet had never been so terrified.

Trembling from head to toe, she turned when she heard someone behind her.

Giannis stood there, his eyes taking her in with a wide smile. "It is time, Your Highness," he said with a nod that acknowledged everything he saw in her eyes.

Head high, Ariana walked to him. On an impulse she couldn't deny, threw herself at him. The good man that he was, Giannis not only caught her but ran a hand over her back comfortingly.

Ariana straightened and nodded, more than grateful for a friend who saw and understood everything.

She was ready for Drakon and its King.

Ariana realized something was wrong the moment she came down the huge, curving staircase and looked into Andreas's dark eyes.

She faltered on the last step and he caught her. His grip was so tight that she was sure she'd have bruises on her hips from his fingers. A fact he wasn't even aware of, she knew, as his gaze swept over her from head to toe.

Her body rang like a pulse at his slow perusal, at the stark possession in his eyes.

A cold hand fisted her spine.

He knew.

Somehow, he knew what she'd hidden.

"Andreas, I…"

"Did you know that I have been prepared all my life for this moment?" The catch in his throat stunned her, scared her. "To be the King of Drakon, I'd been taught, was my only duty in life. My only purpose.

"And now that the day is here…you have destroyed everything, Ari. Even my belief in myself."

"Andreas…wait, please. How did you know?"

"One of my aides thought it would be a good idea to make sure you had no surprises in your past. The media has a way of getting to those skeletons. And my team always tries to stay two steps ahead of them.

"Imagine the poor man's shock and his nerves when he had to bring that hospital report to me… Can you imagine what you have done to me?"

The next few hours were the most torturous of Ariana's life. Not one of her father's passive-aggressive punishments, not even the pain of premature labor and not knowing if she and the baby would come through, nothing could equal the agony of smiling at people she neither knew nor cared about, when Andreas wouldn't even look at her, nothing could trump the fear that she had, once again, ruined her happiness with her own hands.

But where she normally would have shattered and screamed at the unfairness of it all, she stood ramrod straight by Andreas's side on the ramparts of the King's Palace and waved at thousands of people lining up the streets of the city.

She never let her smile slip as she accompanied him in an armored car through the streets, never let the tension tying her belly into knots show as they posed for pictures outside the palace.

When she saw Maria Tharius, who seemed to be the very embodiment of poise and patience and every other virtue Ariana didn't possess, and Andreas speaking to each other, his body language utterly relaxed with her, she didn't rant and rave like a lunatic.

The one time she thought she would humiliate herself

and the House of Drakos was when they had returned to the ballroom for the first ball given in their honor. When the string quartet began playing and Andreas and she were supposed to open the dancing.

For a few knee-buckling seconds, she thought he would not ask her. Five hundred distinguished guests watching their every interaction like vultures waiting to pick at her flesh. If he didn't ask to dance with her… Nausea rose up.

A harsh exhale left her when he finally uncoupled himself from Maria Tharius and came to stand before her. The perfectly nice smile he had been wearing didn't slip one bit. Only the cold chips of his eyes betrayed his emotions.

The string quartet started a sonata and with a fluid grace she should have expected, he pulled her onto the dance floor. Her heart dipped to her knees and stayed there when he held her as if she were the most precious thing on earth.

Their bodies, which had always fit each other like two puzzle pieces slotting into one, moved in perfect sync. Ariana didn't have to look around to know that they had captured everyone's attention. She wouldn't have to look at the media reports tomorrow to know that the King and Queen of Drakon, unprecedented in the history of Drakon, were madly in love with each other.

When the dance ended and there was a thunderous applause, he pulled her to him and kissed her in complete contrast to the propriety that protocol demanded.

Her heart lurching painfully in her chest, her mouth clinging to his, only Ariana realized what it truly was.

There was no softness, no passion. He punished her with that kiss. Fingers crawling into her sophisticated up-do, he ravished her on the dance floor there. His tongue pushed into her mouth, enslaving her.

Even knowing what he intended, Ariana still clung to him. Her breath hung on a serrated edge, her body teased into painful arousal. Made even more cheap by his poisonous remark against her ear. “Welcome to our future life, my Queen.” Color slashed his high cheekbones. “It never fails to amaze me how sweet you taste even when you are filled with the bitterest lies, *agapi mou*. Good thing, too. Because all we have left between us is lies and lust.

“At least conceiving our children should not be as odious a task.”

Like jagged thorns, his words pricked Ariana. “What are you talking about?”

A feral gleam erupted in his yes. “I do not give a damn about your timeline, Ari. We will have children and we will have them whenever the mood strikes me.

“Smile, Ariana. You have won over all of Drakon with your perfect act. Someone should benefit from the sordid game you play with our lives.”

Swallowing back the tears and the ache from his words, Ariana turned to the guests and smiled. Until her jaw hurt. Until the knot in her throat seemed to cut off the very breath from her lungs.

Andreas was a consummate politician. It was a kiss that generations of Drakonites would talk about.

The romance of a century for their future King and Queen.

The twist that Andreas had wanted to start his reign with had paid off perfectly.

The whole world believed in their love story. And it was in ashes at Ariana’s feet.

CHAPTER ELEVEN

IT WAS PAST midnight by the time Andreas, along with Ariana and his brother and sister, had been able to see off the last guest.

As he'd told Ariana, the evening had been a tremendous success on one measure.

Drakon and the crème de la crème of its society had bought the story of his romance, hook, line and sinker.

They had seen what they had wanted to see—their stoic, emotionless King, made too much in his father's mold, and his beautiful wife with whom he'd irrevocably fallen in love.

It was the stuff of fairy tales, and Drakonites loved their tales more than air.

He had done his duty toward Drakon. More than that, he had given Drakonites something to look forward to after decades of his father's cold, impersonal rule.

Somehow, he'd kept a lid on his exploding temper through it all. No, not somehow. He'd been programmed to behave like this, to put duty to the crown and Drakon above everything else. He'd been programmed until it became a second skin to bury his own emotions, to pretend as if nothing had happened even when he stared at a clinical, cold summary of what his eighteen-year-old wife had suffered.

To find out that she had not only been pregnant when she had left him but that she had almost died delivering his son—his stillborn son—in some godforsaken little village at the foot of the Rocky Mountains with no one around her, it was a picture Andreas could not wipe from his eyes.

And yet, he had carried on like the automaton that he sometimes felt like.

Even Nik and Eleni hadn't suspected anything as he conversed with cabinet ministers and Crown Council members alike.

But now, in the deafening silence of the cavernous palace that had been a prison in so many ways, another chain around his ankles, a sense of utter unreality descended on him. As if something inside him was disconnecting from everything that had always shackled him.

He took the stairs three or four at a time. But there was no running from the very thing that was fracturing inside of him. Propelled by a whirlwind of emotion he had never felt, much less understood, Andreas strode into his suite and came to a standstill.

The massive doors flew back and crashed together at the force with which he had burst them open.

In the gold dress that rippled over every high and dip of that sensuous body, Ariana stood leaning against his vast bed, his downfall and his salvation together in those stricken brown eyes.

As if she belonged in here.

For a minute, all he could do, even now, was stare at her. Drink her in so that maybe it would keep other ghastly images of her at bay.

She had never looked so breathtakingly beautiful, so poised and perfect as she did tonight.

It was no wonder the media and his very discriminating guests had lapped up the story they had been fed. With that mystifying combination of confidence and innocence, strength and vulnerability, Ariana made it very easy to buy that any man, even he whose heart was made of stone, would tumble recklessly into love with her.

That any man would defy conventions and propriety to own her. And it was not just how she had looked today. It was how she had engaged people. No amount of coaching or being prepped by his team of aides would have made her look more like the genuine article.

Would have made her speak up with more passion about serving the people. About joining her husband in seeing to it that Drakon emerged victorious again after the last decade in a funk.

Against all odds, it was clear that Ariana had finally accepted Drakon. That she had finally come into her own for the role he'd always wanted her in.

She had become everything Theos had wanted in the future Queen.

She'd almost died, something inside him screamed again. It was as if the loss that had nearly destroyed him when he'd returned from the oil summit, he'd have to live through it again.

His brain provided vivid images of her pale and unconscious lying in some wretched hospital, surrounded by strangers.

Afraid and alone, yet determined to not return to him at any cost. Consigning him to a life of loneliness, destroying the little joy she had brought him.

"Get out of my suite."

"I'm not going anywhere." Defiance and something else screamed from every angle of her body. "Never again. I..." She looked away and then back at up him again. "I was going to tell you today. It's been killing me to hold it inside. Please, believe me that I was going to tell you today."

"Your words mean nothing to me anymore."

The intensity of the fury building inside him, the jagged edge of betrayal, threatened to take him out at his knees.

Was this what he had dreaded ten years ago? Had he always known that she would reduce him to this—the lowest denominator of himself—that his father had worked hard to beat out of him? Had Theos known that Ariana would have the power to bring him to his knees like this?

Her hands went around her midriff, her body faintly swaying from side to side. “No. I want to discuss this.”

Ignoring her, he walked toward his closet and she blocked him. Like a drug addict, he pulled the scent of her skin deep into his lungs.

“Get out of my way, Ariana.”

She stood in front of him, tension radiating out of every pore.

“If you don’t move out of my way, I will not be responsible for what I do.”

“I’m not afraid of you, Andreas. I was afraid of what… I became around you, of what our lives would become if I stayed. I was immature, reckless.”

“Nothing you say or do today is going to change the way I feel.”

A jagged laugh fell from her mouth, far too close to the sound a cornered animal would make in its last bid for freedom. “If only I had known that this last piece of bitter truth was what I needed to spill to get you to talk about your feelings, then I would have done so a long time ago.”

Rage clawing through him like a tsunami, Andreas backed her into the wall until she was caged by his body against it. “What the hell is wrong with you that you would joke about such a thing? How dare you mock me about hiding the fact that you had my son and nearly—” his throat felt like there were pieces of glass in there “—died in the process?”

Finally, she must have seen something of what he was feeling in his eyes for her brown eyes widened. And even that lasted only a few seconds before she tilted her chin up and looked him square in the eye. “I lived through that, Andreas. I know what I suffered.” Tears filled her eyes and ran down her cheeks. “The guilt that something in me made that happen, the grief that drowned me for months… they will not leave me in this lifetime.”

She ran the back of her hands over her cheeks roughly and swallowed. "I'm not defending my decision making at that time. I was—"

"A pathological liar? A woman incapable of thinking maturely?"

"By the time I found out that I was pregnant, you were already engaged to another woman. Think this through, I had already signed papers agreeing to dissolve our marriage.

"If I had come back, if I had told you back then that I was pregnant, you would have made my life miserable as hell. Loving you with nothing in return was already half killing me.

"The fact that I even got pregnant when it was the last thing we needed in our lives is not my fault. The fact that you thought bringing a child into a…rocky relationship would fix everything…that was your fault."

Every word out of her mouth was truth that raked its claws through him. "I asked you to get off the pill because it was the only other way I could convince Theos to accept you. I knew, in the back of my mind, what he was doing to you. I saw the stricken look in your eyes, I saw how subdued you were becoming. I thought I was losing you.

"If you became pregnant, then I could convince him. Then we could give each other a chance…"

Shock made her lips flatten. Hard. "So my choice was to lose myself or to become your broodmare?"

"At the time, you were good for nothing else, so yes. If I wanted to keep you in my life, those were my choices."

She flinched at his words but he didn't care. God, nothing mattered except that he hurt her back as she had hurt him. Nothing mattered except to assuage the pain ripping him open inside.

Even caged against him, she was not feeble. Not fragile. Something glowed in her face, as if there was a light in her again. As if she was that girl who could conquer anything with her very will to live. With her laughter. "How about the simple reason that you loved me just as I was? That you needed me in your life, just as I was? How about standing up to the mighty King Theos and telling him that you were so desperately in love with me that you couldn't go on without me?

"That despite his every cruel treatment, despite his every effort to make you into stone, you still felt so much for me. That you…you loved me and it made you so off balance, so disconcerted that you immediately tried to push me away when we returned?

"That you're, after all, human, Andreas."

Bitterness was a rock in her throat. A jagged-edged one. She was truly lost if she thought he had loved her. "*Christos*, I ruined your life, Ari. Isn't that what you've been trying to tell me for weeks now?

"If you want to call it love, then you're as screwed up as I'm, *glykia mou*. Do you not see that?"

"I loved you so much and your incapability to handle what you felt for me…your inability to accept it for what it was, that's what drove me away. That's what terrified me about coming back.

"The fate of becoming my own mother again…dying inside a little every day."

Andreas turned away from her, just the act of breathing hurting his lungs.

Did it drill down to that as he'd always known, always feared? Did it come down to the fact that even now, he could not process or admit to his own feelings?

She pressed against his back, her body trembling. "I was afraid of what you and your father would do to our child. I was afraid that if I came back to you, you would…"

He turned with a vicious snarl. *Dios*, he just couldn't take anymore. But she was determined to rip him up, she was determined to prove that there was something in him worth loving. "We would do what?"

"I was terrified that King Theos and you would repeat history. That it would be another person your father would control. I was terrified that you would turn our son into… another you. That like my own mother, I would have no say in the bringing up of our child. I stayed away for the baby, Andreas."

The bare truth of her words fragmented the last thread of his self-possession.

He crushed his mouth to hers, for he couldn't stave off that fear spreading through him. Couldn't find a way to hold off the anger, the desperation and worst of all that hurt that seemed to saw through him.

She was right. Theos had made him into this and there was nothing he could do. He could not love her. He still had nothing to offer her.

All the rage he felt at himself, his father and Ariana mutated into this raw, overwhelming need to possess her, the only time in his entire life when he felt something.

The only thing in his life he still had, the only thing that was real and constant in his tilting world.

He poured everything he had ever felt into that one kiss, dragging his mouth over hers desperately. As if she was air and he would expire if he let go of her.

Her mouth was sweet and soft, a cavern of welcoming heat. A place where he'd always found something he didn't know he was missing.

"Andreas, please—"

A sob burst out of her mouth when he buried his hands in her hair and tugged roughly. He had no control anymore and he didn't give a damn. He tangled his tongue with hers, licking in and out of her mouth. The more he kissed her, the more he wanted.

In some portion of his mind, he was aware that she was

trying to talk. That she had more to say. But he didn't want to hear any more. He didn't want excuses. He didn't want more accusations even though he knew most of what she said was true. He wanted nothing but to drown himself in sensation.

So he took her mouth again and again, rough and hard.

He bit her lip when she tried to argue.

He licked at that nip when she sobbed.

He thrust his tongue into her mouth when she moaned.

He molded her body with his hands when she thrashed against him.

At some point, she had stopped trying to get him to listen and began giving as good as she got. Slim hands were clutching him, pushing back his suit jacket. Nails digging into his nape. Fingertips gripping his buttocks.

He laughed against her mouth, a bitter, twisted sound. He'd forgotten how much she loved his body. How many hours she'd spent kissing and licking him. Testing and teasing. Theos's excruciatingly rigorous physical regimen had come in handy in this.

Desire banishing any sense, he picked her up and ate up the few strides to his enormous bed. The French doors were open, he could hear the whisper of the staff walking back and forth across the courtyard. But he didn't care.

All he needed was to be inside her.

He devoured her and she devoured him, their focus so completely on each other that the outside world melted.

"Andreas...you didn't let me finish. Please, let me—"

His questing hands found the zipper of her dress and half pulled, half tore it away from her pliant body. Bra undone, her breasts spilled against his hands. The tips engorged when he ran his knuckles over the nipples. He pushed her onto the bed and her hair billowed on his pristine white sheets like burnished copper.

A string of silk was the only thing that separated him

from the warmth he needed. From the moment Theos had let it slip that she was alive, he'd needed this. Only with her had he ever been like this. An animal that let instinct rather than reason drive him. Years' worth of need burst through him like water through a dam.

He saw so many things in her body. So many things she'd given him with her generosity and all he'd done…

Only staring at her gorgeous body held off the pain. The ache of how much they'd lost. The fear…the stabbing fear that he was still that same man.

That he would only destroy her again.

With his palm splayed on her lower back, he pushed her onto the bed.

He ripped off the flimsy piece of silk from her body. Dizzying need. Glorious freedom.

The taut curves of her buttocks. The neat little indentation of her waist. The fluid arc of her spine. The long, trembling muscles of her thighs. The toned arms that she had spread under her. The fingers digging into the silky sheets for purchase.

He let his gaze rove up and down her body like a starved man staring at a feast. Goose bumps were rising on her skin, exposed suddenly to the cold air.

There was no mercy in him tonight.

She laid her head on one cheek, her shallow breaths making the air near her head fly in a mesmerizing rhythm. Their eyes met and held. There were tears in her eyes, unspilled, making them huge in that gamine face. Her already pouty lips were swollen and a voluptuous pink.

He might as well have been a predator holding down prey for the continual shudders that coursed through her body.

Exposed to him like this, she should have looked feeble. At least fragile. Yet there was a fire in her eyes that dared him to take her like that. To continue on the explosive path he seemed to have pushed them to, even as she quivered like a finely tuned string under the softest of his touches.

"*S'agapo*, Andreas. So much. Always." *I love you, Andreas.*

The words seared him like lashes against bare skin. Like lightning striking things to ground. Like hot spewing lava burning up everything in sight.

The true meaning of those words terrified him, bound him when all he'd wanted was to walk away.

Just once, he promised himself. He would take her for this one night. He would let himself revel in those words this one time.

Holding her gaze like that, he unzipped his trousers and pushed them and his boxers down. His erection sprang free and he saw the tiniest flicker of something—hunger, fear, he didn't care what the hell it was—in her eyes. Heard her breath quicken.

His arousal lengthened at the greed in her eyes. With a growl he couldn't contain, he shed his shirt and undershirt. "Spread your legs, *agapi mou*," he whispered and she complied like a nice, docile wife.

Legs straddling hers, he bent his body over hers. The skin-to-skin contact sent heat ripping between them. She was like spun silk against his rough chest. Her buttocks an inviting cradle for his rock-hard flesh. When she tried to move against him, he locked her movements with his hands on her wrists, using a bit of his own superior strength against hers.

Sounds ripped out of their mouths in unison, a hoarse symphony of need and desire. Sensations they had both long forgotten shimmered close. Fluttered in and out in their harsh breaths as their bodies recognized things their minds hadn't.

God, he loved her like this. He needed this submission from the woman who constantly defied him, who again and again set his world upside down. He needed her willing and wanton beneath him because it was the only place where there was complete honesty between them.

Where she couldn't hide anything more from him.

Where she couldn't retreat behind lies.

Where he was enough for her.

He dug his teeth into her upper shoulder. She bucked under him, thrusting into his hardness with a sob. "More, Andreas. Everything you can give."

The sheets whispered and slithered around them as he grazed a few more spots on her lovely back. He licked the tender spots, already bruising. Sensual and all woman, her taste licked through his veins, incinerating.

His erection caught between their bodies was like velvet-encased steel.

She was moaning and clawing at the sheets when he slipped his hand between her legs. Her slick warmth was like molten fire over his fingers. He felt her writhe under him, trying to arch her pelvis into his hand, searching mindlessly for the rhythm that would bring relief.

He stroked her long and leisurely, opened her up and sank his fingers into her, never giving her the pace she wanted. Stringing her along until she was one long pulse of sensation underneath him.

In a flash of movement, she turned under him, until she was facing him. "Don't retreat from me, please. Andreas. Don't treat me as if I'm nothing but a body to you."

"But you're just that, Ariana. I can give you nothing but this. I have never given you anything but this, *agapi mou*. When will you learn?"

"No, no, no," she said, thrashing against him. Bringing her body flush against his, she brought her mouth to his in a crushing kiss. Her breasts were crushed against his arm, her legs tangled with his. She kissed as if she meant to hold him to her with it.

"I was wrong," she whispered against his mouth, pressing kisses all over his face. "We are both different now, Andreas. We have a chance and I will not—"

He slammed his mouth against hers. Kicking her legs apart, holding her with his hands on her hips, he entered her welcoming warmth with one deep stroke. No warning, no waiting.

A groan ripped from his throat. Her snug sheath closed around his hardness like a glove.

Like they'd never been apart. As if in this moment, in this place, they were not two but one.

Anchoring her with one arm, he palmed her breast with another. The tip was an erotic contrast surrounded by the lush softness. Pleasure coiled and corkscrewed in his groin, and shivered down his spine. Lost to the demands of his own body, he pulled out and thrust back in slow, hard thrusts that had her silky body sliding up against the sheets.

Sensation spiraled through him, erasing the grief and guilt and betrayal, the only thing that could wash away the powerlessness he felt.

Mouth buried in her neck, he slammed in and out, branding her, making her his in every way. She was perfect under him, around him, the one woman who had always made him feel that he was not alone. That made him dream that he did not have to be alone.

S'agapo, *Andreas. So much. Always.*

The words mocked him, taunted him. Charged the moment with so much more than the pure carnality of it all.

He wrapped his hand around her neck, and pulled her up, until on each thrust in, her sex felt him. All of him. He increased the pace just as her body was tensing up around him. Her muscles clenched and released around his hardness, her body bucking and throwing. She orgasmed with a soft moan, her eyes open and holding his, daring him—

oh, how they dared him—always to make nothing of this moment.

It was the fire in her eyes that pushed Andreas over the edge. Lost to desire, he plunged into her with hard, rough, desperate strokes.

His climax was violent, explosive, moving through him like a storm he would never survive. This connection between them had always made everything worth it. Had somehow made sense of everything else.

Heart pounding inside his chest, he stilled. Loath to give up her warmth, he stayed inside, swallowing away the aftershocks of her orgasm still rocking through her.

Sweat-dampened, her skin glistened and invited. Her mouth looked like it had been stung by bees. Faint bruises on her hips showed where he had held her down while he had thrust into her.

Long lashes flickered up slowly. The musky scent of their sweat and sex filled his nostrils.

He couldn't walk away, even though it was exactly what he'd intended to do. Still intended to do.

CHAPTER TWELVE

WHEN ARIANA WOKE up the first time, morning had come. Even through the light-blocking blinds, she could see the world outside had started on its day. Every inch of her body was sore in the most glorious way. A muscular, hair-dusted leg lay possessively over hers, hindering her movement. The oversize T-shirt she wore bunched up to her midriff thanks to the arm curled around her waist holding her caged against the hard muscles behind.

She tried to shift to a more comfortable position and gasped at the unfamiliar sting between her thighs.

The night before came back in a rush. Instinctively, her gaze fell on the darkly handsome face sharing the pillow. His other arm was under her head, his biceps muscles curling tight. Faint shadows under his eyes, even in sleep, Andreas looked like he had the weight of the world on his shoulders.

Or was it the weight of her lies?

Had she lost him forever this time?

Only now, when it was too late, did she realize the destruction she had caused with her secrets and her cowardice.

But the stinging throb between her legs, the faint bruises on her body said something else. She had been terrified that he would throw her out. Or walk away.

Last night, she knew, was the first time Andreas Drakos had ever lost complete control of himself. There had been no finesse to his lovemaking. *Thee mou*, it hadn't even been lovemaking. It had been sex in its most primitive form. It had been pure possession, as if he meant to steal something away from her.

It had been his incapability to walk away from her even at the worst moment of their lives.

The rough graze of his teeth over the most tender spots of her body, the flash of emotions, too fast for her to even notice, in his eyes. The frantic, animalistic thrusts, uncaring of whether he hurt her. Ariana reveled in every ache and pain that her body sang this morning.

She had wanted, desperately needed, every sensation he'd evoked in her.

She had loved every minute of it.

For it meant that she could still hold on to a thread of hope. That meant that despite what he thought was the biggest betrayal, Andreas still couldn't help himself.

He had carried her to the shower, she remembered faintly. While she had stood there numb, her body sore, he had washed her, wrapped her in a towel and brought her back to bed. Dressed her in his T-shirt.

When she had thought he would leave her, she had clung to him, she remembered now, even her subconscious mind knowing that to let him walk away then was to lose him. She had begged him to stay with her, at least until she had fallen asleep. She had begged him to give her one night.

His dark hair fell onto his forehead. He needed a shave and sleep and rest in that order. God, Andreas needed to be loved. Needed to be showed that he could love, too.

She ran her fingers over the defined line of his jaw, the sharp bridge of his nose. Her fingers shook at the soft give of his mouth. The scent of sex and him lingered in the air, an anchor Ariana needed in the chaos she had created.

Anxiety curling through her, she ran her hands over warm, olive skin stretched taut over lean muscles. Every inch of him was precious to her. Every inch of him was a map to her own happiness, to her joy.

She pressed her mouth to his chest, listening to the quiet thunder of his heart. She began to whisper words and phrases that made no sense yet meant everything to her. Things she should have told him before about her life in Colorado. Times when she had missed him so terribly that it had been a physical ache.

Nights when she'd craved his arms, even in the last few weeks.

Moments during the past week when all she'd wanted was to walk into his bedroom and climb into his bed. When all she'd needed was to be held in his arms.

At some point, the words had begun to tumble out without any conscious plan. His body lost that languid sleepy warmth. Tension filled the very air, the quiet hitch in his breath the only sign that her words had begun to register. Without meeting his eyes, for Ari was terrified he would walk away the moment she acknowledged him, she kept talking. The dark helped. The physical intimacy aided. Running her hands again and again over him kept her sane, as if touch were her only tether to keep him there.

She was on her side, and he on his, facing her. She spoke the words into his chest, words she should have uttered the moment she'd seen him standing in front of the church.

The moment she'd realized that without Andreas, she would always be incomplete.

She didn't know if he was listening. She just kept talking, her throat hoarse, her body sore. "By the time I realized my period was far too late, even worse than usual, I was three months pregnant. I… I took four different tests, and they all came back positive." He was so tense around her, suddenly so cold. As if someone had injected him with ice. She rubbed his arms and his chest with her palms, her tummy a tight knot. Expecting him to any moment push her away. "I…should have been terrified and yet I was not. I know you will call it another sign that I was immature and juvenile, but I wasn't. I felt an instant connection to the baby. I…felt like finally I had a part of you with me.

Just for me. Something no one could take away from me. Not even you.

"I…had already found an apartment. Until then, I'd proudly refused to use the money Theos gave me. But that night, I went into the bank, checked my account.

"For months all I did was eat, sleep, wait. I was determined to take good care of myself. I…put on so much weight," she said, her throat catching at the memory.

"Everything was perfect until one afternoon it wasn't.

"Rhonda drove me to the hospital because pains had started and showed no signs of relenting.

"I was knocked out by the drugs and when I finally woke up…" her tears soaked Andreas's chest. Her throat burned. Her lungs felt as if they were being crushed. "I screamed at the doctor, demanding to know who had decided that my life was more precious than his.

"I was hysterical.

"They told me he'd never had a chance. I insisted on seeing him and fell apart at the sight of that tiny bundle."

Soft sobs began to shake through her body and Ariana could no more stop them than she could stop breathing. Andreas's arm came over her and crushed her to his chest. He held her hard and tight, in an almost bruising grip. The heat from his body was a blanket over her, warm and comforting.

It was exactly what she'd needed for so long. This grief, it was his, too. And she had cheated him out of it, because she had been so…afraid of never being loved in return.

"Shh…*agapi mou*," he finally said. Shaken and hoarse, as if he had damaged his throat, too. She felt his fingers move through her hair, his mouth breathing the words into her temple. "I would have made the same choice if it had come to that, Ari. I would have chosen your life…"

"I did everything right, Andreas," she said, needing to tell him this. Needing his forgiveness in this above everything else. "I was careful. I ate well. I took walks. I slept well. I went in to see the doctor for every twinge and ache. I… But I still failed at protecting him. I…never wanted to—"

His fingers were now digging into her arms, but holding her together, too. "Ariana, listen to me. He was…he was not meant to be. But it is not your fault, do you understand? All the things I said about you being reckless… I can comprehend how much you must have loved…that baby. I know how you love, *agapi mou*."

Ariana lifted her gaze, her heart beating rapidly in her chest. Grief made the planes of his face harsher, even more stark. He ran the pad of his finger against her cheek, hesitant. Naked emotion fluttered in his eyes, for the first time since she had known him. "You… How long were you out for?"

He had been so afraid for her last night, she realized now. She saw the nightmare of it in his frenzied movements, in his shattered self-control. The words in that clinical report had been enough for him to imagine what she had been through. "Two days. They said I had lost too much blood."

He nodded, a far-off look in his eyes. A look she knew very well. His detachment look. His "burying away emotion because he didn't know what to do with it" look.

His retreat look.

"After they discharged me, after I came back to my apartment, one evening I sat with the phone in my hand, my fingers hovering over the numbers. I…had never felt so alone in the world. Not even when they came to our house and told me that my parents' car had crashed.

"I…desperately wanted to see you, wanted to be held by you. To just give myself over. To let you mold me into whatever you needed me to be. Anything felt better than what I had done with my life."

"Why didn't you? *Thee mou*, Ariana, why did you not call me? Had you no trust in me at all?"

"There was nothing good left by then. Everything was in ashes and I… I realized I had to move on. I had to make sense of my life. I had to change how I lived it.

"I always used my father's rejection of me as motivation to ruin my life. To do as I pleased. I realized… I was just proving him right. I decided that night that I wouldn't let him be right.

"The next morning, Rhonda got me a job at the agency. And I never looked back."

"I saw it in your eyes the first moment I laid eyes on you. I knew immediately you had changed."

Ariana nodded, dismay coiling up at how…unangry he sounded. So much like the normal Andreas. As if he had gone through the entire range of emotion from fury to grief and was now back to his default state of feeling nothing. "I think a part of me died with our son. I…never wanted to love like that again. I didn't want that pain again. I thought…"

She cupped his face in her hands, desperate to make him understand. "Andreas, when you found me standing at the church, I… I was about to call Magnus. I was about to call it off."

His dark eyes held hers. Wariness and something else she couldn't even identify. "Call what off?"

"The wedding. I realized I just couldn't go through with it. After everything I thought needed to change in me, it seemed nothing had changed where it mattered. I knew you were going to announce your alliance with… You were going to announce your choice for a wife.

"You…would be King and have a new Queen.

"Whether you knew it or not, whether you were in my life or not, it didn't matter. You still had a part of me. You still had possession of my heart after all those years." She felt the tension that rippled through his hard body. Every inch of him screamed rejection. Every inch of him wanted to walk away.

The very instinctual gesture sent deep shivers of fear through her.

He had always wanted her love. Thrived on it. Even a week ago, he'd challenged that he would win it back.

All she was now was an emptiness in his eyes. A resignation that was clawing through her. "I…realized the happy, safe, grown-up life I thought I had with a nice man… I just didn't want it, after all. That you had ruined me for any other man."

"Ariana…" A warning.

She pressed her finger against his lips, desperate for the right words. "I was not ready to admit it to you when you showed up. I wasn't ready to admit it to myself, but I… I never stopped loving you.

"I love you, Andreas.

"I have always loved you. I just… I needed to be worthy of you. Worthy of standing by your side, to rule Drakon. I needed to be more than the train wreck my father thought I was before I could truly understand the meaning of loving you."

The moment stretched, his silence deafeningly heavy in the wake of her words. It was as if she was trying to hold on to this moment between them, trying to freeze time, and it insisted on getting away from her.

"Andreas…please say something. Curse me. Rage at me."

Turning away from her, he pulled up on the bed. Face buried in his hands, he exhaled roughly. "What we have, this, is never going to be enough, Ariana. We might as well accept it.

"The choice is yours."

Fear was a bitter taste on her tongue. "What choice?"

"Whether you want to stay with me or not." Black eyes became opaque pools, reflecting nothing. As if there was nothing. He took her hand in his, traced the veins on the inside of her wrist. As if he was asking her out to dinner while in reality, he was shredding her to pieces.

Rising to her knees, Ari pleaded with him. "Punish me all you want, Andreas, but please give me a chance. Give me a chance to prove that you can forgive me."

"Punish you? Forgive you?" He shook his head. The bleakness in his eyes made nausea rise up in her throat. "Do you still not see, Ari? Do you not see how much we've lost, how much we… Every time I close my eyes, *I see you*. Lying on some stretcher, pale, out of it. Alone. I drove you to that.

"Even if I forgive you, I cannot forgive myself.

"Even if I trust you, I can't trust myself. To not destroy you all over again."

The shudder that went through his powerful frame sent Ariana through a spiral of desperation. "You've changed," she whispered, her voice husky and rough from all the screaming. "I've changed. We have walked through fire, Andreas. And we have both come out strong."

She traced the angles of his face with shaking fingers. Wet, warm, open-mouthed kisses, she spread them over his torso as if she were sprinkling her own brand of fairy dust.

As if she could somehow make him believe that he could love her, too.

Hands fisted by his sides, he closed his eyes. His breath became harsh, falling on her like soft strokes. She pulled away the duvet that was tangled around their legs and straddled him.

Sinking her hands into his hair, she kissed his temple, his eyes and finally his mouth. He didn't move, he didn't react.

A sob rising through her, Ariana dug her teeth into his lip. Moved her mouth down his throat, licked the velvet rough skin of his shoulder. "You love me, Andreas. I will believe it enough for both of us, until you do. You love me, you love me, God, I was such a fool to not see it then. I was such a fool to not stand and fight for you." She whispered into his skin, the love she felt for him overflowing out of her.

Pushing onto her knees, she pulled off the oversized T-shirt he'd put on her. Arms wrapped around his back, she vined herself around him. His chest crushed her breasts, the angular ridge of his hips digging roughly into her inner thighs.

And then she kissed him. Softly, slowly, stroking and tracing every inch of his sculpted mouth. Pouring everything she felt for him into that kiss.

Only then did he open his eyes. Dark color slashed his cheekbones, his breath out of rhythm. His hands descended to her hips and spread her open, wicked desire glinting in his eyes.

Her breath hitched. Every particle in her stilled as he delved his fingers into her slick flesh. "This proves nothing, Ari. You were right. You have always been my weakness." One finger and then two penetrated her sensitive flesh. He licked circles around her nipple, never touching the tip.

Making her crazy for more. "You want to be a part of my life? *Kala.* You want me to continue—" his mouth closed over her nipple and he suckled so deeply that Ariana rocked her pelvis into his washboard stomach "—giving you this mindless pleasure that is the only real thing between us, *kala*. I'm more than happy to, but that's all it is, Ari.

"Your destruction, *agapita*, will not be at my hands this time."

Sensations spiraled through her. Her spine arched, and Ariana tried to hold on to her thoughts. To not give in to the riot of pleasure that forked through her lower belly. Breathing hard, she stilled his fingers wreaking havoc inside her sex. Just the way he knew would drive her over the edge. "You came for me. After everything I did, you still came for me. You searched for me for two years. That counts—"

His thumb pressed at her clit in erotic circles. Daring her to continue. Drowning her in delirious sensation. Sweat beaded on her skin. All rationality was lost again.

The second he rubbed the thick head of his erection against her swollen flesh, Ariana screamed. Tears gathered in her eyes but there was no turning off the kaleidoscope of sensations arrowing down her lower belly.

"This is all I can give you. This and the status and the respect that I would give any woman I'd have married. I would not cheat on you, but I would not love you, either.

"I will not care what you do with your life, you could learn cabaret for all I care, but I would not love you."

Ariana bit her lip hard, wondering if actual physical pain could arrest the climax building through her.

"But—"

Holding her gaze, he wrapped his fingers over her buttocks, lifted her and then sank her down onto his rock-hard flesh. So fully and completely. It stung first and then fire spread through her muscles. He pushed up into a sitting position, his thighs pressing hers inward, one hand locking her wrists.

His mouth buried between her breasts, his voice ragged. "Move, Ari. Move as your body wants you to, *pethi mou*." His eyes closed as her body did its own instinctual, age-old thing to relieve the ache there. "This I will give you, Ariana." With that promise, he took her nipple in his mouth, wrapped his tongue around it.

There was no way to control her body's response. Ariana moved up and down sending guttural groans out of their mouths. His hips surged up, cleaving through her, his eyes glittering in the dark. Stark possession shone in them. "We should not have ever come together, Ari. I…should have never married you."

Tears streaming down her cheeks, her body racing toward the peak, Ari bent down and kissed him softly. "I will choose to believe it was love that brought you to me.

"I will believe for the rest of our lives if that's what it takes. I will be here day and night. Waiting for you. And wanting you."

She repeated the words again and again as pleasure skewered through her body and he covered it with his own, chasing his own climax. He filled her completely, utterly.

And yet Ariana had never known such loss.

When she woke up again, among cool sheets, sticky and sore between her legs, he was gone. The huge room was dappled in afternoon light, bright and pricking her eyes. She didn't have to get up and ask his secretary to confirm what she already knew.

He would have already left the King's Palace.

CHAPTER THIRTEEN

ARIANA HAD FORGOTTEN. Or had she given up counting the number of days since Andreas had left the King's Palace? After the third day, nights and days began to merge.

There were no tears this time. She hadn't ranted and raged after he had walked out.

She lost herself in studying for the bar exam. In developing the contacts she'd made at the ball that would aid in her starting her own legal agency. Under Petra and Giannis's expert guidance, she gave an interview about the work she was going to take up once she was licensed to practice law in Drakon.

She visited two different organizations in the city, who provided relief and shelter to abused women, and came up with action items to tackle the poorly funded shelters. Eleni, she was slowly realizing, was a veritable mine of information on the topic of fund-raisers and charity auctions.

Taking her advice on board, Ariana threw herself into organizing her fund-raiser.

She worked from sunup to sundown, trying to exhaust herself. But when her head hit the pillow in that big king bed of Andreas's, sleep still eluded her frantic mind.

If Ariana had thought him unapproachable before, he was nothing short of the arctic freeze now.

He was utterly polite to her. He constantly checked with her to make sure she had everything she needed to realize her own dream. He respected her opinion, he even let her accompany him on a short trip to some of the key rural areas where Gabriel's firm was investing in the economy by building world-class resorts.

He treated her like he would have treated any other

woman he could have married. With the utmost civility. As if she were a complete stranger he was sharing his life with. As if there was no more to him than the perfect ruler, or the polite husband.

The worst part was that Ariana had no idea if he was doing it to distance himself from her, or if he truly felt nothing. The probability that she had lost him this time…had robbed her of a single night's peaceful sleep.

After the first three weeks of being simply stonewalled, she'd lost her patience one night. Clearly, giving him space and time wasn't working.

Nothing, it seemed, was working.

In an attempt to talk to him, to confront him, she had crawled into his bed one night, knowing that he'd returned at midnight from another trip. After waiting for hours, she had finally fallen into a restless sleep. She had woken up to realize it was his mouth on her neck, his hands on her legs that had hurtled her out of sleep.

He'd hardly even greeted her before he covered her mouth with his. He gave her hardly a chance to breathe when he pushed her legs apart, rid her of her panties and pressed his mouth to her sex.

Ariana didn't remember how many times he'd made her climax that night before he had pushed her face down, spread her legs and taken her from behind. He had exhausted her so deeply that her bones had been jelly, her entire body so sensitive and sore that finally she had fallen into a deep sleep.

When she'd awoken, showered and dressed on buckling knees, he had been gone again.

The pattern continued for two months. Every time he went on a trip, he stayed away for longer. He sent her the most exotic, expensive gifts. He barely even met her eyes anymore. If he found her in his bed, he made love to her. If she wasn't there, he didn't seek her out.

Sometimes they barely got their clothes off, he was that desperate and rough. Sometimes, he made love to her with soft, soothing words. So tenderly, as if she was the most precious thing he had ever beheld. As if he couldn't help himself.

Nikandros and Mia, Eleni and Gabriel had even stopped inquiring about what was wrong. Said only that she looked like a wraith and that Andreas was…well, more unapproachable than ever. She heard the staff, even Petra, who was as loyal as they came, say that he was even more unforgiving than before. That anyone who made one mistake, one misstep with him, got their head chewed off. While to the outside world, they couldn't be happier and more in love. More perfect for each other.

And slowly Ari began to lose hope.

The whole palace was in a mad rush because Eleni had gone into labor all of a sudden.

Ariana had wrapped the little booties and sweater she had knitted in soft tissue paper, eager to visit the little infant, when she heard two aides talking.

Andreas was returning tomorrow, was cutting his trip short to see Eleni's little girl. Eleni had already told Ariana that she wanted Ariana and Andreas to be their little one's godparents.

When Ariana had argued they were the last couple who knew anything about babies, Eleni had shook her head and said she trusted her little girl with the both of them.

As always, Ari's heart thundered at the thought of his return. Longing twisted through her, entangled with hope that, this time, things would be different. That this, the distance, would have been enough for him to see she was here. And that she had no thought of leaving him.

Slowly, as if someone was siphoning away life from her, she lost steam. Coming to rest against a dark mahogany door, she tried to catch her breath past the glass in her throat.

Was she just deluding herself?

He would smile and nod at her with those dark eyes. Tell Eleni that she would make the perfect godmother. Then walk away, especially because this was about a child.

A matter that would always be raw and guilt-ridden between them. A matter it seemed he could not get over.

Then, if she was fortunate, he might come to bed. And if he did, and Ariana tried to talk, he would make love to her until she forgot her own name.

Come morning, all she'd have was a sore body and a crushed heart.

Maybe he was right. Maybe things between them were so broken that they could not be fixed again. But *Thee mou*, she could not live like this.

She couldn't be near him and love him and live day after day knowing that he might never accept his love for her. This was even worse than what she'd run away from. She couldn't bear this…any longer.

Tired and beaten down, all she wanted was to run away. To escape.

But she couldn't. Andreas hadn't given up on her in ten years and she hugged the fact to herself.

She wiped her palms over her mouth, instructed one of the staff to give her present to Eleni and then went back to her suite. Dismissing everybody else, she took Giannis into confidence, told him how to reach her in an emergency.

Like Andreas raising a palace-wide search for her. But no, she was sure he would hardly even notice for a month or two.

She packed a small bag personally, throwing in just enough necessities. Had a car brought round to her, got into the driver's seat and drove away.

She was not running away, she told herself. She was playing the only card she had left to win him over.

Andreas walked away from Eleni's suite, his gut a hard coil of twisting emotions. His new niece, Maria Drakos Marquez, had fit into half his forearm.

She had smelled like baby powder, and new life, and utter joy.

Her eyes glittering like Gabriel's, her mouth stubborn like her mother's, she had been the most absolutely precious thing Andreas had ever beheld.

The infant's little smile felt as if it had clawed into his chest and thumped his heart into a thunderous roar.

His vision had shimmered so dangerously for a second that he had quickly given her over to Nikandros, who was a proud and wonderful dad to his twins.

All he'd been able to see for a few seconds had been another child. With dark hair, and dark eyes like his, as Ariana had told him.

A boy, his son.

His heart thumped painfully in his chest and he couldn't even breathe.

Seeing Eleni and Gabriel ecstatic over their little girl, seeing Nik and Mia offering them advice, he had felt a cold chill pass through him.

As if a ghost had passed through him, his father's ghost. Clearly the pace he had been setting for himself was driving him mad. Finally, he would be like Theos in this, too.

But the laughter he imagined, the mocking *I win* smile that his father would have worn, knowing that he had won in the end—that he had made Andreas as hard and ruthless as him, as he'd always wanted to…it was the thing that broke through his self-imposed punishment.

God, he felt so tired in his heart. So alone and utterly miserable.

He'd tried his hardest to keep away from Ariana, used every tenet he'd used in life to stay strong enough for his father, but nothing worked.

He loved her so much. He missed her so much. Even when she'd hated him, his life had felt more alive than like this. Being near her, sleeping wrapped up around her, smelling the scent of her on his sheets—it had been hellish.

Walking away every time was like losing a limb.

A torture treatment designed just for him.

He wanted to protect her. He wanted to give her a chance to walk away. To find life away from him. To find her happiness without him.

But *Thee mou*, the stubborn woman didn't go. She was in his skin, in his blood, in his soul. With her, he felt complete. He felt joy unlike anything he'd ever known.

He had snubbed her, avoided her, stonewalled her for two months, ripping away his own heart in the process. But she was nowhere near gone from his mind or body or soul.

He had tried to live without her. And it was slowly, but surely, unraveling him. Heart pounding in his chest, Andreas walked toward their private suite. His long strides were just not long enough today.

He went through her suite and then returned to his own. The silence screamed over his nerves. There were no staff members, nor her, nor any of her friends.

Determined to find her, he turned. Giannis, her aide, stood at the door, his chin lifted high. "Looking for something, Your Highness?"

Andreas felt his knees buckling under him. Had she left him again? Had he finally driven her away?

Giannis knew. Of course, her little friend knew. And whose fault was that when he wouldn't even give her the time of the day? When he had used her for pleasure but wouldn't even meet her eyes?

Ariana needed so much, deserved so much in life and once again, all he'd done was starve her.

"Where is she?" Panic made getting the words out so hard.

"She left," Giannis said with something like sympathy in his eyes.

Andreas nodded and gritted his teeth. "She left me then."

"No, she…she said she needed a break. That she needed time to think. She…said she would go back to the only place in the world where she'd been happy.

"Delirious with joy," he said, imitating Ariana's fondness for superlatives.

Ariana and he had both been happy, delirious with joy, in only one place.

Only one place where the world had been at bay. Where it had been just them. Made for each other.

Andreas stilled against the door, his heartbeat slowly returning to normal. At least she hadn't run away. She hadn't left him. He extended his hand to the other man, who looked on it with complete disbelief in his eyes. Finally, when he shook his hand, Andreas smiled. "Thank you for always being her friend, Giannis."

Giannis gave him a completely unnecessary bow of his head. "I would give my life for my Queen, Your Highness. She is worth it, even when she had been just a friend who asked about my *ya-ya*."

"She is," Andreas whispered.

New life breathed in his veins. He knew where she was. He would find her and he would tell her how much he loved her. He was a weaver of words, a teller of past tales, a world-class orator.

How could words be hard to come by in the most important thing of his life?

Within minutes, he asked for a chopper. Since no pilot was available in the last minute, Nikandros volunteered to give him a quick "lift." Andreas had a feeling Nik was only coming along to see Andreas suffer.

"Thank God, Andreas. Eleni and Mia were planning another intervention for you, and only Eleni's labor put a stop to that. Gabriel thought we should simply knock you over the head with a club. Repeatedly, until you came to your senses."

A long time ago, Andreas would have been extremely uncomfortable with the conversation. He wouldn't have seen the point in it, even. What point was there in discussing and pouring out one's feelings to a brother or a friend when those feelings had to be suppressed anyway?

He laid his head back against the seat rest and smiled. "I would not have minded that, Nikandros. I would even go so far as to say I probably needed that. But you tell Marquez that and I will deny it."

Laughter boomed in his ears. "Only loyalty to my King forbids me to tell him that, Andreas. Gabriel would love nothing better, believe me.

"You deserve happiness. Did I ever tell you that?"

His eyes flew open, he stared at Nik. "No. But Camille has. A lot of times. Whether I paid attention to her or not, she repeated it again and again. That it was okay for me to feel anger, want, affection, jealousy, even inadequacy. I don't think I ever told you this, Nik, but I thank you for sharing your mother with me. I would not have known any kindness if not for Camille."

His blue eyes glittering, Nikandros looked away. "Among all three of us, you deserve it the most."

"I'm sure Mia would not agree with that."

"I think she would. You walked the hardest path with Theos. You could have become like him. I worried it was already too late for you. I was terrified you would never know the happiness I know with Mia.

"All because of him."

"I almost didn't. But Camille and you and Eleni…and Ariana…" He swallowed the emotion that sat in his throat like a boulder. Gabriel, the smug bastard, had been right. "Ariana saved me." She had done it even then.

He just hadn't been able to see it. Or understand it.

With one smile, and an outrageous question, she had melted the ice around his heart.

She was right. He was ready. He was a different man. A man who could love the extraordinary woman his wife had become.

Soon, they were up in the sky. Andreas clutched the book in his hands, his book. It was the only thing he had to give her, other than his heart, the only thing that would be valuable to her. The only thing she would truly appreciate.

Ariana had spent most of her first day trying to locate the owner of the old log cabin. The sleepy fishing village had no registration office to speak of. So she had just haunted the old café where she had worked.

But before she could ask a single question, she had been recognized. As the King's wife, Ariana Drakos. The Queen. Thankfully also as the girl who had worked there for one summer a long time ago. She had instantly been mobbed by the friendly crowd, for whom her appearance was a once-in-a-lifetime thing.

In the end, she had eaten dinner there, made a reservation at a nearby hotel, but had no more knowledge about the owner.

The second day had gone with more useless searching and then sleeping away the rest of the day because she had been exhausted.

Tears filled her eyes. Damn it, all she wanted was to have a quick look inside. To bolster her faltering faith in Andreas and her.

She dashed away the tears as she dressed on the third morning. She cried over every small thing these days.

Dressed in jeans and a thick sweater, oversized and falling to her knees, she had stolen from Andreas's closet, she pulled on knee-high boots. She thought she was hungry until she stopped at a coffee shop. Instead the smell of it sent her hurrying away from the cute café. She wasn't able to get much dinner into herself, either.

She grabbed a map instead. She knew the trail through the forested woods pretty well, but it had been ten years.

Pulling a knit cap tight on her head so that a bit of her hair was covered too, as she had totally forgotten about being recognized, she made her way past the first sign.

The air was redolent with scents of pine. She slid her hands under her armpits. She had also forgotten how cold it got here during winter, so close to the mountains. Her spirits lifted as she realized she could make out the path without referring to the map at all.

Fifteen minutes later, she was breathing hard—something else she *had* forgotten about was the steep climb at the end—but standing in front of the log cabin.

The red exterior was gleaming as well as it had been back then. The area in front of it was as always neatly cleared. A huge pile of freshly chopped wood sat on one side. Smoke came out of the chimney.

Her eyes filled up again. But she was extremely glad that someone had lived here all these years. Had taken such good care of it.

Now that she was here, she couldn't return without a look inside. Heart beating with a renewed energy, she walked up the small steps to the porch and knocked on the door.

"Kalimera..." She began her practiced speech before the door swung open completely. "I'm so sorry to bother..."

Andreas was standing inside the cabin, his arm on the

top side of the door, his eyes devouring her with a tangible hunger.

"*Kalimera*, Ariana. Will you not come in?"

Stunned, lost for words, Ariana nodded and stepped inside. Suddenly, she didn't at all feel brave. She felt vulnerable and lonely. And juvenile, if the look in Andreas's eyes was anything to go by.

She caught the groan that rose. Why hadn't she realized he would just see it as another ploy for his attention?

Did she really care if he did?

Taking in his long legs and taut behind, clad in tight jeans and the sheer breadth of his masculinity, she also felt deprived. As if the most delicious dessert was placed in front of her but she was not allowed to touch it.

His hair was curling over the collar of his shirt, over which he had worn a thick sweater like her. The scent of sandalwood soap that he used left a thread in the air and she hungrily followed it into the lounge.

Her eyes wide, she looked around the cozy hall. Everything was gleaming and polished. Everything was exactly as they had left it. There was even a reference book of Andreas's and a magazine of hers. Not collecting dust. But neatly arranged.

She frowned. Wait—what was Andreas doing here? So soon after she had left, too?

"You look beautiful," he said in that deep voice behind her and she turned.

Far too fast apparently, because she was suddenly dizzy and would have knocked herself into the pillar if he hadn't caught her.

She shook her head trying to find her balance again while he watched her from under those thick lashes. Scowling. "I don't know what happened." She cleared her throat, and stepped back from his grasp of her hands.

Which didn't go unnoticed.

"I… I just came by to see this place." A lump lodged in her throat as she spotted the shiny silver frame on the mantel. It was still here? She had bought it in a junk shop in this very same village.

She plucked it off the shelf and once again, breath left her. Another picture of her. This one in her wedding dress—or rather the pink, frilly dress that she had worn that morning.

She looked absolutely, utterly in love. And full of happiness.

Hands shaking, she put away the frame and turned. To find him leaning against the pillar, staring at her. "What are all these things, our things, doing here? I tried to find out who had bought the place but no one really knew. I… I thought it would have become a relic. Like us," she said, and looked away.

She was not going to cry. She was not going to beg.

"I own it," he finally said, and her head whipped up. "I should say, we own it."

"When? When did you buy it?"

"The moment we left here." He looked around at the high ceilings just like she had done. Rubbed the smoothly polished wood with affection. "It took a while to convince the old guy who lived here…but finally he caved."

"Of course—the Crown Prince want something and not get it?"

In two quick strides, he reached her, crowding her along the wall. "What is that supposed to mean?"

She licked her lips, suddenly nervous. She had never seen him like this, so blatantly aggressive. "I… It's not like you're used to being denied what you want, Andreas."

He frowned. "True, but I never used the weight of the crown to persuade this guy. I just told him it was the place where I spent a week trapped with my future wife, the one woman I was going to spend my life with, and that persuaded him.

"It turned out he was an utter romantic."

She nodded, working hard to keep her gaze on his face when the column of his throat beckoned. "You never told me."

A sigh fell from his lips. "I meant for it to be a surprise. I thought we could come back here regularly, but…"

"But everything fell apart when we returned to the city," she finished. God, she had had enough of these games. "Well, I'm sure it would have been a nice gesture." She slipped away from his grasp and faced him. "It works out for me, at least."

"What works out for you?"

"I… I'm not returning to the Palace with you, assuming that's why you're here, *ne*?"

"For what?"

"Stop answering questions with questions."

He put up his hands, as if she was the one being unreasonable. She was totally not prepared for dealing with him here. Any more of this and she'd dissolve into a puddle of tears. "You're here because you think I'm throwing one of my fits and you need to chase me back to the palace for some weighty matter that requires your wife.

"There's four days before the next state dinner and I'll be by your side that morning."

He shrugged. "*Kala*. I will inform Petra we will both return that morning."

"You're crazy. There must be a hundred details to see to."

"As you've pointed out in the past, I have three teams to do my bidding and to arrange my life and one of them will see to the hundred details. I was going to write the speech myself anyway and I can focus better here."

Tears filled her eyes. "Why are you playing with me,

Andreas? What is it you want of me?" Her heart felt like it was shattering anew.

He pulled her into his arms instantly. "I didn't mean to make you cry. *Thee mou*, do not cry, *agapita.* I just… You looked so beautiful, so painfully lovely standing there that I forgot what I meant to say.

"I have not come to take you back. In fact, to hell with the dinner if you just want to hole up here for a couple of months. I have enough wood and food to see us through the winter." Now Ariana was alternately laughing and crying into his sweater.

"Why are you here?"

"I…came to give you something." He plucked a book, his book, from the coffee table and handed it to her.

Smiling, Ariana opened the jacket, read the dedication. Again. "I saw it in your bedroom months ago. I… I've been even reading it when you're…" She looked up and flushed. "When you're not there.

"It made me feel like you were still there with me. Especially, the part of you that I fell in love with."

He nodded and swallowed. "Ariana, will you ever forgive me?"

Words did not come, choked by the tears. She shook her head, then nodded, a deluge of emotions drowning her. "If you forgive me."

His mouth came down on hers. Frantic words fell from his mouth as he kissed her, and tasted her. Ariana didn't know whether she was crying or laughing.

Her heart jumped into her throat when he went to his knees in front of her and looked up at her.

He was so tall that his head still reached her abdomen. She buried her hands in his hair, her heart bursting to full.

"I love you so much. My life is empty of joy, of laughter, of everything without you, *glykia mou.*

"Will you come back to me, Ari? Will you come back because I love you and I can't live without you?"

Ari nodded and fell to her knees. He caught her in his arms and she burst into sobs. Pitiful, wrenching sobs that she could not stop no matter what she did.

Andreas felt as if his heart would shatter all over again. God, he couldn't bear her tears. He couldn't stand the wretched sound of her grief. How heartless he had been to bring her to this?

He pulled her into his lap as he'd done once, a long time ago. Fingers stealing into her hair, he pulled her face up, until she was forced to look at him. "I promised myself I would never again hurt you, Ari. Not at any cost.

"Rage at me. Punch me. But forgive me, *pethi mou*. Forgive me for taking this long to understand this thing between us.

"I adore you. I love you so much that I'm still terrified of all the tumult I feel."

He kissed her mouth and she sighed against him. "I would like to answer one of your questions."

She frowned. "Which one?"

"About why I hadn't publicized that manuscript."

"I know why," she said wiping her eyes. "You didn't want to take away the faith and fantasy it gave the people. I even understand how hard it must have been because it was your life's work, your real passion."

He shook his head. "No. I…think I didn't like it myself. I didn't like that he so easily sacrificed the woman he loved. Even when I didn't understand why, it didn't sit well with me.

"It almost felt like if I revealed it, it would become true. Almost a sentence, a fate for all the rulers of Drakon.

"Even when I thought you were gone, I needed the happy

ending. I needed to believe that I'd had my chance of happiness. That I had grabbed it with both hands while I could.

"But since I learned what price you paid for my—"

It was her turn to shut him up. She did it by kissing him softly, slowly, her entire being soaring with that kiss. By pouring all the love she felt for him into the slide of her mouth. "No, no past, Andreas. Only future."

He nodded and wrapped his arms around her. His big palms came to rest on her tummy and suddenly Ariana knew. The dizziness, the nausea at the smell of coffee when she usually needed an IV of it, the lack of hunger…

She shivered violently and he was instantly in front of her. Concern etched in his face. "Ari? What is it?"

"I'm not sure. But I think…" She pulled his hand to her tummy and held it there. "I think we're pregnant."

The silence, which lasted maybe only ten seconds truthfully, stretched her nerves taut. "I don't know how it happened. It's not something I planned without telling you, I mean—"

With a soft growl that made her laugh, he plucked her off the ground as if she were a featherweight. "No more disappearing without telling anyone. No more eating at strange times. And definitely no more sudden twisting and twirling."

He wasn't even out of breath when he put her on the bed and came on top of her. His lower body flush against hers, he propped himself on his elbow. "Is this okay?" he asked, signaling to his body over hers.

Ariana nodded, determined to hold back the tears. Deep grooves etched around his mouth, a wary concern in his eyes. It was clear that the King of Drakon was absolutely terrified. Thankfully, with him by her side, she was not. She stretched like a cat under him and arched into the arousal she could feel against her leg. "You can do whatever you want to me."

A gleam in his eyes, he kissed her tenderly for a long time. Torturously slow when all Ariana wanted was to feel him inside her.

When he let her come up for air, Ari pushed him back on the bed and laid her head on his chest. She didn't know how long they lay like that, staring at each other, smiling sometimes, nibbling at each other's lips other times. Not needing words.

"Do you want a boy or a girl?" she finally asked.

He placed his palm on her tummy, and lifted his eyes to hers. "I do not care. I just want you both safe. I just… I can't imagine my life if something were to happen to you, Ari."

She kissed his temple, his brows, the tip of his arrogant nose, trying to soothe the raw fear in his voice. "Nothing will happen. Not as long as we're together."

He nodded and swallowed. Looked away. Another silence followed, his fingers tight against hers.

She knew he was processing all this. Knew that the emotion he felt for her, the depth of his love for her…it was not an easy thing for him. So she waited, her heart full of tenderness and love. She would wait an eternity for the privilege of being loved by Andreas.

He looked down at her, a fierce light in his dark eyes. "All I know is that you will be a fierce, wonderful mother and I… This child will be so lucky to have you.

"I am so lucky to have found you, Ariana."

Ariana nodded, and reached for his kiss again. "And I'm honored you chose me, Andreas, of all the countless gorgeous, accomplished, beautiful women that have the hots for you all over the world."

He laughed, and she laughed because she loved his laugh. Covering her body, still smiling, he pulled her sweater off. A devilish gleam in his eyes as he realized the sweater was his.

"You have to stop filching my clothes," he said, with his wicked mouth buried against her neck.

"Never," she replied arching into the sensuous warmth of his body.

"*Kala.* You can have my sweaters, my shirts. And my heart."

She loved him so much that her heart felt like it would never settle down. "And you have mine," she managed to whisper somehow just as he licked the puckered crest of her nipple.

Sinking her hands into his hair, she held him tight.

He was the people's man. He had duties to so many. So many responsibilities. Even his time was not his own.

But his kisses and his laughter had always been hers and only hers.

She didn't need anything more than that.

EPILOGUE

Seven months later

THE KING OF DRAKON jumped out of the chopper mere seconds after it hit the tiled terrace of the King's Palace, heart thundering in his chest.

He was late. Damn it, he'd promised her he'd be by her side and he was late. He'd gone half-crazy being stuck in a cabin on the other side of the world, locked in by a hurricane while she had needed him. Even their communication had been cut off and once her labor had started, Andreas could not distract her just to reassure himself.

At least she was not alone, he consoled himself. Nikandros and Mia, Gabriel and Eleni and even Nik's mother, Camille, had been with her. They would have seen to her every need.

The knowledge that she had delivered and both she and the baby were fine was the only thing that had kept him from going utterly mad.

She and the baby had even been transported back to the palace. When Nik would have spilled the beans to the public, Andreas had forbidden him.

He wanted to see her first. He wanted to see for himself whether his wife had given him a boy or a girl. He needed, desperately, to be a husband and a father, at least for a few minutes, before he had to think like a King. Before he had to make an announcement that Drakon had its heir.

Without breaking his stride, he handed off his laptop case, his long jacket and gloves to his waiting teams. He checked his phone and let another curse fly.

A day, he was late by a whole day.

Long strides took the stairs three and four at a time and by the time he reached his wife's suite, his heart had crawled up into his throat.

The silence hit him hard, ratcheting up his pulse, forming all kinds of scenarios in his head. Uncaring of the sounds he made, he rushed to the huge bed in the center of the room.

Only when he saw her did his breath return to normal.

She lay in the center of the huge bed, a little pale, dark shadows under her eyes, far too thin in his mind. And absolutely beautiful in that glowing, tired kind of way. He was about to reach for her when he heard the soft cry.

A gurgle to be exact.

Like a man possessed, he followed the sound to the tiny crib sitting in the corner of the room. Breath punched through his throat as he looked at the tall infant staring up at him with jet-black eyes.

Long lashes. A thin blade of a nose. Thick hair the color of a raven's wing.

It was like looking at his own reflection—except pudgy, toothless and utterly adorable.

Another gurgle. Almost a command.

His knees buckling, Andreas had to hold on to the wall beside him. This was a part of him—his own flesh and blood. And the emotion that filled his body threatened to take him out at the knees.

"Pick him up," said a husky voice behind him. "He wants you to pick him up."

Andreas jerked around, tears blurring his vision. "Him?" he whispered, past the lump in his throat. "It's a boy?"

Her own eyes luminous with tears, Ariana nodded. Hauling her into his arms, he pressed a rough kiss to her mouth. The taste of her exploded through his body, an anchor, a siren's call. Home.

He tried to swallow her grief—the memory of the son

they'd lost—into him when she trembled. When tears leaked out the corners of her beautiful eyes. "We'll always have his memory," he whispered against her temple and felt her answering shudder.

He crushed her to him, uncaring of how feeble she was. God, he needed the warmth of her body. Needed to hear the hitch of her breath as he peppered kisses all over her face. "Have I told you how much I love you?" he said, his throat gruff and scratchy. "I'm so sorry, *agapita*. I'm sorry I wasn't here when you needed me."

Sinking her fingers into his hair, she brought his face up. "No apologies needed. Not if you promise to be here for the next three."

Laughter burst out of him at the running joke between them. He'd said one, terrified of losing her, and Ariana had said they would have four. Flushed and breathtakingly beautiful, she made it look so easy that for the first time, four seemed like a splendid idea.

"It's a deal," he said against her mouth, wild with love. Crazy with a soul-deep longing that he knew would never abate.

That he knew was his strength in all things.

A loud growl came again from the crib and Ariana dissolved into giggles against his mouth. "Your son demands your attention, Your Highness."

"Does he?" Andreas asked, stalling for time.

And she knew. Somehow, his wife knew how terrified he was. By how much he wanted to do right by his tiny son. By how much he already loved that little infant. By how inadequate he felt for the task.

Leaning her forehead against his, she met his gaze. "If you love him half as much as you love me, Andreas, he will know it. He will know it and he will love you back just as much," she said with a confidence that unmanned him. Another quick kiss over his lips. A tug in his hair. "Go hold your son, before his numerous cousins descend upon us."

Nodding, Andreas stood up and walked toward the crib. *His son.* It was as if the entire world had tilted on its axis and refused to return to normal.

Hands shaking, he lifted the chubby body that was only as big as his forearm. Heart in his throat, he walked to the bed and climbed into it. His son wailed as Andreas settled him snugly against Ariana, his forehead all scrunched up.

"He's a little high-maintenance, isn't he?" Andreas whispered, awed by the tiny fingers that had latched onto his mother's breast.

"Like someone I know," Ariana said with a glorious smile. A blush climbed up her chest and her neck as Andreas unabashedly watched his son suckle at her breast. He had thought he couldn't be any happier these past months. But now his family was complete.

Theos had had all this with him, Eleni and Nikandros. But he had ruined it all with his own hands.

Andreas would never let that happen to him. His life, his fate had delineated from the moment he had seen Ariana in that café and he was thankful for that moment a million times over.

Sliding down on the bed, he buried his nose in her neck, the ever-present desire a thrum under his skin.

"How long is he going to do that?" he asked, a wicked growl in his voice.

She frowned. "A few months at the least. Why?"

Andreas licked the pulse at her throat, tasted the salt and scent of her. His body's tiredness melted away, his world tilting on its axis again. "I just don't like sharing what's mine. Even with him," he whispered, and laughed when his wife blushed.

She was his Queen, a lawyer with a fierce reputation and now a mother. But when she looked at him like that, she was only the woman he loved with all his heart. The woman who'd made his life worth living.

"I'll always be yours first, Your Highness," she whispered against his mouth, and Andreas fell all over in love again.

* * * * *

IN THE SHEIKH'S SERVICE

SUSAN STEPHENS

Thanks to the late Penny Jordan, and to Lucy Mukerjee, my first editor at Mills & Boon, for believing in me.

CHAPTER ONE

A POLE-DANCING CLUB across from the Michelin-starred restaurant where he was dining with his ambassador was an unhappy coincidence. He should have known what to expect when his people booked the ambassador's favourite table for dinner. This was Soho, London, England, where strip clubs coexisted happily with top-end eateries, but the ambassador was an old friend, and Shazim had fallen in with the old man's wish to try something new. The downside was that the ambassador's son had come along too.

Sitting still seemed beyond the edgy thirty-something. Girls dancing in the club across the road had grabbed his attention. It wasn't just the guy's blatant lack of good manners Shazim found appalling, but something more nagging at his senses. Whatever happened, he would not allow the ambassador's son to harass the girls.

'Have you finished eating?' The ambassador's son stared imploringly at him. 'Can we look in across the road?'

He was like a puppy on a leash. Shazim had to grab a glass to steady it as he lurched away from the table in his hurry to leave the restaurant.

Shazim caught up with him at the door. His security guys hovered. With a look, he ordered his men to stand down.

'Aren't you a bit old for this?' He angled his chin towards the rose-tinted windows of the club, where shadowy forms were undulating back and forth.

By this time the ambassador had joined them, and there was real danger of a scene. 'Go with him, Shazim,' the ambassador begged. 'See that he doesn't get into trouble, will you? Please? For me?'

Tasking one of his team to escort the elder statesman home, he thrust a bundle of notes into the maître d's hand and followed the ambassador's son out of the restaurant.

Oh, for goodness' sake! This was ridiculous. Her friend Chrissie wasn't exactly lacking in the bosom department, but Chrissie wasn't exactly overabundant, either, Isla fretted as she attempted to squeeze her ample frontage into the microscopic bikini top.

If someone had asked Isla to name the very last thing on earth she liked to do, it would be to make herself look provocative in front of a room full of men—and there was every reason for that, but Chrissie was a good friend and Chrissie had a family emergency tonight.

The past couldn't reach out and hurt her, Isla told herself firmly, not unless she allowed it to, and tonight it wouldn't.

Her mother's death eighteen months ago had left her shaken to the core, and what had happened directly after the funeral could still send her reeling, but tonight was Chrissie's night, so she would get on with the job—if she could force her breasts into submission. Turning this way and that, she measured the risk factor of her breasts going one way while she went the other. Here was living proof that no one could squeeze a quart into a pint pot. Nor could they make a plain, stocky woman into a sugarplum fairy overnight. She was a down-to-earth mature student in the veterinary sciences department. Far from being the glamorous type, she usually had grime of unspeakable origins beneath her fingernails. On the plus side, the costume was gorgeous. She loved a bit of twinkle, and the bikini was a deep, rich pink, exquisitely decorated with glittering crystal beads and sequins. It would look fantastic on Chrissie, as it would on any woman with a normal figure, but on Isla's super-sized, top-heavy figure?

It looked like a sparkling bandage wrapped around a bun.

One of the many jobs Isla had taken in order to pay her fees at the university was to lead a class of enthusiastic children in gymnastics at the university gym, but she wore a sports bra for that, not an unfit-for-purpose sequinned bikini. This was the first time she could remember having a flexible body and the ability to use it being both an advantage and a disadvantage. She would never have agreed to do this if Chrissie's need hadn't been greater than Isla's fear of ever making it seem that she was trying to lead a man on. Once upon an ugly time, that accusation had been cruelly levelled at her, and it had left a lingering doubt.

She had to hope the apprehension she was feeling went away once she lost herself in practising her moves for the Christmas concert at the gym.

Get over yourself and get out there—

She swung around at a knock on the door.

'Five minutes, please,' a disembodied male voice informed her.

Five minutes? She'd need five hours to make this disaster fly! She took a last look in the mirror and wished her breasts would shrink.

'I'll be there,' she called out, slipping on her high-heeled shoes with agitated fingers. She'd kick the heels off once she got started, but Chrissie had said first impressions were all-important to the audience, and she had no intention of letting Chrissie down.

* * *

There were certain things that came with ruling a country Shazim could do without. Tolerating the offspring of loyal subjects was one of them. Entering a pole-dancing club in order to prevent the ambassador's son hitting on one of the girls was another. Most clubs ran a strict 'no-touch' policy, but the ambassador's spawn was the type to do as he pleased and then hide behind diplomatic immunity.

As he negotiated the mass of men in the overheated club, he thought about his elder brother, and the strength it had taken him to wear the yoke of duty. There were a lot of things about being a king that held no appeal.

Shazim had not been trained to be a king, but the tragedy in the desert, for which he held himself responsible, had thrust him into the role, opening his eyes to a burden his brother had carried so lightly. Following his brother's death, Shazim, the reckless brother, had become poacher turned gamekeeper, and there was no way he would allow shame to fall on his people's heads because of the ambassador's son.

'Can I get you something, sir?'

He eyed the girl. Beautiful. Slender. But with a wary gaze beneath her glossy shell. 'No. Nothing. Thank you.' Removing the ambassador's son from the club with the minimum of fuss was his only goal.

'A seat, sir?'

He glanced at the second girl. Her eyes were as dead as those of the girl currently working the pole. 'No, thank you.' He continued to hone in on his target.

His work in London was crucial, and he would not allow some brash, overindulged diplomat's son to get in the way of it by attracting adverse publicity. Creating a nature reserve where endangered species could breed safely in their natural habitat required specialist knowledge, and he had found all he could need at the nearby university where he was investing millions in research and new buildings in order to bring his late brother's dream to reality.

Waving his security team away, he took the ambassador's son by the arm. The man resisted him with a violent shake and a lot of cursing, but then, realising who he was swearing at, he went limp and began to stutter some excuse that Shazim had no interest in hearing. Ushering him away with a not so subtle warning, he sent him back to daddy with a flea in his ear.

He had intended to follow the ambassador's son out of the club when something made him stop and look around at the stage where another girl was about to start dancing. She was different from the rest, if only because she was smiling. He felt irritated on her behalf when the man next to him commented, 'She's sensational. What a rack—'

There was no denying that the girl was attractive. She was full figured and proud of it. Her skin was honey pale and as smooth as silk, but it was her happy face that held him. She seemed lost in thought, but her uplifting aura was enough to hold every man in the club transfixed as she worked her body enthusiastically on the pole.

Leaning back against a pillar, he stayed to watch. She was skilful and sexy, with both flair and talent, but there was nothing vulgar about her. The men around him had stopped leering, and were staring at her more in wonder than in lust. In another setting, she could have put on the same performance for the Mothers' Union, and would have held them in the palm of her hand.

With the spotlight firmly fixed on her, Isla was determined to put on the best show possible for Chrissie. There had been one brief disturbance. She had been in the middle of a complicated move—one of several she was trying out for the gym's Christmas display—when someone was thrown out of the club. Chrissie had warned her this could happen, but had also reassured her that security was tight for the girls, so Isla had nothing to worry about.

At the gym Isla was always lost in her routine, but tonight her attention kept wandering, mainly because of the man who had come to lean against a pillar to stare at her. All the men were staring at her, but he was watching with particular intent.

She wasn't sure how she felt about him. He was exotic-looking and powerfully built, but unthreatening, possibly because he possessed an unusual air of dignity and presence. Tall and dark, he was beautifully dressed. His crisp white shirt provided a striking contrast to his exquisitely tailored dark suit, and links that might have been black diamonds glittered at his cuffs. As he obviously wasn't going anywhere she continued on with her routine.

She was safely back in her tiny dressing room when the knock came on the door. 'Yes? Come in…'

She was halfway changed, with her jeans and boots on, and grabbed a robe to throw over her bra. She was expecting a visitor. One of the girls had promised to drop off Chrissie's schedule for the next week.

'Oh!'

Shooting out of her seat when she saw the man, she backed instinctively against the wall with fear lapping over her. It was an old fear, but no less severe for being a haunting memory from the past. One, thankfully failed, sexual assault had left Isla with an instinctive fear of men. That it had happened after her mother's funeral when her emotions were strung out had made the fall-out all the keener. Dragging in a shaking breath, she reminded herself that security was only a shout away.

'Forgive me if I startled you,' the man who had been leaning against the pillar murmured in a deep, intriguingly accented voice. 'They said I'd find you here.'

She calmed herself, telling herself rationally that every man wasn't out to hurt her. She also had to think about Chrissie, who depended on this job. She wasn't going to make a fuss unless she had to.

And, if she had to, she could shout louder than most.

'Can I help you?' she demanded in a tone that sounded scratchy and tense. The man seemed to take up most of the available space in the small room, so there was nowhere else for him to be but close. He was a stunning-looking individual, not that that made it any easier to be alone with him.

'I wanted to apologise for the disturbance to your act.' His dark stare remained steady on her face. 'A man was ejected from the club while you were dancing. You're very good at your work, and I wanted to say how sorry I am for the interruption.'

'Thank you.' Smiling thinly, she reached for the door handle to show him out.

'May I give you a lift home?'

Her eyes widened in shock. 'Oh, no, thank you. I catch the bus. But, thank you for the offer.'

'You catch the bus alone at night?' he demanded, frowning.

His reaction brought a faint smile to her lips. 'Public transport in London is quite safe. The bus drops me at my door.'

'I see.'

He was still frowning, giving her the sense that this was a man who was used to being obeyed.

He might be a devastatingly good-looking individual with an air of command and a custom-made suit, but she was an independent woman who could look after herself.

'So. No lift?' he queried, raising a brow as if he thought he could change her mind.

'No lift,' she confirmed. She had a keen sense of self-preservation. She always had her bus fare home, and she would be using it tonight.

'Perhaps I'll see you again,' he suggested.

'Perhaps,' she agreed lightly. Taking a firmer hold of the door handle, she swung the door wide and stood aside.

'Goodnight, Isla.'

Alarm bells rang. 'You know my name?'

His firm mouth slanted. 'The manager told me when I asked to speak to you.'

Isla's brain cogs whirred. The manager would not allow a customer near a girl without a very good reason. So what was this man's excuse? Making an apology for a disturbance at the club? She didn't think so.

'Who are you?' she demanded, feeling unsettled, as well as slightly annoyed by this blatant breach of club protocol.

Her question seemed to amuse him. 'My friends call me Shaz.'

'Goodnight, Shaz,' she said pointedly.

She remained outside the door, pressed against the wall, wanting to keep some distance between them. The fact that he had made enquiries about her had only added to her unease—that and his sheer, brutal machismo.

'Goodnight, Isla.'

His eyes had turned warm and humorous, prompting her to soften enough to say, 'I'm glad you enjoyed the show.'

Her body tingled when he gave her one last appraising look. She was relieved he was leaving, and yet almost regretful knowing they would never meet again. When he rested his hands lightly on her upper arm, she gasped out loud, but he wasn't done with her yet. Leaning forward, he brushed his lips against her cheek—first her right cheek and then the left.

Kissing on both cheeks was the usual greeting and

leave-taking gesture in many countries across the world, she reminded herself as her heart went crazy, both with alarm, and something else.

Pulling herself together fast, she moved out of his way and stood stiffly to attention as he left. Her senses were in turmoil. Wherever life took her from here on in, the man in the club wouldn't be easy to forget.

CHAPTER TWO

SINISTER HIGH-POWERED LAUNCHES announced the arrival of the Sheikh's team. The lead launch was sleek and black, while smaller vessels swarmed like mosquitoes in attendance as they cut a foaming path up the River Thames. The vessels were all heading for the same pontoon, about a hundred or so yards from the café where Isla was working at one of several part-time jobs that helped to pay her tuition fees at the university.

'Hey, Chrissie—come and look at this,' she called out.

Staff and customers alike were held riveted by the sight of the fleet arriving. A sight like this was just what Chrissie needed to cheer her up. The family emergency had been resolved—sort of—but Chrissie was still worried to death about her father, who had been brought home by the police after being arrested for drunk and disorderly conduct. The only blessing was that last night had ended so well for both girls, with a better than expected pay-out from the club.

A mystery benefactor had left the extra money, the manager had explained to Isla, to make up for the disturbance at the club. She guessed it must have been the man who had introduced himself. The money couldn't have come at a better time, as she had been able to hand it all over to Chrissie to pay her father's fine.

That wasn't the only good thing about last night, Isla recalled, touching her cheek. It was the first time in years she'd come into contact with a man who hadn't given her the creeps, and this was especially odd, as the man last night had been a paean to masculinity.

It was just a kiss.

Yes, but it was a kiss she would never forget.

'What's up?' Chrissie said, joining Isla at the window. 'Oh, wow...'

Isla rubbed her sleeve across the heat-misted window so they could both get a better view of the powerboats as they slowed in preparation for docking. She was glad to see Chrissie looking more relaxed as they crushed up comfortably against each other. Just dealing with the fine had been some consolation, though the problem with Chrissie's father was unlikely to go away.

Men were leaping ashore to secure the ropes on a pontoon as new as the fantastic new development springing up next door to the café. This was all part of the same Thames-side university campus being funded by His Serene Majesty, Sheikh Shazim bin Khalifa al Q'Aqabi, a legendary philanthropic figure in a world weary of shallow celebrity. At thirty-five, the Sheikh was not just one of the richest men in the world, but was also practically invisible to the media. His immense power and wealth allowed him to remain beneath the avid radar of celebrity, which made any sighting of him all the more exciting. The new buildings he was funding included a veterinary science department, which Isla was particularly excited about as she had recently won the most amazing prize for her research project into endangered species. The prize included a trip to the Sheikh's desert kingdom of Q'Aqabi to see for herself his world-beating nature reserve. And to work there one day, she hoped.

'Isla! Chrissie! Stop daydreaming and get back to work!'

Both girls jumped into action as their boss, Charlie,

yelled at them. Prize winner or not, Isla was still impoverished after so many years of study. She had yet to secure her first position as a veterinary surgeon and, like many students, her finances were precariously balanced. If she lost even one of her part-time jobs her future career could be in jeopardy.

The activity at the pontoon proved addictive, and Isla glanced repeatedly out of the window as she worked. The uniformed crew had moored up, and rain had begun to pelt down as a party of men disembarked. Dressed disappointingly in traditional western work clothes, rather than the flowing robes of her imagination, they strode up the pontoon in arrow formation towards the building site.

'Do you think the Sheikh's at the head of them?' Chrissie asked, breaking Isla's spell as she leaned against her.

'Who knows?' Isla replied, studying the figure in the lead. He was too far away to see his features clearly, but there was something about him—

'Isla—Chrissie,' Charlie called out sharply, reminding both girls that there was work to be done. 'Get that order for the Sheikh's team together now!'

Flashing a willing smile in Charlie's direction, Isla hurried to obey. The Sheikh's office had called ahead to make sure that an order of coffee was delivered to site as soon as the Sheikh's team arrived.

'I don't think he's with them,' she whispered to Chrissie as she squeezed past her friend behind the counter. 'I expect he has more important things to do.'

'More important than supervising the building of his new facility?' Chrissie's expressive mouth pressed down with amazement as she shrugged. 'Seems to me, he should be here, if only to make sure his billions aren't wasted on coffee.'

Isla laughed. 'They won't be wasted. The new vet school is going to be amazing. I've seen the plans in the university library.' And it was Isla's dream to be part of those plans. Endangered species were her passion, and she was aching to do what she could to help out. The thought that very soon she would be flying thousands of miles to the magical-sounding kingdom of Q'Aqabi to visit the Sheikh's nature reserve still seemed like a fantasy too far—

'Isla!'

'Coming,' she promised Charlie.

'I'll take it,' she added to Chrissie, grabbing the cardboard tray that was waiting to be loaded with coffee.

'Knowing your luck, the Sheikh will be there,' Chrissie complained, pulling a comic face. 'I can just see the drama unfolding now: the fast-food flirt and the autocratic Sheikh. That should be a fun ride, shouldn't it?'

'After last night?' Isla grimaced. 'I'm all for the quiet life. I don't want any more hunter-gatherers pushing me over the threshold from safe to insanity.'

'It wasn't so bad,' Chrissie pointed out. 'You met a great guy—'

'I said, I met a guy—'

'Don't tinker with the detail. Main thing is, we got paid a fortune.'

'Danger money.' Isla laughed, hiding the fact that it had taken more than Chrissie would ever know for her to shed her clothes in front of a room full of men. The fact that Isla's brush with the sickening danger of a sexual assault had happened years ago had left her no less wary. 'And I'm not a flirt. I'm just friendly,' she teased before Chrissie could see the shadow of that memory in her eyes.

'Whatever,' Chrissie intoned with a wry look. 'You get bigger tips than me, that's all I know.'

'Which I share,' Isla reminded her friend with a laugh. 'And, as for the Sheikh—I doubt we'll ever see him. If he comes to cut the ribbon when his new building is opened, I'll be surpri—'

'Will you girls stop gossiping and get back to work?' Charlie rapped impatiently.

Exchanging glances, both girls quickly returned to their duties. Chrissie busied herself with the orders on hand, while Isla reluctantly shoved all thoughts of the exciting projects and sheikhs to one side so she could concentrate on finishing the coffee order for the building site.

'Isn't your shift almost over?' she asked Chrissie as they bustled past each other.

'Yes, Mum,' Chrissie teased with a wink. 'But I'm happy to stay on while there's a rush and you're taking that outside. I can't afford to lose this job.'

'I can't afford to lose any of my jobs,' Isla agreed.

They shared a rueful grin. Juggling studies and holding down multiple jobs wasn't easy for either girl, though, while Chrissie had the looks and figure to strut her stuff for loads of money at the pole-dancing club, Isla's second job was working quietly in the university library. That was when she wasn't working her third job, teaching basic gymnastics to keen youngsters in the gym. Not that she was complaining. She loved the quiet of the library, where she could snatch a study break along with her lunch, while the children in the after-school gym club kept her fit and motivated with their enthusiasm—

'Isla!'

'Yes, boss!' Conscious that Charlie was watching her, she quickly loaded the last of the coffees. 'The site order is ready to go.'

'Then, get it out there before the coffee gets cold,' Charlie grumbled, doing his best to look as if he'd just sucked on a lemon.

Glancing at the rain battering the windows, Isla grabbed her jacket and tugged it on. 'Yes, boss—'

'This is a coffee shop, not gossip central,' Charlie grouched, deepening his frown as she walked past him.

She countered Charlie's bad mood with one of her usual cheery smiles. 'You know you love me, really.'

'The only reason I employ you is for that smile,' Charlie grudgingly admitted.

'That man,' Chrissie exploded. 'Who does he think we are? Smiling puppets?'

'Employees?' Isla suggested with her usual good humour. 'We need this job, Chrissie,' she discreetly reminded her hot-headed friend.

'You're going to get soaked,' Chrissie objected, brow wrinkling thunderously as she stared out of the window.

'Yes,' Isla agreed, 'but, the sooner I get out there, the sooner I get back.'

'Okay, Ms Capability—say hi to the Sheikh, if you see him.'

'Like I'm going to get close.'

'If he's there he'll have security surrounding him,' Chrissie agreed. 'Oh, well, you can still drop a few hints to his team that you're a star student at the university, and you'll be over in Q'Aqabi very soon, when you'll be only too glad to offer your services—'

'I beg your pardon?' Isla acted shocked.

'Okay, Miss Prim—you know what I'm talking about. Get out there before the coffee goes cold. And don't forget to drop that hint,' Chrissie called after her.

Was she wrong to hope that, if the Sheikh had chosen to visit his billion-dollar building site, the white-chocolate mocha with the extra caramel shot and a double squirt of cream wasn't destined for him? Isla smiled as Charlie opened the door for her. A girl had to have her fantasies, and Isla's involved real tough-guy sheikhs—impossibly handsome, riding imperious white stallions… The Sheikh would be clad in flowing robes, and he would live in a Bedouin tent that billowed gently in the warm desert breeze—

'You're lucky I don't dock you girls' dreaming time from your wages,' Charlie rapped as she went past him. 'If you don't watch out, I'll charge you for breakfast.'

Charlie was a kind old thing really, with a bark that was far worse than his bite. And no way was she going to lose out on breakfast, when it was her one decent meal of the day.

Head down, she speed-walked through the driving rain to the mud bath next door. There was no easy way to walk across a building site other than to do it as fast as she could without spilling the coffee.

'Stop!'

She stopped dead and almost dropped the tray. She had reached a steel mesh gate manned by an unsmiling security guard, but, as the gate was open, she had walked straight through.

'You're not allowed on the site,' the guard informed her brusquely.

'But I have instructions to be here,' she tried to explain.

'No one is allowed on the site without protective clothing. And I have to check your identity—'

As the guard reached towards her she flinched. An instinctive reaction. Just one of the many leftover side effects from the attempted assault… It made her creep to have any man touch her, with the exception of Charlie, who was like a grumpy old uncle, and the man in the club last night—

'I'll take over here.'

She jerked alert as a second man spoke. *Oh, no! Shoot me and bury me now.* 'It's you,' she said lamely, recognising the man from the club.

'Quite a surprise,' he agreed drily, and with maximum

understatement. 'I'll see to this,' he said, dismissing the guard.

The guard's reaction was impressive. He practically stood to attention and saluted. 'Yes, sir,' he said, taking a giant step back.

Before she had chance to say anything, two strong arms had snapped around her waist.

'What are you doing?' was about all she could manage as the air shot from her lungs. She had to concentrate on balancing the coffee as the giant of a man led her away. And, for the second time, strangely, there was no fear, no creeps, just quite a lot of affront that the people on the site were making it so hard for her to deliver coffee.

'I'll drop the tray if you don't slow down.'

Not that it would do him any harm in his steel-capped boots. Gone were the black silk socks and highly polished shoes and in their place was a hard hat and a high-vis' jacket. If he'd seemed big last night, he was positively enormous now. And he didn't look the type to yowl if hot coffee should happen to land on his naked skin.

His naked skin...

Stop that now!

She had never known anything like it. Her mind was permanently closed to all thoughts of men's physical attributes—or so she'd thought up to last night. And now she had enough to do, balancing a tray of red-hot coffee while keeping up with the man's ground-eating stride. By the time they reached one of several mobile homes on the site, she was well and truly rattled, and when he angled his chin towards the door she stopped dead and refused to go a step further.

Reaching in front of her, he opened the door. Jerking his chin, he indicated that she should go first.

'Everyone on the site has to wear proper clothing and

carry a security pass,' he explained. 'Health and safety,' he added brusquely.

She stalled, playing for time. She didn't feel uncomfortable with him, as she had with other men, but going into a building where she would be alone with him was a step too far. 'I've never encountered a problem before,' she protested with some justification. 'Like most of the people at the university, I use the building site as a cut-through when I'm walking between the campus and the café.'

'That doesn't make it right,' he said flatly with a stare that ripped through her like a shot of adrenaline. Since he'd arrived, things had obviously been tightened up. She'd spread the word.

The sooner she left the coffee, the sooner she was out of here, but she couldn't deny that the all-embracing warmth inside the mobile building was welcome. The man called Shaz had started rifling through a rail of high-vis' jackets. Blowing on her hands, she wondered if he felt the cold. As part of the Sheikh's team, she guessed he didn't have to suffer it for too much of the year.

'Here—try this one,' he said, holding out a jacket.

Seeing her difficulty, he took the tray of coffee, brushing his hand against her frozen skin as he did so. 'It should be better,' he murmured, holding her gaze a disturbing beat too long. 'This one is smaller.'

He put the tray down and then came back to help her out of her wet coat. This time his hand brushed her neck. She had just moved her wet hair out of the way, leaving her skin exposed. It was an accident, she told herself firmly. It had to be an accident.

Leaving her to fasten the jacket, he started work on her security pass.

'Is there anything else you need?' she asked politely.

He raised his head and stared at her. 'Should there be anything else?'

The expression in his eyes pinned her. He was definitely interested—no doubt about it—and he was curious about her, which made her skin prickle. He had the most incredible eyes, and it wasn't just the fact that they were dark, and heavily fringed with jet-black lashes—they were quite simply the most expressive eyes she'd ever seen… and right now, they were warming as he stared at her.

'A pastry, perhaps?' she suggested with a gulp.

With a faintly amused look, he turned back to his work. 'I'll need a photograph,' he said, coming to stand between her and the door.

He fixed her printed image inside the pass. 'You'll need this next time you visit the site,' he explained, pressing it into her hand. The brief moment of connection between them sent a sizzle up her arm.

Closing her hand around the pass, she stepped back. 'It might not be me bringing out the coffee for you next time,' she felt it only fair to point out.

'It will be you,' he stated. His face grew grim. 'I have no intention of equipping every member of staff at the café with a pass and protective clothing.'

'So I drew the lucky straw,' she commented ruefully.

'Seems so,' he agreed. His expression softened minutely.

'Thank you, anyway.' She slung the lanyard holding the pass around her neck.

'Wear it every time you visit the site,' he said, standing up to tower over her.

'I will.' If she ever visited the site again. By now her curiosity was well and truly piqued. Who was he? He was obviously important enough to be in overall command of the site—an architect, perhaps, though his hands were a little rough for that. He was no stranger to manual work. She liked that idea. She had this irrational belief that a down-to-earth man would be safer and, though he certainly looked tough enough to handle a team of men, he didn't strike her as a man who would ever resort to bullying tactics.

'Thanks for the coffee,' he said as she turned to go.

She flinched back, then realised that he was only stepping forward so he could reach out and turn her badge around, so her details were facing outwards.

He raised a brow at her overreaction. 'Protective clothing,' he reminded her. 'Wear it every time you come to the site.'

Her heart thundered a tattoo at the instruction. She guessed he was the type of man who would be accustomed to provoking a reaction in susceptible females. It was just that she had never thought herself a susceptible female before. She was more the plain, forthright variety…

'Boots might be a problem,' he said, bringing her back down to earth with a bump.

'I'm only walking through the mud, not laying bricks,' she said, frowning as she followed his stare to her feet.

His expression instantly hardened, as if no one argued with him.

'Honestly,' she added, softening her comment with a smile, 'I think you can safely forget about boots. And hats,' she added as his stare switched to the row of yellow hard hats lined up on a shelf. 'I'm sure there must be something in your rule book that allows visitors a certain leeway…?'

He turned to stare at her with real interest in his eyes—interest that sent shock waves rolling through her, but then he curved the suspicion of a smile as if his affront at her rebellion had turned to grudging admiration. 'You do have tiny feet,' he allowed, 'and a lot of very long hair to fit comfortably beneath the hat.' He paused a moment, while she got used to the idea that he had given her a pretty thorough once-over, and was remembering her long hair from the club last night, as it was currently screwed up in a work-appropriate do on top of her head. 'Though the high-vis' jacket will keep you warm if it's raining when you come out here again.'

And he cared.

She shuddered in a breath as he took the sides of the jacket in both hands and settled it properly on her shoulders. It was as if he were touching her naked skin, rather than the heavy waterproof jacket. He was so careful with her, and yet his touch was firm and sure.

'You are tiny,' he said.

She frowned a little at that. No one in their right mind would call her tiny. Though, compared to him…

Her cheeks flushed red as he stood back. His gaze lingered on her face, and for a moment she didn't know what to say or do. She sucked in a swift breath as he reached out to brush some damp straggles of hair from her face. She had not expected that and, for once in her life, found herself wishing she were beautiful. Usually she didn't care one way or the other about her looks, or lack of them, but for once it would have been nice to have a man brush wet hair from her face because he wanted to take a better look at her, rather than simply keeping her hair out of her eyes. If she had been beautiful, maybe she could have progressed a fantasy into a moment of pure romance: the chance meeting, love at first sight, and with a man who wouldn't be rough with her—

'That's it,' he said with finality.

His sharp tone brought her back to reality. Checking the fastening on the jacket, she raised the hood, ready to step out into the rain.

'Excellent,' he approved in a tone that suggested he had also sprung back into work mode.

She had definitely overstayed her welcome. But as she hurried to the door she managed to trip over a table—or would have done if he hadn't reached out whip-fast to catch her. She rested for a moment, startled in his arms, and only realised when he settled her back on her feet that she hadn't felt threatened by him at all.

CHAPTER THREE

A GREY DAY in London had taken on a rosy hue, thanks to the unexpected reappearance of a woman who had intrigued him from the first moment he saw her. From pole-dancer to barista was quite a journey. Whether the rush of blood to Isla's cheeks was awareness of him and how close they were standing, or pique that she had only been doing as his office had requested, delivering coffee, when he had ordered her off site for a breach of Health and Safety regs—

Health and Safety regs?

Was that why his hands had expertly skimmed her body? He already knew what lay beneath the bulky safety jacket. Her fuller figure was his ideal. The temptation to back her against the door and strip her down to last night's curves was overwhelming—fortunately, there wasn't time and he had more sense. The one thing that did amuse him was the thought that if Isla had known who he was, he doubted it would have made a jot of difference. This was not a woman to be wooed with status and wealth. She liked you or she didn't. And right now, she didn't.

'Do you mind?' she said, pushing him away.

That in itself was an intriguing first for him. For such a self-possessed woman—and he had to remind himself that this was the same woman who had conducted herself with such dignity in the undignified surroundings of the club—she was surprisingly jumpy, acting almost like an innocent now that they were one to one.

Yes. He'd stopped her falling; Isla allowed with an appropriate amount of gratitude as she brushed herself down. *But, let's not get carried away.* He couldn't hold onto her until her bones turned to jelly, and she had no more sense in her head than a moth flying into a flame. She flashed a warning stare—and had to acknowledge that he was a gentleman, as he'd let her go. And fate had dealt him a more than generous hand. Douse any other man in a rainstorm, and they would look like a drowned rat. Douse this man and he still looked spectacular. His thick black hair glistened with raindrops, while her hair was plastered to her face—and she probably had panda eyes from knuckling rainwater out of them.

'Here, Isla…take it.'

She stared at the money in his hand.

'It's the least I can do,' he insisted, thrusting a wad of notes towards her.

'There's no need for that. I'm just doing my job.'

The job you want to keep?

'I don't mean to be rude,' she added. 'If you would like to leave some money at the end of the week for everyone at the café to share, that would be great.'

What was she doing? Could she afford to turn down such a generous tip?

No. Absolutely not, but something felt wrong about accepting such a large tip from a man she hardly knew—and particularly from this man. It was too much, and after last night at the club when she suspected he had doubled Chrissie's pay, she couldn't take any more from him.

Cut him some slack, Isla's inner voice intoned wearily. *No doubt everyone who works for the fabulously wealthy Sheikh has more money than they know what to do with.*

Maybe. But that wasn't the point. A small show of gratitude was acceptable, but flashing a twenty? She wasn't comfortable with that.

'Thanks anyway…' She shot him a thin smile and left it at that before braving the icy wind with the memory of his fleeting touches branded onto her mind.

Knocking mud off her boots, she walked with relief into the steamy heat of the busy café. It was good to be back on familiar ground. She felt safe from conflicting feelings here. The customers liked her and she liked them. Charlie said she invited confidences with her easy manner. The truth was Isla needed company as much as anyone else. Since losing her mother and paying off all their debts, she had lived alone in one room above a shop, and she loved the contrast of her busy life at the café. All that company and chat, with breakfast thrown in? What was not to love?

Customers that shook her up, like the man from the building site?

She should forget him. He'd probably be gone by tomorrow.

Forget him?

Maybe not, but she would do her best to keep her mind on the job.

The aromatic air inside the café made Isla's mouth water. Charlie was a good cook and he fed his staff well. No wonder she was smiling, when she had such a great day to look forward to. Once she finished her shift here, she was due at the university gym. Gymnastics had been one of Isla's childhood passions in the days before her father walked out and her mother got sick, and now she was grateful to make money out of her skill. She worked every hour she could to fulfil her mother's dying wish and make her proud.

'My shift is nearly over,' Chrissie carolled happily as she joined Isla at the counter.

'Mine too,' Isla said with a grin.

After the gymnastics classes she could look forward to a long, peaceful evening. That might involve wearing every jumper she possessed with her feet drawn up as close as she dared to her three-bar electric fire, but at least she had a home to go to. A quick glance at Charlie to let him know that she was back was repaid by a hard stare. Understandably. She'd been gone a long time. But once Charlie took in her new outfit, he began to smile. Charlie wasn't the only one. She was so wet, and it was so hot in the café that her clothes were starting to steam. Tipping Charlie a wry look, she explained what had kept her so long. 'I'm to be the Sheikh's team's regular gofer. I think they're going to need lots of coffee while they're here.'

Charlie was pleased to hear it. 'Well done for encouraging business.'

'And look out for the Sheikh when you go back next time,' Chrissie called out.

'Of course I will,' Isla teased Chrissie. Privately, Isla doubted that the Sheikh would be seen until His Royal Sereneness turned up to cut the ribbon on his new buildings and declare them open. In her imagination, the Sheikh of Q'Aqabi was as hard as nails, as rich as Croesus, and as tall, dark and sinister as could be—but compulsively enthralling, all the same.

Realistically, Isla reflected as she got back to her work, the Sheikh was probably shrivelled, pot-bellied, and grumpier than Charlie.

Young. Challenging. Proud. Interesting. But too innocent for him, and he didn't have time to waste on challenges. Interesting? Isla was certainly interesting.

Would he pursue his interest in her further?

Stuffing the twenty away in the back pocket of his jeans, he stared after her. She was proud, and he got that.

She'd been offended by money. How would she react if he offered more? Money could buy most things in his world…

But could it buy him everything he wanted?

He doubted that any amount of money could buy Isla. Her grey eyes had flashed fire when she'd seen the twenty. She'd no doubt guessed he was responsible for padding her wages last night. She was resourceful and adaptable. She was also an innocent who had trespassed unwittingly into his dark, sensual world. He wondered about her past experience with men. She was attractive, so there must have been some, though her air of innocence suggested that none had breached either the defences of her body or her heart. He should know better than to play games with a girl like that, but she attracted him. Mild on the outside, she reminded him of a volcano about to erupt, and he wanted to be there when that happened.

He found her beautiful, with that particular peach-like complexion so common in this part of the world. Her hair was rain-soaked, but he remembered it from the club, when it had been long and unruly, and had glittered gold beneath the lights. Her eyes were grey and expressive. Small and lush, she warmed him in a way he hadn't been warmed in a long time, and her strength of character warned there would never be a dull moment. He liked that idea. As a mistress, she showed definite potential, but could he take her innocence and then discard her when he'd had enough?

A casual affair was unthinkable for him. He had everything to prove to his country. His reckless youth, and the tragedy that had detonated, would take a lifetime to repay. He would do nothing to rattle the sound foundations he was building in Q'Aqabi. His duty was to find a suitable bride. He did not have time to waste thinking about a new mistress. He must harden his heart to Isla, even as another part of him hardened in lust.

He summoned his colleagues in the hope that work would distract him, but, however many lectures he gave himself on the subject of forgetting Isla, he couldn't help but anticipate the next coffee break, and another encounter with the spirited barista.

She didn't go back to the building site. She came up with another plan. Coffee could be left with the security guard, and he could deliver it. Charlie readily agreed to this. They were so busy, he couldn't spare his staff for any more lengthy visits.

The following day Chrissie took over for her, as Isla had to be at the library. She wasn't exactly avoiding a certain person, but she wasn't exactly courting trouble, either. She wasn't used to handling such a compelling man, and she didn't want to appear as if she was overly interested in him. She had the best of excuses. As the prize winner, she was expected to be on duty at the library when the Sheikh of Q'Aqabi finally arrived to tour the university facilities. The head librarian welcomed her with particular enthusiasm as Isla knew more than most about successful breeding programmes of endangered species, having majored in that subject on her course.

The Sheikh's visit had provoked great excitement, and Isla was up earlier than usual getting ready for her duties at the library. She didn't want to let anyone down.

Having tied her hair back neatly, she viewed her pale face in the mirror. She'd missed sparring with the tough guy from the building site, but today wasn't a day for daydreams, but a day when she could do something to help repay the university that had been so good to her. Checking the lapels on her plain grey suit, she told herself firmly that her racing pulse had everything to do with finally meeting 'the invisible Sheikh', and nothing at all to do with the fact that she might have to cross the building site to get a coffee at some point in the day.

To give herself confidence, she slipped on her red high-heeled shoes. She loved them. They were a sale buy, and so unlike her, but what better day to wear them than today?

She wasn't the only one who was excited, Isla discovered when she arrived at the library and the air of anticipation was infectious. It had transformed the customary silence of the hallowed halls into a tense and expectant waiting room.

The Sheikh of Q'Aqabi was pouring money into the university, and had donated several ancient manuscripts from his private collection. The head librarian explained that he would want to view them, and that was where Isla would step in.

She glanced at the entrance doors yet again. Whatever he looked like, the Sheikh was obviously a fascinating man. Closing her eyes, she drew a steadying breath. Being in the library usually soothed her, but not today. And then she heard a buzz of conversation, heralding the arrival of the vice chancellor and his party. She prepared herself for the sight of a sheikh dressed in flowing robes, and was quite disappointed when the tweedy academics arrived with a group of men in business suits.

But spearheading that group was—

She lurched to her feet, the scrape of her chair screeching through the silence.

Everyone turned to look at her. The man from the building site stared straight at her as if she were the only thing of interest in the entire, echoing space.

Why hadn't he said?

Why was she so slow on the uptake?

She realised now that the man who had told her to call him Shaz was, in fact, His Serene Majesty, Sheikh Shazim bin Khalifa al Q'Aqabi, the major benefactor of the university, and her number one sparring partner.

And he was definitely not pot-bellied, or shrivelled, nor could his expression be called grumpy. Commanding, maybe. Faintly amused, definitely. And no wonder when he'd seen her in so many guises.

Maybe he'd known all along. Maybe he'd been playing games with her. His security team had surely supplied His Majesty with a full breakdown of everyone he was likely to meet on campus.

And now he was here in *her* library—the place she loved and felt safest and most at home in; the world of books, where adventures were safely contained within their pages—

There was nothing safe in His Majesty's eyes.

She stood stiffly as he approached, glad that he couldn't hear her heart beating.

'Your Majesty…' She couldn't quite bring herself to curtsey.

'No need to curtsey.'

Her head shot up, and they exchanged a look—challenge, repaid by challenge. She could see the burn of humour in his dark, luminous eyes. He'd known she wouldn't curtsey—and not because her manners were lacking in any way, but because she was frozen to the spot with surprise, and every inch of her was tingling with awareness.

'And here we have our very own Athena,' the vice chancellor stated with enthusiasm, forcing Isla to break eye contact with the royal visitor.

She was standing to attention like a soldier on parade, she realised, trying to relax. She was never this tense. Forcing herself to look into *His Majesty's* mocking eyes, she saw the flare of calculation in them as the vice chancellor continued to sing her praises.

'Isla is our goddess of good order and wisdom, as well

as strength and strategy,' the vice chancellor continued, warming to his theme.

'And warfare,' the Sheikh added in an all too familiar husky tone with the faintest tug of a smile at one corner of his mouth. 'Athena was also the goddess of warfare,' he explained with a lift of his brow when Isla shot him a look.

'You two know each other?' The vice chancellor glanced with interest between the two of them.

'We met on the building site,' Isla explained, holding the Sheikh's burning stare steadily. 'I work at the café, Vice Chancellor, and I took out some coffee for His Majesty's team, though I had no idea who he was at the time.' Her stare sharpened on *His Majesty's* amused eyes.

'And would your manner have changed, if you had known?' the ruler of Q'Aqabi enquired mildly.

She thought it better not to answer that.

'Forgive me, Your Majesty,' the vice chancellor interrupted, obviously keen to break the awkward silence. 'Please allow me to formally present Isla Sinclair...'

For a second time, Isla dipped her head politely without sweeping the impressive giant standing in front of her a submissive curtsey.

'You two may well be working together,' the vice chancellor said with delight, oblivious to Isla's sudden intake of breath. 'Isla is our prize winner, Your Majesty, and, according to the conditions of your very generous gift, Isla will be travelling to Q'Aqabi as part of her prize.'

'Oh, really,' Shaz murmured as if this were news to him. 'My people organised the contest, Vice Chancellor, but be assured that we will welcome you with open arms, Ms Sinclair.'

Isla stared at the hand that Shaz was holding out in formal greeting. She remembered the touch of that hand, and she wasn't too keen on risking the thrill of it with an audience watching.

Muscle up! She was a serious-minded woman; a scientist, a veterinary surgeon—her hand had been all sorts of places. She certainly didn't balk at shaking Shaz's hand, even if she knew now that it had a title attached to it.

'Your Majesty,' she said crisply, giving him a firm handshake.

'Shazim,' he prompted, still holding onto her hand. 'If we're going to be working together we should at least be on first-name terms, Isla.'

'Shazim,' she repeated politely as shock waves travelled up and down her arm. She loved the sound of his name on her lips—and knew she had to pull herself together. But not just yet…

They were still hand-locked when the vice chancellor coughed discreetly to distract them. Quickly removing her hand from Shazim's grasp, she linked her hands safely behind her back.

'Ms Sinclair thrives on challenge,' the vice chancellor offered with enthusiasm, which didn't exactly help the situation.

'You have some interesting students, Vice Chancellor,' His Majesty commented. 'I'm impressed by how hard some of them, like Isla, work to pay their fees. We must talk more about grants and endowments, so that everyone who wants to can enjoy the benefit of an education here.'

'Whatever you think,' the vice chancellor agreed, flashing a grateful glance at Isla. 'I know Ms Sinclair works harder than most. Apart from her day jobs, Isla holds a gym class in the evenings for the children of parents who work or study here.'

'A gym class?' Shazim's eyes were alive with laughter as he stared down at her, though his face remained commendably still. 'You must need to be supple and fit for that, I imagine, Ms Sinclair?'

'First names, please,' she implored sweetly with a

warning flash in her glance. She didn't want to spend the next half an hour trying to reassure the vice chancellor about her pole-dancing exploits at the club.

'Isla runs from praise like a gazelle from a lion,' the vice chancellor praised her with a smile.

'A fitting comparison, Vice Chancellor,' Shazim agreed, flashing her one final mocking look before moving on.

CHAPTER FOUR

It hadn't escaped Isla's attention that His Serene Majesty was also known as the Lion of the Desert, but she was no gazelle. She was more of a doughty old warhorse, tough and thick-skinned—

A warhorse?

She was more like a mole blundering blindly about on the fringes of a royal world she knew nothing about, Isla reflected with a frown as she sank down with relief at her desk as the vice chancellor and the royal party moved on. Winning the prize of a trip to Q'Aqabi was the opportunity of a lifetime. She still couldn't quite believe that she'd been chosen. She'd worked so hard, but had always known that it wasn't a guarantee. The opportunity meant everything to her, and she couldn't afford to be distracted by her attraction to Shazim. She had to concentrate on preparing to be plunged into the desert, a world that would test her like no other. She knew it bore no relation to her fantasies, and she welcomed the hardship and danger. She had never been under any illusion where her work was concerned. Working with animals wrenched her emotions this way and that, and Shazim's project would demand every bit of skill she possessed. But if she could do anything to help, she would gladly devote her life to it.

It was hardly likely that they would work together, Isla reassured herself. The Sheikh of Q'Aqabi must have royal duties by the score—

She sprang to her feet as the official party came into view again.

'Coffee time,' the vice chancellor carolled with enthusiasm, rubbing his hands together in anticipation.

'You will excuse me, Vice Chancellor, I hope?' His Majesty intoned graciously. 'I have a wish to see my manuscripts.'

Isla's heart beat like crazy as Shazim stared at her. He must know that she had been detailed to show him the exhibits.

The tiniest adjustment to Shazim's glance was enough to turn his congenial exchange with the vice chancellor into something very different for her. He could seduce her with a look—if she were a different woman. Though she was surprised that the Lion of the Desert was interested in her at all.

'Of course Isla must accompany you,' the vice chancellor enthused. 'You couldn't have anyone better to accompany you, Your Majesty. I have it on good authority from the head librarian here that Isla brings order to our questing minds.'

'Indeed?' Shazim queried, staring at her with veiled amusement.

'By which our vice chancellor means that I keep the catalogue here in good order,' Isla explained primly.

Shazim's eyes sparkled with humour as he dipped his head with approval. 'I look forward to learning more about how you maintain such an ordered catalogue.'

As Isla led the way he noticed with interest the sassy heels. Everything about Isla Sinclair intrigued him. More than ever he got the sense of the ice maiden with a molten core. It was that heat that made him want to take her to the furthest reaches of the library, to the shadowy, dusty nooks, where no one ever strayed—

'Your Majesty?' she prompted him. 'The tour?'

'Of course. Please, lead on…' He had become distracted watching her walk away. The high heels made her hips sway rhythmically, while her buttocks strained the seam of her skirt. Discovering that Isla was the prize winner was the worst outcome possible. A short affair could be managed discreetly, but she was coming to Q'Aqabi, not just to tour the nature reserve and veterinary facilities as part of her prize, but to offer her expertise and work there for a while. Under those circumstances, there could be no affair, short or otherwise.

'And here we have the illuminated manuscript of the Canticle of…'

He wasn't listening. He knew everything there was to know about the manuscript. Isla could have been spinning him any old yarn, and he'd still be enthralled. His good intentions where restraint was concerned were under pressure already. They were alone in this part of the library, the academic party having moved onto the room where refreshments had been set out. Isla was doing everything she was supposed to, with apparently no personal interest in him. She appeared so contained, when he knew that nothing could be further from the truth. She wasn't docile or tame. Isla was like one of his wild animals, free and spirited. She was ambitious too, and just as driven to succeed as he was. His ambition to be everything he could be to his people to make up for past sins had an obvious cause, but what was driving Isla?

His gaze strayed to her shoes. There was more than a hint of the rebel about her, and he wondered how that would translate in bed.

'I've got a better idea,' he said when she paused in front of a glass cabinet housing another of his priceless illuminated manuscripts.

'Oh?" said, turning with a frown.

'Have dinner with me tonight.'

'What?' She looked at him as if dinner were another word for sex. 'Oh, no, I don't think—'

His suggestion had thrown her. For the first time she was flustered. Her cheeks were red and her breathing sped up. He guessed she wanted to have dinner with him, wanted to spend time with him, but didn't want to do anything to threaten the practical opportunities he could offer Isla in terms of her career.

'I would like to discuss the new veterinary school with you,' he said, making it hard for her to refuse.

'With me?' She touched her chest with surprise, then turned instantly suspicious.

'I would appreciate hearing a recent student's forthright point of view. You would be forthright with me, wouldn't you, Isla?'

'Of course, but—' Her intelligent grey gaze sharpened on his.

'Then, shall we say eight o'clock? I'll have my driver pick you up—'

'But you don't know—'

'Where you live?' Angling his chin, he smiled into her eyes.

'You had me followed?'

He cancelled out her affront with a glance. 'The vice chancellor supplied your address, along with all other information I might need, so my people could get in touch with the prize winner to arrange transport to Q'Aqabi.'

'Of course,' she agreed, biting down on the swell of her lip as she thought about this.

While Isla settled her mind, he wrestled with ideas that had never concerned him before. Discreet arrangements could be made when he wanted a woman in his bed, with mutual agreement the only condition. But when Isla was in Q'Aqabi where he had duties and responsibilities, he could not please himself. He was pledged to his country, and, if he had judged Isla right, she would want more than a brief affair, and that was something he could never give her. Would things change when they reached the desert? Would he make an exception this one time and mix business with pleasure? Would Isla be prepared to pay the price for that pleasure, or would it break her when he sent her away?

And maybe him?

No woman had the power to do that.

His senses sharpened as Isla drew a tense breath and shook her head. 'I'm afraid dinner tonight isn't possible.'

'You have a prior engagement?'

'Yes,' she admitted, meeting his gaze with candour, 'with my studies.'

'But that's what I want to talk to you about. I know your career hopes are pinned on specialising in the preservation of endangered species—'

'Not hopes. I *will* specialise,' she corrected him with a verve he could only admire.

'There is nowhere better than Q'Aqabi for you to pursue your work. We have species on the verge of extinction, and a programme specifically designed to save these animals.'

'Are you offering me a job before I even arrive in the country?'

Her look was both a challenge and a provocation.

'I think I'd better try you out first, to see how you shape up.'

She met his amused stare with distinct lack of humour and a lift of her brow, as if to ask if they were still talking about her career prospects.

The project meant the world to him, and he turned serious as he decided that if Isla was as good as they said she was, she would get the job.

'The team that will be working on my new nature

reserve has not been finalised yet, but your up-to-date knowledge and your obvious devotion to your work puts you in a very good position.'

She visibly relaxed, making him wonder again about her past experience with men. When it came to her love of animals, Isla couldn't be shaken, but when it came to flirting with him, it was always one step forward and two steps back.

'You want to have dinner with me,' she confirmed with a frown. 'And this is so we can discuss your nature reserve and the new veterinary school?'

'Amongst other topics,' he agreed. 'I'm sure we won't be short of things to talk about.'

'I hope I don't let you down…'

Even he couldn't be sure, as Isla grew thoughtful, if she was talking about her appeal to him as a person, or as a vet. One thing was certain, he had waited long enough for her answer. 'Do you accept my dinner invitation, or not?'

Her eyes briefly flared, but she had more sense than to take him on. She would not risk antagonising him, when visiting Q'Aqabi was everything she longed for, and had worked so hard to achieve.

'What's your answer, Isla?'

Lifting her chin, she met his stare candidly. 'Thank you, Your Majesty. Yes. I will have dinner with you.'

CHAPTER FIVE

He was just relaxing into victory, believing Isla had not only agreed to have dinner with him, but quite a lot more, when she added three crushing words: 'But not tonight.'

'When, then?' he demanded curtly.

'In Q'Aqabi,' she said, delivering her final surprise. 'I'll have dinner with you in Q'Aqabi, when we have worthwhile things to share. I'd only bore you to death otherwise.'

Nothing could be further from the truth.

'Your audacity in refusing the invitation of the man who has donated this prize you care so much about is—'

'Breathtaking?' she agreed, nodding her head. 'Yes, I suppose it must seem that way, but, you see, this course means everything to me.'

'So blackmailing me is your way of showing this?'

'I'm just asking for a chance,' she argued passionately. 'I'm asking for a role in your project—a real role. I'm begging, actually. I can't afford to be proud when this is all I've ever wanted. And I know I can help you. I've learned all the latest techniques, and I'm certain I can add value to your plans. I'm already excited—'

'Aren't you taking rather a lot for granted?' he interrupted.

'Am I?'

Despair showed in her eyes. He had no intention of withdrawing the prize. According to the vice chancellor,

Isla had been an outstanding student, and he didn't doubt she had a lot to offer. Her only downfall was that beneath that cool exterior, she was headstrong and passionate—

Wasn't that what he liked about her?

Everything in his life was predictable and rigidly controlled—by him. Isla had turned everything on its head. And she had other admirable qualities. His most recent information said she had been forced to suspend her studies in order to nurse her sick mother, and when her mother died Isla had moved heaven and earth to find the money to get back on the course. She was undoubtedly a force to be reckoned with, and in time might prove a real asset to his project. She would certainly be an asset in his bed.

He had never concluded a bargain quite like this before. Women wanted his money, his power and his influence. They wanted to share his bed. They wanted good sex and a trophy lover. Isla wanted his permission to work the hardest shift on earth in the desert alongside his veterinary rangers. For once in his life, he couldn't be sure if she wanted that more than anything else, but he looked forward to finding out.

'Perhaps you should listen to my terms before you get too excited,' he suggested.

'Your terms?' She was instantly wary.

'You will be going to the desert, which is not the place you imagine.' When her face fell, he added, 'It is far, far more beautiful. But it can also be a hellhole,' he warned, his face growing grim as hers grew rapt. 'Paradise one moment, it can be transformed in a matter of minutes into the most dangerous place on earth, and you, as an expert in your field, must learn the ways of the desert, and how to survive it.'

'I'm up to it,' she stated firmly.

'You will be shown everything you need to know. If you don't prove your worth, you will leave.'

'Will you be there?'

He guessed she had spoken without thinking, as her cheeks were now burning red. But would he be in the desert? Would he retrace that reckless youth's footsteps to the site of the tragedy?

'Prove to me that you are the most willing and able of all my recruits, and you can stay on in Q'Aqabi and work with my other willing recruits,' he said, moving past the question.

As she gulped convulsively, he guessed that Isla's hidden fiery depths encouraged her to picture harems stuffed to the brim with his *willing recruits*. 'You are the most promising of all the students here,' he said, to put a balm on her vivid imagination, 'or you wouldn't be getting this chance. If your theoretical studies are matched by your practical application of them—'

'Oh!' she said before he even had chance to finish. 'Thank you—thank you!'

It was as if all her tension had released at once, and as she took a step forward she looked for an instant as if she was going to fling her arms around him and hug him tight. Fortunately for them both, she curbed the impulse, and remained instead vibrating with excitement in front of him. Physical contact that wasn't initiated by him was alien in the world he inhabited. He had never known affection as a child, having been brought up in a nursery of royal offspring from several wives. His brother had tried to make up for the lack of parental love by being more like a father to him, but his brother had been dead for many years.

He found himself relaxing, even smiling at Isla. Her unselfconscious show of gratitude had touched him more than he'd realised. It had also aroused him.

'Please forgive me, Your Majesty—'

They both turned as the vice chancellor spoke. Shazim

couldn't be sure how long the party of academics had been back, but he guessed long enough to see Isla move as if to hug him, as his elderly host was staring at him with concern, no doubt wondering if she had breached royal protocol, and possibly damaged the excellent relationship between Q'Aqabi and the university.

'I hesitate to remind you about our busy schedule,' the vice chancellor ventured, anxiety ringing in his voice.

He quickly reassured the older man. 'You're quite right, Vice Chancellor, and I apologise for taking up so much of Ms Sinclair's valuable time, but she has been a font of information, and a fascinating companion with a novel take on so many things.'

'On that we are agreed,' the vice chancellor told him warmly, his relief clearly visible.

Isla carefully avoided looking at him when the vice chancellor said this.

'She has the highest marks ever recorded,' the vice chancellor added in a conspiratorial stage whisper. 'You couldn't have anyone better on the team.'

'I'm sure you're right,' he said mildly, raising his brow a fraction as he turned to look at Isla—who clearly wasn't sure whether she should smile or remain expressionless beneath the barrage of praise, but at least she didn't simper.

'I won't let you or the university down,' she told them both with feeling.

'I know you won't, my dear. Your Majesty…' Standing back to allow him to go first, the vice chancellor indicated that it was time for them to join the rest of the official party.

'I'll see you in Q'Aqabi, Ms Sinclair,' he murmured.

His senses stirred as Isla lowered her gaze. When she bit her lip, he wondered if she was reflecting on what exactly she had just talked herself into.

* * *

She was in trouble and sinking fast, Isla reflected later, swirling a sweetener into the coffee on her desk. Not that she had changed her mind about going to Q'Aqabi. She'd worked her socks off to even get a sniff at the prize. Shazim's offer of a possible job after her visit to his country was like all her best dreams coming true at once. And she would prove herself, whatever it took. Her only question was, could she work with him? Could she see Shazim every day, and not be distracted by thoughts that had no connection with the project that meant so much to both of them?

Look at it this way—you're a newly qualified vet with grime beneath your fingernails, while Shazim is an all-powerful sheikh with more sex appeal than there are grains of sand in his desert.

They weren't just incompatible, they were quite literally worlds apart. Shazim hadn't answered her question about whether he would be in the desert at the same time she was, but she doubted it somehow. He'd have many other things to do. Of course she wished he would be the one to show her the hidden secrets of the desert. She couldn't ask for anything more than to see the dangerous wilderness through his eyes. But that sensual world of billowing Bedouin tents, and endless passion beneath the stars on the shores of some tranquil oasis with only the sound of the night hawk to disturb them, was just a fantasy, as he had reminded her, and had no bearing on what she was likely to see.

But if she did see anything like that...and if she did spend some time alone in the desert with Shazim...

That wasn't going to happen, but if it did, and if by some incredible chance she learned to trust again and they had an affair, heartache in exchange for all of that didn't seem too bad a deal—at least, not from this safe distance.

* * *

Isla's arrival at Q'Aqabi International Airport on a commercial jet was a disappointment. Not because the airport was short of anything, but because it had too much of everything. It was the slickest, most efficient, most opulent and impressive airport terminal Isla had ever been through, when she had hoped for a little romance, and perhaps some mystery and magic.

And there was no sign of Shazim.

Of course there was no sign of Shazim. His Majesty had left London long before her, on his private jet the size of a super-airliner, according to the brief news feature she'd watched, detailing the Sheikh of Q'Aqabi's benevolence towards the university. Did she expect the ruler of the country to roll out the red carpet for one newly qualified vet and her mound of unattractive-looking baggage?

No, but maybe she had expected to detect the hint of sandalwood on the air, and perhaps a few grains of sand on the pristine white marble floor—

And camels instead of cabs?

Get real. This was twenty-first-century oil money, polished to the highest sheen. There was a lake of black gold beneath her feet, and a nature reserve somewhere deep in the desert, waiting for her to start work.

'Welcome to Q'Aqabi, Ms Sinclair—'

She whirled around to see a young woman around her own age with the friendliest dark, almond-shaped eyes.

'His Majesty has asked me to meet you and show you to the palace…'

The palace?

'My name is Miriam, but my friends call me Millie,' the girl explained.

'Pleased to meet you, Millie.' The two girls smiled as they shook hands. 'I thought I would be staying in a hotel?'

'His Majesty thought that you, as the prize winner, should have the honour of staying at the royal palace.'

Near Shazim? Her heart sank at the reality of being close to him. Dreams were one thing, but this was all too real.

'That's very kind of His Majesty,' she made herself say.

'He is very kind. Our King is the best of men,' Millie assured her, stirring Isla's curiosity as to how Shazim's countrymen saw him. 'And you'll soon be in the desert,' Miriam added, sensing something of Isla's disappointment that she wouldn't be going straight to the reserve. 'Though I expect you're looking forward to the award ceremony tonight.'

'Oh, I am,' Isla enthused, deeply conscious of the honour. 'Will His Majesty be accompanying our party to the desert?' She hoped not, as the only thing in her head was Shazim, clad in flowing robes with the setting sun burning fiery red behind him, when she needed all her concentration on her work.

'I'm not sure,' Millie said—guardedly, Isla thought. 'His Majesty only travels into the desert when it is absolutely necessary.'

'Oh, I see.'

She didn't see at all. The ruler of a desert kingdom who only went into the desert when it was *necessary*? How did Shazim oversee his nature reserve? How did he visit his people in outlying villages? There was some mystery here, and it was one she felt she must get to the bottom of, though for now she had to content herself with climbing into the sleek black limousine so she didn't keep Millie waiting.

Millie said goodbye and closed the door, leaving Isla sealed inside the luxurious interior. She had gained nothing more than a passing impression of snow-white skyscrapers silhouetted against the bluest of skies, before getting into the vehicle. Looking out of the window, she was fascinated by the lush green spaces and wide squares she could see; the view left her with a sense of order and purpose that she told herself could only have been created by Shazim. Everything he did was in honour of his late brother, she had read somewhere, and this immaculate city was certainly a wonderful tribute. It did make her wonder if Shazim was so shackled to duty he made no time for himself. For all his wealth and power, and even his occasional flashes of humour, he had struck her as a remote man.

Her deepening feelings for him worried her. They couldn't go anywhere. She was wasting her time. Worse, she was allowing herself to become distracted, when this trip was so vital to her future. She had to try and put Shazim out of her mind…though how she was going to do that, she had no idea.

Her next concern wasn't as pressing, but it was very real. As the limousine slowed before sweeping through a pair of enormous golden gates, she wished she had worn something more elegant than her practical travelling clothes.

They had arrived at the palace. And, realistically, she didn't think that any outfit would quite match up to it. Craning her neck, she stared out of the window.

The palace was incredibly beautiful, like something out of a fairy tale, with turrets and domes and minarets. The stone—marble, she guessed—was sparkling white and veined in the palest pink. And the building was so vast that, even when she tried looking every which way out of the limousine, she couldn't see all of it.

The driver had stopped the vehicle in front of a wide sweep of marble steps, where a committee of men and women in flowing robes was waiting to greet her. There was no sign of Shazim, but as the driver opened her door and stood back a man dressed in a long white robe with the traditional headdress, which she had learned before she arrived was called a keffiyeh, stepped forward to greet her.

'His Majesty welcomes you, and hopes you will find your stay here pleasant.'

When he bowed over her hand, rather than shaking it, Isla's throat dried at the enormity of the task that lay ahead of her.

'Please thank His Majesty, and tell him that I am delighted to be here.'

She wasn't used to such formality, and would have to rise to the occasion, Isla realised with mounting apprehension. It was just that everything around her was on such an incredible scale. Nothing could have prepared her for this. She was escorted past guards in jewel-coloured ceremonial robes, with sabres flashing at their sides, and then she was introduced to the personal maid who was to take her onto her suite of rooms.

The splendour inside the palace as they walked deeper into its fragranced interior took her breath away. The exquisite marble, the gilding, the intricate marquetry, the jewels glinting in the doors, and the light, furnishings, space—ceilings stretching away to the heavens, and rooms the size of football pitches, corridors decorated with priceless objets d'art. There were shaded internal courtyards with orange trees and secret nooks where birds carolled as loudly as they would in any park. It was all quite incredible, and far beyond anything her feeble imagination might have conjured up. The talents of countless craftsmen must have been employed to create such a beautiful palace. And, yes, she acknowledged with a secret smile, the scent of sandalwood and spice was everywhere, just as she had always dreamed and hoped it would be.

Once she was installed in her lavish suite of rooms,

Isla's major concern turned to what she was wearing for the ceremony. She didn't have any money to spare for new clothes, and had cobbled together an outfit with Chrissie's help. The outfit consisted of the plain grey suit she wore when she was working in the library, with the addition of a cheap lace blouse. She had chosen a pair of sensible low-heeled shoes, and tied her hair back neatly in a low ponytail. The modest outfit had seemed appropriate in England, but here it just looked cheap.

She felt even more uncomfortable when she finally left the relative sanctuary of her suite, accompanied by the group that had been sent to fetch her. They were all decked out in the smartest of uniforms, or robes and silken gowns. She felt like a dowdy sparrow in an aviary packed with birds of paradise.

She told herself firmly that it was time to pull herself together. She wasn't a little girl now, standing outside the kitchen door at Lord and Lady Anconner's house, where her mother had used to work. She was here because she had worked hard to be here, and her life wasn't one of luxury and privilege. She'd be heading out to the desert soon, and that was where the real work would begin.

Her little group stopped at the grand double doors of the hall in which the ceremony was to be held. The doors were entirely made of gold. They stole her breath away, but her big adventure had only just begun. The walls inside the ceremonial chamber were gold, and the floor was marble inlaid with gold. There was a throne at the far end of the room, and that was also gold. A plush red carpet led up the steps to the front of the throne. A shiver of awareness coursed through her, for there, already seated waiting for her in imperial splendour, dressed in flowing robes of unrelieved black, was His Serene Majesty, Sheikh Shazim bin Khalifa al Q'Aqabi.

As her attendants dropped back, trumpeters sounded a fanfare, and she set out on the longest walk of her life.

He rammed his body back against the throne. Seeing Isla again shook him to the core. Frustration was eating him alive. He was used to satisfying his smallest whim at once, not putting it on hold like this. She looked more beautiful than ever. Her sombre suit was so appropriate for the occasion. His project wasn't flippant in any way, but vitally important, and it deserved the serious approach she had taken. In his view, she couldn't have pitched her appearance any better, and he appreciated the concern she'd shown.

She walked steadily towards him, her gaze fixed on his face. He stood as she mounted the steps, and inhaled deeply when she came to a halt in front of him. He could smell her familiar wildflower scent, and the soap she had used in the shower. She was beautiful. She was special. She was Isla.

'Congratulations,' he said formally, holding out the scroll due to the prize winner. 'I look forward to you bringing new ideas to our work.'

'That is all I want,' she said steadily, staring him straight in the eyes.

'That, and dinner, I imagine?' he prompted in a low voice.

'I beg your pardon?' she murmured so that only he could hear.

'Dinner,' he repeated in the same low tone. 'You do remember your promise back in England—to have dinner with me when we have something to discuss? I think your upcoming journey to the desert merits that, don't you? I imagine you have been studying and planning, and I certainly have a lot of *worthwhile* topics to discuss with you.'

Something flashed in her eyes as he reminded Isla of

the phrase she had used at the university as an excuse not to have dinner with him right away, but she quickly masked her feelings. She was too shrewd to throw away her opportunity on a point of pride.

'How gracious of Your Majesty to invite me to eat with you, and give me the opportunity to discuss the nature reserve with you,' she said, bowing her head. 'I would be delighted and honoured to have dinner with you.'

She had brightened and looked more confident. Dinner was harmless, especially when she had no doubt heard of the official banquet tonight, when there would be other notable achievers present. She couldn't know that he had something different in mind.

'I will send for you,' he said.

'At what time?'

He drew a breath. Being questioned wasn't usual for him. He gave an order and it was carried out. 'At nine,' he said abruptly.

'But the banquet's at eight—' She stopped, and he saw understanding flare in her eyes. 'Your Majesty?' she queried.

'Nine o'clock,' he repeated as the trumpeters delivered a closing fanfare, signalling that the ceremony was over, and Ms Sinclair must return to her suite of rooms to ready herself for dinner with the Sheikh.

CHAPTER SIX

HE ORDERED A lavish buffet to be laid out on the balcony overlooking the oasis. With the help of his head gardener, he had personally selected the flowers from his temperature-controlled orangery. There were white roses, blue sapphire-like agapanthus, luxury soft, pink sweet avalanche roses, with peachy spray roses and pink veronica—all the colours of the sunset. Standing back, he took pleasure in the finished effect. The long table was laid with snowy-white linen. Candles glowed in silver sconces, while the finest crystal glittered in the moonlight. They would sit on cushions, as was the custom in his country. Traditional musicians, sitting in a group some distance away, would play softly to an accompaniment of desert cicadas, and the occasional hooting call of an eagle owl. As bats flittered overhead, even he, the most unromantic of men, had to admit that what his team had created for him was breathtaking. He had never gone to so much trouble for anyone before.

'The prize winner must have the best,' he told his chamberlain as the old man bowed his way out of Shazim's presence, taking everyone with him, having checked that everything had been completed to His Majesty's satisfaction. 'Every person who comes here to help Q'Aqabi and the nature reserve must be shown every possible courtesy and gratitude.'

'Yes, Your Majesty,' his elderly advisor agreed in his

gently modulated voice. 'I'm sure Ms Sinclair will be most grateful.'

He didn't want her to be grateful. He wanted her to be happy.

One of them should be.

But, would she come?

Why shouldn't she have doubts? He wasn't being completely honest about this dinner *à deux*. Yes. This special night was a gift from him, and from his country, but would he have gone to this trouble for anyone else? There was an official banquet to honour the high achievers, but he had not even stayed at that long enough to eat, and had returned here to be with Isla.

And he couldn't even be sure of her, when any other woman would have rushed to have dinner with His Majesty, the Sheikh.

Old habits died hard, he discovered, as, rather than glancing at his functional, top-end wristwatch, he stared up at the stars, the moon, and their relative positions in the sky. He had shunned desert lore for too long, because that subject, at least contained within a book, had been his brother's preserve. Shazim believed his right to use those skills had died with his brother on the night of the tragedy, but now the ability was back, and the sky was once again his timepiece.

It was nine o'clock. So, where the hell was she?

Luxuriating in an unusual abundance of spare time, Isla was bathing in a scented bath. The bath had been run for her by the same smiling maid who had escorted her to her suite of rooms. There was everything she had ever dreamed of for her comfort. Even the big fluffy towels were softer and warmer, while crystal flacons filled with perfumed oils and emollient milks were things of beauty, rather than functional, like the plastic tubs she was used to. The walls of her bathing chamber—she couldn't even begin to think of it as a bathroom—were lined with lapis lazuli in a rich shade of blue that reminded her of the night sky. Even the taps gleamed silver like the stars. The maid had insisted on lighting hundreds of tiny candles to make the whole process a stunning experience. And now, she discovered, that same maid had laid out several silk chiffon gowns for her to choose from.

'For the heat,' the maid explained in broken English, with a smile so open and warm Isla couldn't find it in her to refuse.

She had never been treated so well. Her only experience of wealth and privilege had been with her mother's employers, but Lord and Lady Anconner had treated them both like machines—people without feelings, and not worthy of their care.

This was the starkest contrast possible, Isla concluded as she stared with bewilderment at the selection of gowns.

'I'm hopeless at this. I don't have a clue which one to wear—can you help?' she asked the maid, miming her request at the same time. She only owned one dress, and that was the plain grey one she had worn for her graduation. These gowns were in rainbow shades, and she didn't know where to start.

The maid rushed to help, and picked out two. One was in a soft blush rose, the colour of the sky at the horizon at dawn, and the other was a soft blue, decorated with silver.

Either one, the maid mimed back, holding up first one exquisite dress and then the other.

'Which one would you choose?'

The maid held up the sky-blue dress, and, drawing an arc above her head to represent the sky, she next drew the bowl of the sun, from which all life came. Then, she touched her heart, and brushed her stomach with her hand as if she were carrying a child.

Isla tried hard not to let her surprise show. She had to arrive at a decision fast.

'I love the one you've chosen.' But not for the reason the maid had used to make her choice.

Apprehension stormed through her. She was being naive if she thought Shazim had invited her to a private dinner in order to quiz her about her work. It might not seem possible to her that he looked at her with interest in anything other than her professional skills, but to everyone else…

The maid coughed discreetly, and glanced pointedly at the beautiful little French ormolu clock on the console table.

What could she do? She had left it too late to let him down.

He was staring out over the oasis. Flat and empty, it could have been a symbol of his life. It was how he'd seen his life when he lost his brother. Behind him was the table loaded with delicious things, but he couldn't be sure Isla would join him.

His senses flared as he heard her behind him.

'Isla—'

His face as he turned must have betrayed the fact that he wasn't simply greeting the prize winner who could give so much to his country, and to his brother's project, but a woman he wanted in his bed. She looked exquisite and, for a moment, he was too stunned to speak. He had half expected Isla to wear her usual jeans, or perhaps the sober grey suit she had worn for the ceremony, but this most practical of women was floating towards him in the most glamorous gown he had ever seen. Ankle length, it was composed of several layers of the finest silk chiffon that undulated and drifted around her as she moved. And she'd left her hair loose. Did she have any idea how beautiful she was?

He thought not. Isla was as unaffected as the day was long, and as direct and as uncompromising as ever.

The scene he had created for her enjoyment stopped her in her tracks.

'Shazim, this is…'

She started to speak, but for once words failed her and she gestured helplessly instead. 'I can't describe it,' she admitted. 'I had no idea there was an oasis behind the palace, and this candlelit setting against the night sky is just so unbelievably beautiful. I had no idea you could be so romantic,' she added as she took it all in.

'My team are responsible,' he retorted with a self-deprecating shrug. 'They wanted our prize winner to have the best experience possible while she's here.'

He couldn't even speak of her as if this was his idea, and Isla was standing in front of him. His heart was ice. He had flashes of longing to be different, but the ice must stay. He didn't deserve anything more.

'You've gone to far too much trouble—or your team has,' Isla insisted. 'But I'm really grateful.'

From the little he had come to know of her, he knew how pragmatic a woman she was, and so he was surprised to hear the shake in her voice, as if she had been touched by the effort that had been gone to on her behalf, so maybe Isla had problems demonstrating her feelings too.

Or maybe the trouble he had gone to made her nervous. There was that possibility too.

'Please thank your team for me,' she said, polite as ever as she leaned forward to inhale the bewitching scent of the floral displays.

As she moved her silken hair briefly covered her face and, when she straightened up again, he couldn't have been more surprised to see tears in her eyes.

'I know I'm being silly,' she said, facing him, 'but no

one has ever done anything like this for me before, and I wish—'

She stopped and turned away.

Walking up to her, he put his hands lightly on her upper arms and, standing behind her, he stared out as she was doing across the flat oasis.

'You wish your mother could see it,' he whispered.

'You know?' She blinked the tears away and stared at him. Then she must have remembered what he'd said to her in the library about receiving information regarding her from the university.

'Of course your people will have researched every tiny detail regarding those you would meet,' she murmured, frowning a little.

'You must miss your mother.'

'Oh, yes…so much,' she admitted.

Isla wasn't sure how long they stood together in silence. She only knew, as emotion ravaged her, that Shazim seemed to understand her grief. She was angry with herself for showing him any weakness, but sometimes the grief she felt at her mother's passing was hard to hide. And then, confusingly, there was happiness too, knowing she had fulfilled her mother's dying wish by going back to university to continue her studies. She couldn't let her mother down now, but if she failed to meet her expectations in any way, she would.

And then there was also a totally unrealistic yearning for Shazim to put his arms around her, and she had to tell herself to stop wanting things she couldn't have. All this heart-searching would only distract her from her true purpose…

'Shall we eat?' he suggested.

The distraction of such a down-to-earth suggestion was a relief. She had opened her heart for a moment, showing him her true mixed-up feelings, and she could only be glad that he didn't pity her. He felt her sadness, and had recognized it as his own. In that they did share a bond. Perhaps they were coming to understand each other a little.

'I'd love to eat—I'm starving,' she said, turning around. Her heart leapt as Shazim smiled into her eyes at this sign of her spirit returning. 'Everything looks so delicious.'

'My team has worked hard,' he agreed. 'We mustn't disappoint them.'

Shazim put her at her ease. They sat side by side, but not touching each other, on cushions overlooking the oasis. It was only as the night progressed that Isla began to realize that what at first had appeared completely empty was in fact full of life… Birds silently skimmed the surface, while bats cavorted overhead. Fish leapt, their scales iridescent in the moonlight, while fireflies hovered like tiny dots of light against the darkness. There was a whole busy world, just waiting to be explored.

'This is the most beautiful place I've ever seen,' she told Shazim.

While she was still trying to get her head around eating supper with a sheikh in such fabulous surroundings, they ate and talked at a leisurely pace.

Isla had been right in waiting, as she had put it, until they had something worthwhile to say. She'd done her homework on Q'Aqabi, and forced him to revisit details he hadn't considered for years. He had wanted to blot out so much of it, that now he could only be glad that she had prompted his recollections, and that they were as vivid as they had always been.

'And now you've got to show me the desert,' she insisted. 'I want to see it through your eyes—'

Her eyes were avid with eagerness, but his tone was sharp. 'No.'

She had asked him the one thing he could not do, and recoiled with surprise at his response.

'I have excellent rangers—the best in their field,' he explained to soften the blow. 'They will show you everything you should see.'

It took Isla a few moments to recover. She was clearly baffled and embarrassed by his sudden change of manner. When she spoke again she had changed too. She was circumspect, and almost reverential to the point where he could have roared with frustration. He didn't want reverence from Isla. He wanted her honesty and the frank and easy way in which she had previously spoken her mind to him.

'I apologise, Your Majesty. I realise that you must have far more important things to do than show me around.'

Nothing could be further from the truth. What could be more important than visiting the project that would have meant so much to his brother? He had hired the best brains, the best rangers, and the best equipment. Money was no object to him, and no effort had been spared. He had sat up late into the night for years, discussing the best outcome for each stage of the scheme with acknowledged experts in the field.

But had he seen the results of that endeavour first hand?

Wasn't it time to face his demons and go back into the desert?

Had this extraordinary woman pointed out the one flaw in his plan? Had she shown him in a single night that a scheme without a beating heart was doomed to fail—that it wouldn't inspire, it couldn't thrive, it couldn't last?

Springing to his feet, he stared down at her. 'I'll have the appropriate items you will need for your journey into the desert delivered to your suite. I will be ready and waiting to leave at dawn tomorrow morning.' And with that he strode away, leaving her staring after him in surprise.

After a restless night, tossing and turning as she wondered if she had insulted Shazim, Isla was up before dawn. She was excited at the prospect of visiting the desert, *and with him*, and a little apprehensive too. All her knowledge and understanding came from books. Would she be equal to the task when she faced reality?

Shazim offered no reassurance. When she joined him at the foot of the palace steps, she doubted she had ever seen him so grim and intent, or so remote from her before. Something had rattled him. Was it her? Dressed down in jeans and a figure-hugging top, with the polarised aviators pilots favoured shoved back on his thick black hair, Shazim looked more like a stuntman in a movie than a hard man of the desert. He was too good-looking to be real, but then appearances could be deceptive, and from everything she'd seen and heard about him Shazim was tempered steel.

They took an elevator to the roof of the palace where a squat black helicopter was waiting. She had never flown in a helicopter before, and had to admit to a flutter of nerves. It was only Shazim's air of command that calmed her enough to climb in. He was piloting the aircraft, and she tried not to look at the floor as he strapped her in. She'd had no idea it was see-through, but, of course, that made sense, though it wouldn't pay to have a fear of heights.

Having organised her headset and her microphone, Shazim made some last-minute checks and spoke to air traffic control. Seated next to him, she could see everything, and his confidence helped her to conquer her nerves as they lifted off. She relaxed to the point where she could enjoy the view...and not just the desert that stretched like an endless sea all around them, but the man at her side. He was like a rock beside her, powerful, certain, and calm. His shoulders had the span of a warrior's shoulders, but he was the protector of his people…and his lean, tanned hands, hands that had been so gentle on her arms last night, made her long to be in his embrace. She wanted to know everything about him—what made him sad, happy, and what made him smile. She had never felt like this about a man before and, after her experience at the hands of her attacker, she'd never thought she'd be able. She was sensible, practical, and competent. She had her fantasies, but had never considered bringing those fantasies into her life before.

Having Isla at his side and in his head was like salve on an open wound. He might have put off this trip for ever without her. Revisiting the desert was a pilgrimage for him. He owed it to his brother to bring Isla and her new ideas to the project. That was what had driven him here, and now his hunger was growing to have the hands-on role he had denied himself for too long. As their shadow crept over the desert he was impatient to be down on the ground. He wanted to feel the sand beneath his desert boots again. He'd want Isla on his team, regardless of whether or not he wanted her in his bed. She was loyal and she was tough, and she wasn't fazed by anything… least of all him. She had stood up to him every step of the way, and was strong-minded, always doing what she believed to be right.

Too strong-minded, possibly?

He smiled a little. He liked the challenge she gave him.

He glanced at Isla. She gave him a guarded smile, but he could sense her excitement. She was about to visit the nature reserve she had been dreaming about. Checking in with flight control, he signalled his intention to land.

'Oh,' she exclaimed, clinging onto her seat as he swooped lower. 'Are we landing?'

'Yes.' He made a mental note not to fly as he usually did, but to have some concern for his passenger. He had grown tense at the thought of revisiting the site of the tragedy, and was flying on the edge of what was possible.

He shouldn't even be thinking about a woman who could only be the briefest of distractions in his life when he had so much more to accomplish, he told himself firmly as he landed the bird.

The briefest of distractions?

Was that why he had dispatched his security team to watch over Isla when she had left the club in London? This was a woman who had revitalised him like a bolt of lightning to his core. She had shaken up his life when he had thought everything would be at an emotional standstill for ever. She'd made him see things differently, to the point where he knew now that Isla wouldn't be seeing the desert through his eyes, but he would be seeing this land he had once loved so deeply through hers.

CHAPTER SEVEN

ISLA WAS A child of nature, drawn to new experiences and adventure, as he had been as a youth. They had barely landed when she asked if she could visit the clinic. The Jeep was waiting for them, so he drove her there. He had barely switched off the engine when she crammed her hat onto her head and leapt out to brave the sun. It amused him to think that, for once, he wasn't taking the lead; nor was he the greater attraction. He followed her into the building, where he watched her take stock. He didn't need to introduce her; she'd already done that herself. He stayed just long enough to watch her roll up her sleeves and get to work.

She was still at the clinic three hours later working alongside his rangers. He knew they'd be grateful for her expertise. He was at the coral, where animals awaiting release into the wild were housed. A stab of very masculine jealousy hit him as he worked alongside his men. His rangers were all tough, good-looking guys, and Isla had brought grown men slavering to their knees at the pole-dancing club. His warrior genes had detonated at the sight of them devouring her with their eyes, though she'd handled them all with the same cool aplomb—handled him the same way. Even when she'd discovered who he was, it had made no difference to Isla.

Isla Sinclair. Warrior woman. The thought made him smile. He admired her guts, and her sheer, stubborn determination to do the work she loved, and to help those around her. Even at the club, the manager had told him how Isla had stepped in last minute to help a friend, and had been such a sensation that he wanted to offer her a job. Shazim had killed that idea, and for no reason he could fathom at the time—just gut instinct that told him there was some vulnerability beneath Isla's can-do attitude. He didn't know the root of it, but wouldn't countenance other men taking advantage of her—

'Your Majesty? Is everything all right?'

Seeing the expression on the rangers' faces, he realised how grim he'd become and had to clear thoughts of Isla from his mind. With a brief dip of his head, he said nothing as they walked past the spot he had avoided for so many years. The precipitous ledge where his life had changed for ever was part of the reserve. It was the heart of it. He would never avoid it again.

The desert was working its magic on him too, he mused as he stopped to stare around. Could Isla resist the magic? Anticipation roared through him at the thought of finding out.

Her first experience of the real desert did not disappoint in any way. The palace had been fabulous, and the extraordinary new experiences in a place of such opulence and craftsmanship had been a real eye-opener for her, but this wild, dangerous place was where Isla knew she belonged. And though her dreams had been mini-adventures, nothing could have prepared her for this reality. The immensity of the landscape, and the great bowl of electric-blue sky arcing over the seemingly boundless ocean of sand, made her feel very small and very insignificant, but, oh-so eager to begin. She loved the clinic, and the rangers, and the animals. She slotted right in, and had never been happier in her work.

She stayed long after everyone else had left, and when she walked outside, it was twilight. The colours of the darkening sky were extraordinary, and she took a moment to give thanks for where she was. Purple, pewter, pink and aquamarine vied for supremacy, filling her with a sense of happiness, a sense of belonging. Stretching out her arms to touch the air, she shook them to loosen her muscles. She needed it after concentrated working for so long. There was only one thing missing now, she reasoned wryly, and that was Shazim, though she doubted he would have time for her. Her assistants had told her that he had taken another group of rangers deeper into the desert, so he could observe the progress of the latest animal release programme.

Isla's imagination was only too eager to supply romantic images for this. Shazim would be dressed in flowing robes, and seated on a prancing stallion as he stood for a moment silhouetted against a darkening sky.

When he actually arrived, it was in a convertible Jeep, and he was wearing the same jeans and top he'd been wearing all day. Shazim was driving, and the group of rangers with him looked tired but happy, while Shazim looked more alive than she had ever seen him. His fierce stare sought out hers immediately, and when the rangers went their own way he came up to her.

'What?' he asked, no doubt seeing the bemused look on her face. 'Were you picturing a desert sheikh dressed in flowing robes, with a *howlis* wrapped around his head, riding towards you through a shimmering heat haze?'

'At night?' she said, curving the suspicion of a smile.

'Perhaps there was a prancing stallion involved,' he suggested with more than a suspicion of irony.

'In fact, there was,' she said, blunt as ever. She was glad of the new ease between them, and didn't want to do anything to put a spoke in that.

'So how did I look?' he asked.

She shrugged. 'Pretty good, considering there's no prancing stallion in the mix.'

He smiled. 'Only pretty good?'

She felt the heat of Shazim's smile in every part of her body as they walked side by side, back to the clinic.

'Anyway, welcome again to Q'Aqabi,' he said as he opened the door. 'I hope your first working day went well?'

'I couldn't have asked for more,' she said honestly.

Breath hitched in her throat as Shazim paid her the compliment of the traditional Q'Aqabian greeting, touching his forehead, his lips and then his heart. 'I hope you will be very happy here, Isla Sinclair.'

For the first time, she felt like curtseying to him, but a shiver of arousal soon chased that thought away, and she confined herself to a circumspect response. 'Thank you, Your Majesty.'

'Shazim,' he reminded her, fixing his stare on hers.

'Shazim,' she repeated softly, thinking his eyes were as deep and dark as the ocean—and her heart was going crazy.

If Shazim had been attractive before, he was a devastating distraction in the desert. He seemed more primal here, and his power was undeniable in a land where physical strength and understanding of the wilderness could save lives.

She also knew what she was doing, Isla reassured herself. She might not know the desert as well as Shazim, but she was confident in her ability, and in her common sense, and all she asked for was to be a small but vital cog in the engine that drove Shazim's conservation project.

'Well,' she said when he closed the door behind them. 'What now? Are we heading back to the palace?'

'Not yet.'

A ripple of alarm attacked her, until Shazim explained.

'Now we relax, swim, celebrate—there's a village nearby where a new underground spring has been discovered. I thought you'd like to come with me and join in the celebrations. You'd be meeting some of the people you'd be working for. This is their land. We are only their servants, and you should meet them.'

'Of course.' She was eager to meet the local people… though the thought of going deeper into the wilderness with Shazim was daunting.

'Oh, no—I don't ride,' Isla protested when they went outside to find that one of the rangers had brought up two horses.

'You must ride. You have to for this trip,' Shazim insisted. 'It's the quickest way for us to reach the village.'

His reproving stare acted like a firm hand moving slowly across her body, until the desire to see more of the desert with Shazim became an irresistible urge.

'You'll need some suitable headgear,' he said, staring with a frown at her safari hat.

Before she'd had chance to refuse, he had deftly wound a long scarf around her face and neck.

'No more excuses,' he commanded. 'Mount up.'

She could do this, Isla told herself firmly as she eyed up the horse with suspicion. The horse eyed her back with matching suspicion. She loved animals. She loved being able to help them when they were sick, and seeing them recover best of all, but could she, who had never ridden a horse in her life before, ride through the desert alongside a sheikh, who was about to spring onto the back of the prancing stallion of her dreams?

'What are you waiting for?' Shazim prompted.

She sucked in a shocked breath as he put his big hand over hers, but he was only showing her how to hold the reins. He guided her other hand to the pommel of the saddle, and now his big frame was just a breath away. Her entire body was trembling. If she made the smallest movement she would touch him.

'Put your foot in my hand,' he instructed, marshalling her straying thoughts. 'I'm going to lift you, and then you must settle gently onto the saddle.'

She was anxious, and the horse knew it. She got there somehow, and used every muscle she possessed to ensure she didn't land heavily in the saddle. But now she was too high off the ground.

'This isn't going to work,' she exclaimed. 'He knows I'm nervous.'

'Then, your only option is to ride in front of me,' Shazim instructed curtly as he picked up his reins.

She only had to take one look at his warhorse to change her mind. 'I'll manage,' she said grimly.

'Better not—'

She yelped as he lifted her off the saddle, and lowered her onto the saddle in front of him. She barely had chance to open her mouth to protest before the stallion lunged forward. And then it was too late. She was pressed up hard against Shazim, and they were moving as one. A shuddering breath shot out of her body as she registered every hard muscle in his powerful frame—

Shazim was a sheikh, the ruler of this land, and she worked for him. There was no romance. There were no billowing tents, no sandy shores of an oasis, no silken cushions, or pierced brass lanterns casting a honeyed light, waiting for her. There was just hard work, and the joy she always found in helping animals. She must keeping reminding herself of this… She was *not* here to lose her head—and heart—to a sheikh!

'I can't understand that you've never learned to ride,' Shazim said, frowning as he eased the powerful animal into a rolling canter.

It was a moment before she could reply. She was scared, she was thrilled—who wouldn't be? She was on the back of a mighty horse in the arms of a powerful sheikh.

'Why would I learn to ride?' she managed at last on a tight throat. She was still getting used to the unaccustomed gait. 'You live in a different world from me. You ride for necessity, while I take a bus. I've done plenty of fantasy riding as a little girl, but never in the arms of a sheikh—'

He laughed. 'You need to relax,' he said, binding her even closer.

And how was she supposed to do that?

It was only one small step from growing tense again, to wondering if fate had thrown them together for a purpose, and she had to remind herself yet again that she was a hard-working vet, while Shazim was a king, and master of all he surveyed. When her time in Q'Aqabi was done, she'd go home and he would stay here. There was no point wondering where the Lion of the Desert was taking her, or what they'd do when they arrived.

He should have left Isla to travel with his rangers. He was enjoying this too much. He had wanted her to share this special moment of triumph with his people, to help her understand the country she was here to help.

He moved her hand away when Isla tried to collect her hair and tie it back. Her scarf had flown off, and she was concerned that she didn't lash him in the face with it. But seeing that glorious hair flying behind her like a banner was all the impetus he needed to urge his stallion on. He leaned forward and she leaned with him, making the temptation to brush her hair aside and kiss her neck overwhelming.

CHAPTER EIGHT

HE WAS PRESSED up hard against her when Isla caught her first sight of the village lights twinkling in the distance. Her face lit up the night as she swung around to exclaim, 'Oh, Shazim, it's so beautiful!'

And so was she, he thought, though the glow of pleasure on Isla's face only emphasised her innocence, which made her seem more vulnerable than ever.

'And there's an oasis!' she said with excitement.

'Of course. All settlements are sited close to water—'

'Which is why they're so scarce in the desert,' she added.

Her excitement touched him. He had never noticed how beautiful her pure energy was before. It went beyond the physical to something that shone in her eyes. Seeing everything through those eyes was like seeing it for the first time for him.

'Look, Shazim…' She pointed out across the oasis. 'The water's so smooth, it's like a silken veil covered in spangles of moonlight.'

He smiled at her romantic description but quickly forced his mind back to practicalities. 'Put your scarf back,' he said. 'There's a wind kicking up, and you don't want to get your hair all clogged with grit and dust.'

'Thank you,' she said as he helped her to arrange the folds of cloth. Her voice on his skin was like a soft caress.

* * *

The touch of Shazim's hand on her neck had made her quiver with arousal and she could only hope he hadn't noticed. She didn't want to do anything that could be misinterpreted by him, or that might threaten their professional working relationship. She didn't want to do anything to spoil this perfect night—

Don't feel too guilty, her inner cynic warned her, *because perfect doesn't last...*

'People have come from miles around,' Shazim explained, distracting her from this troubling thought. As they drew closer to the village she could see how many campfires were studding the darkness with pinpoints of light, and she thrilled at the thought of meeting his people, but it was Shazim's breath, warm on her neck, that made her body thrill.

'Are you cold?' he asked as she shivered with awareness of him.

'I'm excited,' she answered with a healthy dose of truth. 'I'm excited to see something so new to me, and to join in the celebrations.'

'Don't worry,' Shazim assured her in the deep, husky voice that made her tremble again. 'You'll be safe with me.'

Would she? Was Shazim a safe haven, or was he a dangerous destination for a woman who knew so little about love?

Love?

Sex, Isla conceded ruefully. She knew so little about sex. Shazim, on the other hand, was a totem to physicality, and she doubted there was much he didn't know.

So...would she be safe?

She'd only find that out when she got there.

'I'm happy for you—' She turned to flash a look into

Shazim's heavily shadowed face, and felt another thrill of awareness. 'I'm happy for Q'Aqabi, and for your people. I know what this latest discovery of a new water supply must mean to everyone.'

He hummed in reply, and the vibration of that sound transferred from his body to hers.

News of the important discovery had spread like wildfire, and the city of tents made the small village appear to sprawl for miles. The sound of music and laughter, and conversation, constantly rose and fell like the murmur of surf on a distant shore.

'Dreaming again, Isla?' Shazim prompted as she sighed.

Realising that she'd leaned back against his chest to enjoy the moment, she huffed a smile and pulled away again fast. 'I'm a very practical woman,' she argued. 'You must know that by now.'

'Should I? And does your practical nature mean that you are forbidden to dream?'

There was humour in Shazim's voice, and his comment raised a flutter of alarm. It was as if he had a window into her mind.

'What was your childhood like, Isla?'

She tensed at the unexpected question.

'Relax,' Shazim insisted. 'The stallion has to tackle a steep incline, and he doesn't need you tensing up, making it harder for him.'

No. Only his master was allowed to do that.

'Didn't your investigators tell you everything about me?' she queried, hoping the question would let her off the hook.

'Bare facts only,' Shazim said. She felt him shrug. 'I receive a briefing for everyone I'm likely to meet on a tour.'

So he was unlikely to know more than those bare facts about her, which was a relief. She didn't want to think back to the time Shazim was asking about, and remained silent as his horse picked a path down the dune.

'Everyone has a story to tell that goes beyond a cold-blooded report,' Shazim elaborated once they reached safe ground. 'I'd like to hear yours.'

'Well, I don't know anything about you,' she defended, then realised that she had definitely overstepped the mark. She could tell by the way Shazim had tensed. It wasn't her place to interrogate him, but as her employer he had the right to know more than those plain facts he had mentioned.

She wasn't the only one with pain in her past, and that should make her more understanding, not less. 'I was an only child, studious and serious,' she began. 'I'm sure you're surprised to hear that,' she teased, trying to make light of it. 'I read a lot.'

'And cultivated a vivid inner life thanks to your reading, I imagine?' Shazim suggested.

She smiled. 'I wouldn't deny that. I certainly had a vivid imagination. I still do. I've read that many only children have a lively inner life to take the place of all the adventures they might have had with their siblings—'

Shazim cut her off. 'What about your father? You never mention him.'

A chill ran through her at Shazim's prompt. 'I can hardly remember him,' she said truthfully. Having successfully shut out the beatings and her mother's screams, the best she could come up with was, 'He left when I was very small. There was never another man in my mother's life.' It wouldn't have helped to add that the police took her father away, or that he was later locked up for assaulting several other women.

'And then, while you were studying at university, your mother became sick.'

'Long before that, but the illness became critical when I went away.'

'So you came back.'

'I broke off my studies, yes.'

'Though they mean so much to you,' Shazim prompted.

'Nothing meant more to me than my mother.'

His eyes clouded briefly as if he understood. Some had said her mother's illness and premature death had been the result of the years of cruelty at Isla's father's hands. Isla could never think back without wishing she could have taken on her mother's pain.

Shazim waited until she was ready to continue, and then he said, 'I apologise if my bringing up the past upsets you.'

His voice was gentler than before, but he had opened a wound that had never properly healed. 'Why do you want to know these things?' She sounded defensive.

'I'm interested in the welfare of everyone on my team. Do you find that so strange?'

'No,' Isla admitted. And it was up to her to handle the emotional fallout. It wasn't Shazim's fault that his questions had cut so deep. 'My mother was sick for most of my childhood. As I grew older, her illness progressed—'

'Until you became her full-time carer,' Shazim supplied when words choked off in her throat. 'You nursed her selflessly until the day she died, and gave up your education to do so.'

'Gladly.' Isla flared up as remembered pain lanced through her. 'Because I loved her—love her,' she amended passionately.

It was a relief when Shazim didn't attempt to shower her with sympathy, and simply stayed quiet until she spoke again. 'It was a bad time,' she admitted then, and with a considerable understatement.

'Yet you pulled yourself together and went back to university.'

'It was my mother's dearest wish. She insisted that I must.'

'She must have been a wonderful woman.'

'She was.'

'She would be very proud of you,' he said quietly.

'Thank you.'

They rode on in silence after that, with the simple village growing ever closer, until he said, 'And you grew up in a castle.'

'Not exactly inside the castle—that was a cold, unfriendly place. Not like this village,' she added as the warmth and music from the celebration washed over them. She only had to think back to the years of debauchery at the castle to know that this simple life had to be better. 'My mother was the cook at the castle,' she explained, 'though I suppose that's another fact you already know.'

'It's good to hear your side of things,' Shazim said. He had slowed the stallion to a lazy walk and had let his reins hang loose, as if he really wanted to hear her side of the story, and was making time to do so before they entered the village. 'All I know is that you were raised in the grounds of a castle in Scotland, alongside a family that could politely be called eccentric.' He gave an easy shrug. 'Who wouldn't be interested in that?'

'The Anconners held drug-fuelled parties,' Isla stated bluntly. 'I suppose you've heard that too. They cared nothing for their reputation, or for that of their staff. My mother stayed on out of a misplaced sense of loyalty, and we lived in a staff cottage on the estate.'

'But you had to leave—I don't understand. Why was that?'

Isla was silent for quite a while as she thought back. Shazim's grip tightened around her waist as if he wanted to reassure her. 'We left the cottage when my mother became too ill to work,' she explained. 'We had to,' she said when Shazim gave a jerk of surprise.

'You *had* to?' he said in a bemused tone.

'If my mother couldn't work, we had no place at the castle.'

'Is that why you moved into the room where you still live now?'

'Yes.' She didn't want to talk about it. It hurt too much to think of her mother uprooted when she had needed the familiarity of her own home the most.

But Shazim refused to let it go. 'One room must have been a bit of a comedown after a castle?'

'We made it home. It was our home, and we were safe there. No one was going to throw us out.' Her voice reflected her emotion as she remembered the tiny room that she had shared with her mother in the last days of her mother's life.

Isla had made it safe, Shazim concluded. Isla had protected her mother like a lioness with a cub, reversing their positions when it became necessary—the cared for becoming the carer in her mother's hour of need.

'I loved our cottage on the castle estate,' she murmured wistfully. 'It wasn't much, but it was home—my mother made it home, so I did the same when we moved into that room. We didn't have anything much, but the funny thing is I don't remember going without anything. We were warm and safe…'

'But you missed the cottage,' he pressed when she became silent.

'Nothing could match that,' Isla admitted. 'I was born in the cottage, and I lived there all my life. It never once occurred to me that I wouldn't be able to always call the cottage home.'

'That's how it should have been,' Shazim insisted. 'I

can't believe you didn't have a right to tenancy after living in the cottage for so many years?'

'We couldn't have afforded it, and Lady Anconner explained quite clearly to me that the cottage went with the job.'

'When did she tell you this?'

'Lady Anconner visited us after my mother's first hospital admission. I was so thrilled for my mother when her ladyship knocked on the door, but I was puzzled too—Lady Anconner wasn't exactly noted for her kindness, though I knew my mother would appreciate the gesture.'

'And did she?' he quizzed.

'My mother was so excited to be remembered by the people from the big house that she wouldn't hear a word against her ladyship—even when Lady Anconner explained that if my mother could no longer cook for them, then we would have to leave the cottage so they could hire someone else, and that someone else would live there instead of us.'

He was appalled. 'She threw you out, knowing your mother was so ill?'

'It was pure economics—at least, that's what Lady Anconner said, and my mother agreed with her. She said that was how things had always been at the castle.'

'And this so-called lady couldn't change the status quo for someone who was desperately ill, and who had lived in the cottage all her working life?'

'Lady Anconner didn't want to—she couldn't, really. All those colourful stories you've heard about the Anconner parties were true. How could they host them without staff to wait on their guests?'

They could have tidied up one of the unused attic rooms for a new member of staff to use, and left a dying woman in the only home she'd ever known. That was what he thought, but he kept his feelings to himself. High passion was too little too late, and it wouldn't help Isla.

'I hear the Anconners are bankrupt now,' he said instead.

Isla eased her shoulder in a hesitant shrug before answering, and then she said, 'I haven't really had time to follow their story.'

He doubted that was true, but he let it go. There was too much hurt in Isla's voice, and that hurt was as fresh as the day Lady Anconner had shattered her mother's dreams. How anyone could be so cold-hearted was beyond him. However aristocratic this Lady Anconner might think herself, in his view she had no claim to the title 'lady'.

'You grew up in a royal nursery,' Isla reminded him, jolting him out of his preoccupation with her past. 'That couldn't have been easy for you—being distanced from your parents?'

'I had siblings,' he said thinking back. 'And my elder brother was like a father to us.'

'And now?' she prompted softly as if she knew she was treading on hallowed ground.

He ignored the question, and turned instead to a subject of his choosing. Looking around at the crowds gathering in the tented city, he commented, 'Mixing with my people was always a joy to me.'

'Have you been spending too much time in your ivory tower, Shazim?'

He laughed, and shook his head at Isla's disrespect. 'Too much time looking at schedules, balance sheets, and architects' drawings,' he admitted.

'Someone has to do it.'

'Are you making excuses for me, Ms Sinclair?' He leaned forward to murmur this in her ear, and felt her quiver with awareness. The connection between them pleased him. He'd never experienced it with anyone before, and was grateful to Isla for bringing him down to earth and reminding him that he was in danger of forgetting where he came from, and who he was.

'Shazim?' she prompted when he fell silent.

'Tell me more about your life,' he insisted, keen to swerve the spotlight from himself.

She didn't want to talk about her past, and closed her eyes to shut it out. She didn't want to remember the humiliation of a little girl, forbidden entrance to the castle where her mother was working, or being shooed away like an untrustworthy urchin, who wasn't even good enough to enter by the back door. And though the two things weren't connected, she certainly didn't want to remember what had made her so wary of men.

'Thanks to my mother I had the best of childhoods,' she insisted, glossing over the more unpalatable facts. 'We got through just fine.' That was a lie too, but how would it help her mother now, if Isla dwelled on all the comforts she hadn't been able to give her mother?

'The castle is up for sale, I hear,' Shazim prompted.

He said this without expression, but she was wary. 'I hope you're not thinking of buying it. It was such an unhappy place.'

'If I do, I'll raze it to the ground,' he promised harshly. 'My world is here in Q'Aqabi, with my people, and my projects.' He paused for a moment, and then said, 'You've done really well in achieving what you have, Isla.'

'As have you,' she said with her usual forthrightness.

'We do share some similarities,' he conceded on a laugh. 'Trust you to point them out to me.'

'I just follow my heart,' she admitted.

'And has your heart never led you astray?'

Isla fell silent. She didn't speak again until they arrived in the village.

CHAPTER NINE

THE VILLAGERS CLUSTERED around Shazim's stallion. News of the Sheikh of Q'Aqabi's arrival had quickly spread, and a great crowd followed them into the village. What they made of the woman seated in front of the Lion of the Desert remained to be seen. Shazim didn't appear to be remotely concerned, but Isla was. Her only experience of wealth and privilege had not been a good one, and this event, thrilling though it was, was a stark reminder of the power Shazim wielded. Coupled with his immense wealth, it left her at an extreme disadvantage. She had almost relaxed with him during their ride through the desert, but now she was growing tense again.

He had become acutely conscious of Isla's smallest reaction while they were pressed up close on the horse. He would have had to be asleep not to register every nuance in her body language, and he had felt Isla shrink defensively into herself as people stared at them. He guessed that this was partly because he had prompted her to talk about her unhappy childhood, when she had been belittled and humiliated by people who should have known better. She had certainly felt awkward riding into the village in front of him, and probably thought his people would be critical of her, when he knew they would welcome her as a guest of their Sheikh. His people would have been more surprised if he'd kept such a beautiful woman away from them. Isla was different, special, he reflected, scanning her slender shoulders and the tumble of hair that had escaped her scarf, and they would see that, as he did.

Would bedding Isla ease her tension? Maybe, but he wanted more of her than a single night, and could he risk indulging himself and potentially losing a valuable member of his team? Isla might be newly qualified, but she had an outstanding record at the university, and he would be risking all she was on the altar of lust.

Those were his virtuous thoughts, but another part of him wanted to take Isla's softly yielding body and awaken her to pleasure.

'You're very quiet,' she said.

'I was enjoying the silence,' he commented drily.

'Oh, I see,' she said, responding to his mocking tone. 'You should maybe have left me behind if you wanted silence.'

He hummed in agreement. He needed a distraction fast. Isla was soft and pliant against him, and her hair was fragrant against his lips. Her wildflower scent was intoxicating—there was just one problem. He had never ridden a horse with such a painful erection before.

The crowd followed them to a recently erected pavilion reserved for their King. It soon became evident that in honour of his visit the vast tent had been sited directly over the new water source in the shadow of a towering cliff. The pavilion was quite private. Clustering palms and the discretion of the villagers would make sure of it.

Isla was impressed. If this wasn't quite the billowing Bedouin tent of her fantasies, it was close. Maybe it was even a little better than her fantasy with the Sheikh's personal pennant flying from the topmost point. The flag, with its ground of cerulean blue, bore a lion rampant in gold with crimson claws. A shiver tracked down her spine as she stared at the rearing lion, towering over its helpless prey.

Yes. Well. She wasn't exactly helpless, and she wasn't about to become anyone's prey.

Shazim's royal house...his royal privilege...his castle...

She had to close her eyes and close her mind to the feelings from the past that threatened to intrude now and spoil everything.

'The pavilion is yours to use as you wish,' Shazim said, distracting her as he reined in his stallion.

'Mine?' she queried with surprise.

'I'm going to greet my people, and then I'm going for a swim before the festivities begin,' Shazim announced as he sprang down to the ground.

'But I thought you were sleeping here?' she said as he reached up to her.

'I'll find somewhere else. Take it,' he said impatiently. 'It's yours for the night.'

Scientist or not, she couldn't help but feel rejected, with her fantasies lying flat on the ground. 'If you're sure?' she said, dismounting carefully so she wouldn't join them.

'I'm sure,' Shazim insisted, holding the big horse steady as she got off.

It had looked so easy when Shazim sprang down that she launched herself into thin air with every confidence that she would land safely on her feet. Unfortunately, that didn't go too well, and as the stallion pawed the ground with the same impatience as his master she was thrown off balance. She would have landed on her face if Shazim hadn't reached out to catch hold of her. He steadied her, but now her muscles protested after so much unaccustomed horseback riding, and she stumbled, almost falling to her knees, forcing him to catch hold of her again.

'You'll get used to it.' His black eyes were burning with amusement.

'Will I?' She gave him a hard stare, which failed to

counteract the feelings flooding through her as Shazim held her safe in his arms.

'I guarantee it,' he murmured. 'Meanwhile, I suggest a massage.'

'What I need is a hot bath.' She flared up as all her old fears regarding men came back to haunt her. Then, realising what she'd said, and how insensitive it must have sounded when water was such a precious commodity in the desert, even more valuable than oil, she added, shamefaced, 'Forgive me. I do know how thoughtless that must have sounded.'

'You can take as many baths as you want.' Shazim shrugged. 'This new water supply makes everything possible. In fact, I'll order water to be drawn for your bath right away.'

'Please—no. I'm perfectly capable of doing that myself. I don't want anyone going to any trouble on my behalf.' Though she did need Shazim to let her go right away before her senses went into permanent meltdown.

'Whatever you want,' he said with his face so close to hers, her cheeks tingled.

A pulse of something warm and seductive throbbed inside her. It was definitely time for her to make her move—out of his arms. 'Thanks for the save,' she said matter-of-factly.

Testing her legs only proved that she wasn't ready to let go of him, and hanging onto Shazim was dynamite to her senses.

'Are you sure you can do without me?' he mocked her softly.

'Of course I can.' Letting go, she set off again, and this time managed to stagger a few steps. Shazim's expression as he watched her was both intimate and sexy. It warmed her. He warmed her, and in all sorts of dangerous ways.

They were employer and employee, Isla told herself

sternly. She'd had a few flings with boys at school and university, but the Sheikh of Q'Aqabi was definitely not a boy. There had been no time for romance in her life while she was caring for her mother, and then she'd been too busy studying to get back into college as she'd promised her mother she would. After the near attack, she was grateful for the excuse to avoid relationships. She was an innocent throwing herself to the lion, while everything about Shazim suggested his experience of things like sex was beyond her comprehension.

'I think you'd better get that massage,' he suggested as she yelped and stumbled again. Before she could say no, he swung her into his arms. And, pausing only to free the fastening on the tent flap so that it fell into place behind them, he carried her to a bed of silken cushions and laid her down. Straightening up, he turned to go. Pausing briefly by the entrance, he recommended, 'Take a bath and work those muscles.'

She'd been dumped—literally, like a sack of potatoes. Perversely, though, she hadn't wanted him to stay; Shazim being in such a hurry to leave had left her feeling plain and undesirable.

She'd got everything she deserved. She wasn't living out a fantasy. This was real life, with real aching legs. It would take time to work those muscles, and that was what she should do. She was no use to anyone until she could get about.

And it wouldn't help to imagine Shazim carrying out the massage…starting at her calves and working up. The faster she returned to full working order—and that meant her brain too—the sooner she could explore the village and see if there was anything in the veterinary line she could help out with.

As soon as she could she went exploring. She started with the pavilion, which was huge, and pleasantly shaded.

It was faintly scented with some delicious spice, and packed full of craftsmanship. The colours were muted, and everything looked well loved, as if nothing was too much trouble for the people's Sheikh. The tent was full of ethnic treasures, many of which bore the patina of age, and should probably be housed in a museum, Isla mused, running her fingertips across the intricately carved surface of an ancient chest. And Shazim had given all this up for her.

The huge bed in the centre of the pavilion had been made ready for him. Dressed in white silk sheets, it was shaded by gossamer curtains. Alongside the bed there were low tables laden with jugs of juice, and bowls of fresh fruit—there was even a brass campaign bath, she saw now, full of warm, scented water. Hugging herself, she smiled as she glanced around. One option was stay here all night, and live the dream… The other was to go into the village to see if there was any work she could do.

'She's doing what?'

'Working, Your Majesty,' one of his rangers assured him.

Any pictures he might have conjured up of Isla waiting for him, soft and fragrant after her bath, could take a hike. Apparently, she had freshened up, and then taken a walk through the village to find the animal clinic. Having run a quick assessment of need, she had asked one of the rangers to show her where they kept their stock of medical supplies.

Isla couldn't be stopped. She was exceptional. But this wasn't a work detail. On this occasion, she was his guest.

A regular guest, or a special guest?

Beneath her can-do ability, Isla was a green shoot waiting to be trampled. She deserved more than the cliché of a moonlit night with the desert Sheikh. Inevitably, she would be sidelined after serving his needs. He could offer her nothing. His duty was to his country. The debt he owed his late brother demanded nothing less of him. He wasn't totally without heart. He would make Isla's time in Q'Aqabi enjoyable—if she stopped working long enough for him to do so.

A glint of amusement flared in his eyes when he found her. Brow pleated, lips firmed, she was intent on her work. The challenge of distracting her was something he looked forward to.

'The celebrations?' he reminded her.

She glanced up. Her cheeks pinked and her eyes darkened as she stared at him. Betraying more than she cared to, he suspected.

'Just a few more minutes and I'll be done,' she said.

He shrugged and pulled away from the door. They were both driven. He could accept that, but she should chill out. One of them needed to.

The last thing Isla had expected when she returned from the clinic was that the women of the village would want to thank her for treating their family pets alongside those on the Sheikh's programme. Isla had thought nothing of offering her services, beyond the fact that all her patients were creatures in need, but now the women were offering to share their best clothes with her.

Staring down at her travel-worn outfit, she had to agree that a change of clothes was in order. The safari suit she was wearing had been recommended by an outdoor clothing store in England, and was way too hot and heavy for the desert. It had far too many pockets bulking it out, for one thing, even for someone who customarily carried a wound-suturing kit alongside her lip balm.

And she could do with another freshening up after her work in the clinic, Isla concluded as her new friends drizzled fragrant oil in the bath they had prepared for her. She only balked when they brought out coffers of family jewels for her to wear. She couldn't do that, she explained with mimes and gestures, as they were far too precious.

After bathing, they insisted on massaging scented oils into her skin, and then they dressed her in a delicately embroidered robe of floating silk chiffon in a soft peach shade. She had never worn anything quite so beautiful. Even the gown the maid had chosen for her at the palace hardly compared to this, for this was a lovingly preserved gown that had been passed down through the generations. She could see that in the tiny darns and repairs, which she believed made it more precious than the most expensive couture gown, for every stitch had been sewn with love.

So this was her second time in a flowing gown, when she could count the number of times she had worn a dress on the fingers of one hand. She'd always been a tomboy, rather than a girly girl, but this dream of a dress, beaded in silver and hung with tiny bells that sang as she walked, was more than enough to convert her. She felt like Cinderella dressing up for the ball.

Hadn't she sworn off Cinderella?

Anyone would make an exception for this gown, and she had no intention of offending the women of the village by refusing their kindness and generosity in lending it to her.

At the first touch of the cool silk gliding over her naked body, Isla wondered if the gown might be the key to holding Shazim's interest for longer than five minutes. There were things she wanted to talk to him about—improvements to the clinic, for instance.

For a moment, she forgot about work. The gown was transforming, and she turned full circle to show it off to the women, laughing with them as she stared at her reflection in the full-length mirror. She doubted she would ever get the chance to wear a gown like this again.

'You're very generous. Thank you...'

She went to each of the women in turn, smiling her thanks into their eyes. But they hadn't finished with her yet. Her hair had to be polished, and then scented before they placed a dramatic and very beautiful veil on her head. They left her hair loose beneath the veil, and pinned it in place with tiny jewelled pins. Even her hands and feet had to be softened with fragranced cream, and then they persuaded her to slip her feet into dainty sandals.

All good so far, but could she lose her tomboy strut?

As she watched the village women flitting around the pavilion like so many beautiful, graceful scented moths, Isla felt like a clumsy oaf. Perhaps this was all a dream, and she'd wake up to find that she was snoozing beneath a pile of bandages, or a page of notes.

When the women were finally satisfied with her appearance, they gathered around her so they could lead her to the celebration. She was thrilled, and also self-conscious. She'd done it once before, but that was just with Shazim at his palace. Could she pull off this new and very different identity in front of a crowd?

She'd played roles before, Isla reminded herself sensibly. In fact, she'd played so many roles they must have made Shazim's head spin. This was just one more.

Thoughts of her mother reassured her as the women led her out of the pavilion. Her mother would have loved to see Isla dressed like this. She had always tried to get her to wear pretty dresses when she was a little girl, and would have laughed with sheer joy to see her ragtag daughter dressed like the princess she had always wanted her to be.

She would hold her head up high and wring every drop of happiness out of each moment, Isla decided. It was a privilege to be here, and to be part of this celebration. That was the only way she knew to thank the women for all the trouble they'd gone to on her behalf, as they tried to make a silk purse out of a sow's ear, though what Shazim would think of their handiwork remained to be seen. Her heart gave a bounce as she thought about him.

A vast crowd had gathered in the centre of the village. The women led her forward towards the large bonfire in the centre that had been lit to ward off the chill of a desert night. Everyone was sitting cross-legged on cushions around Shazim, and every age group was represented. His audience was rapt, and she stopped walking for a moment to listen to him. She couldn't understand the language, but the tone of his voice affected her, and she found herself imagining how it might feel to have Shazim talk to her in that same profoundly caring way.

Nothing in her fantasies could compare with this, Isla decided as she looked around. There were camels instead of cars beneath the palm trees, and cicadas chirruped in the background as night owls swooped overhead. The air was warm and fragranced with wood smoke, while the fiery sky above her head was fading to magenta on its way to impenetrable inky black. She was beginning to understand what people meant when they talked about the magic of the desert. Q'Aqabi was a very special place, with special people, and a special man to rule over them. Shazim, she knew now, was both a force to be reckoned with, and a man to admire.

He startled her by looking up and staring directly at her. All her confidence drained away when he beckoned to her, but the women took hold of her hands and drew her forward to sit with their Sheikh.

CHAPTER TEN

THE CAMPFIRE SEEMED to blaze higher than ever as she approached. The hot light emphasised Shazim's chiselled cheekbones and his regal profile. The women backed away respectfully, and, though there was a crowd of hundreds surrounding them, for a few moments Isla felt that she was alone with Shazim. His stare, so dark and commanding, pierced hers, drawing her towards him, until with a gesture he pointed her towards the cushions at his side. She had to remind herself that this regal figure was the same man she had met in London on a building site, but here he seemed so much more. Like her, Shazim was dressed in traditional robes. His were night-blue silk, and the soft folds pressed insistently against his powerful frame. He might as well have been naked. She could all too easily imagine him naked, and swallowed deep. To have that huge, muscular body looming over her—

What was she thinking?

But it proved impossible to sit next to him without that idea flashing through her head.

She had sat down awkwardly. There wasn't much room and she was hampered by skirts. There was such a press of people around Shazim that she was pressed up hard against him. That was all it took for her to remember how it felt to be in his arms—though she had only been there by default—on his horse, and then when she'd tripped over. Imagining how it would feel to be in his arms, if it were planned, should not even make it into her wildest fantasy.

But it did. And she felt her cheeks flame when Shazim turned his attention to her. It didn't help when everyone fell silent to watch, and she could only be thankful that it was dark so her red cheeks were hidden from the villagers.

'I was just telling the elders of the village what an asset you are to our project,' Shazim explained.

She drew a sharp breath in. His words were innocent, but his gaze had drifted to her lips. 'I will do anything I can to help,' she heard herself say, staring at Shazim's mouth. She couldn't help but remember his chaste kisses on each cheek, only now she was wondering if they'd been quite as chaste as she had imagined.

'You are a very talented woman,' he said, directing this comment to the crowd, and then translating for them into Q'Aqabian. 'We want you to feel that you can spread your professional wings here—'

At his mention of her professional wings she was able to relax.

'Anything you need, I will see you have,' he said.

Again, his words were harmless on the surface, but there was something in Shazim's eyes that spoke of different needs, and different rewards for her compliance, and she grew instantly tense again when he added, 'Your every wish is my command, Ms Sinclair.'

Try as she might, she could not subdue the pleasure pulses that his words alone could produce, and when Shazim smiled into her eyes it was as if the great Sheikh of Q'Aqabi could read her mind.

Leaning towards her, he whispered so only she could hear, 'Don't look so worried. I'll keep you safe.'

Safe?

There was nothing safe about Shazim. She would be

naive to think so. He might look like a figure from a fable: remote, and too principled to take advantage of this situation, but underneath he was just a man…a man whose head was uncovered, and whose thick black hair was unruly as it always was, and slightly damp, as if he'd been swimming in the oasis. Luxuriant inky waves had caught on his sharp black stubble, and as he smiled faintly there was intimacy and promise in his eyes; she knew he wasn't thinking of her veterinary skills.

'I approve of your outfit,' he said, lifting one brow. 'It's a great improvement on that ugly safari.'

'Though this is not as practical for working in the clinic,' she pointed out.

'True,' Shazim agreed with a dark look that made her senses soar. 'And your legs—'

'My legs?' she queried, and had to remind herself not to speak so loudly, as everyone had quietened again to listen.

'Are your legs recovered after your ride?' Shazim asked smoothly, and in a few moments, realising there was nothing wrong, people started chattering amongst themselves again.

'Like the rest of me, my legs are resilient,' she said, which made him laugh.

'I'm pleased to hear it. I intend to give them a lot of work while you're here.'

The look was back again, and she was still trying to fathom out how to handle Shazim in this mood when he turned to talk to the elder on his other side.

'Don't worry—'

She started as Shazim swung around and interrupted her. 'I've told everyone how much they can expect of you.'

'Ah,' she said as he turned away again. But what did Shazim expect of her?

Thanks to the press of people, his thigh had remained

pressed against hers, and the contact between them was having all sorts of powerful effects on her body. She felt his heat, and the brush of his arm on her breast when he leaned across her to find her some delicacy to try was just too intimate.

She was about to get up, to see if there was somewhere else to sit, when he offered her a sweetmeat dripping with honey.

'No more, please,' she begged, not trusting herself to take it from his fingers.

She couldn't take much more of his sensual torture, and decided she must go to bed. She started to explain that she was tired after her journey, but Shazim's frown stopped her. 'The women have gone to so much trouble, and now you're going to bed?' he demanded.

Put that way, he did make her sound rude. She sat down again. She could hardly admit to Shazim that it was the survival of her professional identity troubling her now, and that he was the cause of her concern. But then, some of the women who'd helped her to dress looked across and smiled encouragement, and she knew she had to stay for them.

Experience burned in Shazim's eyes every time he looked at her, and, while she could be sensible, her body refused point-blank.

Entertainment after the banquet provided some distraction. This included horse riders performing incredible stunts, and there were fire-eaters, acrobats, and jugglers, as well as traditional dancers of both sexes. It was a wonderful evening and, in spite of all the troubling thoughts where Shazim was concerned, she could only thank her lucky stars that she was here.

Her heart leapt with fear when Shazim was challenged to ride a dangerous race, in which the riders were expected to snatch a flag before their opponents could reach it. Shazim didn't hesitate to join in, and called at once for his great stallion.

Wishing him good luck hardly seemed enough. Shazim was a great horseman, but he would be given no quarter here, no allowances for being a king. Every man was equal in the race.

She leapt to her feet and held her breath along with the rest of the crowd, as Shazim urged his mighty stallion forward. Just as the race was about to start a cloud covered the moon. A collective sigh went up, as if this was a portent of what was to come, and Isla's heart thudded as the sky turned black as ink.

Flambeaux were quickly lit to light the way, casting giant shadows across the sand. It was like watching a film, she thought as the cheers of the crowd became deafening. But this was all too real, and suddenly she was frightened for Shazim.

The flag went down and horses plunged forward. Riders risked everything, and there were too many, too close. She needn't have worried about Shazim, Isla saw with relief. Having taken an early lead, he was well ahead of the other riders, an advantage that allowed him to avoid the death-dealing jostle around the flag. A great cheer went up as he dipped low over the side of his horse to snatch the prize. Isla was weak with relief, though she was cheering with the rest when Shazim wheeled his stallion around so fast it reared up and, controlling it masterfully, he galloped back victorious, holding the flag on high.

Closing her eyes briefly, she sent up thanks to all the fates for keeping him safe, and when she opened them again Shazim was in front of her on his mighty stallion, which snorted and stamped as it eyed her imperiously.

'Take it,' he commanded, still high on the adrenaline of victory as he held out the flag.

She grasped the pole still warm from his hand and, stretching as high as she could, she waved it above her head.

When Shazim turned to acknowledge the cheers of the crowd, she was exultant for him. He was a rock to his people, and a force for good that she was only just beginning to understand.

When the excitement had died down and they returned to their cushions, she felt that Shazim's triumph, and her small part of it, had changed their relationship in some small, but significant way. It was as if, by handing her the flag, he had made a public declaration of her importance to him. She knew that was only in the field of veterinary sciences, but still…

She was more aware of him than ever, and while Shazim appeared more interested in chatting to the man on his other side, his body seemed to be speaking to hers, and those messages didn't need an interpreter. They were intimate, and on the rare occasions when he did look at her there was new heat in Shazim's eyes.

When the evening drew to a close, and people started heading off to bed, she waited until Shazim was free for a moment so she could say goodnight to him. So many people wanted to speak to him that she had to stand in line, but it gave her chance to smile and thank everyone for such a wonderful evening. And then it was her turn to speak to His Majesty, the Sheikh.

'Thank you, Shazim. I can't remember ever having such a wonderful night. I'll never forget it. And you were great,' she added with a cheeky twinkle. 'Congratulations on your victory, Your Majesty.'

'Did you doubt me?' Shazim demanded. His stern face softened into a smile.

'Not for a moment,' Isla said honestly. 'You had the best horse,' she added with another cheeky look.

Throwing back his head, Shazim laughed. 'Trust you to pop my pompous balloon.'

'You're not pompous—you just take yourself a little too seriously at times.'

The look he gave her this time made her heart race.

'I'm glad you've enjoyed yourself, Ms Sinclair.'

Shazim's voice was dark and husky, and his tone was tinged with the humour that could always make her toes curl, if only because it was so rare, and seemed to be reserved for her, as if everything else in Shazim's life were deadly serious.

'I will escort you back to the pavilion,' he said.

'I'm fine. I know my way,' she said, brushing off Shazim's offer as politely as she could. She knew where her boundaries lay, and while sitting next to him at the celebration was one thing, having Shazim accompany her to the isolated pavilion was very different.

'I insist,' he commanded, indicating she should go ahead of him.

She couldn't cause a scene in front of hundreds of Shazim's loyal subjects.

'The desert has more dangers than you know,' he added, sending shock waves down her arm as he began to guide her through the crowd. 'Landmarks can be deceiving. The weather is unpredictable. Everything can change in seconds.'

'Between here and the pavilion?' she queried in her usual down-to-earth way.

Thinking to put some sensible distance between them, she now only succeeded in having Shazim place his hand in the small of her back to keep her on track.

'You'd be surprised,' he said, urging her on with fingers slightly spread. 'There are rumours of a sandstorm on the way.'

At this, she shook the random thoughts of pleasure out

of her head and paid attention. 'Surely, we would have heard something—some warning on the radio?'

'There are signs that only those who are familiar with the desert can interpret.'

'For instance?' she pressed, trying to concentrate with sensation streaming from Shazim's hand to her core.

'That unexplained gust of wind tonight that blew off your scarf? That warned me to be vigilant,' he explained.

A lot of people were leaving at the same time, and the crowd had become a jostling mass. Putting his other hand on her shoulder, Shazim guided her safely through. Everyone fell back for him, she noticed.

'Storms can creep up slowly,' he said, his grip sliding slowly down her arm, 'or they can roar in on a following wind—'

She gasped as he pulled her close when she almost drifted into a camel.

'If you should stray out of the village, even by chance, during one of these turbulent episodes, I might never find you again.'

'Would you care?'

'Of course.' There was humour in his voice. 'How would I ever explain that to the university?'

'Thanks,' she said drily. 'But wouldn't a tracker solve the problem?'

'I wish you luck with your tracker in a sandstorm.'

'All right,' she conceded as they turned onto the quieter path leading to the pavilion. 'You can rest assured that I won't inconvenience you tonight by leaving the pavilion. I promise I'll stay there all night. And now, as it's such a short walk from here—'

'I will come with you.'

Shazim had stepped in front of her. A few remaining villagers turned to look. She did the only thing she could.

She bid them goodnight with a smile, and allowed their Sheikh to lead her on. She would deal with Shazim when they reached the pavilion and were alone.

CHAPTER ELEVEN

SHE WAS TENSE, but needn't have worried. Her overactive imagination was destined to be confounded at every twist and turn. Far from following her into the pavilion, and seducing her at great length and pleasure on the silken cushions, Shazim left her at the entrance with the sketch of a mocking bow, as if he knew exactly what she was thinking, and her naivety amused him.

Which only made her feel more frustrated than ever, fool that she was! Why was she having so much difficulty controlling her fantasies? Since the assault she'd not been able to think about such things, as the thought made her stomach knot, so the effect Shazim was having on her was altogether confusing!

Allowing the tent flap to fall back, she closed her eyes in disappointment. Any thoughts of fending him off resided solely in her mind, where they had to stay. And what a joke, when Shazim wasn't even interested.

And an affair with him would be crazy.

Yes. It would be crazy.

She began to pace. She wasn't even sure what she wanted, but it wasn't this after the excitement of the evening. She wasn't ready to go to sleep yet. She'd seen so much, experienced so much, and now she wanted more. Even this grand and special space was meant for sharing. There was so much here to enjoy and appreciate. Patterned carpets in jewel colours covered the floor, while the walls boasted hangings, embroidered with the royal emblems, as well as many other symbols she presumed were associated with Shazim. The silken cushions did indeed gleam beneath a honeyed light, just as she had always imagined, while the regal bed had been prepared for the night, and looked more than inviting—this huge, beautifully dressed bed, in which she would sleep alone.

Peeling off the diaphanous robe, she draped it carefully over an intricately carved ebony chair. Slipping on the simple nightshirt she'd brought with her 'just in case', she climbed into bed and tried to settle. The sheets held the scent of sunshine and sandalwood…

Like the man who ruled here—

With a frustrated growl, she thumped the pillows in an attempt to bounce Shazim out of her head. Making herself comfortable again, she turned her face into the cushions. She wouldn't think about him. She had no intention of compromising her professional standing in Shazim's eyes by doing anything she might regret.

Which wasn't enough to stop her body from longing for things it couldn't have.

Like Shazim, she mused groggily as she drifted off to sleep.

She was in the middle of a frenzied erotic episode, starring a shadowy figure clad in flowing robes, when she was rudely jolted awake. Catapulting off the bed, it took her a moment to realise that what she was listening to was the howling of a furious gale. This was the ear-splitting roar of nature at her most destructive. The sandstorm Shazim had talked about had arrived. When she'd read about storms like this on the Internet, they had made Shazim's homeland seem even more exciting and challenging, but to be in the middle of one, and to know that there was only camel skin and tent poles between her and the deadly wind, was a terrifying thought. The walls of the pavilion weren't billowing, as per her fantasy; they were straining to the limit of their resistance. It was as if some giant hand were trying to pluck the massive tent out of the ground. For a moment she was struck by panic, but then she remembered the animals.

Tugging on her clothes, she wrapped Shazim's scarf around her face and neck. Then, raising her arm to protect her eyes, she forced her way out of the pavilion. She had to battle a wind so strong she could only lurch crazily from one solid structure to the next, grabbing hold of whatever came within reach to keep her balance.

Propelling herself forward took all her strength. Her goal was the clinic, and nothing was going to stop her from getting there. If she was frightened, the animals would be terrified. Some of them might even have been injured when they were thrown into a panic.

The clinic was only a short walk away under normal conditions, but with the lack of visibility, and the power of the wind, it seemed to take for ever to get there. It was only when she reached for the door handle, she realised, that any uncovered skin had been all but flayed by the driving sand. She was relieved to find the rangers in attendance, a little less so to see Shazim standing in their midst, staring at her with disapproval.

'What are you doing here?' he barked.

'My job,' she fired back.

'You need to dress those wounds,' he said in a tone that suggested she had caused more trouble than they needed by braving the storm.

'I'll do that later,' she said briskly. 'I'll wear gloves for now.' She was already pulling them on. 'You'll have to get out of my way,' she added, assuming command of the emergency clinic. 'Can you handle the bigger animals outside?' she asked Shazim, ignoring his look of surprise. 'If

I have to, I'll do it, but it will stop me from working here,' she said impatiently in answer to his enraged expression.

'You should not have risked your life to join us,' he said coldly. 'We need you alive and uninjured. I thought I'd made that clear?'

He was right, but she was here, and she was staying here to work. 'Let's get on,' she said, staring up unblinking.

'Very well,' he conceded grimly. 'If you're staying I'll work alongside you.'

'As my assistant?' she challenged.

'As anything you need me to be. We have the same goal.'

'Then, if you will please triage the animals outside, and bring them to me one by one in order of need.'

'I will,' Shazim confirmed, summoning the rangers.

Isla lost all sense of time as she worked. The number of animals needing treatment never seemed to diminish. She rushed outside at one point to check on progress, only to find Shazim working harder than ten men in the paddock where the injured animals were being shepherded into covered stalls. It was quite a bit later before he joined her in the clinic, by which time he was grey with dust, and his eyes were as ringed and sore as hers.

She couldn't have been more surprised when he crossed the room and took her face in hands turned gentle.

'Must you always be such a hero, Isla?'

'This is what I came for. I'm in for everything, not just the celebrations.'

Shazim stared at her. 'You have many scratches. Let me clean them and dress them. You must be exhausted,' he added as he reached for the antiseptic.

'And you're not?' she said.

When Shazim looked at her there were things she didn't want to think about too closely, and the least of those was exhaustion. Their faces were so close as he cleaned her scratches their breath mingled, and when she glanced into his eyes she had to look away. She was in serious danger of getting carried away again. As the seconds ticked by, her entire body seemed to call to his in a way it had never done before.

'Let me clean you up now,' she insisted briskly when Shazim had finished tending her wounds.

'I heal fast.' He pulled away. 'Come with me, Isla. You've done enough tonight. I'll take you back to the pavilion.'

'I won't leave until I'm sure that every animal is calm and settled. I'm sorry, Shazim,' she added with an apologetic shrug when his eyes flared with disapproval at yet another example of her stubborn refusal to do as he commanded. 'I can't automatically obey, unless it makes sense to do so,' she explained. 'Obedience isn't in my job description, you see.' She smiled, and was relieved when Shazim laughed too.

'You are impossible,' he admitted with a shake of his head.

'You'll get used to me.'

'Will I?' He raised a brow.

Suddenly, she was on the back foot again, wondering if she would be in Q'Aqabi long enough for Shazim to 'get used to her'.

She started to protest when he called for one of the rangers to take her place.

'They managed very well without you,' he said firmly, 'and I expect them to do the same when you're not here.'

Straightening up with a hand in the small of her back, she closed her eyes for a moment to try and rattle some sense into her brain, but she was too tired to think.

'Isla?' Shazim demanded with concern.

Their determined stares met and held. She had to admit

she was exhausted—and grateful to Shazim for working so tirelessly at her side. She wasn't going to argue with him for the sake of it.

'Bed,' he insisted, 'or you'll be no use to anyone tomorrow. If I have to throw you over my shoulder and carry you out of here, you're done for the night.'

It surprised her to see the air outside tinged with dawn. The wind had dropped and, though the air was still thick with dust, the visibility had improved. There was no immediate danger to the animals—

'That was a direct order,' Shazim insisted, cutting through her thoughts. 'You rest, or you go back to the city. Your choice, Isla. I won't have anyone working on this project who isn't as committed to safety as they are to doing their job.'

'The building site all over again,' she murmured, smiling faintly.

'The desert is a lot more dangerous than that.'

She had no doubt as Shazim stared at her, and another pulse of awareness joined the rest. Where was he going to sleep? She doubted he'd had time to make those *other* arrangements. She had read somewhere that Shazim was destined to marry in the near future so he could found a dynasty. She guessed he would choose a royal princess, or an heiress who understood the responsibilities that went with extreme wealth and privilege. If she were foolish enough to follow her heart, she might as well lay it on the ground for Shazim to stamp on.

'Bed,' Shazim instructed in a louder voice.

'Fine, fine. Do you trust me to find my way back this time?' She set her fingers flying to box up the remaining liniment and bandages, so she didn't have to look at the answer on Shazim's face.

'I probably should trust you to get back on your own,' he agreed, surprising her.

She glanced up, and knew at once that her disappointed look had betrayed her.

'Thank you for your assistance tonight,' she said primly, in a vain hope that she could deflect the calculating expression in Shazim's eyes.

'It was my pleasure to work with you,' he said. She breathed a sigh of relief at his acceptance of the change of subject. 'You seem to have settled in.'

'Oh, I have,' she enthused. 'It's so wonderful here.'

'Even the sandstorm?' he demanded drily.

'Apart from that,' she conceded. And then she felt prompted to ask, 'Did you find somewhere to stay tonight?'

Shazim had closed his eyes, and now he opened one of them. 'Why? Are you offering?'

'Certainly not,' she retorted. 'But you must be as tired,' she added, feeling guilty.

He raised a brow. 'Are you questioning my stamina?'

Shazim moved so fast, she was in no way ready for it, and she was pinned against the wall before she knew what was happening, with Shazim's fists planted on either side of her face. For a tense few seconds as he caged her, she was certain he was going to kiss her. 'What?' she challenged.

'I'm going to clear something up,' he said. His dark, mocking gaze dropped to her lips. 'You asked where I'm going to sleep tonight. Where do you think I'm going to sleep?'

'I have no idea. Maybe you've got a bed roll?' she guessed, as her heart did its best to beat its way out of her chest.

Was she really going to let him sleep outside in all that dust and fug? Wasn't she bigger than that?

'You're coming back with me to the pavilion,' she said bluntly. 'We both need to get some sleep.'

At least he had the good grace to look surprised by her offer.

'And, if you did have it in mind to seduce me—which I'm quite sure you don't—you'd better know that you'd have to wake me up first.'

'Is that so?' Shazim curved a smile as he pulled his fists away from the wall. 'You're taking a lot for granted, aren't you?'

'Seriously, Shazim—' She put on her most serious work face. 'Come back with me. At least try to get a few hours' sleep. There's plenty of food and drink, and you can bathe in the oasis.'

'Thank you for telling me that.' His smile reminded her who was the expert here. 'I can't think of anything I need more right now than a swim in ice cold water.'

CHAPTER TWELVE

'I CAN'T BELIEVE you're doing this for me,' Shazim murmured in his usual mocking tone as they reached the entrance of the pavilion.

'Shazim, I'd do this for an animal.'

His laugh was so free, so uninhibited, that she began to doubt her decision to allow him to stay. Shazim didn't sound in the least bit tired.

'I'll accept your kind offer, on one condition,' he said, drawing her attention to his shadowed face.

Alarm bells immediately started ringing. 'Yes? What's that?'

'You allow me to check your wounds before you go to bed.'

That seemed reasonable. She could hardly refuse.

'You were so impatient at the clinic, I'm not happy that I dealt with half of them as thoroughly as I would have liked…' As Shazim held the tent flap back and she walked past him into the pavilion, she felt like a piece in a game of chess that had just been held in check.

Bathing wounds should not be this pleasurable, she thoughts minutes later, frowning as Shazim's touch became seductive, rather than strictly therapeutic. 'Haven't you attended to that scratch before?'

'I didn't have this cream at the clinic,' he explained. 'We have special herbal remedies in Q'Aqabi—for just about everything,' he added with a smile, 'and there just happened to be some here.'

She watched as he dipped his big hand into a golden casket containing the healing potion. It was hard to believe he could be so gentle, or that she could remain obedient and still for quite so long.

'You're smiling?' he queried.

And she wasn't about to share the thought. She had sustained quite a few minor injuries during her training, but doubted that any of those big animals had been half as dangerous as Shazim.

'Better?' he murmured. Satisfied with his handiwork, he sat back, but as she went to tentatively touch her face he caught hold of her hand and kept it firmly in his grasp. 'No touching,' he whispered. 'Only I am allowed to do that.'

'Okay,' she agreed with a shrug. As long as it was only her face he was thinking of touching.

'You seem nervous, Isla.'

'Do I?' Was it so obvious? Intimacy between a man and a woman was so far out of her comfort zone she was surprised she hadn't jumped off the bed by now, but she had seen tenderness in Shazim's eyes, and it was hard to be frightened of that.

Was she falling for him?

Certainly not, Isla told herself impatiently. She would never lose sight of the fact that Shazim was the leader of a country, or that she was a vet on a mission to that country.

'We should call a halt to this,' she suggested, 'or I'm going to fall asleep.'

'No, you're not,' Shazim assured her.

Time seemed to stand still. His hands were so soft on her face, and as they moved down to her shoulders, and on her neck, and then her breasts, she didn't find them threatening at all. Shazim mapped her body so skilfully, so confidently, that she could only receive his touch and wonder why she had put this moment off for so long.

'You're not just a vet, Isla, you're a very beautiful woman.'

Easing her neck, she closed her eyes, wanting to believe him. Shazim's touch was like heady wine. He made her feel beautiful, when she feared that wasn't the case. He made her feel womanly, when she'd always striven to be practical and resolute. He made her make time for indulging in sensation and pleasure, which was something she had never done. His hands and touch were so knowing and instinctive that he made her body ache for him, but he knew just when to pull back.

'More?'

The question was in his eyes, and this time she could find no argument.

Weighing her breasts appreciatively, Shazim smiled deeply into her eyes. 'You were made for pleasure as well as practicality,' he insisted with a smile. 'Never forget that, Isla.'

She was never likely to while Shazim's thumbnails were lightly abrading her nipples. She closed her eyes and realised then that she had never known sensation like it. When she opened her eyes again, she decided she had never seen Shazim's eyes so mesmeric before, and realised then that he liked to watch the waves of pleasure building inside her. She'd had no idea that pleasure was such a skill, or that it could be so addictive. He was backing her down on the bed and she wasn't even resisting. Far from trying to find that practical part of her that always saved the day, she wanted it to be lost for ever. There was a very small part of her that questioned her sanity in inviting him to stay the night, but it couldn't compete with the pleasure waves consuming her.

And then he moved and stood up, and reality came flooding back in.

'You'll sleep on the floor?' she asked anxiously, not knowing why he'd suddenly broken away from her. Even to her, her voice seemed to have risen an octave.

He just stood there, looking deeply into her eyes; she felt thoroughly examined…and she liked it.

Slipping off the bed, she reached for the cushions and tossed them on the floor. 'There's no point in being uncomfortable,' she said. 'The floor rugs are thick, and with these cushions to lie on—'

Shazim caught her up in his arms. 'Stop,' he murmured. Nuzzling her neck with his sharp black stubble, he whispered, 'You don't have to hide behind cushions and rugs and excuses, Isla. Free yourself, and stop this now—'

'But I can't—I… I won't!' With a supreme effort, she managed to pull away from him, and, turning her back, she hugged herself tensely.

'Take the bed,' Shazim commanded softly, clearly defeated. 'You're exhausted. We'll talk about this some other time.'

She was so relieved that Shazim had no intention of taking advantage of the situation that she wanted to cry. Her emotions were in shreds, and she was too tired to think anything as she crawled into bed. She barely had the strength to strip down to her top and thong before crumpling on the pillows in an exhausted heap. Pretty much everything after that was a blur. She couldn't even remember pulling the covers up. It was so quiet after the noise of the storm that she slept like a baby. It was only when some goat bells woke her later that morning that she realised she had slept like a baby *in Shazim's arms*.

Catapulting off the bed, she staggered backwards until the walls of the tent prevented her from going any further.

She frowned as she tried to work it out. At what point during the night had Shazim joined her on the bed?

Calming herself, she absorbed the facts. She was still dressed in her top and thong, while Shazim was sprawled…*naked* on the bed. His bronzed skin bore no traces of the sandstorm. He was clean and gleaming, his thick black hair glossy again.

He'd been for a swim, and though she knew she should look away, he was built like a titan, and it was hard—no, impossible—to do the right thing. She couldn't even control her breathing, which was coming hard and fast. She crept closer, taking advantage of his unconscious state. Shazim was as magnificent asleep as he was commanding when he was awake. She was glad he was sleeping on his front, though even his back view was a breath-stealing delight. Now she wondered how they'd both fitted on the bed. With his limbs sprawled, Shazim took up most of it…

That was why she had been curled into a tiny ball.

Yes. But a tiny ball in his arms!

'Are you coming back to bed?' Shazim murmured with his face still turned into the pillows. 'Or, are you going to stand there thinking about it for the rest of the day?'

Was he talking in his sleep? He had to be, surely?

She stared at his back, at the width of his shoulders, and at the tightness of his buttocks, and his hard-muscled thighs, all perfectly displayed for her pleasure. He was quiet again now, breathing easily, his entire glorious, bronzed body hers to admire.

The only excuse she could think of, as she remained perfectly still at the side of the bed, for how she'd ended up in his arms, was that when Shazim had returned from his swim he must have collapsed exhausted on the bed. He had probably taken hold of her while he was sleeping, perhaps mistaking her for someone else—

Her heart lurched and sank as she thought about it.

And what he'd said just now?

He'd said in his sleep, she reasoned. *Face facts.* Shazim could have any woman he wanted. She had probably been having one of her heated dreams, sighing and moaning, so that taking hold of her was nothing more than a reflex action on his part. She could only hope she hadn't been talking in her sleep. Panic struck her now, at the thought of what she might have said—done—to encourage Shazim to mistake her for that someone else. She had to be grateful that the goat bells had woken her, Isla concluded.

So what now? She could hardly get back into bed. She was tempted to go for a swim. It would be the fastest way for her to wake up and clean the sand and grit off her body—and maybe the icy water would knock some sense into her head. With a rushed explanation to Shazim, who might be sleeping, that she was going for a swim, she made her escape outside.

She walked down to the banks of the oasis. There was no one to be seen, but she didn't need to strip off completely, as a thong and lightweight cotton top were fine for swimming. One last glance around, and she let herself down gently, gasping at the change in temperature. She had no fear of swimming alone. She was a strong swimmer, and she would take it steadily as she aimed for the opposite bank. Dipping her head beneath the water, she streamlined her body, and, using a strong, even stroke, she set off. A swim would ease her aching muscles, if nothing else.

It didn't seem to be helping anything else, like cooling her senses, she accepted as her thoughts flew back to the mystery of her night with Shazim.

He hadn't touched her.

She huffed a laugh at that—*As if!*—almost choking herself in the process.

No. Shazim hadn't touched her, and, truthfully, she wasn't sure whether to be insulted or relieved.

Relieved! Of course she was relieved. If he'd made a move she would have run a mile. She had experienced the usual teenage fumbling, but that one terrifying episode at her mother's funeral had finished her where sex was concerned. The man, who had assured her he was a good friend of her mother's, had tried to rape her, and had almost succeeded. She had fought him off, but it was a horror she would never forget.

The abuse he'd heaped on her afterwards had stayed with her ever since: she was unattractive and useless, anyway. No man would ever want her. He'd only been doing her a favour. After losing her mother, she had been at her lowest ebb, and the man's comments had left her devastated and defeated. The only type of sex she had indulged in since was in her head, where she was always in control. Shazim didn't need to know this. He would never know.

She raised her head mid-stroke to look around to check she was still alone. She had swum further away from the pavilion than she had intended, and it was time to go back and think about work. Stepping out of the water, she yielded to one last temptation. Closing her eyes, she turned her face to the sun and, stretching out her arms, she allowed the strengthening rays to dry her.

He watched Isla swimming and admired her strength—in the water and out of it. She was still battling her demons as he was, he suspected, though right now, standing in supplication to the sun on the bank, she looked as free as he'd ever seen her. He didn't want to change that, because it told him that Isla would reach her goal. At one time he might have seen her as a tender green shoot, but on closer acquaintance…she'd been a revelation to him during the storm. Brave and quick thinking, Isla had been as appealing to him in work mode as she had been at the celebration in the village, when she'd had all the appearance of an ethereal butterfly. Once again, she had proved to be so much more than that. At the campfire, she had achieved with smiles and gestures a connection with his people that had won her many friends. During the storm her bravery and resilience had won her the respect of his rangers. And in the early hours of this morning, stretched out on his bed, she had tempted him beyond reason.

And now?

For the next couple of days he would have her to himself. There was no hurry. Delay was arousing.

'Shazim!'

'I'm sorry if I startled you.'

'You didn't,' Isla insisted as she wrapped her arms around her chest. Her top was wet and plastered to her breasts. She'd had the presence of mind to remove her bra before falling asleep last night.

'Last night,' she began, as if picking up on at least some of his thoughts.

'You're not needed this morning,' he cut in.

'Not needed?' She frowned. 'Did I do something wrong?'

'On the contrary. The rangers agree with me that you should take a rest today after working through the night.'

'But that's not what I'm here for,' she argued. 'If there's a problem, we stand together.'

'There is no problem today, and the rangers are content to stand alone.'

The rangers were hardly going to disagree with their Sheikh, she thought.

'Don't worry, you'll be working,' Shazim assured her, seeing her doubt. 'I'm going to take you deeper into the desert, to a watering hole where you can witness the progress of the conservation programme first hand.'

'Will we stay overnight?'

'Is that your first question?'

'There are more.'

'Well, to answer the first one, the length of our stay will depend on what we find when we get there.'

'I'll be prepared,' she said.

'I'm counting on it.' He wisely curbed a smile.

If this was work she couldn't refuse, Isla reasoned as she walked swiftly back to the pavilion to prepare to leave, her main concern was this: Was Shazim trialling her for a job he had in mind, or something else? And what could she do about it, either way?

CHAPTER THIRTEEN

ISLA STAYING ON in Q'Aqabi was now a definite in his mind, rather than a possibility, but how would she feel when he took a bride? *How would he feel?* The villagers might have taken to Isla on sight, but the country was agitating for him to get married. When he did that, his bride would be chosen from a similar background, and would understand that any marriage he contracted would be a transaction to the benefit of both parties. He wasn't free to indulge in the idea of romance. It simply didn't exist in his world. His duty was to his country, and to his late brother, and that called for nothing less than single-minded dedication to the cause.

'I really need to stay here at the clinic quite a lot longer,' Isla said, frowning.

'You're having doubts now?' he queried sharply. 'I thought you were looking forward to visiting the interior with me?'

She hummed uncertainly. 'I'm only just beginning to realise the scope of the job here, and I need time to establish myself at the clinic.'

His male pride was piqued. Isla's eyes were wary and she couldn't hold his stare, suggesting there was a lot more than the clinic on her mind. His best guess was she didn't trust herself to go deeper into the wilderness with him.

'The clinic isn't going anywhere. It will still be here when you get back.'

Her jaw firmed as if she had come to a decision. His mind was made up, and he was impatient now, both to leave, and to have Isla with him. His hunger for her was growing like a sharp, nagging edge. She would come with him. There was no more to be said on the matter.

Shazim had made it impossible for her to refuse to take the trip, but she was going to make a few of her own rules before they set off. For a start, she was going to ride her own horse. She wouldn't risk any more of that pressing up close against him. This was a research trip, not a romantic outing.

Riding her own horse was perhaps an exaggeration. The animal the rangers brought up for her was more of a plodding mule. But it was kind, and its ears were velvety beneath her fingertips. It was just an old horse, slow and steady. They'd get on fine, she told herself confidently, as Shazim rode up on his fire-breathing monster.

'I see you've already mounted up,' he said with the suggestion of an amused smile.

'And *I* see that you are resigned to riding alone without my assistance,' she countered as she gathered up the reins.

'Like this,' he said, leaning over.

He was just gorgeous, and his hands on hers were a seductive delight, but she pretended not to notice as Shazim laced the reins through her fingers.

He was a great guide too, and took trouble to point out all the things she wouldn't have noticed without him as they rode along: ibexes concealed in the shadow of a dune, and animal tracks, and then, most thrillingly, a pair of desert eagles soaring high above their heads. But it was when they rounded the base of a particularly mountainous dune that she got the biggest surprise of all.

'My observation post,' Shazim explained with the flash of a grin and a casual shrug.

She couldn't tell if he was joking or not, for there, sitting on the bank of the most beautiful and tranquil watering hole, was the billowing Bedouin tent of her fantasies.

'Is this what you pictured when you set out for Q'Aqabi?' he demanded, turning in the saddle to take a look at her.

'Pretty much,' she admitted, feeling her cheeks fire red.

'My people will have set up refreshments for us, but I suggest a swim first to cool off.'

'Sounds good,' she agreed. What was she worried about? Shazim hadn't even mentioned sleeping with her last night. He'd been all business since they left the village.

Didn't that make her feel just the tiniest bit disappointed?

No. It did not. This trip was to inform her about the project and nothing more. Shazim's people had been out here ahead of them to set up the equipment they would require for...well, for whatever they were here for.

She soon forgot her concerns when Shazim led the way into the icy water. Her much smaller mount followed his, and soon they were swimming, their horses lunging forward. She was getting the hang of this—

Or, she thought she was, until the force of the water lifted her clean out of the saddle.

Shazim's hand instantly found her thigh and he pushed her deep into the rolling motion of the saddle. She gasped as her body accepted the contact—of him, and of the horse's thrusting gait. Sensations collided: the cold of the water and the heat of his hand, and he didn't take his hand away, leaving his fingertips within millimetres of her core.

'Better now?' he asked.

Was that amusement in his voice? Rather than answer him, she decided to concentrate on staying on the horse.

* * *

'That was great,' she admitted as their horses found solid ground and clambered out. The magic of the desert must be getting to her, she concluded.

Once they were safely on dry land, she dismounted cautiously, determined not to make the same mistake again. She was becoming more confident on a horse. She would need to be, to get about in the desert. Taking the reins over her horse's head, she tethered him where Shazim had left his stallion.

'Isla…' She turned at Shazim's call. And then had to try to appear as if seeing the most beautiful man stark naked was all in a day's work for her.

What had she expected—that he would pull out a pair of designer swimming shorts from his saddlebag?

This was the desert. Life was in the raw. She had known what to expect when she came out here. Didn't she pride herself on being practical and down to earth?

Yes. But she hadn't expected to be confronted by the sight of Shazim diving butt naked into the watering hole.

'Do I have to come there and get you?' he shouted to her from the water.

Please no!

But. There was only one way to handle this. Planting her hands on her hips, she gave him a look, and then, slowly and deliberately, she peeled off her clothes.

He had turned away by this time, but he heard Isla entering the water. He badly needed an outlet for his energy, and had powered away to the opposite bank. He turned to see Isla swimming strongly towards him.

She remained a safe distance away, treading water. 'Race?' she suggested, her face innocent and beautiful.

'I'll give you a head start,' he offered.

'Do you really think I need one?' she queried, lifting a brow.

'I know you do.'

It was only when she turned away and started swimming that he realised she was as naked as he was. And there had been a definite blaze of challenge in her eyes. Now he knew why. With a laugh he powered after her. Isla Sinclair was determined to beat him at his own game. It remained to be seen if she could.

He followed at a lazy pace, knowing how badly she wanted to win. She still felt she had something to prove to him, but she was wrong. Isla had nothing to prove to him.

She stopped swimming in the shallows, trying to decide what to do next. Maybe she wasn't as brazen as she thought she was.

When he reached her, she whipped her arm across the surface of the water, sending a blinding spray into his face.

'Two can play at that game, Ms Sinclair—'

'I certainly hope so,' she yelled back at him.

She was frightened by what she'd started with Shazim; excited and aroused. There was no mistaking her feelings now. Whatever fear there had been had been replaced by a far more primal need, and it was inevitable that what had started out as fun turned serious. They tangled in the water, and Shazim wrapped his arms around her. She could feel every impressive inch of him against her. There was a moment when they stilled and looked at each other…

Isla's eyes had darkened in a way he couldn't mistake. He had an instant to decide if he needed this sort of complication in his life.

'Who knew?' she said, pushing him away. 'You can be fun.'

'You have no idea,' he murmured.

Letting her go, he lifted his hands, palms up flat, to signal once and for all that this was over. But then she did the last thing he'd been expecting. Still laughing, she threw herself back into his arms, and, lunging forward, she planted a clumsy kiss on his lips.

'Don't,' he warned, slowly wiping the back of his hand across his mouth. 'You don't know what you're getting yourself into.'

'Maybe I do,' she argued stubbornly, holding his gaze as they stood facing each other in the shallows.

They looked at each other, daggers drawn for a moment, and then he swung her into his arms and strode with her to the tent.

Shazim didn't speak. He didn't need to. She knew what she was doing. Even knowing what she had here and now with Shazim was only temporary, she had made the first move, and she was quite prepared to see it through.

What exactly did she have with Shazim?

If anyone was going to help her to shake her fear of sex—

She had fallen for him.

Maybe.

Definitely. Was she prepared to pay such a heavy price for what could only be a few hours of pleasure?

She had never been a coward.

She'd never been a fool, either.

Her inner critic's plain talk was wasted. All she wanted was Shazim. For however long it lasted, everything had been leading up to this moment. The desert had awoken something primal in her, and that had freed her as he'd said it would.

Once they were inside the pavilion, Shazim took her face in his hands in a touch so gentle it was almost reverent. He made her feel safe, valued. But then something changed in his gaze that made a prescient shiver trickle down her spine. He was probably thinking the same thing she was: that this was just a moment in time, and that it couldn't last. But while it did…

Linking their fingers, he very slowly drew her close. She breathed deep on his familiar scent with its overtones of sandalwood. She loved his touch. She loved being this close to him. She loved the way her skin tingled with awareness.

When Shazim brushed his mouth against hers, she softened against him. When he deepened the kiss, she clung hungrily to him. He might be a king, and powerful beyond imagining, but in this they were equals.

'I'm glad that fate has brought you here,' he said, removing the last of her doubts.

Pressing her body against his, she was suddenly ravenous for more contact, the ultimate contact. This was her man, her mate. As their tongues tangled and her breathing quickened, her fate was sealed. Shazim was air for her lungs, and food for her soul, and his kisses were a seduction she couldn't resist. Her body ached for him to be deep inside her. He was the missing part of her, and the cure for her deep-seated fears. She answered Shazim's fierce passion with hungry sounds of need, until with a growl he let her go. And when she sank down on the bed, he hooked his thumb into the back of his robe and dragged it over his head. Her eyes widened as she stared at him, naked and magnificent, like a statue cast in bronze. Tossing the robe aside, he threw the covers back and joined her on the bed. He was such a daunting sight. He was so huge, so beautiful—

And was entirely built to scale—

Those old memories made her want to run away…this was too much…

'Isla?'

Crouched on all fours, she was starting to back her way off the bed. Shazim drew her back to him. 'No,' he said.

'That's not the way. You don't run from anything, Isla, least of all me.' And while she was still hesitating, and still unsure, he embraced her again, bringing her close so he could soothe her with unthreatening kisses until she calmed down.

He had been right all along about Isla, but she was far more damaged than he knew. He held her for a long time until her eyes started to close, and then he settled her back on the pillows and stood up.

'No,' she exclaimed groggily, her confidence returning. As he threw on his robe she reached for his hand. 'You're right. I don't run from anything.'

He backed away. This was torture for him, but it was torture he would gladly bear for her sake. He might want Isla with a madness that threatened his usual control, but her need was far greater than his, and he would not take advantage of her fears. She was clearly not ready for this. Not ready for him. She was inviolable until she was strong enough to share the cause of them.

'I'm not leaving you,' he explained, 'but you must tell me who has hurt you. If you don't let the poison out, it will destroy you.'

It was a relief when she began haltingly to explain. He sat in a chair to listen a little way from the bed. He didn't want to do or say anything to interrupt her. He needn't have worried. It was as if she had lanced a wound, and all the foulness of the past poured out. It appeared that, on top of the tragedy of losing her mother, Isla had been further traumatised. He listened to her story in horror, and when she'd finished he went back to the bed and took her into his arms. 'Not all men are like that, Isla. Give life a chance. Learn to trust again, or this will scar you for ever.'

While Isla knew, deep in her heart, that his words spoke the truth, something defensive rose up in her.

'Says the Sheikh with shadows in his eyes,' she murmured.

His whole expression changed in a moment. She saw the hurt and pain in his eyes and instantly regretted her words.

Standing, he turned away. Dressing again, he slipped his feet into his sandals and left the tent.

She didn't call him back this time.

CHAPTER FOURTEEN

ISLA BRINGING UP the past had really thrown him, but work had always been his salvation. Thankfully, there was no shortage of work to do. They were still at the watering hole, where he was separating the pregnant ibexes from the rest of the herd, when Isla joined him. She acted as if nothing unusual had happened between them. That suited him. They'd get more done.

They worked side by side until the sun went down, and they worked on by moonlight. When the moon finally went behind a cloud, he called it a day.

'That's it. We'll start again tomorrow.'

They walked back together to the tent, but he stopped when he reached the supplies he'd decanted from his saddlebags.

'What are you doing?' Isla asked him.

'Preparing to sleep beneath the stars...'

'There's no need for that,' she said awkwardly as he rolled out his sleeping mat.

'I could sleep on the floor of the tent,' he suggested tongue in cheek, 'but I prefer to sleep out here.'

'Then, so do I,' she blurted out.

'You?' He stared at her in astonishment. Even though she'd opened her heart to him, after her last brush with intimacy he had imagined Isla would want to forget being close to him. 'No.' He shook his head. 'You sleep under cover. You're not used to sleeping rough.'

'You'd be surprised what I'm used to—'

He cursed beneath his breath as she disappeared inside the tent, and then stared at the sky and asked for patience when she returned loaded down with blankets and cushions.

'Let me,' she said, dumping them on the ground so she could dip down to help him clear some rocks away. 'I'm sorry,' she whispered, glancing up.

'What are you sorry for?'

'For loading my troubles onto you—can we start again?'

She took his silence for refusal. 'Please?'

She came right up to him, and looked so young and sexy. 'Better not,' he said.

'But our working relationship's still okay?'

Her tone was anxious. 'Nothing's changed,' he assured her. Bed made, he stood up.

'Are you sure you're okay with that?' she asked, flashing a dubious glance at his bedroll.

'Why wouldn't I be?'

Taking hold of her shoulders, he brought her in front of him. The fire he'd made to combat the chill of a desert night crackled on, while the moon beamed down benevolently. Everything was as it should be, but he still got the feeling that everything in his rigidly controlled life was about to change.

'I think you'd rather be with me, in the tent,' she whispered.

'Have you learned nothing?' he demanded, putting her away from him. Impatiently, he toed the cushions into place.

As she reached for him it became clear that she had not. And this time he'd call her bluff.

Catching hold of her hand, he bit her palm gently, and when she gasped out loud he drew one of her fingertips into his mouth.

The air between them was electric as Shazim drew her deeper into his erotic net. Closing her eyes, she inhaled deeply and shakily as he dipped his head to lightly brush her lips with his. His kiss was like a question: Did she want to carry on? Her answer was yes, most certainly. This time she reached up and laced her fingers through his hair to keep him close. Her senses were full of him. He intoxicated her. He tasted of all things good. He smelled of woodsmoke and sandalwood, and the delicate balance between her fear of physical love and the growing sense that she was safe with him reached tipping point. Realistically, she was in the greatest danger of her life. Shazim's destiny called him to greater things than a girl by a campfire in the desert. But she had no intention of spending the rest of her life wondering what a night with Shazim would be like.

When his big hands cupped her buttocks, that delicate balance between safety and danger tipped irrevocably.

She groaned as he pressed her against him, and groaned again when she felt the thickness and weight of his erection. Her body seemed to mould around his of its own accord, and when he cupped her breasts over her fine cotton top she exhaled on a soft and shaking cry. She was glad, for once, that her breasts were so firm and big and full. She wanted him to like them. She was glad that her nipples were uptilted and tempting, and when he removed her top in one easy move and claimed the tight buds, laving first one and then the other with his tongue, she encouraged him to sink his face deep. Arching her back, she thrust her hips towards him to show how much she approved.

'Not yet,' Shazim murmured, slanting a wicked smile as he glanced up at her. 'You must learn patience, *habibti*.'

She had no patience, no self-control, and writhed against him, seeking more contact.

'What do you need?' Shazim murmured, baiting her with his smouldering heat.

'I think you know,' she whispered.

'But you must tell me,' he insisted. 'Those are my rules.'

'*Your* rules?'

'Even now you are defiant?'

He frowned, but she could tell that the thought amused him.

'My rules, or nothing,' he said as he reached for the fastening on her shorts.

'Do you want to take a bet on that?' she said softly as she pushed his hand away. Slowly and deliberately, she lowered the zipper herself.

He loved Isla's defiance almost as much as her self-determination. She was ready, and it had been worth the wait. He wanted nothing to stand between them, least of all the past, or her unreasonable fear. He took over, sliding her shorts over the swell of her hips…slowly. He was in no rush. He intended to relish the sensation of his slightly roughened palms moving over her silky skin as he took her thong down.

He couldn't wait to tease and explore. He had to remind himself, quite forcefully, that delay was always the servant of pleasure.

She gave a sharp intake of breath when he drew his robe over his head. That reaction was echoed by his own response as he stared down at her. The flames of the campfire had warmed Isla's pale skin to blush peach, while he remained in shadow and darkness. The contrast between them was marked and she was half his size.

'Shazim…' She reached for him. 'Touch me. Teach me—'

Pausing only to protect them both, he silenced her

with a kiss. 'Not until you tell me what you want,' he reminded her.

'An end to this torture,' she said, but, as she was still covering herself modestly with her arms, she was doing nothing to convince him to speed things up.

'What torture?' he demanded, continuing to tease her with long strokes down the length of her thighs.

'My legs don't ache,' she said, frowning.

'You're getting used to riding,' he observed with the faintest of smiles.

He carried on stroking her as she sighed with pleasure, and then he moved his attentions to where she needed him, but he was never quite close enough.

'Shazim,' she begged him in a shaking voice.

'Good?' he murmured, teasing her some more.

'Not good enough,' she complained, and then she turned her face into the cushions, as if for once her boldness had gone too far, even for her.

Easing her legs over his shoulders, he made her lie back on the cushions while he knelt in front of her.

She was shocked, and exclaimed, 'What are you— Oh,' she gasped as he cupped her buttocks, holding her firmly in place. She was more aroused than even he had suspected.

Was it possible to survive sensation like this? Isla doubted it, and sucked in a shuddering breath as she clung to the bedroll at her side. Shazim was so good at this, so intuitive. He knew exactly when to draw back, and when to give her just a little bit more. Having dispensed with what remained of her modesty, he was keeping her legs widely spread on the powerful sweep of his shoulders. And she was right on the edge.

His tongue was slightly roughened and he knew just how much pressure to apply. The rhythm was irresistible, and she was just tensing to let go when he stopped.

She exclaimed with disappointment as he lowered her legs and sat back. But then he nudged one hard-muscled thigh between her legs, easing them apart again. She felt so exposed and so aware as he stared down, and she was so very desperate for contact, but all he would give her was the tip of his erection. Drawing it back and forth very lightly, he made her crave release. She hadn't even understood her own body when it came to her capacity to feel pleasure, but now she was hungry for more, and angled her body in an attempt to catch more of him.

'I need you,' she cried out in frustration.

'You need this,' he argued. 'Say it,' he commanded in a firmer tone.

'I need all of you,' she exclaimed, a slave to the hunger inside her. 'And I need it now,' she gasped, thrusting her hips up to meet him.

'I decide when,' Shazim murmured, taking the cry of disappointment from her mouth in a kiss. 'Slowly,' he warned when she fought hard to urge him on. 'I won't rush this, not even for you. I won't hurt you, Isla.'

And she believed him. Trusted him. Which was something she'd never thought she'd be able to do again. And then he touched her with his hand, and took her to yet another level of arousal.

'Tell me,' he whispered against her mouth. 'Tell me what you need.'

'I need you deep inside me,' she said shakily. 'I need you to take me deep. You're so big, I want you to let me get used to you first,' she pleaded on a suddenly dry throat, 'but then, I want you to take me firmly, fast and hard—'

Forced to break off, she wailed softly with excitement as Shazim caught inside her...and this time he didn't pull back. She remained quite still, savouring the moment, and then she exhaled on a gust of pleasure as he sank a little deeper still. He repeated this several times, sometimes withdrawing completely before returning to give her a little more each time. She trusted him completely, knowing now that if she tensed, he would stop. It was a lesson in how to relax, and her reward was Shazim's thick length deeply lodged inside her. When he rolled his hips she almost fell, but as always he knew how to keep her from the brink. He remained quite still, poised over her, braced on his forearms. He withdrew steadily until they were completely parted, and then, after a moment of fear that he might stop, he plunged deep. He moved hard and fast, driving into her with firm, regular strokes, shooting the air from her lungs and the fear from her heart, and with a cry of relief she threw herself into pleasure. When she quieted, he reduced the pace to a gentle and insistent buffeting, until she discovered that, far from her pleasure ending, it was just building again.

'Hold your legs wide for me,' Shazim instructed, staring down to where her enjoyment was all too obvious to him. 'And don't move. Your role is to lie still and be pleasured.'

His promise excited her, and she pressed her thighs apart.

'Relax,' he warned when she began to tense as her climax approached. 'If you don't relax, I'll stop. Now, concentrate your mind on that one place, and no other. Good,' he approved as she stilled.

Turning her onto her hands and knees, he moved behind her. His hands on her buttocks were firm and controlling as her hunger raged on. Anticipation of pleasure had made her insatiable, and when he took her and touched her, she couldn't hold on.

'Greedy,' he said approvingly as she rammed backwards onto him.

She worked her hips frantically to be sure of the last pulse of pleasure. Shazim barely gave her the chance to draw a breath this time before throwing her onto her back and taking her again, firmly and fast.

There was no world outside this, no existence possible outside the two of them, and there was no man for her ever, but Shazim.

He relished Isla's mewls of pleasure, and her final ecstatic cries. Even now she wasn't sated and reached for him. She was a revelation to him. Her appetite matched his. No sooner had she crested one wave than she eagerly sought out the next.

'But what about you?' she asked him finally.

'Me?' He laughed softly against her mouth as he dragged her close for a kiss. 'Don't you think I'm enjoying this?'

'I know you are,' she said, reaching down. He shuddered with pleasure as her small hand closed possessively around him.

'Then,' he instructed, 'you must mount me.'

'Must I?' She gave him a look. 'Do I need another riding lesson?'

'Oh, yes.'

'Then, I'm glad to obey, Your Majesty,' she said with a witchy smile. Rolling away, she changed position, and, arranging herself on top of him, she spread her legs wide. Throwing her head back, she groaned with pleasure as he guided her slowly down.

'You are a witch,' he remarked as she grew in confidence.

'And you're the best stallion I ever rode.'

She laughed, and he laughed with her as she attempted to pin him down.

Coming to Q'Aqabi, to do the job she loved, had altered Isla in one small, but fundamental way. She didn't just know what she wanted now, she knew how to get it. How he would ever let her go, he had no idea.

'Better?' he asked when she was calm enough to speak.

'Almost,' she teased him with a look. 'I feel there might be more.'

'Much more,' he confirmed, proving it.

'You're right,' she agreed with a gasp of pleasure.

Shazim made everything possible. She had never guessed she had such an exhaustive appetite. 'I love it,' she exclaimed in answer to his husky question.

I love you, she thought as Shazim turned her so her back was facing him.

'So I can touch you while I take you,' he explained.

'Whatever you want to do is all right by me.' She laughed softly, realising this was true. There was nothing Shazim could do that would frighten her, or that she wouldn't enjoy—though enjoy was hardly the word for it. There had to be a new word invented for this amount of pleasure. 'Oh, yes,' she breathed when he pressed the flat of his hand into the small of her back, making her even more available to him. 'It's so good…and I can't hold on—'

'You're not supposed to,' he reminded her, continuing to move to the same dependable rhythm. 'Just let go…'

He loved watching her face when Isla lost control, but watching from this angle gave him another view on pleasure. Keeping her buttocks firmly angled with one hand, he worked her sensitive bud with the other. At the same time he thrust rhythmically and deep. But Isla had some ideas of her own, and he groaned as she closed her inner muscles tightly around him.

'Let go,' she urged him, angling her buttocks even more for him to see. 'Let—'

The rest of her words were lost in a roar of mutual release as they fell together.

Pounding into her, he thought she might extract his life force before she'd finished with him. And when they did finally recover, they could do no more than collapse back on the bedroll and sleep.

Some time during the night he woke and watched her sleeping beside him. She looked so peaceful, so young and carefree, and so happy that he smiled in response to the curve of her lips as she slept. He wondered what she was dreaming about to make her smile. Then the fire started guttering, and a cool breeze reminded him that the temperature would dip further still. Gathering her into his arms, he carried her to the tent and laid her down on the bed, and this time he made no pretence of sleeping on the floor. Pulling her into his arms, he kissed her and drew the covers over both of them.

CHAPTER FIFTEEN

SHE WOKE SLOWLY, stretching out a body that had been very well used. She smiled as she remembered Shazim making love to her, and stretched out a lazy hand to touch him.

'Hey, lazy bones—'

She turned to see Shazim, already up and drying his wild black hair on a towel. There was another towel slung around his lean waist. He'd been for a swim, and his bronzed torso was pumped and gleaming. He looked amazing. Burying her face into the pillow, she faced up to the fact that she looked like the same sleep-wrecked, down-to-earth woman she'd always been, a woman who was far too sensible to ever be called pretty. In fact, forget pretty. A man like Shazim would hook up with a genuine beauty. It was one thing having a passionate fling with the ugly duckling, out in the desert with no one to see them, but he'd want the swan for when he was back in town.

'Come on,' he urged, leaning over her. 'It's time to get up and out.'

She pushed her worries aside. 'Kiss first,' she insisted, clinging onto the fantasy for as long as she could.

'We've got work to do,' he said sternly.

She loved his sternness. She loved the work. She loved the way he said, *we've* got work to do. The fact that Shazim was already thinking of them as a team, at least professionally, was all she had ever wanted. And they were a team—a great team.

At least for now.

Turning to face him, she smiled away her fears and reached up. 'This is something special, isn't it?' Now she sounded desperate, but she was too much in love to care.

He laughed. 'So special I may never get enough of you.'

Her heart actually ached with happiness. That was all she had wanted to hear.

He should have known it wouldn't end with a good morning kiss. The moment his hands closed around Isla's soft, hungry body, it was only a short trip to their favourite destination. Making her shriek with excitement as he swung her off the bed, he kissed her deeply as she wrapped her legs around him. Backing her up to one of the sturdy tent poles, he did the only decent thing.

'Oh, yes,' she exclaimed, working furiously to draw him inside her.

In a matter of moments they were working together and laughing softly against each other's mouths.

'One more time,' she begged him, writhing a little to encourage him.

He needed no encouragement and took her again.

These had been the best few days of her life, Isla thought, smiling as she helped Shazim to free some rare desert gazelles into the wild later that morning. They had shared something special. And the best thing about it—the part she couldn't believe—was that Shazim seemed to feel the same about her. He hadn't told her exactly that he loved her, but he had said that he could never get enough of her.

Okay, she was a realist, and Shazim was a king, a lord of the desert. They could never be a cosy couple, but they might work something out.

And when he gets married, as kings do?

She didn't know—she wasn't sure. That was a question for another day.

Forcing unwelcome thoughts out of her head, she got on with unlatching the crates to free the animals. Her heart swelled with love for Shazim as they exchanged a triumphant glance when the animals bounded free.

'And now I must go,' he said, shocking her into silence. 'I'll take a quick swim to freshen up, and then—'

'You're going already?' She had thought she was prepared for this. He'd said something about the rangers coming so she wouldn't be alone, but she'd been too busy working, and hadn't really listened. Shazim had explained that he had some matters of state to attend to, she remembered now, after which he would be meeting with some Q'Aqabian tribesmen. His departure was hardly a surprise. She just hadn't expected it to be so soon.

'An emergency,' he explained, frowning with concern. 'A dispute between some local tribesmen—if I'm not there to pass judgement it could blow up into something big.'

'Then, you must go,' she insisted. 'What?' she said when he hesitated.

'I don't want to leave you, Isla.'

'Don't be ridiculous. Of course you've got to go.' Pushing her hair back, she straightened up to confront him. 'Don't think I can't manage here.'

'The rangers are on their way to join you,' he murmured as if thinking out loud.

'There you are. Everything's fine. Now, go.'

'The last communication I had with the rangers said they'd be no longer than half an hour.'

'Then, what are you worrying about?'

He hummed in answer.

'Look,' she said, pointing out into the desert. 'You can see the dust from their Jeeps from here. They're even closer than you thought.'

'They'll have to leave the Jeeps with tribesmen, and travel on by horseback—'

'I know you wouldn't leave me if you thought there was the slightest danger.'

Only Shazim's eyes were visible now as he wound his *howlis* around his head. He was again the Lion of the Desert, and she knew exactly what she was taking on. They both had a job to do. 'Go,' she insisted. 'I wouldn't have agreed to come to Q'Aqabi in the first place if I hadn't thought I could handle situations like this.'

'There are plenty of supplies in the tent for all of you, so you can stay on and finish the job.' Shazim's stallion was becoming impatient as he added, 'The weather report is good, but remember that the desert is unpredictable.'

'I'll be fine,' she insisted, flinging her arms out wide. 'If I can't survive for twenty minutes on my own, what hope do I have of keeping a job here?'

Shazim still look worried as he made the customary gesture with his hand to his forehead, his lips, and then his heart, and she wondered if his concern had anything to do with those shadows in his eyes. He didn't give her time to ask him as he wheeled his horse and rode away.

Shazim was a king with duties to his countrymen, Isla reasoned sensibly after watching him ride away until he had disappeared from sight. He could hardly take off endless amounts of time to be with her. She had always known that what they had would end abruptly, and maybe this was for the best. Shazim would come back, of that she had no doubt, but by then they would both have had chance to think, and to come to terms with a reality that did not include a long-term relationship between Shazim and his latest veterinary recruit.

The rangers did not arrive. Instead, Isla received a radio message to say that a flood warning had prevented them from taking the route they had intended, and that she must get herself to higher ground without delay. Shazim was already on his way back to her.

'If he's only coming to rescue me, he can stay where he is,' she insisted as her heart squeezed tight with concern for him.

'He's on his way, Ms Sinclair. There's nothing we can do to stop him now.'

She would have said more, but the radio signal crackled and then broke up.

Well, there was no sign of a flood so far, Isla reassured herself, and Shazim was as capable as she was of taking care of himself. But she still worried about him, and kept on checking the sky to be sure there was no sign of a storm. Maybe the flood warning was for somewhere else, she reasoned, somewhere closer to the rangers. If the worst happened, she had been watching the path the gazelles took up the cliff when they were released. They were wily animals and instinct invariably kept them safe. The pathways up the cliff were narrow, but manageable. She could only hope Shazim didn't take any chances with his safety. Dashing worried tears from her eyes, she got on with her work.

He could not believe what he'd done. He'd left Isla alone in the desert. Who knew better than he that conditions could change in minutes in the wilderness? In one final irony, as he'd ridden away he had told himself that he was doing the right thing, and that he should leave Isla for her own sake, to save her from him.

He'd made a critical error. If Isla was in danger, there was nowhere else he should be than at her side. He had issued a declaration to the tribesmen that if they didn't sort out their differences they would be answerable to him. Word from his council had come back immediately to say the warring factions had parted grumbling, but resigned to obey their Sheikh's will.

Shazim was a strong ruler, and he should have known better than to allow his feelings for Isla to go so deep. He could not allow their relationship to progress, but that didn't mean he would knowingly expose her to danger. He couldn't bear to be responsible for another tragedy. And when Isla was involved—

Leaning low over his stallion's neck, he urged his horse to gallop even faster. He would reach Isla—whatever it took.

He reined in abruptly. The outcrop of rock where he'd left her was already awash with water. The dried up riverbed was full. He'd have to go around it. He tried to reach her by satellite phone, but each time the line cut before she could answer; a sign that the weather conditions were deteriorating. He could only hope that she'd had the good sense to movc to higher ground. He scrambled helicopters from the royal fleet, but even he couldn't be sure that they would arrive in time.

If he lost her—

Isla had more courage and can-do in her little finger than anyone he'd ever met. He might be wedded to his country, and to the projects that had meant so much to his brother, but if this was what caring for someone felt like, then he embraced it with all his heart, and the sooner he told Isla how he felt about her, the sooner he might be able to live with himself again. The realisation that she might be in danger had shaken him to the core—it had unlocked something in him and he knew, without a shadow of a doubt, that he had to be with her, because he loved her. She was his life.

There was no sign of Shazim, nor was there any sign of an impending flood. There was an increase in the flow of water in the riverbed, but that was only consistent with a brief rainstorm somewhere else. The sky was sullen overhead, which was new in Isla's brief experience of the desert, but there was nothing else to alarm her. She had one more group of animals to tag before the herd could be left to roam at will, and then she would call it a day.

Or so she thought. But a few of the animals were really wily, and had managed to escape. She caught up with them further down the riverbed on the flat ground that Shazim had warned her to stay away from, as it could flood.

She would be quick, she reassured herself as the deepening river water washed over her sand boots.

She glanced up to where the rest of the herd was waiting. Some of them were climbing higher still. She stopped for a moment to listen, but could hear nothing unusual. Maybe there was some tasty moss on the higher slopes.

It didn't take her long to finish and, as the last animals joined their companions, she shaded her eyes and smiled to see a group of horned faces staring down at her.

The last animal to be released was a fawn. It leapt up the jagged path like lightning, and Isla's stomach clenched when she saw its startled eyes and laid-back ears. She tried telling herself that no animal liked to be captured and tagged, and she had no reason to be fearful. She ducked instinctively as a crash of thunder argued with this. And then the rain came down. It didn't just start to fall, but hit her with the force of endless blows. She was drenched immediately.

So that was why the animals were so spooked. She'd done her homework, and she knew what could happen in a thunderstorm in the desert. After Shazim's warning, she took no chances and raced to the base of the cliff. Starting to scrabble up it, she knew she'd been overconfident and too absorbed in her work. She should have done this sooner. Her nails ripped on the treacherous surface as she struggled to find a handhold on the same path the gazelles had used. Desert sand didn't soak up water quickly, and the walls of water created by a sudden rainstorm could be as much as thirty feet high. She had to keep on climbing or she could drown. More people drowned in the desert than died of thirst, she had also read.

She reached a ledge and took a moment to catch her breath, but she still wasn't high enough. The animals were a long way above her, but they took chances, and she didn't have their blind courage. They would launch themselves into space on a wing on a prayer, but if they fell… She cried out as the fawn she'd just tagged spun past her. Jostled from the ledge by its companions, it had missed bouncing off the cliff face by only a hair's breadth. It landed awkwardly and she breathed a sigh of relief when, having righted itself, it shook its head. But it was dazed, and was bleating with bewilderment.

By this time she was halfway down the cliff on her way to rescue it. And now she could hear the water coming. Just the faintest rumble in the distance, but it was getting louder all the time.

He saw the flash flood coming while he was safe on higher ground. The only way he could be sure that Isla wasn't trapped was to climb the cliff where they'd been working from the other side.

When he reached the top and looked over the edge, the sheer volume and force of the water was far worse than he'd imagined. He had supplies in his saddlebag, including rope, gloves, and a medical kit, all of which was a necessary precaution in the wilderness. And he knew how to climb. He also knew just how dangerous it could be. In fact, who knew better than he, when his climbing had been responsible for the tragedy that had killed his brother?

There would be no more tragedies today. On that he was determined.

Uprooted palm trees were being swept along like matchsticks. Desert storms arrived fast, and subsided just as quickly, but the devastation they caused could have tragic, long-term consequences. Isla would be safe if she had stayed in the tent, but he doubted she would have gone there, as she had been so keen to finish her work. She was still here somewhere, he was sure of it—but where? She would have to climb to at least thirty or forty feet above the riverbed to be safe.

Looping a rope around a rock, he heaved himself up and climbed on, telling himself that she was sensible and resourceful. She had proved herself in the sandstorm, and he'd warned her not to go near the riverbed. She would be safe.

She had to be safe.

He'd climbed high enough to catch sight of the tent through the driving rain, and he scanned the area between there and the oasis.

There was no sign of Isla.

The water was crashing around one side of the rocky outcrop, destroying everything in its wake, while on the other side the scenery was unchanged. He could only hope that Isla's smarts had kept her on the safe side of the cliff.

She was on a ledge, safe for the moment, with the gangly animal in her arms, resting before she pressed on, when a dark shape loomed over her.

'Shazim!'

She couldn't have been more surprised to see him climbing down to her, having come over from the other side of the cliff.

'Are you okay?' he asked, taking in the situation at a glance.

She nodded as his eyes blazed into hers. Without another word, he took the fawn and lifted it onto his shoulders. 'Come on. We can't stay here. The water's still rising.'

'No.' She shook her head as he held out his hand to help her. 'You need both hands to climb—it isn't safe. I won't be responsible for sending the ruler of Q'Aqabi plunging to his death.'

The change of expression on Shazim's face shocked her.

'Take my hand,' he repeated harshly. 'We have hardly any time left before the next wave of water sweeps us away.'

Ignoring him, she crabbed sideways until she found a foothold. Then, launching herself into space, she somehow landed on a narrow ledge. Once she was sure it cold hold her, she instructed, 'Pass me the gazelle.'

'No. You're not strong enough.'

'Pass him up,' she insisted.

He didn't doubt Isla's courage, but she didn't have the strength for this. The gazelle, meanwhile, made its own choice, and coiled around his neck in terror, refusing to move.

'Stay where you are,' he called out. 'I'm coming up.' Having found the entrance to a cave in the cliff face, Isla was taking refuge there. When he reached her she was ashen-faced. Carefully disentangling the gazelle, he set the small animal on the path to freedom. Dragging Isla into his arms, he embraced her with relief. As she clung to him he wondered if he could ever let her go. 'I'm sorry this had to happen. It's my fault for leaving you.'

He pressed his face into her hair, but she pulled back and shook her head. 'I knew what I was doing. I'm not a fool, Shazim.'

'No,' he argued grimly. 'You're anything but a fool, but you could still have been killed.'

'You left me for what you thought was a few short minutes,' she argued. 'If I can't cope in the desert for that long, then I don't belong here.'

'But if anything had happened to you—'

'It didn't. And if it had, *I* would have been responsible, not you.'

'You're wrong,' he said coldly. 'I would have been responsible, because I brought you here.'

'What's really wrong with you, Shazim?' she demanded. 'You don't come into the desert unless you can help it these days, your rangers told me. You set up one of the most important conservation programmes in the world, and then you stand back and let others take the glory, while you micromanage the scheme from a distance. The project only exists because of you—'

'You're so wrong about that,' he said bitterly.

Isla shook her head. 'It exists because of you, and not because some ghost from the past is directing you from afar. This is your project—your work—your triumph.'

'You don't know what you're talking about!'

'Don't I? I know what I see. You didn't bring me here to be a puling milksop who agrees with every word you say. You brought me here to challenge and question, and to add value to your scheme. And I will, if you'll allow me to. But if I can't be trusted alone in the desert, then I don't know where we go from here.'

'By bringing up the past, you are treading very dangerous ground,' he said icily.

'I wouldn't know, as you've never told me anything about your past. I only know what the rangers tell me—that everything you do here is to honour your brother's memory. But how are you honouring him if you can't trust the people you bring out here to help with the conservation programme? Is it because you don't trust yourself?

Is that why you're behaving like this with me—as if I'm not capable of doing anything on my own?'

He made an impatient gesture. 'What's wrong here is that you don't listen to me.'

'Oh?' Hand on chest, she feigned surprise. 'And here's me thinking we would listen to each other.'

'You should have stayed away from the riverbed. You shouldn't have come here in the first place—'

'I shouldn't be here in the desert? Or I shouldn't be here in Q'Aqabi with you? Are you changing your mind about inviting your prize winner to visit your country, Shazim? Is that what this is about? You wanted to sleep with me, so you played along with that aspect of the prize, but now that you've had me I'm in the way. Maybe I'm even a potential embarrassment for you. Is that what you think?'

'This is not what this is about and you know it,' he said, growing equally heated.

'Do I? It seems to me that the ruler of Q'Aqabi gets everything he wants when he wants it, and when he's done with it he turns his back and rides away.'

'It was not like that.'

The shadows of the cave added menacing contours to the lines of Shazim's face, but she wasn't nearly done with him yet. 'What exactly was it like, Shazim? You brought me here to seduce me—and not just sexually. You got me to drop my guard—' Emotion got the better of her, and she made a brief angry gesture of frustration. 'You wooed me with words and with the magic of the desert. You listened to my fears, and plumbed my sorrows, without telling me a single word about yours. Did you feign interest just to get me into your bed?'

Shazim looked shocked and angry, but she couldn't stop now. 'Was this all a ploy to get what you wanted from me?' She gestured around. 'You took my trust and you abused it. You took my sorrow and made it your own—

or you appeared to do so. Now I can only think you were getting me to open up and relax so you could get on with the job of seducing me. Have me, and then send me home. Job done. Well, I've got news for you, Shazim of Q'Aqabi. You're so used to people obeying your smallest whim, you can't see when they're doing something out of genuine concern for you. I admired you and everything you've done for Q'Aqabi, but now I feel sorry for you, because you'll never know what it is to risk your heart—'

'What's my heart got to do with this?'

He might as well have tipped a bucket of icy water over her head. Shazim couldn't have sounded more bemused.

'Exactly,' she said, raking her hair with frustration. 'You don't allow yourself to feel, so your heart has got absolutely nothing to do with this. Our relationship, as far as you're concerned, is purely that of employer and employee who undertook some pleasurable extramural activity. The fact that we slept together—and, I believed, became close—means nothing to you. I was on your agenda—on your schedule of things to do. And when you'd done me—done *with* me—you left for your next appointment,' she roared, all out of words.

CHAPTER SIXTEEN

'YOU'RE SO WRONG, ISLA. I don't know what you expect from me. I never promised you anything,' Shazim rapped with an angry gesture that took in his royal person, as well as her position as a vet on his team, together with the fact that at that moment they might have been talking two very different languages.

Isla gave a grim laugh. 'And you don't disappoint. Now,' she said as she walked to the mouth of the cave to look out, 'do you think we should try and get out of here? Because I do.'

Shazim's hand on her arm was meant to calm her, she was sure. 'I'm just glad you're safe,' he said.

She wanted to believe him and heaved a troubled breath.

'Your emotions are threadbare,' Shazim insisted. 'You need to calm down. If we're going to climb our way out of this cave safely, you need all your concentration.'

He was right about that, at least. 'I am calm—well, at least I am now,' she said, frowning. 'And if my emotions are threadbare, it's because I care for you, you stubborn—'

'Me stubborn?' he said.

'Yes. You,' she insisted fiercely. 'The longer you nurse your wounds, the more they'll fester. Let me in, Shazim—if not me, then at least promise you'll let someone in.'

'Let you in?' he echoed, frowning. 'Do you think I have the luxury of emotion in my position?'

'You said that I'm a woman as well as a scientist. Doesn't the same rule apply to you? You're a man as well as a king, Shazim. You're allowed to feel.'

She gasped as he dragged her into his arms.

'And you torment me beyond reason—'

As Shazim growled something vicious in his own tongue he slammed his fists on either side of her face. Pinning her back against the smooth, cold stone, he thrust his powerful frame against hers, melting her anger with his passion, and turning her frustration into searing heat.

'Stop—stop it—' She pummelled his chest.

'If I thought for one moment you meant that—' Shazim stood back, removing all contact from her. 'Do you?' he demanded. His blazing stare burned into hers.

'No,' she admitted, just as angry as he was as she reached for him.

They came together forcefully, love and desire colliding, dissolving her will in her urgency to be one with him. From there it was a fast road to an inevitable conclusion. Shazim lifted her, and supported her with his hands clasping her buttocks, while she locked her legs around his waist. She was more than ready for him, and while she laced her fingers through his hair to keep him close, Shazim gave her what she needed in firm, deep strokes. Her entire body was one with his, but she was only aware of a mutual and desperate need to reinforce trust in each other. Shazim moved as fiercely as she did in the hunt for release, and when it came it was as powerful and as vital to both of their existence as the air they were so greedily gulping in.

When she calmed, and Shazim was still holding her, he murmured in between kissing her, 'We have to climb the cliff, *habibti*. You must save your strength for that.'

Humour coloured his dark, husky voice, but she wasn't

done with him yet. Shazim was still hard, still lodged deep inside her. She rotated her hips, wanting more.

He was lost the instant she moved again. Dipping at the knees, he took her firm and deep, thrusting to a rhythm as old as time. He wanted this woman with a hunger that would not abate. He thought about her every waking moment. She kept him awake at night. He knew how to bring her to the edge and take her over, and he did so efficiently and fast. They did have to move on. There was no more time to lose.

'Now,' he instructed softly as she groaned with pleasure.

She broke apart in his arms, while he made sure that she enjoyed the very last wave of pleasure, and then he held her until she collapsed, spent in his arms.

'You're amazing,' she said softly.

'So are you.' He smiled against her mouth.

'What are we going to do about this, Shazim?'

'Do?' He lowered her to the ground. 'We've got to get out of here first.'

'That isn't an answer.' But then she removed her hands from his steadying grip as if she had come to a decision. 'But you're right,' she said. 'We should focus on climbing the cliff.'

Her voice sounded strained and had lost all the passion it had so recently held. Isla could always snap back into practical mode, but he knew she was hurting inside and he could offer her nothing. He followed her glance outside the cave to where the water was still roaring. 'Let's make a move.'

'Do you have enough rope?' she asked, checking what little equipment they had.

'It has to be enough.'

'Is it safe?' She stared at the coiled rope, chalk, and climbing gloves.

None of this was safe, but they had no choice. He wasn't sitting around to wait and see. Action was always his preferred option. 'The rope will take our weight easily. I've only got one pair of gloves, so you wear them—they'll protect your hands,' he insisted when she started to argue.

'Yes. Both of my hands in one of your gloves,' she remarked with a look. 'You wear the gloves. I'll take the chalk.'

He could see her now, heading up his team in the desert. Once Isla was fully conversant with all the dangers that team might face, she would make a formidable leader. But could he risk the life of someone like that to a perilous climb?

'I'd rather you stayed here and I bring the helicopter to lift you—'

'No,' she insisted. 'If you're going, I'm coming with you.'

'It's a hard climb, and too much of a risk.'

'That's for me to decide. Coming to Q'Aqabi was a risk, but I'm here. You risked a dangerous climb to come and find me. Are you saying I can't do the same?'

'You're not strong enough.'

'Inaction isn't an option for me, either, Shazim. Let's do this—'

He snatched the rope out of her hands. 'You're staying here.'

'What's really bugging you, Shazim? I know it's more than this or the storm—'

'I'm asking you to wait this out,' he spelled out as they faced each other angrily. 'What's so hard for you to understand?'

'You,' she retorted. 'You're impossible to understand.'

With an immense call on his patience, he tried sweet reason. 'It's much safer for you to wait until I come back with the helicopter rescue team. It will be easier—'

'Easy?' she queried. 'We're not here for easy, Shazim. If we liked easy, you would be on a yacht somewhere, living the playboy life with a supermodel on your arm, and I'd be in a nice, comfortable city practice with a regular wage and drinks down at the pub on a Friday night.'

As they stared grimly at each other, he knew she would never give up.

'Tell me,' she said. 'Tell me what's really bugging you.'

'If I do, you'll beg me to let you wait for the helicopter.'

'Try me,' she said.

Shazim was silent so long she wondered if he could hear the water creeping closer.

'My elder brother was killed saving me from a cliff like this,' he said at last.

She stilled, not wanting to distract him as Shazim stared blindly out of the cave at some horror she would never see.

'He overbalanced and slipped—'

When he didn't say anything more, she prompted him. 'Are you saying that you believe the fall was your fault?'

'It was my fault. He wouldn't have been anywhere near that cliff, if not for me.'

'But he was there and he saved you,' she argued pragmatically.

'I told him I could get down without his help. I was young and wild, and I believed I was indestructible. My brother was a lot older than me, but not nearly as strong. He was the thinker, while I was the reckless brother—'

'He liked to put plans together for the benefit of Q'Aqabi,' she guessed. 'Like the nature reserve,' she added as the pieces of the jigsaw fell into place. 'No one needed to tell me, Shazim,' she said when he stared at her. 'I've seen the way you devote your life to this project. I've seen your face when you discuss your ideas, and I know how far you'll go to advance them. This nature reserve is more than a passion for you, Shazim, it's your life's work.'

She understood him now. Nothing gave Shazim respite from the guilt he felt about his brother's death. That was why he set himself such impossibly high standards and why he gave himself no rest.

'My brother was steady and cautious,' he said, shaking his head as if he still couldn't believe what had happened after all these years. 'He loved the desert he'd been born to rule, but he could never come to terms with its unpredictability. There had to be a rationale, a pattern to everything, he used to say, but the desert defied his best attempts to order it, and, in the end, I think that frightened him.'

She thought so too, and, remembering the theorising of the academics at her university, she knew now that there was nothing to beat knowledge combined with demanding and even very dangerous first-hand experience.

'He'd be proud of you, Shazim. You've turned your brother's dreams into reality.'

'But have I succeeded?' Shazim's fierce face was shaded with concern.

'That's why I'm here,' she said. 'You've not just succeeded, you've created a world-renowned facility that attracts a global audience. As far as I'm concerned, working here would be a dream come true.'

They both glanced out of the cave to see the floodwater lashing at branches only a few yards away from them. They moved as one.

'Just one thing,' Isla said, staring at Shazim's outstretched hand. 'Before we leave here, I want you to accept that the past is the past for both of us. You can't go on blaming yourself for ever—'

'Leave it, Isla. I am to blame.' Shazim's expression blackened as he picked up the rope.

'You came to save me,' she pointed out, standing in front of him so she could meet his fierce stare levelly.

'That's different. I know what I'm doing. My brother should have left me on that ledge to freeze. *I* should have died instead of him—'

'No—' She grabbed hold of him when he collected up the rest of their equipment. 'Don't walk away from this, Shazim. Confront it.'

'What do you think I do every waking moment?' he demanded, swinging round.

'I think you rehash it—I think you replay it over and over to see if you could have done something differently—'

'I've told you all you need to know.'

His eyes were cold, his voice dismissive.

'You've told me the sanitised version,' Isla argued. 'Now tell me the rest.' His brother's death had overshadowed Shazim's life, and this perilous moment might be the only chance he ever got to start healing.

'What do you want to know?' He thrust his face into hers. 'Do you want to hear that my brother tried to save me and that he fell instead?'

'I want you to accept that you're not personally responsible for everything that goes wrong. I will never believe you caused your brother's death intentionally. You're innocent, Shazim. What happened was a tragic accident.'

His black eyes raked her face in fury. His balled fists were bleached with tension. Her heart went out to him, but she wouldn't relent. No one could live through that sort of torment without it destroying him in the end.

With a roar of impatience, Shazim rapped out, 'My brother took a chance to save me, as you risked your life to save that animal. Unlike you, he missed his footing. He held on for as long as he could, and I somehow managed to scramble down to him. I even found a good handhold, and reached out to take hold of his hand. He looked at me and smiled with such relief when I grabbed him, but I knew at once that I couldn't take his weight. He saw it in my eyes… There was such love in his eyes when he let go.'

There it was, laid out in front of her, pain of a type that few people, thank God, would ever know. She had often wondered if she would get over her mother's death, but she couldn't begin to imagine how Shazim must feel, believing himself responsible for what had happened to his brother.

'The nature reserve is your work, Shazim,' she told him gently. 'It's the most wonderful tribute to your brother. You've built a legacy in his name that will last for generations.'

Frowning bitterly, he shook his head. 'All that's left of my brother is the fountain I built in his honour, and my work in his name. Do you seriously think that can make up for his death?'

'No. Of course not.'

'You think I'm doing something admirable here?' His expression was derisive, self-hating, and riven with pain. 'Everything I do, everything I am, is thanks to him. He should be here now, not me.'

'And if he were here instead of you,' she argued, out of patience, out of time, Isla realised as she glanced outside the cave at the rapidly rising water, 'we'd probably die in this cave. I'm sorry to be so brutal, Shazim. I know you loved your brother, and I'm gutted that you lost him, but you can't spend the rest of your life blaming yourself for something you can't change. You're not a selfish youth now, you're a good man. Your brother wanted to prove how much he loved you by conquering his most deep-seated fears. He confronted the desert. He climbed a cliff. His only thought was to save you. He was a hero. At least allow him that.'

Her passionate words rang in the sudden silence and, for a moment, she wasn't sure how Shazim would respond. His expression was fixed and shocked, but to her relief it slowly changed into something more human and alive. It was the expression of someone who could feel. Emotion flashed behind his eyes, and then finally his shoulders relaxed.

'How long are we going to stand here?' she demanded then in her most practical tone. 'Shall we try for that ledge?' She glanced up to a path beyond the ledge that would take them to safety.

Shazim's silence was the longest few seconds of her life.

'Stand on my shoulders.' His voice rang out.

She did so.

He held onto her legs, keeping her steady. As soon as he was sure she was safely onto the ledge, he followed, and he kept on climbing until he reached a point where he could lean down and offer her his hand.

'Grab my wrist, Isla. I'll pull you up. Trust me…'

She didn't hesitate. Holding Shazim's stare, she took a firm grip of his wrist, and he hauled her up to safety.

CHAPTER SEVENTEEN

THE FIRST THING they did when they reached the safety of the tent was to call to reassure people they were safe. Within minutes of that, the sound of rotor blades approaching made talking impossible, and it wasn't until the engine had been turned off that Shazim was able to make himself heard.

'You're going straight back to the city for a thorough medical check-up.'

'That's not necessary,' Isla protested, suddenly suffused with dread at the thought of a second abrupt parting. They had opened their hearts to each other, Shazim had saved her life, and now he was returning to business as if nothing had happened?

'I say it is necessary for you to receive a full medical check-up,' he insisted without emotion. 'Your safety is of paramount importance to me.'

'Really?'

'Yes,' Shazim said grimly as a team from the helicopter filed into the tent. Staring over her head, he issued a number of brief commands in Q'Aqabian, from which she gathered that she was to be escorted away.

'Excuse me just a moment,' she said in a loud, clear voice. 'I haven't finished talking to His Majesty.'

Shocked glances flew to her face. Everyone understood the gist of her appeal, and the fact that she had just disobeyed their Sheikh.

Shazim made a gesture to his men to give them space.

'Thank you,' she said. 'What we've been through was so intense, and now this seems to sudden.' She gestured at the helicopter. 'I just need you to reassure me that you won't go back inside your ivory tower—that you'll remember what we talked about on the cliff, and that you'll always believe—'

'We've said enough on that subject,' Shazim informed her, turning away.

'Have we? If we have, then, who will talk about your brother?'

His eyes when he swung back to look at her were murderous.

'I'm not frightened of you, Shazim, but I am frightened that you'll go back to avoiding the truth about your brother—about us—'

'Us?' he queried coldly. 'There is no *us*.'

'No,' Isla agreed sadly. 'I think you're probably right.'

There was nothing more to say. Shazim strode to the entrance of the tent to summon his men back in. He was right to end things between them. It was up to her to accept that what they'd enjoyed so briefly was over. Shazim had to return to his royal duties, and she had to return to her work. He was already busy exchanging information with his men. No doubt he'd want a progress report on the tribesmen's dispute, along with a whole host of other royal concerns. She could understand the urgency to catch up, but while Shazim could close off his feelings like that, she had no confidence in his recovery, which meant his mission to be the very best of kings might never be realised.

And that was no longer something for her to worry about, Isla accepted as members of the Sheikh of Q'Aqabi's black-clad team escorted her to the helicopter and saw her safely strapped in.

That was an end of it—of the two of them, she thought,

blinking tears from her eyes as the helicopter lifted off and wheeled away. This empty feeling was on her for falling in love with a desert king. They would never work closely together now, as she had dreamed they would. Maybe she would never see him again, except maybe in passing at the university. Though, now that she'd pressed him to talk about his brother, would he even want to speak to her again? Isla doubted it. She had uncovered a pain far greater than anything she could have imagined, and Shazim had no one to share that pain with. She'd been selfish. In trying to help him, her amateur psychology had only succeeded in causing him more pain. And now she was leaving him to cope with that alone.

Isla's official time in Q'Aqabi had ended. It nearly broke her heart to leave the rangers in the desert, her friends in the village, and the animal programme she had so hoped to be a part of. Three weeks after she had returned from her hospital check-up, there was still no word from Shazim. Rumour said he'd gone on a retreat into the desert—without guards, without rangers. This was a first for him since his youth, though his people greeted it with rejoicing, as it spoke of Shazim's commitment to them. Isla was glad too, as it seemed to be a sign of the recovery she had feared he wouldn't make. Shazim had a lot of history to work through, and solitude and thought could hopefully help him heal, as he came to terms with the facts of his brother's death.

A smile broke through her sadness when Millie called to say goodbye to her. 'I'm just downstairs,' Millie explained. 'Can I come up?'

'Of course.' Isla couldn't think of anyone who could lift her heart more. Well, one person, but he had chosen not to be here, which was perhaps just as well. Her heart couldn't take much more battering.

She was still packing up her belongings, ready for the long flight back to London, when Millie knocked on the door. Closing her case, she wheeled it to the door. Her heart was full when she opened it to find Millie waiting outside. They hugged without words, but then Millie stood back.

'Come in,' Isla insisted.

'No. You'll be fine. I just wanted to see you—just wanted to reassure myself—'

'About what?' Isla frowned. 'Shall I call you when I finish packing? I'd like to say goodbye properly—'

Millie was staring down the corridor leading to Isla's suite of rooms. And now she saw why.

'Shazim,' she whispered.

Dressed down in jeans and a plain black shirt, Shazim was walking towards them in silence, Unsure as to why he was here, she backed into the room after acknowledging him with a polite dip of her head.

'Isla…'

Raising her chin, she stared into his eyes as Shazim followed her in. 'Yes.' She heard the door click quietly behind her as Millie left them.

'Can you forgive me?' Shazim asked straight out.

'Forgive you?'

'For being blind… For being thoughtless—'

'Shazim—' Taking hold of his hands in a firm grip, she stared steadily into his eyes. 'I didn't know what to think when you had me airlifted out and you stayed behind,' she said honestly. 'I just hoped that wherever you went, and whoever you were with, you would heal.'

'I am healed, because of you.'

Letting go of his hands, she shook her head and stood back. 'No one could heal that quickly. Not after what happened to you. There is no miracle cure for grief. There are only coping strategies, and time to heal a wound that cuts so deep. You have to face it every day, and you have to work towards healing it, as if it were a real physical wound.'

'Then, I've taken my first steps, thanks to you.'

Isla remained silent. She wouldn't take the credit for Shazim deciding that the time had come to face his demons. She was just glad that he had.

'And now you're here to say goodbye to me.' She nodded her head, as if trying to convince herself that she could accept this and leave Shazim and Q'Aqabi behind for good.

'You didn't think I'd let you go without coming to say goodbye, did you?'

'To be honest, I didn't know what to expect.'

Perhaps she should have been angry with him for sending her back to the city without a discussion, but Shazim had been fighting his own inner struggle. Her impulse even now was to comfort him, but instead she accepted reality, extended the handle on her suitcase, and turned for the door.

'You're not going to let her leave without saying something, are you?' Millie demanded the instant Isla had stepped outside the room.

She was surprised to find Millie still standing there. And even more surprised when Shazim said, 'Please forgive my sister. She always did speak her mind.'

'Your sister?' Whirling around, she stared at him, and then the pieces of the jigsaw rattled into place. Shazim had told her about the royal nursery, and how his brother had been like a father to the royal children. And now Shazim was the father of his country, and had taken over the role of father to his siblings. Of course, he'd chosen his sister to meet the prize winner at the airport. It made perfect sense. Millie was probably as invested in the nature reserve as Shazim. She had lost a brother too, and she would naturally want to honour his memory.

'I would like to hear what you've got to say,' Isla admitted.

'You must,' Millie insisted. Taking hold of Isla's hand, she drew her back into the room. 'We need you in Q'Aqabi. The project needs you. My brother needs you most of all—' Turning, Millie fired a fierce look at Shazim.

'Isla is her own woman,' he commented. 'She will do as she wants.'

'Then let's hope she wants to stay—though, heaven knows, you don't make it easy, brother.'

'I'll do anything I can to help you,' Isla said as she stared into Shazim's eyes.

'You'll need a job contract first. And a decent salary,' Millie added, directing this at Shazim. 'Isla would work here for nothing, but you can't allow that. She can't live on hot air.'

'I'm sure we can sort something out,' Shazim said with amusement. 'Would you give us a moment?' he asked his sister.

'Do you want the job?' he asked Isla as soon as they were alone.

'You know I want the job.' She held his dark stare steadily. 'There is nowhere else on earth I'd rather be, and no work I'd rather do. I'll even put up with you to do it—if you're sure you want me here.'

'The project needs you,' he said gruffly. 'You've got a job for life, if that's what you want.'

'But not as your mistress,' she stated firmly.

'Please—' Shazim's expression suggested that truly was the last thing on his mind.

Okay. She got that. She had already concluded she was hardly mistress material. 'Sorry. That was presumptuous of me, but I had to be sure.'

'At least I can always trust you to lay your cards on the table,' Shazim said drily. 'I wouldn't want you to change. The job I'm offering won't be easy. I want you to act as deputy leader for my project. You'll be a bit of a gofer for the current leader to begin with, but what the man in question knows about desert lore can't be taught. I want you to work closely with him, and learn as much as you can, with a view to taking joint responsibility eventually. I've witnessed your leadership skills, and I've had experience of your courage. I've also seen a great deal of common sense—'

'That man—the leader of the project. It's you, isn't it?'

The hint of a smile softened Shazim's hard face.

'So I haven't offended you?'

'Offended me?' He frowned.

'By speaking my mind?'

'That's one of the things I like best about you. When you're in my position, very few people will speak their mind, for fear of losing royal favour. That's something that's never troubled you.'

She laughed. Even if Shazim only *liked* her, it would be enough if she could work here. It would have to be enough, Isla told herself firmly.

'I read the report from the hospital,' he said. 'I was relieved you were okay.'

'Everyone was very kind, and it appears that, apart from a few broken nails, I got off lightly.' *Unlike you*, she thought, remembering Shazim baring his soul to her on the cliff face. But if that had prompted him to take a pilgrimage into the desert to face up to the past, then everything had been worth it. 'Are you all right?'

'Of course.' Shazim brushed off her concern.

'Are you sure?' she pressed softly.

A muscle in his jaw worked as he admitted, 'I've never told anyone how I feel about the past before.'

'And you chose me. That means a lot to me, Shazim.'

Shazim dipped his head until their lips were just a tiny distance apart. Staring deep into her eyes, he kissed her so tenderly she felt tears pricking. If not completely healed, Shazim was mending. Talking about the past, and how the terrible events had made him feel, must have been a release for him, and for that she was glad.

'So, when do I start my new job?' she asked, staring up with naked love shining in her eyes.

'Right now—if you want to?'

'I can't think of anything I want more,' she exclaimed.

'Can't you?' Shazim murmured.

Her stare steadied on his. 'What do you get out of teasing me, Your Majesty?'

'The same thing you get out of winding me up, I imagine. But, I love you, so…' He shrugged. 'What can I do about it? I don't want to let you go. Will you stay with me?'

For the first time since that encounter on the building site, Shazim was asking—he wasn't instructing or commanding. The all-powerful Lion of the Desert, His Majesty the Sheikh of Q'Aqabi, was simply a man telling a woman that he loved her, and he was putting his heart on the line as he asked if she loved him too.

'I love you more than anything in this world,' Isla said honestly.

Shazim's words were a balm to her aching heart. He was fierce, but she loved his brand of fierce. His arms were strong and he was a natural protector, and, though she was strong, she needed him, more than she could ever express. She would never let him down. She would fight for him, as she had fought for everything else in her life. She would be strong for him, and for Q'Aqabi. They'd be strong for each other. She was complete with him, and flawed without him. She was his, body and soul. She loved him with everything she had. Every moment apart was too long, while every moment with Shazim was perfect.

'I'm so sorry I left you,' he murmured.

'I was so worried about you,' she admitted. 'But you run a country, so I understood…sort of.'

Shazim laughed. 'Will you be so different when you're running my nature reserve?'

'I doubt it,' she confessed. 'We both get lost in our work.'

'But I want more than work from you,' Shazim said, turning serious as he held her in front of him. 'I want a life with you, Isla. I want children with you. And I want time with you in the desert so our children learn desert lore from both of us. Don't look so surprised,' Shazim added as he looped his arms around her waist. 'I want to marry you. I'm asking you to be my Queen. You can't possibly think that anyone else could match up to you, Isla Sinclair?'

She wanted to take it in, and to be deliriously happy. She wanted to shout out loud and perform a happy dance, but instead her frown deepened. 'I'm just not queen material.' All her concern was for Shazim, who seemed to her to be on the brink of making a terrible mistake.

'You are so wrong.' Shazim turned serious. 'My people respect you—I respect you. What better material for a queen could there be than you? But more important, I love you. No one else will ever come close to the way I feel about you.'

'I feel the same,' Isla admitted, her throat burning with emotion. 'I can't ask for anything more.'

'Really?' Shazim lifted one ebony brow. 'You disappoint me, Isla Sinclair.'

As Shazim was backing her towards the sofa, he was probably right.

'Wear no underwear in the future,' he instructed, caressing her and arousing her until she was so frantic to be one with him she could only agree. 'Let me,' Shazim suggested calmly as she yanked at her clothes, and only succeeded in tying herself in knots as she struggled to get them off.

'How can you be so calm?' she demanded with frustration.

'The end game is worth it?' Shazim suggested with a wicked smile as he lifted her in one arm and shucked her jeans and thong off with his free hand.

And then he thrust deep, claiming her as she claimed him. Fiercely.

It was a while before she could speak, and then it was only to urge him on. 'I love that,' she gasped as Shazim held her firmly in place while he buffeted her rhythmically against the wall.

'Something else we have in common,' he remarked, upping the tempo.

'I love that even more—'

'I would never have guessed,' he murmured.

She screamed as he brought her to the edge and held her there.

'Concentrate,' he instructed.

'Please,' she exclaimed in desperation, clinging to him as she panted out her need.

Shazim laughed as he tipped her over the edge. 'I'll never get enough of you, Isla—or of this.'

'Mmm...glad to hear it,' she managed somehow. 'But I still don't think I can be your Queen.'

'Why not?' Shazim demanded, holding her at arm's length so he could stare into her face.

'I'd be hopeless—just look at the facts: I'd never be ready in time, because I'd always have some clinic or other to finish. I'd be with the animals when you needed me most. I'd be covered in mud or worse, when I should be all dressed up for some important function—'

Shazim shook his head. 'There is an answer to all of that.'

'Is there?' she asked, wanting to believe him.

'Sure.' Shazim gave a smile. 'I'm going to keep you locked away in my harem.'

Isla dismissed this idea with a huff. 'You can try. And, no harem,' she added fiercely.

Shazim's smile broadened. 'Leave your fantasies behind for once and consider this. Has it never occurred to you that I love you so much I'm prepared to compromise where your work is concerned, as I ask you to compromise where my duty to Q'Aqabi is concerned?'

'A duty I hope to share one day.'

'You will,' he promised, slanting a smile.

'So, you really do love me?'

'I really do,' Shazim confirmed.

But it still didn't seem right to Isla. She wasn't beautiful. She wasn't tall and elegant like all those princesses and celebrities Shazim could choose from. And she certainly wasn't slim. She was stocky and capable, and far happier wearing rubber gloves ready to go deep, to do whatever was necessary for an animal, rather than flitting about in an evening gown. Could she really see herself in a regal robe and tiara, with her hair neatly brushed, and the right words for every occasion on the tip of her tongue?

'I'm such a klutz. I'd be hopeless at it,' she fretted out loud.

'You're just the kind of hands-on queen my country needs,' Shazim argued.

'But how about you, Shazim?' she asked with concern. 'What kind of queen do *you* need?'

'I was hoping you'd ask that question, because I need you—'

'Be serious. I'm not compliant enough to be your

Queen. I wouldn't fall in step behind you—though I might stumble in your wake. And, if I do take that job—'

'Is there any doubt?'

'No,' she gasped, horrified just at the thought of turning it down. 'But I'll have no free time. You should pick one of those celebrity types—' Isla frowned as she thought about it. 'Or a royal princess…' Her eyes glazed over as she imagined what it might feel like to be that beautiful royal princess on the eve of marrying Shazim…

'Earth to Isla,' Shazim murmured, jolting her out of the daydream. Cupping her chin, he made her look at him. 'You have no idea how much I love you, do you?'

'You should found a dynasty,' she said, still distracted by thoughts of whom he should marry. 'You should marry one of those princesses, settle down and have children. Make your life easy, Shazim, and let me go.'

'What was it you once said about easy? I don't think either of us is happy taking that route, are we?' Shazim's lips pressed down as he shrugged. 'Though my life would certainly be easier if I let you go. But I'm afraid there's a problem with that too.'

'I'm good with problems,' Isla offered. 'Tell me and I'll try to sort it out for you.'

'Marriage with a princess?' Shazim's mouth tugged in a quick grimace. 'That's not a concept I'm comfortable with. I never will be.'

'But—'

It was no use trying to fight him off when Shazim pulled her into his arms.

'What are you doing?' she demanded, putting up a token fight.

'Explaining to you that your life is going to be with me. I'm not sure how yet, but we'll work it out—though I do need your agreement if we're to be married, and you haven't given me your answer yet. How else can you be my Queen?' he prompted. 'Well? Do you agree? What's your answer, Isla? Will you do me the honour of agreeing to become my wife—my Queen?'

As Shazim knelt in front of her Isla was speechless for a moment, but then she did what felt right and knelt too, so they were facing each other. Shazim kissed her mouth, her earlobe, and then her neck…

'What you said,' she managed when she could catch breath enough to speak. 'Do you really want my answer now?'

'I've already guessed your answer, but you can tell me again, if you want to.'

'Yes,' she exclaimed.

'Just as I thought,' he murmured, kissing her again, but this time deeply. 'You're easy to persuade.'

'Depends on what the problem is,' she countered on a shaking breath. 'And now, no more talking. I need you to concentrate.'

'Again?' Shazim murmured, laughing softly against her mouth.

'Oh, yes,' she confirmed. 'Always again…'

It was hard to believe how far she had come in her trust of men, but Shazim wasn't just any man, he was the love of her life, this man she had given her heart to. There were so many times when he had shown her why she should trust him, and though Shazim had battled through terrible issues of his own while they'd been together, he had never let her down. More than that, he had opened up her world to amazing possibilities, and had expanded her horizons in every way.

'How can this work?' she asked later when they were lying with their limbs comfortably entwined in Isla's bed at the palace.

'Let me see,' Shazim said as he moved over her. 'I'm sure if I try hard enough, I can work something out—'

'Stop!' Isla exploded into laughter as Shazim tormented her with kisses and all kinds of unmentionable things. 'All the answers can't be found in bed.'

'But most of the problems can be solved here,' Shazim countered. As he was nudging her legs apart with one hard-muscled thigh at the time, she was in no mood to argue. 'We'll have to dig deep, of course,' he added, 'if we are to find the answer to making this work…' As he was lifting her and positioning her so she was straddling him, it didn't seem the right time to disagree.

'Look at me when I'm talking to you,' Shazim commanded.

'Must I?' She threw her head back on a groan.

'Yes,' Shazim insisted. 'Now, ride me,' he murmured, encouraging her with his hands.

'I'm getting quite good at riding.' She threw him a mischievous smile.

'You certainly are,' he agreed.

And then he turned her beneath him, and Isla, still being aroused from the last time, was ready to fly again, and one firm thrust was all it took.

CHAPTER EIGHTEEEN

'I CAN'T BELIEVE what you've done for me, Shazim.' It was the eve of their wedding and Shazim had promised Isla a wedding gift that would exceed her wildest dreams, but never in all her fantasies could she have conjured up anything as incredible as this. He had recreated the university coffee shop in every tiny detail, but on the banks of a glittering oasis.

'I hope you like it.'

'As temporary structures go, it's pretty impressive,' she admitted, shaking her head.

Shazim laughed and tightened his arm around her shoulders. 'You can keep it as long as you want to—turn it into a refreshment stop for the rangers if you like, or dismantle it. It's entirely up to you, but I do think you should take a closer look at it before you decide to do anything too drastic with it.'

'I can't wait,' she admitted. 'But this is far too much…'

'Money can buy anything, but it can't buy happiness. Isn't that what they say? Nothing I do for you could ever be too much. And isn't it usual for a bride to enjoy a pre-wedding get-together with her friends?'

'My friends?'

Isla was astonished when she walked inside. Just about everyone she knew was sitting at a booth, or at one of the basic Formica tables. Shazim had faithfully recreated every detail, even down to her high-vis' jacket hanging on a hook by the door.

And… No!

'Charlie?'

Bounding up to her grumpy ex-boss, Isla threw her arms around him, and only when she pulled back did she get chance to realise that even Charlie was smiling today.

'Latte? Or your usual double macchiato with a caramel shot?'

'Chrissie!' Hearing the familiar voice, Isla whirled around to show Shazim with a smile how much she appreciated the thought he'd put into this fantastic wedding gift. 'I don't believe this!'

As the two girls hugged, Isla realised that it wouldn't have been a proper wedding without Chrissie to help her dress for the ceremony. 'I don't know how to thank you,' she said, shaking her head as she turned around to look at Shazim.

'Yes, you do,' he murmured so that only they could hear.

Isla's heart flipped at the thought of their wedding night as Shazim gave her one last look before leaving her with her friends. The next time she saw him would be at their wedding tomorrow.

Their wedding! Her marriage to the man she loved... the man she would always love.

It didn't get any better than that. She would have married Shazim if he had been one of the roaming Q'Aqabian tribesmen, with only his horse, his cooking utensils, his bedroll and a tent to his name, Isla thought as she watched Shazim spring onto the back of his stallion and ride away.

'So…how does it feel to be almost Queen?' Chrissie asked her, green eyes wide with wonder as she looked at Isla as if she had never seen her before.

Isla pulled a comic face. 'A bit like sitting my finals all over again.'

'Then, let's not talk about it,' Chrissie agreed. 'Shazim said my job is to distract you, so you don't get nervous about the wedding. So, I've got a great idea—let's talk about me.'

Isla collapsed into laughter. 'Great idea. There are so many people I want you to meet.'

'Hot men?' Chrissie asked hopefully.

'Surprise—she cuts to the chase,' Isla teased, rolling her eyes as she gazed heavenwards. 'As it happens, I've got some very hot men I want you to meet. Shazim's got a lot of friends coming over for the wedding, so you can take your pick. Just don't get too distracted, because I'm going to need your help more than ever when you dress me for the ceremony.'

'I still can't believe you're marrying the Sheikh of Q'Aqabi.'

'How do you think I feel?'

'Loved. At least, that's how you look.' Chrissie studied Isla's face. 'You're all glowing and bright-eyed…' She drew in a long breath. 'You're not…'

'Maybe.' Isla grinned and shrugged. 'We're certainly putting in all the effort required, but it's still far too early to tell.'

Chrissie's face lit up. Reaching across the table, she grabbed hold of Isla's hands. 'Congratulations! You're going to make a fabulous mother. You've had the best teacher, after all.'

Touched by her friend's sincerity, Isla felt tears smarting behind her eyes. 'Thank you,' she said softly. Her mother had been constantly in her mind since Shazim had asked her to marry him, and she was confident her mother would be with her, watching over her daughter every step of the way on the happiest day of Isla's life.

* * *

They were to marry in his palace, and his last task was to persuade Isla to wear his mother's jewels. His people would expect it. The golden casket was to be delivered to Isla's suite of rooms at the palace. This was the same casket that had been placed into Shazim's hands by his mother on the day she had begged him not to throw away his life because of his brother's death. She had told him that that would be no tribute at all, a sentiment he hadn't heard echoed until Isla had said exactly the same thing to him.

Lifting the lid, he stared into the glittering depths, and then grinned. He could just imagine Isla's reaction when she saw them. She was so understated, so dedicated to her work, he couldn't be entirely sure that his bride wouldn't rush to the wedding still dressed in scrubs and overshoes, fresh from the operating theatre.

Mounting up, he turned his stallion towards the palace where thousands were due to arrive to witness their wedding. The palace courtyard was so vast that Isla would ride to the ceremony in a horse-drawn carriage. The matched greys were being groomed even now. He would be waiting for her, mounted on his stallion as tradition demanded.

'Ready for a quick getaway if I change my mind,' he'd teased her.

'Fine. Just leave me to my work,' she had countered with a cheeky grin, which had obviously called for more physical pleasure in order to persuade her once and for all that he would be there.

There wasn't a chance he would change his mind about his wedding tomorrow. He would never find another bride like Isla if he searched the entire globe.

On the morning of her wedding Isla could not believe how her life had changed since that one rainy day on a building site in London. She had asked the women of the village to come to the palace to help her dress, and Shazim's sister, Millie, as well as Chrissie. With all their help, she hoped that she might feel—if not yet a queen, then almost a queen.

'You look beautiful,' Chrissie said as Isla studied her reflection in the mirror.

'I certainly look different,' Isla conceded, turning this way and that to watch the diamond coronet sparkle on her hair.

She couldn't believe the jewels Shazim had given her. There were glittering bracelets, countless rings, and the dainty diamond anklet she had decided to wear today, together with sparkling earrings and, of course, the royal coronet.

She would only have to wear them on state occasions, Shazim had promised—or maybe in bed with him, if she felt like it.

Better confine them to state occasions, Isla had concluded as she'd handled the priceless jewels with reverence. In bed with Shazim was always such a hectic affair she couldn't risk the coronet bouncing across the floor.

He had also suggested she could wear them to work—to impress the animals. She'd known he was only trying to tease her into accepting the riches that came with the job of Queen, and she had lost no time in teasing him back. 'Better not. Can't risk losing them down the sluice—'

Of course she would honour his people by wearing the jewels, as Shazim had explained they had been in his family for generations. She thought about his ancestors as she put them on, and made a sacred pledge to devote herself to Q'Aqabi as they had.

'Let me fasten your dress,' Chrissie insisted. 'We're running out of time.'

Shazim had flown Isla to Rome in his jet for the design and fitting of her wedding dress. It was a dream of a dress in cobweb-fine lace over a close-fitting base of cool ivory silk. There was a long, floor-length veil, lightly embroidered with diamonds and pearls, that billowed out behind her for more than twenty feet, and her hair, having been polished to a honeyed sheen, had been left loose to cascade around her shoulders, because that was how Shazim liked to see it.

A mischievous smile touched her lips when she remembered how he liked to fist a hank of it so he could ease her head back and kiss her throat—

'Isla?' Chrissie chivvied.

She stared at Chrissie blankly for a moment. She had been so wrapped up in her fantasy—a fantasy that, quite incredibly, was about to become reality—that she hadn't heard a word Chrissie had said.

'They're ready for you,' Chrissie prompted gently, standing back.

'Your carriage awaits,' Millie added, leaning forward to kiss Isla fondly on both cheeks. 'Welcome to the family, Isla.'

Millie was in charge of the wedding bouquet that Shazim had had specially flown in, along with all the wedding flowers, from the English Channel Islands. The blush-pink, cream, and ice-white roses had been chilled to keep them fresh, and as Isla brought them to her face to inhale their delicate scent she brushed the tips of the petals against her cheek. They were cool and slightly damp, and she knew at once what she wanted to do with them, and she always followed her heart.

Shazim was waiting for her, mounted on his stallion beneath a flower-strewn arch. Nerves gripped her when she first heard the roar of the crowd. There were so many people. As her carriage drew closer they seemed to form an endless sea. She would have preferred a quiet, intimate ceremony, but had always known what she was getting herself into. This wasn't just her day, it was for the people of Q'Aqabi too, and that was a small sacrifice to put her wishes aside for them and for Shazim.

Shazim's smile was all the reassurance she needed, and as he helped her down from the carriage his expression was so intense and so loving that her world shrank around him, and she saw only him.

Shazim had never looked more astonishingly handsome. Dark and swarthy with his *howlis* covering his head, but not his face this time, he was dressed in black flowing robes, edged in gold. She had heard it said that brides went through their wedding ceremony in a dream, but she'd done with dreaming. Every single atom in her being was fully aware of the reality she was entering into. When she accepted Shazim's ring, she was accepting him as well as everything he represented. She was pledging to support him and his country, to share his life and his duty to the land he loved, and she couldn't have been more sincere when she made her vows.

'Do you like it?' he murmured as he placed the ring on her finger.

She would have loved anything Shazim had chosen for her, with the exception, perhaps, of that safety gear back at the building site. But this platinum band studded with diamonds was nothing short of spectacular. Like the man at her side, she thought, smiling up at him as the ceremony concluded and they were declared man and wife.

They walked through the crowd to their reception at the palace, and were cheered every step of the way. But there was just one small detour she wanted to make…

'What is it?' Shazim asked with concern when she touched his arm.

'There's somewhere I have to go.'

'Anywhere you want,' he said.

Linking arms with him, she walked up to the beautiful fountain Shazim had built in his brother's honour and, kneeling in front of it, she laid her bouquet down.

'For your brother, for your country, and for us,' she said, when Shazim raised her to her feet. 'But most of all, for you,' she whispered.

'How did I get to be so lucky?' he demanded, folding her arm through his.

'You found a high-vis' jacket that would fit me?' she suggested.

'I think it was a little more than that,' Shazim argued softly. 'I love you more than life itself, my beautiful wife.'

'I love you too,' she said with belief in the very brightest of futures shining in her eyes.

EPILOGUE

TICKLE TORTURE WENT on for much longer that night. No wonder the children refused to go to bed when Shazim got them so excited. And it was the same each night, just when she got them calmed down. But when he looked at her and shrugged with that look in his eyes, she would forgive him anything. He was the most wonderful father to their three children, and the most wonderful man to share her life with. He hadn't stopped at recreating the café in London to make her happy. Sensing something of her feelings on living such a public life, he had built them a getaway on the outskirts of the city, where they could enjoy a proper family life. This wasn't just any getaway, but a building he had designed to remind her of the simple cottage where she had lived as a child.

Though Shazim's version of the cottage was at least twice as big, she had to tell him tactfully, and the home she'd grown up in hadn't been packed to the brim with Shazim-style luxuries. But that was one of the benefits of marrying not just a king, but a highly skilled architect who was always creating the most innovative structures. Her children had been born here, and the kitchen was her own—such a small thing, but it meant the world to her, and to their daughter, Yasmin, who was rapidly turning the kitchen into a makeshift clinic for the overflow of pets, having recruited their twins, Darrak and Jonah, to act as her rangers.

'Bed,' Isla insisted firmly. The children reluctantly

obeyed her command. They had already learned that Daddy might be King, but ignore Mummy at your peril.

'Can I come to the clinic with you tomorrow?' Yasmin begged, clinging to Isla's hand while her brothers jumped up and down in an attempt to catch their share of Isla's attention.

Isla's clinic was thriving and, with Shazim's help, she had opened three more. She was still happiest dressed down in work clothes, she reflected wryly as she hugged and kissed her children before they went to bed, but she had learned to act like a queen and to wear the beautiful jewels that Shazim's mother had left him with such love and pride, as she should, to honour the memory of a woman who had known such immense love, as well as such terrible grief.

'If you go to bed now, and I don't hear another sound out of you until the morning, you can *all* come to the clinic with me.'

Luckily, Shazim swept all three of them up, or their shrieks of excitement might have deafened her, Isla decided, laughing as she went to help to tuck them in.

When it was all quiet upstairs, Shazim came to stand with her on the beautiful veranda overlooking the oasis. As he linked his arms around her waist, she nestled back against the man she loved and smiled. They were so close in heart and spirit that, even with her back to him, Shazim could feel the change in her. 'No,' he said in wonder.

'Yes,' she softly replied.

'I think we should go to bed to celebrate the arrival of another child.'

Turning, she smiled into the eyes of the man she loved, and trusted with her life, and all her heart. 'I thought you'd never suggest it...'

* * * * *

OUT NOW!

Available at
millsandboon.co.uk

MILLS & BOON

OUT NOW!

Available at millsandboon.co.uk

MILLS & BOON

OUT NOW!

Available at
millsandboon.co.uk

MILLS & BOON

LET'S TALK

Romance

For exclusive extracts, competitions and special offers, find us online:

MillsandBoon

@MillsandBoon

@MillsandBoonUK

@MillsandBoonUK

Get in touch on 01413 063 232

For all the latest titles coming soon, visit
millsandboon.co.uk/nextmonth